THE

ICE

BENEATH

HER

Camilla Grebe

THE
ICE
BENEATH
HER

Translated by Elizabeth Clark Wessel

ZAFFRE

Originally published by Wahlström & Widstrand, a division of the Bonnier Group

First published in Great Britain in 2016 by Zaffre Publishing by
arrangement with Ahlander Agency, Sweden
ZAFFRE PUBLISHING
80–81 Wimpole St, London W1G 9RE
www.zaffrebooks.co.uk

A CIP catalogue record for this book is
available from the British Library.

Hardback ISBN: 978–1–785–76197–3

Trade paperback ISBN: 978–1–785–76198–0

Ebook ISBN: 978-1-78576-196-6

1 3 5 7 9 10 8 6 4 2

Typeset by IDSUK (Data Connection) Ltd
Printed and bound by Clays Ltd, St Ives Plc

Zaffre Publishing is an imprint of Bonnier Publishing UK,
a Bonnier Publishing company
www.bonnierpublishing.co.uk

For Estelle and Fredrik

You never know friend from foe,
'til the ice beneath gives way.

– Inuit proverb

Peter

I'm standing in the snow by my mother's headstone when I get the call. Her stone is simple, barely knee high, in rough-hewn granite. We've been talking for a while – my mother and I – about how hard it is to be a police officer in this city, where nobody gives a damn about anything but themselves. And – perhaps more important – how hard it is to live in that kind of city, in this kind of time.

I stamp wet snow off my trainers and turn away from her headstone. It doesn't feel right to talk on the phone at her grave. The rolling hills of the Woodland Cemetery lie spread out before me. Mist hovers between the tops of tall pines, and beneath it the dark tree trunks shoot up out of the snow like exclamation marks, as if emphasising life's transience. There's dripping from the treetops and from the gravestones. Meltwater runs over everything. It finds its way into my thin shoes, too, collecting around my toes like a wet reminder to buy those boots I have yet to allow myself. Somewhere in the distance I catch a glimpse of dark figures receding into the pine forest. Maybe they're here to light votive candles or place pine boughs.

Christmas will be here soon.

I take a few steps towards the neatly snowploughed footpath and throw a glance at the phone screen, even though I already know who it is. The feeling is unmistakable. A sinking, pounding sensation that I know all too well.

Before I answer, I turn back one last time to her headstone. Wave awkwardly and mumble something about coming back soon. It's unnecessary, of course – she knows I always come back.

The road stretches out black and shining as I drive into the city. The brake lights of other cars glisten in front of me on the road, lighting the way. Thick drifts of dirty brown snow and squat, depressing, conformist buildings line the road to Stockholm. The occasional illuminated Christmas star brightens up a window, like a torch in the night. It's started snowing again. A rainy slush settles on the windscreen, blurring all the edges, softening the landscape. The only sound is the rhythmic swish of the wipers married to the soft purr of the motor.

A murder.

Yet another murder.

Many years ago, back when I was still a novice detective inspector, getting called to the scene of a murder always provoked a kind of exhilaration. Death was synonymous with a mystery that needed solving, like tangled wool that needed unravelling. Back then I thought everything could be unravelled and explained. As long as you had the energy, the stamina, and knew which threads to pull and in what order. Reality was nothing more than a complex web of threads.

In short, it could be mastered, figured out.

Now I don't know any more. Maybe I've lost interest in the web itself, lost my intuition for which thread to pull. Over time, death has taken on new meaning. Mum, resting in the wet ground of the Woodland Cemetery. Annika, my sister, lying in the same cemetery not far away. And Dad, who's bent on drinking himself to death on the Costa del Sol, will be here soon enough. The crimes that come my way no longer feel as important. Of course, I can help figure out what happened. Put the inconceivable into words – someone has had their life taken from them – and describe the events leading up to it. Maybe find the culprit, too, and in the best-case scenario, help to prosecute him. But the dead are still dead, aren't they? These days, I have difficulty finding meaning in what I do.

By the time I reach Roslagstull dusk is falling, and it occurs to me that it never really got light today. This day passed unnoticed through the same colourless December fog as yesterday and the day before. There's more traffic once I merge onto the E18 motor-way heading north. I pass by roadworks, and potholes shake the car so the Little Tree hanging from the rear-view mirror jumps alarmingly.

Manfred calls again when I'm driving past the university. Tells me it's a bloody mess, some kind of bigwig is involved, and it would be great if I stopped taking so bloody long and just turned up. I peer out into the cement-grey dusk, tell him to hold his horses, the road has more holes than Swiss cheese, and I'll bruise my balls if I drive any faster.

Manfred fires off his familiar grunting laugh, like the snort of a pig. Or maybe I'm being unfair: Manfred is fat; maybe that colours my view of his laugh, makes me think of a voluptuous grunting. Maybe his laugh sounds just like mine.

Maybe we all sound the same.

We've been working together for more than ten years, Manfred and me. Year after year, we've stood side by side at the autopsy table, interrogating witnesses and meeting distraught relatives. Year after year, we've taken on the bad guys and done our best to make the world a safer place. But have we, really? All those people slumber-ing in cold storage at Forensic Medicine in Solna are still dead and nothing will change that. For ever and ever. We are no more than society's cleaning crew, tying up loose ends after the fabric frays and the unthinkable has already happened.

Janet says I'm depressed, but I don't trust Janet. Besides, I don't believe in depression. Because that's how it is: I don't believe in it. In my case, I've just realised the true state of our existence, and I'm looking soberly at life for the first time. Janet says that's a textbook response, that the depressed person isn't able to see beyond his own perceived misery. In return I tell her depression is one of the pharmaceutical industry's most profitable inventions, and I don't have the time or the desire to make obscenely rich pharmaceutical companies even richer. And if Janet wants to talk any more about how I'm feeling after that, I always hang up. After all, we broke up more than fifteen years ago; there's no need to discuss that kind of thing with her. That she happens to be the mother of my only child doesn't change that fact.

Albin, by the way, is the child we never should have had. Not because there's anything wrong with Albin – he's a normal enough teenage boy: pimply, oversexed and pathologically interested in computer games – but because I truly wasn't ready to be a parent. In my darker moments (which are becoming more and more frequent over the years) I think she did it on purpose. Threw away her contraceptive pills and got pregnant as revenge for that thing with the wedding. Maybe that's the case. I'll never know, and it doesn't really matter now. Albin very much exists and lives in comfort with his mother. We see each other sometimes, not often – at Christmas and Midsummer and on his birthday. I think it's best for him if we don't have much contact. Otherwise, he'd probably end up disappointed with me too.

Sometimes I think I should carry a picture of him in my wallet, like the other (real) parents. A clumsy school picture taken against a sepia-toned panel in a gym by a photographer whose dreams have led no further than the Farsta Secondary School. But then I realise that wouldn't fool anyone, least of all myself. Parenthood is something you earn, I think. A right that comes from suffering sleepless nights, changing nappies and all that other stuff you have to do. It has very little to do with genetics, the sperm I unknowingly donated fifteen years ago so Janet could fulfil her dream of being a mother.

I spot the house from a distance. Not because the white, boxy building stands out in any way in this exclusive suburb, but because it's surrounded by police cars. Blue lights flash across the snow and the unmistakable white van of the forensic technicians is parked neatly not far away. I leave my car at the bottom of the hill and walk the last stretch up towards the house. Greet the uniforms, flash my badge, and slip under the blue-and-white barrier tape fluttering gently in the breeze.

Manfred Olsson is standing at the front door. His huge body obscures most of the doorway as he raises a hand in greeting. He's wearing a tweed jacket with a bit of pink silk handkerchief poking out of the breast pocket. His generous wool trousers are tucked firmly into blue plastic shoe covers.

'Bloody hell, Lindgren. I thought you'd never turn up.'

I meet his eyes. His small, impish peppercorn eyes are set deeply in his ruddy face. His thin ginger hair is combed neatly in a style that calls to mind an actor in a fifties movie. He looks more like an antiques dealer or historian or sommelier than a police officer. In fact the last thing he looks like is a detective – something he's undoubtedly aware of. I suspect it might just be a ploy, that he actually loves exaggerating his eccentric style in order to provoke more hidebound officers.

'Like I said . . .'

'Yeah, yeah. Blame it on the traffic,' Manfred says. 'I know how it is when you get hold of a good fucking porno. Hard to tear yourself away.'

Manfred's rough language is in sharp contrast to his elaborate and conservative style of dress. He hands me a pair of shoe covers and gloves and says in a quieter voice:

'Listen. This is some truly fucked-up shit . . . Come on, see for yourself.'

I put on the shoe covers and latex gloves and step onto the transparent plastic foot pads that the technicians have placed seemingly at random in the hall. The smell of blood is so intense and nauseating that I almost retreat, even though I know it all too well. The pounding in my gut is growing stronger. Despite all the crime scenes I've been at, all the corpses I've seen, there's something about being in the proximity of cold, naked death that still makes the hair on the back of my neck stand up. Maybe it's the reality of how fast it can happen. How quickly a life can be extinguished. But then again sometimes it's the opposite – the way a crime scene, or a body, bears witness to unbearably protracted agony.

I nod to the forensic technicians in white coveralls and look around the hall. It's noticeably anonymous, verging on austere. Or is it just very masculine? They're almost the same thing when it comes to interior design. White walls, grey floor. No sign of the personal belongings you would normally find in an entrance hall: coats, bags or shoes. I step onto the next plastic square and peek into a kitchen. Black-lacquered kitchen cabinets, high gloss. An elliptical table with chairs around it that I recognise from some home decor magazine. Knives on parade along the wall. I note that none seem to be missing.

Manfred puts his hand on my arm.

'Here. This way.'

I continue down the hall on the plastic pads. Pass by a forensic technician equipped with a camera and notepad. A large blood-stain spreads out under the plastic. No, it's no bloodstain, it's a sea. A red, sticky sea of fresh blood that seems to cover this entire section of the hall, from wall to wall and further down the stairs to the basement. From this sea there are tons of footprints in different sizes that lead towards the front door.

'A hell of a lot of blood,' Manfred mumbles, and steps forward with surprising agility, even though the plastic pads buckle under his weight. A numbered sign stands next to a bloody bundle of clothing. I catch a glimpse of a leg and a high-heeled black boot, and then the lower body of a woman lying on her back. It takes a few seconds for me to realise she's been beheaded and that what I first mistook for a bundle of clothing is in fact a head lying on the floor. Or rather, it stands there, as if it were growing from the floor.

Like a mushroom.

Manfred groans and sinks down on his haunches. I lean forward, taking in the macabre scene. Letting it in – that's important. The natural reaction is to shrink back, look away from this terror, but as a detective inspector I have long since learned to suppress that reflex.

The woman's face and brown hair are clotted with blood. If I had to guess, which is a little difficult given the condition of the body, I'd say she's around twenty-five. Her body is also soaked with blood, and I glimpse what look like deep wounds on the forearms. She's wearing a black skirt, black tights, and a grey pullover. Beneath her, soaked in blood, I glimpse a winter coat.

'Fucking hell.'

Manfred nods and strokes his stubble. 'She's been beheaded.'

I nod. There's nothing to add to that statement. It's obvious that's exactly what happened. It requires a considerable strength, or at least laborious effort, to separate a head from its body. It says something about the killer. Exactly what I don't know yet, but it was certainly no cripple who did this. The killer was reasonably strong. Or very motivated.

'Do we know who she is?'

Manfred shakes his head. 'No. But we know who lives here.'

'And who's that?'

'Jesper Orre.'

The name sounds familiar, in the way of a retired athlete or former politician. It rings a bell, but I can't remember where I've heard it before.

'Jesper Orre?'

'Yes, Jesper Orre. The CEO of Clothes&More.'

Then I remember. The controversial head of Scandinavia's fastest-growing clothing chain. The man the media loves to hate. For his management practices, for his many love affairs, and for his frequent politically incorrect statements to the media.

Manfred sighs deeply and stands up. I follow his lead. 'The murder weapon?' I ask.

He points silently down the hall. At the far end, next to a staircase that seems to lead down to a basement, lies a large knife, or maybe a machete. I can't see it clearly. Beside it stands a small sign neatly placed with the number 5 on it.

'And Jesper Orre, have we got hold of him?'

'No. No one seems to know where he is.'

'What else do we know?'

'The body was found by a passing neighbour who noticed the front door was open. We talked to her. She's at the hospital now – apparently she's having heart problems from the shock. Anyway, she hasn't seen anything else of note. Unfortunately, she stomped around quite a bit in the hall, so we'll see if the technicians can lift any useful footprints. There's blood in the snow outside too. Presumably the killer tried to wipe it off after the murder.'

I look around. The floor next to the front door is covered with a jumble of red tracks. Along the walls there are blood splatters and bloody handprints. The scene resembles a Jackson Pollock painting: it looks like someone poured red paint onto the floor, rolled around in it, and then splashed paint all over everything else as well.

'The murder seems to have been preceded by a pretty bad fight,' Manfred continues. 'The victim has defensive wounds on her forearms and hands. The coroner's preliminary assessment is that she died between three and six p.m. yesterday. The victim is a female around twenty-five years old and the cause of death is likely the many injuries to the throat when the head was . . . Well, you can see for yourself.'

Manfred falls silent.

'And the head,' I say. 'How did it end up like that, the right way up? Could that be by chance?'

'The coroner and technicians say it's probable that the killer placed it that way.'

'So fucking sick.'

Manfred nods and holds my gaze with his small brown eyes. Then he lowers his voice, as if he doesn't want anyone else in the room to hear what he says, for whatever reason. The only people left in here are the technicians.

'Listen, this is eerily similar to . . .'

'But that was ten years ago.'

'Still.'

I nod. I can't deny that there are similarities to a murder we investigated on Södermalm ten years ago, one we failed to solve, despite being one of the most extensive investigations in Swedish criminal history.

'As I said, that was ten years ago. There's no reason to believe that . . .'

Manfred waves his hand dismissively.

'No. I know. You're probably right.'

'And this Orre fella, the guy that lives here, what do we know about him?'

'Not much yet, beyond what you can read in the papers. But Sanchez is working on it. She promised to come back with something by tonight.'

'And what do the papers say?'

'Well, the usual gossip. They call him a slave driver. The union hates him and has filed several lawsuits against the company. Apparently he's a well-known womaniser, too. Tons of ladies.'

'No wife? Children?'

'No, he lives alone.'

I look around the hall, letting my eyes glide across the large kitchen. 'Do you really need a mansion if you live alone?'

Manfred shrugs.

' "Need" is a relative term. The neighbour, the lady they took to the hospital, said there have been different women living here every now and then, but she's lost count of how many.'

We walk out again, take off our shoe covers and gloves. About thirty feet away, near the side entrance, there appears to be a burnt-down shed, half covered by snow.

Manfred lights a cigarette, coughs and turns towards me.

'I forgot to mention that. There was a fire in his garage three weeks ago. His insurance company is investigating the matter.'

I look at the charred remains of beams sticking up out of the snow and it reminds me of the pines at the Woodland Cemetery. The same silent, dark figures silhouetted against the snow, evoking the same disquieting sense of impermanence as well as death.

During the car ride into the city, I think of Janet again. There's something about the most heinous crimes, the worst horrors, that always makes me think about her. I guess because Janet set me off balance, the way a crime like this does. Or maybe, on some primitive, subconscious level I sometimes wish she were dead, like the woman in the white house. Obviously I don't really want to kill her – she is Albin's mother, after all – but the feeling is there.

My life was infinitely simpler before we met.

Janet worked in a cafe near the central police station on Kungsholmen. We always said hello to each other when I went in. Sometimes, if there weren't many customers, she'd sit with me for a bit, treat me to a coffee, and we'd chat. She had short, blonde, punky hair and a gap between her front teeth that was sometimes charming, sometimes not. It was something to keep your eyes focused on, a fixed point like the picture of a fly in a urinal. Plus she had amazing tits. Of course I'd had women before. Quite a few actually, but no serious relationships. They came and went without making much of an impression on me. I doubt I made much of an impression on their lives either.

But Janet was different. She was stubborn, unbelievably stubborn. I think we'd gone out to dinner maybe three or four times, ended up in bed together about the same, when she started going on at me about moving in together. Of course I said no. I didn't want to live with her. Janet's non-stop babbling had already started to get on my nerves. I found myself wishing more and more often that she would shut up. But sometimes when she was sleeping, naked in my narrow bed, I found her indescribably beautiful. Stillness and silence suited her so much better than nagging. I wished she could always be like that. But it was an absurd wish. You can't ask your girlfriend to be quiet and naked.

At least not all the time.

In the beginning most of her badgering was about small things, like taking trips together. She would come home with a bag full of travel brochures and devote an entire evening to judging which destinations were the best. Mallorca or Ibiza. Canary Islands or Gambia. Rhodes or Cyprus. It might be about where the weather was best, the food was most delicious, or where you could buy the most exciting junk.

In the end, of course, we did take a trip, and it wasn't that bad. There wasn't much to do in that little village on the east coast of Mallorca, and Janet spent most of the week in her bikini reading *The Clan of the Cave Bear*, which meant she was quiet at least. And almost naked.

And then there was the sex.

The sex was incredible, I can't deny it. All that wine and sangria in the heat might have helped. She was like an animal, uninhibited and vulnerable at the same time. Sometimes I caught myself thinking there was something almost masculine about her behaviour in bed. With that demanding, impatient desire that wanted to be satisfied immediately and in a surprisingly selfish way. She took what she wanted, and at that time it was me, my body. And maybe it happened that, in the heat of the moment, I did seriously consider a life with her. Maybe I said so too. I don't remember.

There's so much you don't remember.

But we were hardly home again before she started talking about buying an apartment together. I explained to her as clearly as I could that I wasn't ready to move in with her, but it was as if she didn't want to hear what I said. As usual, she had set her sights on a goal – an apartment and a family – and shouldn't I feel the same since, after all, I was thirty-three?

She had my name tattooed on her lower back as well, 'Peter' on a banner carried by two doves. It made me uneasy, though I didn't really know why. I guess because a tattoo is for ever and just the thought of spending eternity with Janet gave me the willies.

This all coincided with my new job as a detective, so naturally I was busy at work. I took every single case very seriously back then, actually thought I was helping to create a better world. I even believed it was possible to imagine what that world might look like.

A better world?

Now, fifteen years later, I know that nothing changes. I've realised that time isn't linear, but circular. It might sound pre-tentious, but it's really quite banal. Time is a circle, like a ring of sausage. It's not something to spend too much time contem-plating. It is the way it is. New murders and new police officers with a romantic idea of the profession throwing themselves into their jobs. New criminals who, as soon as they're imprisoned, are replaced by even newer ones.

It never ends.

Eternity is a ring of sausage. And Janet wanted to share it with me.

I tend to think I was firmer at the beginning of our relationship. Back then I'd actually stand up to her crazy ideas. But over time she broke down my resistance, or maybe I gave up my defence strategy. Became more evasive. Replied that we 'might move in together next year' when she brought it up. Then found fault with all the apartments she dragged me to: too far down in the building, too high up in the building (it's a fire hazard!), too far away from the city, too centrally located (so loud!), or whatever I could come up with.

She always looked crushed as we walked home from those viewings. Staring down at the pavement without saying a word, her long blonde fringe draped like a curtain in front of her eyes. Holding her bag tightly in front of her chest, like a shield. Lips pressed together into a thin, bloodless dash.

Janet knew all the tricks. Knew that the guilt she provoked in me would make me even weaker and more manageable. Sometimes I wondered where she'd learned all that, how someone so young could be so skilled at manipulation.

Maybe it was my experiences from the relationship with Janet that made me so fascinated with Manfred when we started working together a few years later. Although on the surface he gave an almost comical impression – partly due to the tension between his appearance and his unpolished language – he also possessed an inner strength that I admired immediately. After just a few days he took me aside and explained that he was getting a divorce, and it was probably best that I was informed since it might affect his work.

Manfred was married to Sara at the time, and they had three teenagers together. I remember I asked what Sara thought about the divorce, and Manfred responded, 'It doesn't matter, because I've made up my mind.' Something about that statement got me thinking. He had made the decision on his own, and he was going to get that divorce no matter what Sara thought.

I couldn't quite put it together.

At the same time, it worried me. There was a risk that Manfred, who was so clear-sighted and strong, might see right through me. See my weakness, my ambivalence and my unwillingness to commit myself. Qualities I'd learned were so ugly that you were better off hiding them. Qualities that smelled bad when they surfaced, like rotting leaves floating on a river.

A few years later I actually told Manfred about the wedding thing. At first he looked perplexed, as if he couldn't really understand what I'd said, then he started laughing. He laughed and laughed until tears ran down his round, ruddy cheeks and his double chins bobbed. He laughed until he almost had to lie down on the floor.

There's a lot you can say about Manfred, but he certainly does see the brighter side of life.

It's dark by the time I arrive at the police station on Kungsholmen. It seems to have got colder, too, because instead of sleet, large, downy flakes are falling over Polhemsgatan. If the police station hadn't been so unbelievably ugly, the scene might have been a beautiful one, but instead the gigantic buildings dominate, a reminder of the post-industrial brutalist architectural style that was so in vogue in the sixties. The screens of light silhouetted on the facade reveal my colleagues hard at work inside; the fight against crime never calls it a night. Not even on a Friday evening just before Christmas. And especially not when a young woman has been brutally murdered.

On the stairway to the second floor, I run into Sanchez. 'You look tired,' she says.

She's wearing a cream-coloured silk blouse and smart black trousers that make her look just like the desk officer she is. She has her dark hair in a ponytail, and I can see the tattoo on her neck. It appears to be a snake winding its way up from her back towards her left ear, as if trying to nip at her earlobe.

'You don't look so good yourself,' I answer.

She smiles with deceptive smoothness, and I know immediately that I will have to pay for that comment later.

'I've put together some information on Jesper Orre. I gave the material to Manfred.'

'Thanks,' I say and continue up the stairs.

Manfred is drinking tea in front of his computer and waves me over when I come in. On his desk are photos of Afsaneh, his young wife, and their soon-to-be one-year-old daughter, Nadja.

'Have you eaten?' he asks.

'Not hungry. Thanks.'

'No. That visit wasn't too good for the appetite.'

I think of the head in the middle of a puddle of blood. People do strange things to each other, sometimes for no reason and sometimes because of feuds that last for generations. I remember a TV programme I saw a few months ago, which tried to answer the question: Is man a peaceful or a murderous animal? I thought the question itself was strange. There is no doubt humans are the planet's most dangerous animal; we constantly hunt and kill not only other species, but our own. The membrane of civilisation is as thin and cosmetic as the garish nail varnish Janet loves to wear.

'Get anything on Jesper Orre?'

Manfred nods and runs his thick finger over the text in front of him. 'Jesper Andreas Orre. Forty-five years old. Born and raised in Bromma.'

Manfred pauses and reaches for his reading glasses, while I reflect on this. Forty-five years old, four years younger than me, and possibly guilty of a brutal murder. Or maybe he too is a victim; too soon to tell, though it's statistically likely he's involved in the crime. The simplest explanation is also usually the right one in the end.

Manfred clears his throat. He continues:

'Has been CEO of the clothing chain Clothes&More for two years. He's . . . what we'd call controversial. Not well liked, considered a tough nut. Apparently fired people for being at home with sick children, that sort of thing. According to the union anyway. They've filed several civil lawsuits against the company. He made 4,378,000 kronor in taxable income last year. No criminal record, never married. Often mentioned in the media, mostly by tabloids, and mostly about his love life. Sanchez spoke to his parents and his secretary, and nobody has heard from him in the last few hours. But he went to work as usual on Friday and apparently seemed completely "normal".'

Manfred makes air quotes when he says the word 'normal' and meets my eyes over the top of his glasses.

'In a relationship?'

'According to the parents, no. And the secretary indicated that he's been very reticent about his private life since the media started writing about him. We got contact information for some of his friends, too. Sanchez is getting in touch with them.'

'And what about that fire?'

'Right. The fire.' Manfred flips through the stack of papers again. 'Jesper Orre was in the process of building a garage, but three weeks ago it burnt down, along with two cars he owned. Quite expensive cars apparently. A . . . let me see now . . . an MG and a Porsche. The insurance company is investigating whether the fire was arson. Sanchez is going talk to them, too.'

I look out the window. The snow is falling more heavily, obscuring the view. Manfred sees my expression.

'Soon,' he says. 'I have to go home. Nadja has an ear infection.'

'Again?'

'You know how it is at that age.'

I nod, thinking that I actually don't know. It has been a long time since Albin was little, and when he was I almost never saw him. Ear infections, stomach flu – all that passed me by.

'Peter,' Manfred says. 'It wouldn't hurt to dig around a little in that old investigation again. The method is a little too similar to just ignore it. I could talk to the people involved. Maybe dig up that witch-lady, too. What was her name again? Hanne?'

I turn towards Manfred, slowly. Careful not to reveal the kind of effect that name has on me. How the memories rush out, spreading through every cell in my body.

Hanne.

'No,' I say, perhaps a little too shrilly, I'm not sure. I no longer have control over my voice. 'No, we definitely don't need to contact her.'

Emma

Two months earlier

'Damn, that's a huge rock.'

Olga's skinny fingers snatch the ring and hold it up against light, as if she's trying to make sure it's real.

'Very nice,' she says, and hands it back to me. 'What did it cost?'

'It was a gift. I couldn't ask that.'

'Why not?'

'You just can't.'

There's silence for a moment.

'So tell us,' Mahnoor says. 'Who's the prince?'

'I can't . . .'

'Oh, come on,' Mahnoor giggles. 'You're engaged now. How secret can it be?'

A thick black braid hangs over her shoulder. Around her eyes she's painted a dark ring of eyeliner.

'It's complicated,' I begin.

'My aunt married her cousin. They didn't tell nobody for ten years,' Olga offers helpfully. 'They have two children. That is complicated. For real.'

'I promise. It's not someone I'm related to. There's no incest going on. It's just . . . complicated.'

'Like on Facebook? "It's complicated." '

Olga laughs slyly. 'Maybe.'

Silence falls in the tiny kitchenette, and the fridge turns on with a sigh. I can understand my colleagues' curiosity. I would have reacted the same way. But this is different. This is an exceptional situation. It would be wrong and irresponsible of me to tell anyone, especially Olga and Mahnoor. It could cause trouble for Jesper, and ultimately myself.

Besides, I promised.

Olga sweeps the crumbs on the table into a pile, draws patterns in it with her long white acrylic nails.

'I don't understand why all the secrecy,' she whines. 'It would be one thing if he was married, but obviously he's not, because you're engaged to him!'

Mahnoor raises a hand.

'She doesn't want to tell. Just respect that.'

I mime a thanks to Mahnoor, who returns the smile and moves her plait onto her back.

Olga squeezes her thin lips and rolls her eyes.

'Whatever.'

Silence again. Mahnoor clears her throat.

'How was your mother's funeral, Emma? Did it go well?'

Mahnoor. Always so kind and considerate. A soft voice and a slow, tentative way of speaking. Words like small, soft caresses. I push the ring into place. Breathe.

'It went well. Not a lot of people, just the closest.'

In fact, there were only five people in the small chapel. A few lonely wreaths lay on the simple wooden casket. The organist played some hymns, even though I knew my mother hated everything about hymns and prayers. In death, as in life, you have to bow to tradition, that's what I think.

'How are you feeling now? Are you OK?' Mahnoor looks worried.

'I'm OK.'

Fact is I don't really know what I feel, but whatever it is, it's too hard to explain. The situation is surreal. I can't get it through my head that my mother is dead, that it really was her large, fat body wedged into that coffin. That someone had dressed her, combed her wiry bottle-blonde hair, and laid her in there. That the lid had been closed and nailed shut, or whatever it is they do.

What should I be feeling?

Despair, sadness? Relief? My relationship with my mother was complicated, to say the least, and in the last few years, since she'd started drinking 'full time', as one of my aunts put it, we hadn't seen each other much.

And now this thing with Jesper. Amid all this misery, he gives me the ring, says he wants to share his life with me. I look down at the diamond sparkling on my finger, think that no matter what happens no one can take this away from me. I'm worth it. I've earned it.

The door flies open with a bang.

'How many times do I have to tell you, you can't leave me alone in the shop? You're sitting around smoking while—'

'Nobody's smoking,' Olga interrupts sharply, and runs her hand through her long thin hair.

Her comment surprises me. Arguing with Björne doesn't usually turn out well. He stiffens, stretches his long thin body, and stuffs his hands deep into the pockets of his jeans, which are just perfectly distressed and hang perfectly low on his backside. He switches his weight back and forth on his cowboy boots, stares at Olga, and raises his chin, making his underbite even more pronounced than usual. He looks like a fish, I think. An evil fish that lurks in murky water waiting for its prey. His dark, matted hair hangs low on his neck as he jerks his head back.

'Did I ask for your opinion, Olga?'

'No, but—'

'Well then. I suggest you shut your mouth and help me tag jeans, instead of sitting here admiring your new Russian nails.'

He turns around and slams the door behind him.

'Penis,' says Olga, who despite ten years in Sweden still has trouble finding the right words.

'Guess we'd better get out there,' Mahnoor says, and stands up, pulls on her blouse a bit as if to smooth it, and opens the door.

On the way home I do some food shopping. Jesper likes meat and tonight we're celebrating, so I buy us some tenderloin – the expensive organic kind, even though I can't really afford it. I buy lettuce, cherry tomatoes and goat's cheese to grill on little toasts as well. I spend a long time in front of the shelves at the off-licence. I run my hand over the bulging bottles standing to attention before me. Wine is not my area of expertise, but we usually drink something red. Jesper is fond of South African wines, so I settle on a hundred-kronor bottle of Pinotage.

It's dark by the time I walk down Valhallavägen towards home. A cold wind is blowing from the north and small hard raindrops whip into my face. I look down at the wet black pavement and hurry the final length to the door.

The apartment building was built in 1925 and stands right next to the Fältöversten shopping centre in a posh part of Stockholm. One of my aunts lived here until her death three years ago. For some unfathomable reason I inherited the apartment, which caused quite a bit of controversy among my relatives. Why should I, Emma, who hadn't even been close to Agneta, inherit her apartment in the inner city? How did I trick her into giving it to me?

It wasn't completely irrational. Aunt Agneta had no children of her own and we did meet now and then. All of my aunts got together sometimes, determined to keep their dysfunctional matriarchy alive, and sometimes I would join them.

I unlock the door, press down on the brass handle. The familiar scent of toast and detergent hits me. And something else, something a little stale that I can't quite identify. Something organic and familiar. I set the bags down carefully on the floor, turn on the light in the hall and pull off my wet shoes. I drape my coat on a hanger, then grab a towel and gently wipe the rain off it.

There are two envelopes on the floor. Bills. I pick them up and take them into the kitchen. Put them in the pile with the other ones and reminders. The bundle is alarmingly thick, and I remember that I really need to talk to Jesper about that. Maybe not tonight, but soon. I can't just keep putting the bills in a pile. One day they'll have to be paid.

I call Sigge's name and get some cat food out of the cabinet. As soon as he hears the creaking of hinges he's there, stroking himself against my calves. I bend forward, pet his black fur, chat a bit with him and then go out into the living room.

My apartment is sparsely furnished. I inherited the Carl Malmsten chairs from Aunt Agneta as well. The table and chairs in the hall I bought online and the bed is from IKEA. I have a desk, too, which I found at the Salvation Army. It's covered with books and red notebooks. On top of my job at the shop, I'm studying for my International Baccalaureate. I dropped out of school. Certain things happened to me that made me both unable and unwilling to continue, but school was always easy for me. Especially maths. There's something liberating about the world of numbers. There is no grey area, no subjectivity, no room for interpretation; either you've calculated right or you've calculated wrong.

I wish the rest of life were that simple.

For a moment I think of Woody. His long black hair fastened in a ponytail at the nape of the neck. His habit of keeping his hand on his cheek while he listened – he always seemed to listen with astonishing intensity. As if all of us had something truly important to say. And maybe we did. I shiver and go out into the living room.

One day I'll stop thinking about Woody, I tell myself. One day his memory will fade like an old Polaroid, and I'll continue on as if he'd never existed.

There's one object of real value in my home – a painting by Ragnar Sandberg hanging in the bedroom. A naive composition of football players in yellow and blue. I like it a lot. Mum often suggested I sell it, so we could split the money and she could drink her share, but I refused. I liked keeping it there on the wall, where it had always hung.

Aunt Agneta left me a little money, too. One hundred thousand kronor, to be precise. Carefully wrapped bundles of hundred-kronor bills that I found in the linen cupboard. I never told my mum. I knew all too well what she would have done.

I go over to the window and look out.

Five floors below me Valhallavägen stretches out like a giant black artery feeding traffic to Lidingövägen and the centre of the city, part of the gigantic circulatory system of roads criss-crossing Stockholm. The rain seems to have grown heavier. It's beating against my window, leaving oily streaks behind. It must be cold out, almost freezing, I think, and shiver.

I unpack the food, cut the goat's cheese into pieces and put them on small toasts. Turn on the oven and prepare the salad. Then I take a shower. Feel the warm water slide over my body. Breathe in the hot steam. Carefully wash every inch of my body with the soap I know he loves. My breasts feel tender and swollen when I massage them. I reach for the shampoo, wash my hair before stepping out of the old-fashioned sitting bath.

The bathroom is filled with steam. I open the door a crack, wipe the mirror with a towel and lean forward. My face looks swollen and flushed. Freckles stand out clearly against pale skin, hundreds of small islands scattered haphazardly across a sea. Some larger, some smaller. Some are fused into clusters, forming irregular continents of reddish skin on the pale sea.

I gently start to straighten out my long reddish-brown hair with a wide-toothed comb. I examine my breasts. They're big, much too big for my body, with wide pale-pink areolas. I have always hated them, ever since those small, hideous protrusions started to become visible, like boils on my pale skin. I did everything I could to hide them: wore baggy shirts, walked with a hunched back. Ate too much.

Jesper says he loves my breasts and I believe him. He lies between my legs, caressing them like two puppies, and talks to one and then the other, infatuated. It occurs to me that love isn't just what you feel for another human being, it's also seeing yourself through your lover's eyes. To see beauty where before you saw only flaws.

I put on my make-up painstakingly. Jesper doesn't like too much make-up, but that doesn't mean no make-up, just the appearance of no make-up. It takes a lot longer than you'd think to get that natural look. When I'm done, I dab a little perfume in all the strategic places: my wrists, between my breasts, my neck. Put a little near my groin, too. Then I pull on my black dress, with nothing underneath, dry my feet carefully on the bath mat and go out.

Jesper is usually punctual. I'm tempted to put the canapés into the oven at seven, but they only take a few minutes so it's better to wait until he comes. The rain is still beating against the dark pane of the window, with undiminished intensity. Outside, the sound of sirens fades away. I light candles on the table. The draught from the leaky old windows makes the flames flutter, and the shadows in the room seem to come alive, start to move. They wave across the shabby kitchen doors and table. For a moment it feels as though the entire room is rocking, and it's as if it's contagious, because suddenly I feel a slight nausea.

I close my eyes and steady myself against a chair. Think of him.

Jesper Orre. Of course I'd heard of him, seen glimpses of him on TV and in the tabloids. And, of course, sometimes we talked about him at work. We knew our CEO was controversial, both in business and other things. He was basically the bad boy of the fashion industry, with a reputation for being both tough and unscrupulous. When he became CEO, he fired the whole management team within a month and brought in his own gang. More changes followed quickly. Twenty per cent of the employees were let go. New directives for how customers should be treated were sent out. Stricter dress codes for staff were enforced. Shorter lunches. Fewer breaks.

When he came into the shop that day in May, I didn't recognise him at first. There was something a little confused about his whole appearance. He stood in the middle of the men's department and spun round and round slowly, like a child standing in the middle of a circus ring staring wide-eyed at the audience.

I walked over and asked if I could help. It's my job to do that, and the company has manuals with scripted lines that employees should use – another one of Jesper's ideas that the union didn't like.

He turned towards me, still with that confused expression, ran his hand over his chest with embarrassment and pointed to a large orange stain on his shirtfront.

'I've got a board meeting in half an hour,' he said, while continuing to avoid my gaze, eyes darting around the shop. 'I need to find a new shirt.'

'Spaghetti bolognese?'

He froze and a hint of a smile crossed his tanned face. Then he met my eyes and at that moment I recognised him. Luckily, he looked away again, because his presence suddenly felt so overwhelming, so palpable that I didn't know what to do. And he left me alone in that silence, incapable of handling the situation.

It took a moment or two. Eventually I collected myself. 'What size?'

He looked at me again, and now I noticed how tired he looked.

Dark circles under his eyes, wide streaks of grey at his temples and a sad frown pulling down the corner of his mouth gave his face an almost bitter cast. He looked older than in the pictures. Older and more tired.

'Size?'

'Yes – your shirt size that is.'

'Sorry, of course.' He told me.

'And what colour would you like?'

'I don't know. Maybe white. Something neutral. Something appropriate for a board meeting.'

He turned his back to me and peered across the shop. I grabbed three shirts I thought might work. When I came back, he was still standing there. 'Do you think you could help me decide?' he asked.

'Of course.'

There was nothing strange about that question; it was part of the job; helping customers to find clothes that looked good. I waited outside the fitting room until he came out in the first shirt, the white one.

'Does it work?'

'Absolutely. It fits perfectly. But try the other ones too.'

The curtain swung noiselessly back. Two minutes later he came out in the next shirt: a blue-and-white-striped one with a button-down collar.

'Hmm.'

'You don't like it?'

He looked so worried I almost started laughing. 'No, no, it's just not right for a board meeting. You should probably wear something a little more . . . formal.'

He nodded as if ready to obey my every whim and stepped into the fitting room again. 'Should I try the third one on too?' he said from inside the stall.

'I definitely think you should.'

I was starting to be amused by all of this. It was like a fun little game I was playing with our CEO, who had sneaked into the shop incognito. Like a king in a fairy tale who dresses like a beggar to blend in with his subjects.

The fitting-room door opened, and he stepped out in a light-blue shirt.

'That's perfect. You should take that one,' I declared. 'It's serious, but not as boring as the white one.'

'So . . . we sell boring clothes in this shop?'

There was a new light in his eyes, and he looked at me with an entirely different focus from before.

'Well, sometimes our customers need boring clothes.'

'Touché.'

He smiled and stopped halfway into the fitting room. 'I like your style. What's your name?'

'Emma. Emma Bohman.'

He nodded and disappeared behind the curtain without saying another word.

When I was ringing up the shirt, something happened that would change my life for ever. Jesper started frantically searching for his wallet. It was clear he was becoming increasingly embarrassed.

'I don't understand. It should be ...' He searched his pockets, then shook his head in resignation. 'Damn,' he muttered between his teeth.

'Listen, it's fine if you come back with the money later. I know who you are.'

'Absolutely not. Then your till will be off. I really don't want to cause problems for you.'

'Well, if you try to trick me, I'll send the police after you.'

The joke seemed to escape him. I could see drops of sweat forming at his hairline. They sparkled like crystals under the harsh artificial light.

'Damn,' he repeated, and somehow he made it sound like a question, as if he wanted my advice on this awkward situation.

I leaned forward, put my hand gently on his arm.

'Listen. I'll lend you the money. Here, I'll write down my number for you. Pay me back when you can.'

And that's how it happened.

He took my phone number with relief. On his way out of the shop he waved my note in the air, as if I'd given him some kind of diploma, and smiled at me.

I glance at the clock hanging above the television. Twenty past seven. Where is he? Maybe he got the time wrong. Maybe he thought he was supposed to come at eight rather than seven. But something feels off. I have never met anyone as punctual as Jesper. He's always on time and always arrives with fresh flowers in hand. He is, in short, the perfect gentleman. He can seem rude and arrogant, almost brutal at first, but in actuality he is emotional, empathetic and as playful as a child.

And punctual.

I pour myself another glass of wine and turn on the news. French farmers have dumped tons of potatoes on the ring road around Paris to protest against some change to EU subsidies. A tornado hit Sala this afternoon and seriously damaged a new school. Chinese scientists have found a gene that, if it is defective, causes prostate cancer.

I turn off the television again. Fiddle impatiently with my mobile. I don't like to bother Jesper, but I'm worried he's misunderstood something: time, place, date?

I send him a short text message, asking if he's on his way. Hopefully I don't seem too persistent.

Jesper Orre. If Olga and Mahnoor only knew.

If only Mum could have known.

Something twists insides my stomach. Don't think about Mum.

But it's too late. I can already sense her presence in my small living room. Smell the mixture of beer and sweat. See the pale flesh pouring out over the sofa where she sits slumped, snoring loudly in front of the TV, a half-empty beer can planted firmly between her knees.

Mum always made a big deal about never drinking anything stronger than beer. Lena, one of my aunts, used to point out that an alcoholic who only drank beer was the most tragic, most inferior addict of all, with one leg in the grave and the other on the way to the off-licence to fill the fridge.

But the saddest part of all was that Mum hadn't always been like that. At some point, long ago, she'd been different. I still remember it clearly, and sometimes I wonder if I mourn the loss of the person she once was more than I do her death.

One early memory. I'm sitting with my mother on my narrow bed. The room's walls are dirty, covered with the prints of fingers and hands and even feet. 'How do you manage to climb these walls like a monkey?' Mum used to say, then sigh theatrically as she'd try to rub away the prints with a damp cloth.

It was dark outside. Someone was shovelling snow in the court-yard. I could hear the sharp blows as the shovel penetrated through the snow and hit the cobblestones below. It was cold inside, and both Mum and I were wearing long-sleeved pyjamas and socks. The book about the three bears was resting in Mum's lap.

'Keep going!' I said.

'OK, but just a little longer,' Mum said, yawning, and turned a page that was mended with tape in one corner. She looked at the text with a serious expression on her face.

'"Who has been sleeping in my bed?"' I read, following the words with my index finger.

I was seven years old and in my second year at school. I'd learned to read before I started school.

I don't really remember how I learned. I guess some kids just pick it up, crack the code on their own. In any case, my teacher had been very happy when she called and told my mum I was way ahead of my classmates when it came to reading. And since, as the teacher pointed out, 'reading is the basis for all other learning', that meant things would go well for me in the future.

'And the next line?'

'The little bear looked at the big bear and sho . . . shook his head,' I read.

Mum nodded in concentration. It looked like she was pondering some complicated maths problem. At that very moment there was a light knock on the bedroom door. Dad peeked in. He was holding a book and a packet of cigarettes in his hand. His longish hair fell across his face in a soft wave. I always thought that Dad looked a little like a rock star with that floppy hair and his relaxed style. He was cool in a way that none of the other mothers or fathers were, and I used to wish he would take me to school rather than Mum.

'I just wanted to say goodnight,' he said and came into the room. He walked to the bed, leaned over and kissed me on the cheek. His stubble felt scratchy against my skin and the smell of cigarette smoke stung my nostrils.

'Goodnight,' I said and followed him with my eyes as he walked out again. His skinny back, combined with his hairstyle, or lack of hairstyle, and the distinctive way he moved his arms as he walked made him look like a teenager.

I looked at Mum again. She was truly Dad's opposite. Her body was large and spool-shaped, like an animal that lives in the sea, maybe a sea lion or a whale. Her bleached hair stuck out in every direction, and her breasts threatened to burst through her flannel pyjamas every time she took a deep breath.

'Now it's your turn,' I said.

Mum hesitated for a second, then moved her index finger slowly along the text. ' "I hav . . ." '

' "Haven't", I filled in. Mum nodded, tried again.

' "I haven't slept . . . in your bed," said the li . . . li . . . little b . . . b . . .'

'Bear,' I said. Mum clenched her hand hard.

'Drat. "Bear" – that's a hard word.'

'Soon you'll think it's easy,' I said seriously. Mum looked at me. Her eyes suddenly looked shiny and she squeezed my hand.

'Do you really think so?'

'Of course. Everyone in my class can read.'

That all their mothers and fathers could also read, I didn't say to her. Even though I was only seven, I knew it would make her sad. I was the only one who knew. Not even Mum or Dad's colleagues knew about her shameful secret.

'We can keep practising in the morning,' Mum said and kissed me on the cheek. 'And don't say anything to Dad about . . .'

'I promise.'

She turned off the light and left the room. I lay there in my bed, a warm, soft feeling spreading inside me. It was the feeling of being not only loved but also needed.

What if Mum were still alive; what if she'd had the chance to see me with Jesper? What would she have thought? Something tells me she wouldn't have liked the attention our relationship is likely to attract. She would have pursed her lips, given me a disappointed, self-pitying look, and mumbled something about how I didn't care about her any more, but what else could she expect since I'd never helped her with anything. Then she would have started talking about that hag Löfberg's daughter, who still lived at home, even though she was thirty, and took care of her old mother.

I glance at the clock. Nine-thirty. A vague feeling of unease is building in my chest and before I can put words to it, I know what it is: fear. What if something has actually happened to Jesper? It's dark and windy and the roads are surely covered with a thick layer of freezing rain. I think about it for a few seconds, then pick up the phone on the table. Hesitate. It's strange how hard I find it to call him. It's as if my value is in some way dependent on him wanting me more than I want him – or at least wanting me as much. Only desperate women pester you, I think, and desperate women are hard to love.

In the end, I ring anyway.

The call goes directly to voicemail and I wonder if he's turned off his mobile and why. I empty my wine glass, pull the blanket over me and close my eyes.

It took a week for Jesper to call me about the loan and to invite me to lunch as well.

We met one Saturday close to his small pied-à-terre on Söder-malm. The restaurant was crowded and noisy. I almost didn't recognise him at first. He was wearing jeans and a T-shirt, looking considerably younger than he had in his suit that day in the shop. His whole attitude was different. The somewhat awkward, confused expression was gone. His back was straight. He smiled and looked confidently at me.

'Emma,' he said and kissed me on the cheek.

I felt embarrassed. No one kissed me on the cheek, not even my own mother.

Especially not my own mother. 'Hi,' I said.

He leaned back and gazed at me in silence, sat like that until I felt embarrassed, compelled to say something, if only to puncture the oppressive silence.

'So how did the board meeting go?'

'Good.'

He smiled. There was something greedy, almost hungry, in his eyes, as if he saw something edible when he looked at me. Suddenly I felt uncomfortable with the whole situation.

'Why did you invite me to lunch?'

The question just popped out unbidden. His behaviour confused me so much that the only way I could think of to handle it was brutal honesty.

'Because I'm curious about you,' he replied without hesitation and without taking his eyes off me.

I stared down into my lap, examining my new jeans which I'd bought specifically for this lunch. So silly. As if Jesper Orre cared what I wore – a shopgirl.

'I was curious about you because you treated me like an equal,' he clarified.

I met his eyes. For a moment I thought I caught a glimpse of something hidden in there, pain perhaps, or disgust, as if he'd taken a bite of something bitter.

'An equal?'

He nodded slowly. A collective roar came from the bar. I turned around. On the wall-mounted TV screen Arsenal had just scored against Manchester United.

Jesper leaned forward across the table, putting his face close to mine, so close that I could smell his aftershave and the beer on his breath. Again I felt discomfort creep over me. 'When you are . . . When you have the job I have,' he corrected himself, 'few people behave normally around you. Most people treat you with exaggerated respect. Some don't even dare to talk to me. Few say what they really think and feel. It's exhausting. And kind of lonely, if you know what I mean. But you said what you thought. You treated me like a normal person.'

I shrugged. 'Aren't you?'

He laughed and took a sip of beer. His arms were sunburnt and covered in golden hairs.

'Call it crazy, but I felt some kind of connection with you. If you're honest . . .'

'Yes?'

'Aren't you also the kind of person who feels lonely? Odd? Different from the people around you? An . . . observer?'

I nodded slowly. He was right. I had always felt different. Ever since I was little. Always had the strange feeling that I was playing a supporting role in my own life. That I was sitting in a bubble, looking at myself from the outside. The question was how the hell Jesper Orre could have seen that from ten minutes in the shop with me.

Dejected sighs came from the bar. 'It hit the post,' said Jesper.

'How . . . do you know that?'

'What?'

He glanced in confusion towards the TV screen, as if my question was about the game.

'About me. You bought a shirt from me and now you're claiming we're alike. And that we're lonely. You don't know anything about me. Not who I am, where I come from or what I want from my life. Yet you're saying . . . all of this. As if you think you can read me like a book.'

He raised his beer in a toast and winked at me.

'As I said, I like how you treat me like an equal. And you're fearless. Like me.'

I left the restaurant on shaky legs. My cheeks were hot and my hands sweaty. I don't know which I felt more strongly: irritation that he had accurately described me after so little time spent in my company, or the attraction that was already there. And besides all that, I couldn't help but wonder if he was right. Were we alike? Was there a connection, an instant sense of belonging that cut through all the barriers of class and age and profession?

It was just after four as I hurried towards Slussen. The afternoon was warm, and I had only a tank top on. Despite that, sweat was running down between my breasts, and halfway up Götgatan I had to stop to catch my breath. People passed by: pedestrians and shoppers, beggars and veiled women on their way down to the mosque. I felt as if I was in the middle of a flooding river, as if I'd suddenly lost the ability to steer and was bobbing like a stray boat in a sea of people.

When I got to the entrance of the metro, I saw a familiar silhouette in the doorway. Jesper Orre. Somehow he had anticipated where I was going and got there before me.

He took my hand. 'Come,' was all he said.

He pulled me along with him and I couldn't protest, couldn't argue. The feeling of powerlessness was numbing, yet oddly liberating. A release from responsibility and the guilt that comes with it. I followed him. Closed my eyes and let him lead me through the sea of people.

When I wake up it is three o'clock in the morning and I am in a weird half-reclining position in the armchair. My neck is stiff and hurts when I stand up. Darkness has formed a black wall outside my window and the wind has picked up. It's whistling through the cracks and I can feel cold air around my ankles.

For some reason, it makes me think about my dad and the insect I found. I must have been ten or eleven years old.

The caterpillar, which was strikingly plump and pale green, reminded me a bit of a gummy bear with hair on it. It had the same round shape and semi-transparent guts. A bunch of small legs extended from its stomach and on its tail was a small barb. It tickled as it crawled along my freckled hand and up onto my arm.

'Does it bite?' I asked.

Dad shook his head. 'No, the little spike at the back of its body is its anal proboscis. It's completely harmless.'

The caterpillar kept crawling and I turned the underside of my arm upwards so that the dusty ray of sunlight that cut through the window illuminated its small green body. Suddenly it was almost transparent. Like a sparkling, perfectly polished gemstone resting on my wrist.

'Where did you find it?' Dad asked.

'In the bush by the swings.'

He nodded, then said, 'It eats leaves. Come on. Let's go and get some food for it.'

We sneaked through the hall so as not to wake Mum. Dad nodded to me to follow him out and the front door closed behind us with a click. The buildings that surrounded the small courtyard embraced the sparse greenery with their tall concrete bodies. The sun hadn't made it above the rooftops yet and the courtyard lay in shadow. It was also deserted. The swings hung abandoned from their metal bars and the sandpit lay empty in anticipation of the children who would soon be let outside to play. A few cracked plastic shovels lay scattered on the gravel path beside it. In the distance Middle Eastern music played and a child screamed. The scent of coffee hovered in the early summer air.

'Here,' I said and pointed to the bush with the jagged branches.

Dad broke off a few dew-damp twigs in silence, then looked at me seriously. 'Now we're going to build a little nest for it.'

We put branches from the bush into a glass jar, then slipped back into the building as quietly as before. It was dark in the hallway and smelled faintly of Mum's cigarettes. I could hear her snoring in the bedroom next door. Dad was searching a cupboard. The toolbox rattled. When he came back out into the hall, he had a small, sharp object in his hand.

'This is an awl,' he whispered and pushed it through the metal lid several times, making little breathing holes for the green inhabitant of the jar. The caterpillar seemed to accept its new home. Apparently it didn't ask much from life – a branch and some leaves – because it immediately made itself comfortable on one of the thorny twigs.

'What happens now?'

'Something amazing,' Dad said and wiped a few drops of sweat from his sunburnt forehead. 'Something completely amazing. But you have to have patience. Do you have that?'

I reach for my mobile. No missed calls. No text messages. Jesper has skipped our engagement dinner without any explanation. Should I be angry or worried? I decide that unless he's in A&E with his legs in casts, he deserves to be yelled at.

With a blanket wrapped around my shoulders, I shuffle into the kitchen. Put the salad, canapés and wine into the fridge. Then I call for Sigge and go to bed.

Grey-blue morning light filters through my thin curtains. The room feels cold and I crawl further under the covers in search of warmth. Sigge, who is rolled up into a small ball at my feet, wakes up, licks his paws. For a few seconds my mind is empty of everything but his pleasant warmth and the faint sound of raindrops pattering against the window.

Then I remember.

Jesper never turned up yesterday. For some reason he didn't come to his own engagement dinner and I ended up alone in the kitchen with a plate overflowing with canapés and wearing nothing but a low-cut black dress.

My mobile is on the floor. Still no missed calls. No text messages.

I sit up in bed. The room is cold and a draught leaks in. Even though I wrap the duvet tightly around me as I go over to the window, I can feel cold air seeping through the cracks.

I watch the morning traffic creep slowly forwards on Valhallavägen. Tiny people, barely bigger than ants, make their way towards the metro. I go out into the living room to turn on the news. If something has happened – an accident, a crime – maybe they'll mention it. As I sink into one of the green armchairs, I'm overcome with nausea. How much did I drink yesterday? Maybe I should eat something.

I go to the kitchen and open the fridge.

The canapés are lined up neatly on the plate. I grab two, go back to the living room and turn on the TV. But the screen is black and a brief yellow text states that there's no signal. I push one of the canapés into my mouth and go back to the kitchen again, feeling fairly sure what's happened. I carefully move the stack of bills to the table, shove the second canapé into my mouth and start tearing envelopes open. I pull out reminder after reminder from utility companies, my mobile provider and credit-card companies.

In a way, all of this is Jesper's fault. A month ago I lent him some money and since then I've been putting the bills in a pile rather than paying them. My salary isn't enough – it never has been – but before I always had a little nest egg to dip into.

I open the last envelope. It's from the cable company. I glance through its letter threatening termination of my television and broadband subscriptions if I don't pay my bill within ten days.

The letter is dated two weeks ago.

I toss the envelope aside and pick up the stack of bills. Hesitate a moment, not really knowing what to do with them. Then I push them into the empty bread bin. It squeaks as I close the lid.

On the metro, I read the news on my phone. A knifing in Rinkeby, riots in Malmö, but nothing about Jesper Orre. There's also nothing about any traffic accidents that might have occurred during the night.

The metro carriage is packed and the heat and smell of crowded bodies bring on the nausea again. I am forced to get off at the Östermalmstorg station, where I take off my jacket and sit down for a moment on a bench. I put my face in my hands. From the corner of my eye, I see commuters looking at me with puzzled, even anxious, glances but no one stops to ask how I feel and I'm grateful for that.

All I can think about, all I want to know is, where is Jesper and why didn't he turn up last night?

Hanne

Those who claim that unhappiness is the result of having too-high expectations from life are wrong. I've never had any special expectations, didn't expect happiness, money or success. And yet here I am, filled with a disappointment that I can't quite put into words, can't define, that goes beyond what words can describe. Perhaps it's bigger than I am. Maybe I live inside the disappointment rather than the other way around.

As if it were a house that I'm locked inside.

Part of this is of course because I can no longer trust my own body. My intellect, my memory, is disintegrating, fragmenting into small, elusive crumbs that no longer join into any meaningful whole.

I look at the pill organiser on the counter. At all the small white and yellow pills lying in compartments marked with the days of the week. I wonder if any of those pills even have an effect. At my last appointment, the doctor said it was impossible to say anything definite about the course of the disease. It could go fast or slow, take months or years for me to sink into oblivion and confusion. The medicine might work or might not – that too was unpredictable – but the fact that the disease struck me at a relatively young age, only fifty-nine years old, suggests it might become aggressive.

When he said that last bit, about how the disease could become aggressive, I put down the notepad of questions I had prepared. I didn't want to hear any more.

Sometimes it's better not to know.

I take the dog food out of the cabinet and immediately hear the patter of paws approaching from the bedroom. There she stands in front of me on the floor, looking up with her dark eyes. Her head is slightly bent forward and her eyes attentive, pleading. You're ingratiating yourself, I think. Why? Have I ever failed to give you food?

Then I realise that it's actually possible I have forgotten to feed Frida. I forget things all the time now without even knowing it. I look around the cosy kitchen. The cabinets are covered with small yellow Post-it notes, which I use to remind myself of things. Owe hates those notes. Perhaps because he hates my illness, what it does to me, but I suspect he hates what the disease does to him more. How it threatens his self-image and his life's work: the perfect home; the beautiful, intellectual wife; dinners with friends that go on long into the night. He has hinted that he'd rather not invite anyone over with the kitchen looking like this, and deep down I know that he's ashamed. Because it is shameful, losing control of yourself in this way, shameful.

I go out into the living room. Examine my well-ordered life: soft, inviting cushions; antique candlesticks carved from whalebone; bookshelves that stretch from floor to ceiling. Masks and small statues from all over the world are scattered among the books, which bear witness to the trip that never was: *This Cold Heaven: Seven Seasons in Greenland, Inuit Art* and *Eskimo Essays – Tales from the Top of the Earth.*

Owe doesn't share my fascination with Greenland and the Inuit people. Can't understand what's so interesting about that inhospitable, uncivilised Arctic continent. You can't play golf there, the food tastes like shit (Owe's words) and, to add insult to injury, it costs a fortune to get to.

I suppose I've given up hope of ever seeing Greenland. I'm not sure I'd dare to go on a trip like that alone. Not now, when the disease lies in wait for me wherever I go. Waiting to devour me, just like the sea devoured Sedna, according to legend.

The beautiful but vain Inuit maiden Sedna ran away from her father with a storm bird to become his wife. The bird promised

Sedna he'd take her to a fabulous country where she would never be hungry, where tents would be made from the finest hides and where she would sleep on the softest bear skins. But when the girl arrived the tent was made of old fish skins that let in the cold and wind, and she had nothing more than old, hard walrus skins to sleep on and nothing but raw fish scraps to eat.

When spring came, the father went to visit his daughter and found her despondent and exhausted in the storm bird's country. He killed her husband and brought Sedna home in his kayak.

But the birds retaliated. They whipped up a mighty storm and the father was forced to sacrifice his daughter to the sea in order to appease the birds. He threw her overboard into the icy water and when she didn't want to let go of the boat he cut off her fingers one by one. As each finger fell into the sea, it turned into a whale or seal. Finally the sea devoured Sedna and she became its mistress – the goddess of the sea.

The ancient legend of Sedna is a warning, of course, to young Inuit girls about the dangers of vanity and disobeying your father, but it is also about the relentless elements, which we cannot control, but must appease in order not to perish.

I myself have food on the table and a warm bed to return to every night, but still the disease is always there, waiting to devour me. To make me his mistress in the emptiness, in the life of no memory that awaits.

Owe doesn't think we should tell our friends about my illness. Not yet. He repeats it irritatingly often, but always adds that he'll be there to care for me. Just like you always have, I think, but I don't say anything. Because that's exactly how it is: Owe has always taken care of me. Ever since we met when I was nineteen and he twenty-nine, he's taken care of me. Picked me up on the motorway when the car broke down, paid my bills, taken me home from parties when I drank too much. Even pulled me gently out of strange beds, whenever I seriously attempted to revolt by cheating on him. And afterwards, he has always been understanding. Understanding but patronising. He's given me pills that numb and calm. Explained that he knows I'm feeling bad, but that jumping into the arms of a colleague or some peripheral acquaintance won't make my problems go away. I don't understand what's good for me but he loves me anyway.

Years of cloying care have left me feeling suffocated. It's like I can't really breathe in his presence, as if he takes up so much space there's no oxygen left in the room for me. Sometimes I tell him that, and he explains that if I hadn't been so immature and irresponsible, he wouldn't have been forced to act the way he did. I made him like this.

It's my fault. Again.

I tend to think there might be some truth to that, but it's hardly the whole truth. His need for control is pathological and permeates all aspects of my life: what I eat, who I associate with, and yes, even what I think.

Ten years ago I was very close to leaving him. If everything hadn't gone to hell that day, I wouldn't be living with Owe now. But you can't think like that. It will drive you crazy. So much of life doesn't turn out as you expected but it's no excuse for bitterness. So I fight against disappointment as if it were a cluster of weeds, refusing to allow it to take hold in earnest. I try to grab on to all the positives: my work, the research I've dedicated the last ten years to, my friends – the ones who became my family in place of the children who never came.

I set the bowl on the floor and watch Frida gulp down her food. Wonder if maybe life as a dog might not be better after all. Then I pack up my things. Grab my notepad and write, 'IKEA cafe, 2 p.m., help Gunilla choose furniture.' A simple reminder in case I forget where I'm going. Not that it's that bad yet. I remember where I'm going and I can still drive a car. But I dread the day when I have to ask Owe for help with that.

The temperature has dropped well below zero over the weekend, so I put on my down coat and warm boots. I lock both locks on the door (yes, I still remember that too) and go down to the car, which is parked on Skeppargatan, on the hill that leads down to Strandvägen. Everything is blanketed by four inches of snow and it takes me a while to clear enough away from the windscreen so that I can drive.

The clouds hang alarmingly dark and heavy over Nybroviken, and the gently billowing surface of the water seems almost black. The weather forecast calls for more snow, so I decide I'd better get going as quickly as possible – start up the car and drive north. I have to be back by five. Owe and I are going to a Christmas concert at Hedvig Eleonora Church.

Being cultured is very important to Owe. Music, theatre and books aren't just hobbies, they constitute the subject of most of the conversations we have with our friends. If you don't stay up to speed on cultural life, you'll end up embarrassed and silent at our dinner parties.

Just more proof of Owe's excessively controlling behaviour: his need to be in charge of what is discussed when people get together. Sometimes I'm overcome with an almost irrepressible urge to start talking about something completely different. Frivolous topics that would embarrass Owe and make him yell at me after everyone's gone home. Mention how I just got an amazing facial with essential oils or start talking about clothes or jewellery or beach holidays. Or, most unthinkable of all, with feigned seriousness insist that I both read and enjoyed *Fifty Shades of Grey*.

As I exit near Barkarby, I summarise all the reasons I hate Owe: Self-righteous. Egocentric. Narcissistic. Domineering. Smells bad.

Gunilla is already sitting at a table in the cafe. She's hung her little fur jacket on the back of her chair and seems to be studying her nails. Her mid-length strawberry-blonde hair is perfectly blow-dried, and her polo shirt fits her slender frame to a T.

There are several reasons Owe doesn't like Gunilla. First of all, she's one of those superficial people he despises so much: the kind who paints her nails, wears make-up and buys expensive clothes. Also, she laughs too loudly and too long when she visits us, and at all the wrong things. But most important of all, she left her husband after twenty-five years of marriage. Just like that, because she was tired of him. That's just not done. Not in Owe's world anyway.

Not if you're a woman.

Her hug is long and warm and she smells like expensive perfume. 'Here, sit down, I'll go and buy us something,' she says.

I nod and sink into the chair opposite her. Pull off my heavy winter coat and look around. It's remarkable how many people are crowded into the cafe at IKEA. It smells like wet wool, saffron buns, sweat and food. There's scattered laughter and the low hum of conversation coming from nearby tables.

Gunilla returns with a red plastic tray, some saffron buns and two cups. Their spicy scent is unmistakable.

'Mulled wine? Is it alcohol-free?'

She laughs indulgently. Tilts her pretty face.

'No, I thought we should treat ourselves today. Celebrate that I've bought an apartment.'

'But I'm driving.'

'Oh, it's just a tiny cup. And we'll surely be here for a while?'

I shake my head. 'You're funny. Celebrate? At IKEA?'

'Why not?'

'Is there anything more tragic than celebrating at the IKEA cafe?'

Gunilla takes a sip of her hot beverage and looks around. Observing the people sitting at the tables around us. Her bright eyes settle on an elderly couple sitting in silence, each eating their respective child-sized serving of meatballs.

'I can think of worse things. How are you feeling?'

Gunilla is the only one besides Owe who knows. In fact, I told her about the disease before I said anything to Owe. Maybe that means I'm actually closer to her than to my own husband. I guess that's so.

'I feel fine.'

'What did the doctor say?'

'The usual.'

She nods and all at once looks very serious. Takes my hand, squeezes it gently. I can feel her warmth flowing into me.

'You'll tell me if you need any help, right?'

'I don't want any help.'

'That's exactly why.'

Her face looks so serious that I have to laugh.

'And what about you?' I ask. 'How's your love affair going?'

Gunilla smiles and stretches like a cat. Sets her cup of mulled wine on the table, leans over and whispers, as if she's about to reveal a secret.

'Absolutely fantastic. And we're so incredibly . . . attracted to each other. Horny, to be vulgar about it. Is that allowed, at our age?'

'Oh, please. You have no idea what I'd give to be a little horny.'

Owe and I don't have sex any more but I don't want to tell that to Gunilla. Not because she'd have any opinions on it but because I think it's so pathetically tragic to live with someone you don't desire. Only weak people stay in bad relationships. And I don't want to be weak – not even in Gunilla's eyes.

I hear my mobile buzzing in my bag. Pick it up and glance at the screen. I don't recognise the number.

'Go ahead and answer,' Gunilla says. 'I have to use the ladies' anyway.'

I answer as Gunilla stands and walks off, limping slightly. She suffers from sciatica and I suspect she's in more pain than she wants to admit.

The man who's calling has a soft, rich voice. He introduces himself as Manfred Olsson and explains that he's a detective at the National Police. It's been a long time since I've heard from them.

I stopped working for them five or six years ago, when I decided to concentrate full time on my research and end my consultancy work for the police. Or, actually, Owe decided that for me. He thought I was working too much, said it made me surly and grumpy.

Also, we didn't need the money.

'We worked together about ten years ago,' says Manfred Olsson. 'But maybe you don't remember.'

I have no memory of any Manfred Olsson but the last thing I want to do is talk about what I do or don't remember, so I say nothing.

'It was in connection with the investigation of a murder on Södermalm, here in

Stockholm,' he continues. 'A young man was beheaded. The head had been—'

'I remember,' I say. 'You never arrested anyone for that, right?'

Dementia or not, the image of how that man's head had been placed on the floor is etched into my memory. Maybe because the murder was so brutal, maybe because we all worked so hard to find a suspect. By the time I was called in, the investigation had already been going on for a few months. Back then the National Police didn't have any criminal profilers, so I was hired as a consultant to assist the investigation team in creating a psychological profile of the perpetrator.

I'm a behaviourist, but over the years my research has increasingly focused on psychological models for particular crimes. I stumbled into police work and then worked for them regularly for several years.

'No, that's right. We never caught him. And now there's been a similar murder. Eerily similar. I wonder if you'd be willing to meet for a coffee. I remember finding your thoughts on the matter very interesting.'

Gunilla is back. She sits down opposite me and downs the rest of her mulled wine in one gulp.

'I don't work with the police any more,' I say.

'I know that. This wouldn't be a consultancy. I'd just like to pick your brain on the subject. Over a coffee. If you have time, that is.'

There is a silence and Gunilla raises her eyebrows. 'I'll think about it,' I say.

'You have my number,' he replies.

When I get home, Owe is standing in the hall as if he were waiting for me. His thinning grey hair is combed to the side in an attempt to hide his bald spot. His stomach stretches out his shirt, his face is bright red and his skin is shiny with sweat, as if he's just come home from a jog. He throws a meaningful glance at his watch (which is expensive without being ostentatious and sends just the right message to his acquaintances).

'We've got ten minutes,' I say.

Owe turns around without a word and walks towards the bedroom. In a minute he'll return with that cardigan on. I put the bag of tea lights and napkins from IKEA on the floor and greet Frida, who's jumping around my legs trying to catch my attention. I run my hands through her curly black fur which resembles sheepskin.

Owe comes back into the hall in his mustard-yellow cardigan. The ugly one. Puts on his coat and boots and looks into my eyes.

'We have to leave now if we're not going to be late.'

The snow plough hasn't been down Kaptensgatan. I try in vain to avoid getting snow in my boots by walking down an already beaten path as we move through the darkness towards Artillerigatan.

'I got a call from the National Police today,' I say.

'OK,' Owe says in a neutral voice that doesn't reveal his feelings on the matter. But that's how it is with Owe: he's like a steam engine, holding in his emotions until the pressure has built up. Then he explodes.

'They want to meet me.'

'OK.'

We start to go up the hill towards the church, pass by the Army Museum's restaurant, where we sometimes have lunch.

'There's been a murder similar to an investigation I was involved in ten years ago.'

'You've got to be kidding me, Hanne. Tell me you're joking.'

'What do you mean?' I ask innocently.

He stops mid-step, still not meeting my eyes.

Instead he stares in the direction of the well-lit church rising up in the snow in front of us. The steeple points into the black night sky towards eternity. I can see that Owe's hands are in fists and I know exactly how angry he is. In some strange way it excites me, fills me with primitive, mischievous joy. Like a teenager who's finally managed to provoke a reaction from a restrained parent.

He turns around, puts his hand lightly on my arm, and there's something in that subtle gesture – which signals both indulgence and ownership – that infuriates me.

'What?' I say. 'What is it?'

'Is that really appropriate?'

He's lowered his voice now and I know he's struggling to regain control. Owe loathes losing control, loathes it almost as much as when I lose control.

'What isn't appropriate?'

'Taking on a lot of work in your . . . condition?'

' "Condition"? You make it sound like I'm pregnant.'

'If only that were the case.'

'And who says I'm going to work for them?'

'Oh, Christ. You know how it always ends when they call you in.'

'And why shouldn't I be able to work?'

He raises his chin as he looks down at me, in that way I detest, and takes a deep breath.

'Because I say so. You're not healthy enough to take on something like that and as your next of kin I have to be the one to tell you.'

I know I should give some scathing reply or perhaps just slap him, or at the very least turn around and go home to Frida. Light a fire, pour myself a glass of wine. But instead I say nothing and we continue walking in silence and darkness towards the church.

Emma

Two months earlier

'So, how was last night?'

Olga's gaze is curious but kind. She keeps her grey eyes on me while she folds the jeans lying on the long table next to the checkout.

I don't know how to answer her. Part of me wants to say that it went well, that the food was good and we had amazing sex all night long. Another part of me wants to tell the truth but maybe I'm not up to it.

'He didn't turn up.'

'He never turned up?'

Olga puts down a pair of jeans without folding them and looks at me more attentively. 'Nope, he never came over. And I couldn't get hold of him either, so I don't know what happened.'

'He never called?'

'No.'

The silence that follows is uncomfortable. I can see that Olga is having a hard time comprehending the situation and doesn't really know what to say.

'But does he usually call you if he's late or not coming?'

I hesitate a moment. 'He's never late. And it's never happened that he couldn't meet me.'

Suddenly the room feels cramped, even though we've just opened and almost no customers have come in yet. The bright artificial light hurts my eyes and there's a dull throbbing at the back of my head.

I lean against the jeans table and feel tears burning behind my eyelids. 'What if something's happened?'

Olga's voice is quiet, almost a whisper. Between those painted-on eyebrows, a little wrinkle has emerged. I can't speak, so I nod instead.

'You tried calling today?'

'Yes. Just now. Just before we opened.'

She says nothing more, instead starts folding jeans again as she glances around the shop.

'Here he comes!' she whispers without looking at me.

I grab the closest pair of jeans and start to fold. Lay them on top of the pile but already it's too late.

'Are you two just hanging out again? Emma, take the till!'

Björne has cut his hair. The dark wisps of hair on his neck are gone. He's combed a long flap down over one eye. His bow-legged appearance, combined with his new hairstyle and waistcoat, makes me think of the Lone Ranger. An arrogant, ageing Lone Ranger.

I turn around and go to the checkout without answering him. Thinking about my mother. About my mother and my aunts and everything else that no longer exists. About how terrible it is that those brittle, beautiful memories have been dispelled like smoke in fog and replaced by Björne and stacks of jeans and thongs.

I begin to recall a particular Saturday and the sound of laughter gurgling and rolling through Aunt Agneta's small apartment on Värtavägen.

The smell of freshly brewed coffee hung in the air along with smoke from my mother's cigarettes. Aunt Christina, who'd just given up smoking, sighed and pointed out that Mum wasn't being very supportive. I wondered if she was angry but then she laughed her husky laugh and I decided it was some kind of joke.

My aunts and my mother always had lunch together on the first Saturday of the month. It was a loud, calorie-rich affair to which only the sisters and I were invited.

Voices were lowered to a murmur, occasionally interrupted by a giggle. I didn't need to listen to know what they were talking about: Lena's new lover, Christina's foolish husband and Mum's bad back.

My mother was the youngest of the sisters. She was the wild, bad-mannered but beloved baby of the family who horrified Grandma and Grandpa by getting pregnant with me when she was just eighteen. More laughter filled the rooms, a wave of primitive joy and delight. Agneta snorted; it sounded like she was about to start coughing but then I heard some dishes rattling.

I sat motionless on the wooden floor of the bedroom with my legs crossed. The glass jar with the caterpillar inside rested in my lap. The leaves had withered long ago and fallen to the bottom of the jar, one by one, and the naked branches now resembled a ball of barbed wire. The pale-green caterpillar was no longer visible. Dad had explained what happened. Inside the small smooth cocoon hanging from one of the branches, something amazing was taking place. The caterpillar was transforming and if I was patient and lucky, I'd be able to watch as a completely different animal hatched from the cocoon.

That worried me a little; I wanted so desperately to be there when that new, transformed animal hatched, but I didn't know when it would happen. So I made sure I always had the jar with me. The first thing I did when I woke up and the last thing I did before I fell asleep was to carefully investigate the cocoon, to see if I could detect any changes.

I'd asked Dad why the caterpillar couldn't just stay the way it was, forget about weaving itself into a shiny greyish-brown shell, but Dad just shook his head sadly.

'It has no choice, sweetie. It has to change or die. That's how nature works.'

I thought about what he said for a long time, tried to imagine how it would feel to be faced with a choice like that – change or die. But no matter how hard I tried, I couldn't put myself in the caterpillar's place.

When I looked up from the jar, I was looking straight at Aunt Agneta's narrow bed. She hadn't shared it with anyone for a long time, Aunt Lena had whispered to Mum in the stairs on the way up. Adults always thought children didn't hear them or that if we did we didn't understand. Neither of which was true, of course. I had to work hard to keep my expression uninterested and childishly uncomprehending every time I was able to hear my aunts' secrets.

A small painting of football players hung above the bed. I didn't understand what was so special about it, what made the aunts talk about it with eager, quiet voices when they stood in a semicircle smoking and admiring it. I didn't say so for fear of making them sad, but the painting was actually quite ugly. The figures lacked any sharp contours, seemed to flow into each other; the artist hadn't succeeded in reproducing them in a realistic way. I probably could have done a better job. But I didn't say so, because despite everything I had better manners than that.

'Sweetie, why are you sitting on the floor?'

Aunt Agneta appeared beside me in the doorway. She squatted down next to me. Her thick legs looked even thicker close up and her knee socks cut into her calves in an unflattering manner.

'Don't you want to sit in the armchair instead? Or on my bed, maybe?' I shook my head without answering and Aunt Agneta sighed quietly.

'Oh well. You do as you like. What do you have in that jar, by the way?'

'It's a cocoon. It's what a caterpillar builds in order to transform itself.'

'Ahh. Where exactly is the cocoon?'

I pointed it out to her. She gently took the jar, held it up to the light, squinting until her small blue eyes disappeared under heavy eyelids.

'You can barely see it.'

'That's the whole point. Otherwise the birds would eat it up. They like caterpillars.' She looked at me gravely and nodded.

'That makes sense. I've never thought about that before.'

Up close, Aunt Agneta looked older than her age. Her cheeks hung down on her neck and her breasts rested heavily on her knees as she squatted.

'In nature, everyone eats each other up as fast as they can.'

Agneta stroked my hair with her calloused hand. 'Little Emma,' she said in a voice as smooth as chocolate. She made it sound like a question, as if somehow I could answer her unspoken enquiry. She handed the jar back to me and I put it down gently on the floor.

'How are things at home, Emma?'

Aunt Agneta suddenly sounded worried; there was some strain in her voice that I didn't really recognise.

'What do you mean?'

She paused and looked across the room. A quiet murmur could be heard from the kitchen. The absence of laughter was a sure sign they were discussing somebody's husband. All the sisters' husbands were either nasty or stupid, so Agneta was actually the luckiest one to have skipped getting married.

'Do your mum and dad drink a lot of wine and beer, Emma?'

It was a question I didn't really know how to respond to. Obviously I understood the words but I didn't know what 'a lot' meant. Was she asking me if my parents drank *too much*? There were always beer cans in the sink and in the living room in the morning but was it a lot? Was it too much? How many beers and bottles of wine did other mums and dads drink in the evening? These were things I really didn't know, so I answered truthfully.

'I don't know.'

Aunt Agneta sighed again and stood up with difficulty, her knees creaking and cracking as if they were made of dry birch instead of tendons and flesh and bone and blood.

'Jesus,' she said, stifling a little belch. 'Don't you want to come out and eat some cinnamon buns with us, Emma?'

'Later. Maybe.'

Once Agneta was back in the kitchen, the murmur fell to a whisper. That usually meant something interesting was being discussed, so I took my jar and crept out into the hall to lie on the floor and listen. I could just make out fragments of what they were saying. I heard Agneta's raspy voice: 'The child's different.'

And then I heard Mum, her voice a little louder now: 'Different isn't necessarily bad.'

None of my aunts said a word.

Just as I was about to crawl back into Agneta's bedroom, something in the jar caught my eye. The cocoon was hanging from its branch, just like before, but something had happened. It was as if the shell had started to become translucent, like scratched glass or dirty ice. And inside the glossy shell I sensed a quivering movement.

The metamorphosis had begun.

The man standing at the checkout extends his hand towards me and smiles broadly. 'Anders Jönsson. I'm a journalist.'

I hesitate, take his hand and smile cautiously. 'I'm Emma.'

His eyes are bright blue and his thinning hair is the colour of dog pee in snow. He's wearing a dirty-green military parka and jeans, and looks to be in his thirties.

'Can I help you?' I ask when I realise he doesn't seem to want to let go of my hand. He grins widely.

'I'm doing a story on the working conditions here. They say you're forbidden to speak to journalists, is that true?'

'Forbidden? Nah, I don't really know . . .'

'And you're barely allowed a toilet break,' he prompts when he hears my hesitation.

There is something to what he says, of course. Sure, the company has been going through some tough times since Jesper took over, as the media is quick to point out. But I can't talk about that, especially given my relationship with Jesper.

'I don't want to talk about this,' I say and feel the colour rising in my cheeks.

'We can meet somewhere else if that feels better,' he says, leaning forward. Those watery eyes are fixed on me. 'You can remain anonymous – no one will know.'

'I'd rather not.'

I catch sight of a figure approaching from the side.

'She told you she didn't want to talk to you. What about that don't you understand?'

The reporter stretches up to his full height.

Björne is standing beside me now. I can see that he's angry. His hands are fists and his jaw is clenched. He sweeps his fringe into place behind one ear with a practised gesture, sticks out his jaw and slowly says, 'This is the second time you've come in here to harass my staff. If you don't leave now I'll call the police. Do you understand what I'm saying?'

'I have every right—'

'Hey, did you hear what she said? Do I have to spell it out for you? She doesn't want to talk to you.'

Small droplets of saliva fly out of Björne's mouth as he splutters the words. Then he turns around and starts walking away. Before he disappears, he shouts at me over his shoulder, 'Good work, Emma.'

I look at the journalist again. The broad smile is gone. His face is completely blank. He roots around for something in his jacket pocket, puts it on the counter and pushes it towards me slowly with his index finger. It's a business card. His light eyes meet mine again.

'Here. Call me if you change your mind.' Then he leaves.

I bend forward and cautiously pick up the card, examining it before slipping it into my pocket.

Jesper Orre. Those large warm hands. That soft, slightly wrinkled face. The stubble, a mixture of brown and grey, which spreads out over a strong chin. The way he looks at me, like a starving man staring at pastries through a bakery window.

What does he see in me anyway? I'm just an ordinary person with a boring job and an uneventful life. Why does he spend so much time with me? What is it that makes him able to lie for hours in my arms, running his hands up and down my body? Finding his way to parts of me I have never given much thought to before.

I remember our meeting a few weeks ago at my apartment.

'We're so alike, Emma,' he murmured. 'Sometimes it almost feels like I can read your mind. Do you know what I mean?'

I thought that, no, I actually didn't. I feel no telepathic affinity with him, don't know at all what he's thinking. I love him but don't get what he means when he starts babbling on about our connection.

But I didn't say that to him.

'I'm so lucky,' he whispered as he hoisted his heavy body on top of mine. He spread my legs with his knees, pressed himself closer, closer.

'I'm the luckiest man in the world.'

He penetrated me before I was ready. Kissed me on the neck, ran a finger across my breast.

'I love you, Emma. I have never met anyone like you before.'

I still said nothing, not wanting to ruin this magical moment. Wanting to stay inside this feeling for as long as possible. It burnt. He was being rough and it wasn't pleasurable but it was still magical somehow.

To be loved. Desired. Like a raspberry pastry in a bakery window.

He moved more violently inside me. His grip on my arm tightened. Drops of sweat fell on my cheek like tears. He whimpered; it sounded as though he was in pain.

'Emma?'

It sounded like a question, or maybe a request. 'Yes?' I said.

He stopped, his breathing heavy. Kissed me. 'Emma, would you do anything for me?'

'Yes,' I said. 'I would.'

Would I do anything for Jesper Orre? The question is theoretical. He has never asked me for anything, except when he borrowed money from me to pay his contractors. And really, I was the one who insisted he take it. I was the one who wanted him to stay with me rather than going to the bank.

I remember he kissed my eyelids.

'Honey. You know I want to stay, but I promised to pay my contractors today. Cash. And I don't have a hundred thousand kronor on me. So, unfortunately, I have to go to the bank.'

A lunch fuck.

The expression was Olga's. She'd laughed out loud when I said I was going to eat lunch with my guy. At my house. Olga was blunt. Forthright. Provocative. She always said what she thought and she wasn't ashamed of it.

Jesper propped himself up on his forearms.

'I have to go, Emma.'

'You can borrow the cash from me,' I suggested.

'From you?'

He looked surprised, but seemed to ignore my suggestion because he got up, walked over to the window and looked out while scratching his crotch.

'I have money at home.'

He turned towards me, amused.

'You have a hundred thousand at home. Here, in the apartment?' He made a sweeping gesture with his hand around the room.

I nodded.

'I have money in the linen cupboard,' I said, then got up out of bed and giggled. Then I pulled on a T-shirt, not because it mattered if Jesper saw me without clothes, but out of habit. I didn't feel comfortable showing off my breasts in broad daylight. Not to anyone.

Not even to Jesper.

He followed me over to the cupboard, watched in silence as I took down a basket of tablecloths and carefully unwrapped a red Christmas tapestry to uncover bundles of banknotes. ''Tis the Season' was embroidered in cross-stitch.

'Are you completely fucking crazy? You have a hundred thousand at home, in your linen cupboard?'

'Yes. So?'

'Why don't you have that money in the bank? Like a normal person.'

'Why?'

'What if you get robbed or something? Only old ladies keep their money under mattresses and in linen cupboards.'

I reminded him that I inherited the apartment from exactly that kind of old lady. He laughed softly and shrugged.

'OK. You'll get it back. Soon.'

Then he kissed my neck, embraced me from behind, slowly ran his hands over my breasts.

'I want to fuck you again, you rich slut.'

Peter

Manfred leans over the body, seemingly unaffected. His gaze slides from the neatly stitched incision across the chest and abdomen to the deep wounds on the forearms.

'So she put up quite a fight?'

The coroner nods. Fatima Ali is in her forties, originally from Pakistan, educated in the US. I have worked with her several times before. Like most coroners, she's precise to an almost absurd degree and terrified to speak in overly strong terms. But I trust her. She has never missed anything. And there seems to be nothing her big dark eyes and dainty hands recoil from.

'She has crush injuries on the back of the head and on the face, and a total of eighteen cuts on the forearms and palms. Mostly on the right side, suggesting that she was attacked from the right.'

Fatima leans forward, spreads the edges of one of the deepest cuts on the arms, which exposes the red flesh, and points.

'Look here,' she says. 'The wounds are deepest in this direction, so the murderer is probably right-handed and stabbed like this.'

She raises her hand, encased in a blue rubber glove, and makes a sweeping motion towards Manfred who instinctively steps back.

'Can you say anything about how long they fought?' I ask. Fatima shakes her head firmly.

'I can't say for certain. But none of these injuries are the cause of death. She died from the injuries to the neck.'

I lean forward and look at the woman's head, resting on the stainless-steel counter. Brown hair clumped together with dried blood. Well-shaped eyebrows. And under them a shapeless mass of flesh and tissue.

'And the injuries to the neck?' I ask.

Fatima nods and wipes her forehead with the back of her arm. Blinking under the bright lights as if they were irritating her eyes.

'She received numerous stabs and cuts to the throat. Just one of them would have been enough to kill her, but the perpetrator seems to have been determined also to remove the head from the body. The spinal cord has been severed between the third and fourth vertebrae. It would have required considerable force to do it. Or stubbornness.'

'How much force?' Manfred enquires and leans over the head too.

'Difficult to say.'

'Would a woman or a weaker person be able do this?'

Fatima raises her eyebrows and crosses her arms across her plastic apron. 'Who says women are weak?'

Manfred fidgets a little.

'I didn't mean it like that.'

'I know what you meant,' Fatima says and sighs expressively. 'Yes, a woman would be able to do this. Or an elderly person. Or a young, strong man. That's your job to figure out.'

'Anything else?' I ask.

Fatima nods and looks down at the pale body.

'I would say she's between twenty-five and thirty years old. She is one hundred and seventy-two centimetres tall and weighs sixty kilograms. A normal body composition, in other words. Healthy, fit.'

The smell in the room is starting to make me feel sick. I'd like to think that I'm hardened to it after all the years, but there's something about that smell that you never get used to. It's not exactly bad, more like a mix of week-old flowers and raw meat, but I feel the urge to get out of there. A sudden longing for the cold fresh air outside.

'There was one more thing,' Fatima murmurs. 'She has given birth or at least been pregnant.'

'One child?' Manfred asks.

'That can't be determined,' Fatima says and pulls off the gloves with a smacking sound. 'Are we done?'

*

Manfred is driving us back to Kungsholmen. A dusting of snow falls over the dense traffic. Even though it's only three o'clock, it's starting to get dark.

'Good-looking woman,' Manfred says and turns on the radio.

'Fatima?'

'No, the one without a head.'

'You're fucking disturbed.'

'Am I? You saw for yourself. She must have been beautiful. I mean, what a body. Those breasts . . .'

I ponder his comments as I look out the window.

'Do we know anything more about who she is?' I ask.

'Nope.'

'And we haven't been able to reach Orre?'

'No. Didn't show up at work yesterday, apparently.'

'And today?'

'Don't know yet. Sanchez was going to check. But half of Sweden is searching for him by now, so he won't be able to avoid us for very long.'

'And the preliminary forensic report?'

'On your desk. There are no signs of a break-in, so either someone let the murderer in voluntarily or he lived in the house. In other words, Orre did it. They found urine on the floor. And a number of hand- and footprints, but that neighbour trudged around so damn much in there, it's hard to tell what they'll end up getting from them. Then there were a ton of fibres of various kinds, but nothing remarkable. The murder weapon was a machete, by the way. They sent it to the National Lab; we'll see what they find. And they've brought in that splatter guy, Linbladh, who works with bloodstains. Apparently he'll be able to help us reconstruct the course of events.'

It's quiet for a moment. Manfred is drumming his fingers on the steering wheel in time to the music, and I get the feeling that he's stressed. His stubble is longer than usual and his eyes look tired.

'Is Nadja feeling better?' I ask.

He glances at me and runs his hand over his camel-hair overcoat.

'Spent the whole fucking night screaming. Afsaneh was going crazy. She had to get up early. One of her students was defending their dissertation. And in the middle of all this misery, she starts talking about getting married. Why do women do that?'

I have no answer to that. I remember only too well what happened with my own wedding.

I had been with Janet for maybe a year when her nagging about marriage started to become almost unbearable, and in all honesty I don't really know how it happened, but somehow she got the impression that I said we should get married. I should have corrected her from the beginning rather than being so wishy-washy and evasive. But I guess I didn't want (or dare) to disappoint her.

So I let her have her way.

During the months that followed, she obsessed over flower arrangements, menus and guest lists. She brought home cakes to taste-test, made seating arrangements on large sheets of paper and played entrance music on her ghetto blaster.

And dieted.

I became almost worried about her. She was eating like a bird to fit into a special dress. One that I absolutely couldn't see until the wedding itself. That was apparently very important.

Meanwhile, I escaped into my job. We were investigating the murder of a car park attendant in Tensta, and since I'd just been promoted, it was especially important for me to prove myself. I can't say Janet was very understanding. Instead she demanded even more time and dedication from me. We had to look at churches, book honeymoons and practise our vows (which she'd written).

One evening she came to me with a bundle of envelopes. I remember she looked excited, in that way she only did when she bought something too expensive or maybe found a holiday in one of those catalogues she lugged home. Her eyes shone and her short bleached hair stood on end.

She explained that the invitations were ready, handed me the letters and asked if I could post them. I don't remember exactly what
I said. Probably something like we'll talk about it later but, as usual,
she didn't listen to me.

What I do remember is sitting in the armchair at home later that
evening with the invitations in my lap, wondering what the hell to
do with them. I knew I should post them. It would be the easiest
thing in the world to do – just go down to the junction and stuff
them into the yellow letterbox – and then I wouldn't have to think
about that shit for several more weeks. But I couldn't. I wasn't ready
to do anything that definitive, to take such a decisive step towards a
coupledom that I hadn't chosen for myself. For a second, I had the
impulse to talk to Janet, tell her how it was: that the whole wedding
thing scared the shit out of me and I really wanted to postpone it.
But when I went into the bedroom to talk to her, she was already
asleep. So I put the invitations in the drawer of my desk and decided
to have the conversation later.

And then it just happened. I can't say that I quite forgot about the
invitations in the drawer; it was more like I didn't have the energy
to broach the subject. Every time I decided to talk to Janet something got in the way: she was too angry or stressed or didn't want
to talk. She could be like that, curt and grumpy. Often for reasons I
didn't really understand.

When I think back on that time, I notice how I try to justify my
behaviour, even to myself. But really there is no excuse. What I did
was stupid and immature, and it hurt Janet in a way that I never
imagined it would and really never intended it to.

I didn't want to hurt Janet. I just wanted her to leave me alone.

Either way, as the wedding approached – I think maybe there
were three or four weeks left – she came in and sat beside me on
the bed one evening. Her hair, which she was growing out in order
to be able to wear it up, fell in wisps around her sad face and her
breasts were hanging alarmingly far down on her emaciated chest.

'No one has RSVP'd yet,' she said and turned her face to me. 'Isn't that strange?'

I was reading through a preliminary investigation protocol which I'd promised to get to the prosecutor by the next morning, so I had no time to discuss it with her right then. But I remember it upset me. Made me feel ashamed, even.

'Do you think they might have got lost in the post?' she asked quietly.

Something about her slumped posture and the unusual toneless quality of her voice affected me deeply. Made me realise the extent of my betrayal.

I felt truly bad.

But I still couldn't manage to tell her. Not then. Instead, I decided to take it up with her the following morning. But that's not what happened, and I know I acted badly but hindsight has twenty-twenty vision.

That night while I slept, Janet started searching the apartment. It was as if she sensed what had happened, as if she had some kind of fucking sixth sense. I woke up to a scream so terrible that I have never before or since heard anything like it. At first I thought she was being beaten to death, that someone had broken in and was raping her. I jumped out of bed and stumbled over a chair, fell onto the coffee table and slashed a deep cut into my chin. With blood pouring from my face, I continued through the apartment. Found her finally in front of the desk. The envelopes lay scattered like dead leaves over the floor, as if she'd hurled them into the air. She kept screaming. She screamed and screamed, but I took her in my arms and rocked her like a child. And when I held my hand in front of her mouth in an attempt to silence her, she bit me.

I remember I felt such relief, despite the pain. With my hand in front of her mouth at least she couldn't scream any more.

Manfred, Sanchez and I are sitting in the small conference room on the second floor, to the right of the kitchenette. It looks just like every other conference room in this building: white walls, blonde-wood chairs with blue seats and a white laminate table. There's a candlestick in the window that Gunnar brought from home in an attempt to give the room some festive cheer. On the wall hangs a faded poster illustrating how to give CPR.

We have to prepare for tomorrow's meeting with the investigation team and the leader of the preliminary investigation – one of the new prosecutors, Björn Hansson. I haven't met him, but according to Sanchez he's 'smart but has his head up his backside and far too high an opinion of himself'.

Manfred has brought in the coffee pot and Sanchez is cutting up saffron buns with a butter knife. Pictures of the crime scene are spread out all over the table. I try not to look at the severed head when I reach for a bun.

Two days have passed since the murdered woman was found in Jesper Orre's house in Djursholm, and we still don't know who she is. Somewhere her loved ones are going on with their lives, not knowing that their daughter or sister or mother has been murdered.

Somewhere, a killer is on the loose. Sanchez summarises the situation:

'Jesper Orre was last seen at work on Friday. According to his colleagues he appeared quite normal and nothing out of the ordinary happened. He left the office at half past four and then, according to statements he made, headed home. He didn't tell anyone what his plans were during the weekend, but he'd taken time off until Wednesday, so it may be that he was planning to go away on a trip. His phone and his wallet were found in the house. No withdrawals have been made from his accounts since last week. The technicians have lifted a bloody footprint from the hall and outside in the snow that is a size forty-three footprint, which might indicate that he actually left the house after the murder. They also found footprints from the neighbour and our unknown victim. Plus several other as yet unidentified prints. The analysis of the fingerprints on the machete has not been finished yet, but the National Lab said there is some kind of print on the weapon.'

'What's he like as a person, this Orre?' Manfred asks, then takes a loud slurp of coffee.

'He seems to be pretty popular with his colleagues on the management team, but the other employees at the corporate office seem to think he's pretty tough, and many are actually afraid of him,' responded Sanchez. 'Elsewhere in the organisation, however – on the floor, so to speak – he's despised for his toughness. And the union hates him. But you know that already. His parents are both retired teachers and live in Bromma in the same house where Jesper Orre grew up. They describe Jesper as energetic, athletic and happy. He has no psychological problems that they know of. His parents also confirm that he's been single for many years, but has what they call an "active love life".'

'What the hell does that mean?' Manfred asks.

Sanchez leans across the table and looks into Manfred's eyes. Stuffs the last of the bun into her mouth.

'It means he has a hell of a lot more fun in bed than you do, Manfred.'

'That's not saying much,' I interject, which causes Sanchez to start giggling until pieces of bun fall out of her mouth and down onto her short black skirt.

Manfred doesn't seem overly amused by this discussion. He takes off his checked jacket, hangs it dramatically on the back of his seat and pounds lightly on the table with his big fist to get our attention.

'If we could collect ourselves a little, maybe we'll get out of here sometime today. Sanchez, what's your theory?'

As the most junior officer at the table, it's logical that Sanchez would be asked first. That's how it works. The older, more experienced investigators teach the younger. It's part of the cycle. Sanchez sits up straight and suddenly looks serious. Clasps her hands in front of her on the white table.

'It's pretty obvious, right? Jesper Orre is at home with one of his girls when something goes wrong. A fight breaks out and it ends with him killing her. After the murder, he flees the scene.'

'Why doesn't he take his mobile or wallet?' Manfred asks and brushes away some invisible crumbs from his pink shirt.

'Because they were in the living room, and he didn't want to walk around too much on the crime scene,' Sanchez suggests. 'Or he forgot. He had a lot of other things to think about.'

'I'm wondering about the killing itself,' I say, pointing at the picture of the head which seems to be growing out of the floor. 'Why so brutal? Wasn't it enough to just kill her? Why did he have to decapitate her, too?'

Sanchez knits her eyebrows.

'He must have been really fucking angry, maybe actually hated her. I also wonder if the position of the head means something special. It seems to be looking at the door, towards whoever might come in. Have you thought about that? I wonder if he wanted to say something with that.'

'Like what?' Manfred asks.

We look at the photo again. The woman's eyes are closed and her bloody hair hangs in wisps over her face.

Sanchez shrugs slightly.

'I don't know. Look! This is what happens if you deceive me, or lie to me, or whatever it was that he thought she'd done.'

Manfred's mobile rings and he picks it up. Listens and then says:

'We're sitting in the small conference room on the second floor. Can you show her up here? Good. Of course. OK.'

Then he gathers together the photos from the crime scene, turns them over and puts them in a neat stack beside him. Takes a deep breath and leans back in his chair.

'We have a visitor,' he says. 'Remember we talked about that murder ten years ago that was so similar to this case? I've taken the liberty of inviting one of the people involved in that investigation to speak to us. Not necessarily because there might be a connection, but because I think she could help us to understand a little more about our murderer.'

There's a knock on the door and I feel myself go cold; all the heat leaves my body instantly and is replaced by an icy feeling and a pounding in my chest. The room shrinks and the ceiling starts to lean, as if it might collapse inwards on top of me.

The door opens and there she stands, wearing an ill-fitting puffy black coat and boots that look thick enough for an expedition to the North Pole. But clothes were never her strong point. Her thick light-brown hair has broad swathes of grey in it now, and she's wearing a pair of glasses that make her look a bit stern. Otherwise, she looks the same. Exactly like she did ten years ago. If possible, she's even more beautiful. There's something about the fine web of wrinkles around her eyes and her slightly leaner face that makes her look vulnerable. As if time has only made her a little more fragile and thin.

'This is Hanne Lagerlind-Schön,' Manfred says.

Emma

Two months earlier

There is a particular kind of exhaustion that overcomes you when you work in retail. The bright artificial light and the ever-present background music have a strangely hypnotic effect. In fact, I could swear that sometimes I'm actually sleeping as I slowly circulate around the shop with a busy look on my face. Sometimes entire hours just disappear, as if deleted from memory. I can come back from lunch, gather up some clothes and realise it's time to close, without knowing where the day went.

Outside, people pass by wearing wet coats with umbrellas in their hands. Mahnoor is putting sale tags on shirts from the summer collection. She moves slowly, in time with the music. Her long dark hair flows down over her shoulders and back, a black river across her red tunic. Her skinny jeans-clad legs make small, subtle dance steps. Olga is nowhere in sight. Maybe she's outside smoking; maybe she's gone to lunch early.

I haven't heard a word from Jesper.

He remains missing, and whatever happened is still a mystery. I assume I would have heard something about it on the news if he'd been in a serious accident. And if something prevented him from coming he would have told me, right?

He's never stood me up before.

The shop is empty. My eyes feel dry as I blink into the white light. The speakers are pumping out the same music as an hour ago;

the playlist which the marketing department updates once a month plays on a loop every day.

Doesn't it drive you crazy? Mum asked me once. The truth is that you get used to it. In the end, you don't even hear the music any more. That's when you start being able to sleep and work at the same time, move through the shop without thinking. Floating above the notes without being swept into the melody, all higher intellectual functions turned off, like a leaf floating on water.

'Do you like working there?' Jesper asked the first time we went out for dinner.

I fidgeted a bit, not knowing what to say. We'd just sat down at a restaurant on Stureplan, one I'd passed many times without ever entering it. I decided it was probably better to lie. I hardly knew him then, and what was the point in confiding in someone who was basically your boss.

'Absolutely,' I said. 'I like it.'

'You don't sound entirely convincing.'

A waitress in sky-high sandals came over with menus. She squatted down next to us and took our drink orders. Her skirt was so short that I caught a glimpse of her knickers through her gauzy tights. I was grateful for the distraction because I didn't feel comfortable with this topic of conversation.

'What would you like?'

'I'll have whatever you're having.'

He raised his eyebrows, looked me at me for a moment, then turned to the waitress and ordered two drinks. Then he loosened his tie and sank further down in the deep chair with a sigh.

'I really hate my job sometimes,' he said emphatically, looking out the window. The low, early-summer sun painted golden streaks onto the wet pavement outside.

'Seriously? I never would have imagined that.'

'Why not? Just because I have a ... prestigious position. An important job. At least on the surface.'

He suddenly looked tired. Tired and cynical and not at all like a high-level executive.

'No, I . . . I don't know.'

'Because that's what people think. That my job is fucking awesome and interesting. You know, it's a myth. It's not like that at all.'

'What is it really like then?'

The drinks arrived. I was nervous, noticed my hand shaking as I lifted the glass to my mouth. I had to hold it with both hands, but the liquid still splashed out. My fingers got wet. Sticky. Stuck to the cocktail glass. I tried to wipe them off with the napkin, but small pieces of paper stuck to my hands instead. Jesper didn't seem to notice anything. He was smiling in an introspective, almost uninterested way.

'Honestly?' he said.

'Honestly.'

He took a sip of his drink and leaned towards me. A strange expression glimmered in his eyes, something I didn't recognise. Tiny wrinkles appeared around his eyes. How many years older was he than me? I reckoned he was in his forties. So: fifteen? Twenty?

'It's lonely,' he said.

'Lonely?'

'You don't believe me, do you? I promise. There's nothing lonelier than the limelight, than being on television or in newspapers. Being the boss. Everybody knows who you are, but you don't know anybody. Everybody wants to be your friend, but you can't trust anyone. Not for real. Do you understand?'

'I understand.'

He smiled. A joyless grimace that revealed his unnaturally white teeth. What did he do to them anyway? Bleach them?

'I knew you'd understand. We're the same, Emma. We feel the same.'

Again I got that creepy feeling that something wasn't right, that he saw things, qualities in me that weren't there. He'd decided I was something that maybe I wasn't. Another feeling was pushing its way inside too: fear. Would he be disappointed when he discovered who I really was, if he got to know the real me? Was I just a way for this powerful man to amuse himself? Would he dispose of me afterwards, like an old toy?

'What about privately? Don't you have any family?' I asked.

The question was, at least partially, rhetorical. I knew very well that Jesper had no wife or children. Girlfriends had come and gone.

Anyone who could read knew that. In fact, you didn't even have to read. It was enough to look at the pictures on the front pages of the tabloids.

Jesper's smile fell a fraction of an inch.

'It's never worked out,' he said curtly. 'Should we look at the menu?'

We ordered.

Outside the window a couple were kissing in the evening sun. I felt embarrassed, didn't know where to look. I tried in vain to remove the little pieces of paper from my sticky hands.

'And what about you?' he asked. 'Do you have family?'

'Me?'

He smiled.

'Yes. You, Emma.'

I felt my cheeks turn red and cursed myself for not getting a grip faster.

'If you're asking whether I have a boyfriend, the answer is no. As for family . . . I have my mother.'

'Ah. Do you see her often? Are you close?'

'We see each other a couple of times a year, so I guess I can't say we're particularly close.'

'OK.'

I had a sudden impulse, a desire, to confide in him. I didn't usually talk about my mum, but for some reason it felt appropriate at this moment, with Jesper.

'My mother is an alcoholic,' I said.

He rested his dark gaze on me, leaned forward and squeezed my sticky hand. 'Oh. I'm sorry. I didn't know.'

I nodded, looked down at the table, suddenly couldn't speak, couldn't meet his eyes.

'Has she had alcohol problems for a long time?'

There was a pause while I considered how honest I dared to be. 'As long as I can remember.'

I thought back. Was there a time when Mum didn't drink? I couldn't recall one. But she was happy and full of energy when I was little. We'd sneak out late at night, long after bedtime, and chase each other barefoot through the snow. One time we went to the pet shop and bought a puppy when Mum was drunk. She wobbled so much on the way there that I had to support her. And then there was that time we were out of money and went shoplifting together at the supermarket.

Good memories, despite everything.

'What about your father?' Jesper asked.

'He died when I was fourteen.'

'Do you think about him often?'

'Sometimes. I dream about him.'

He nodded as if he understood exactly. 'Stepfather?'

An image of Kent popped in my mind and I shuddered immediately.

Mum had been with him for several years. I never understood what they had in common, besides drinking.

'It has to be hard growing up with an alcoholic parent.'

Jesper's hand rested on mine. Warmth flowed from him like sunshine. 'It was . . . lonely.'

'You see,' he said triumphantly and squeezed my hand even harder.

'What?'

'You're lonely too. Just like I said. I knew it.'

On my way home from work, I get off at the Slussen metro station. A cold wind is blowing, pushing leaves and cigarette butts down Götgatan. Small ice crystals have formed on the damp ground.

They sparkle under the streetlights. It's slippery, and I almost lose my balance when I turn left at Högbergsgatan. A faint smell of food streams out of the cheap restaurants and cafes. Two guys are sharing a cigarette in a stairwell. They look at me as if I'm bothering them, as if I'm interrupting something intimate. Their eyes seem almost threatening. I pull my leather jacket tighter around me and pass by as quickly as I can with my eyes fixed on the frozen ground.

Then I'm in front of the apartment building on Kapellgränd.

I recognise it immediately. The withered rose bush outside, the coloured glass panes in the door. Just as I'm about to go inside, an elderly man exits with a dog. He greets me and holds the door open. I nod back.

I don't recognise him.

There's no name on the door, just a little sign that says 'No Junk Mail' which Jesper wrote himself and which tells me that I've come to the right place. I always thought it was strange that he didn't want his name on the door, but he said he preferred anonymity. To avoid nosy neighbours and journalists. I press the doorbell. Nothing happens. I wait a little, then press it again, maybe hold the button down a little too long. The bell rings angrily through the door. Somewhere inside I hear steps and the door flies open.

'Yes?'

The man is wearing a sleeveless vest and sweatpants and holding a beer can in one hand, his arms covered with tattoos. But there's something else that surprises me: the furniture in the hall is completely different from what Jesper had there before. The red chairs and the small sideboard have gone. Instead, paintings are leaning against the wall and there's a heap of coats in the corner. The rug, which Jesper's mother wove herself, has also gone.

'Excuse me, is Jesper here?'

'Jesper? Which Jesper?'

The man pops open the can of beer. It snaps, then hisses. He puts it to his mouth and takes a deep swig while keeping his eyes on me.

'The man who lives here. Jesper Orre.'

'Never heard of 'im. I'm the only one who lives here. You must have the wrong address.'

He starts to pull the door shut, but I'm faster, pushing my foot into the gap. 'Wait, is this the only apartment on the ground floor?'

'Yes.'

'Do you know if a Jesper lived here before you moved in?'

'No fucking clue. I've only lived here for a month and I'm moving out soon. They're demolishing the place. There's some shit in the walls. And if you'll excuse me, I've got things to do now.'

I back away. Apologise. The man closes the door without saying another word.

I go home and walk around my apartment. Pace back and forth on the creaky wooden floors. The darkness outside is dense. From inside, it seems as if someone has bricked up the windows. Wind howls around the house, almost making it sway, and the windows rattle with each gust, protesting against the harsh treatment.

My apartment is the kind you can walk around in, and it strikes me I'm behaving just like when I'm at work. I circle around aimlessly, as if that will help me sort out my thoughts.

No calls, no text messages.

I've even been keeping an eye on the post. But it's just junk mail and bills. I don't have the energy to open the letters, just stack them on top of the others in the old bread bin.

I sink down into one of the green armchairs. Twisting my engagement ring. It feels big and it chafes a bit. Carefully, I slip it off, hold it up against the light. It has no inscription. We agreed to arrange for that later.

The stone is ridiculously large.

In fact, I've never seen such a large diamond in real life before. I think about Olga, who asked what it cost. It's a legitimate question, even if etiquette forbids it. What does a ring like this cost? Jesper made very sure I wouldn't see the price tag. And I thought it was romantic, felt like Julia Roberts in *Pretty Woman* sitting there on the jewellery shop's worn velvet sofas.

At least fifty thousand, I think. Given the prices on the other rings in the shop with smaller stones, it must have cost at least fifty thousand. The thought is dizzying. I have never had so much money to spend on something so completely unnecessary, and I don't think anyone else in my family has either. With the exception of my aunt, of course.

I'm walking around with a fortune on my finger, but the man who gave it to me has gone up in smoke. Why would you say you love someone, give them an expensive engagement ring and then disappear? Is there any explanation apart from an accident, a sudden illness, an urgent business trip, a lost phone? Could he have done it on purpose? Does it give him some kind of sick pleasure to know I'm worried, that I'm at home waiting with no idea what's happened?

I push the thought away.

Of course he'll come back. I just don't know when.

I brush my teeth and crawl into bed, feel the cool sheets against my skin. Despite the thoughts crowding into my head – the argument I'm having with myself – I fall asleep almost at once.

I dream that he's standing by my bed, stock-still, staring at me without saying a word. The moon shines through the window but although I strain my eyes, I can't see his face. He's just a black silhouette against the silver-white light, the contours of a man I no longer know. Whom I may never have known. I want to talk to him, make him explain, but when I try to open my mouth I discover that my body is paralysed. And when I try to scream no sound makes it out through my lips.

Then he's gone.

Grey morning light filters in through the window. I'm standing up in bed, my hand on the faded wallpaper. Trying to sort through my thoughts and make some sense of them.

The Ragnar Sandberg painting is missing.

There's a bright rectangle on the wallpaper where it hung. The nail is still in the wall. Even though I know it's an unlikely place for it to be, I drag out the bed and look behind it. There's nothing there, just balls of fluff and an old receipt from the off-licence.

I look at the floor again, slowly formulating the question to myself: Did someone come in here and take the painting while I slept, or was it gone when I came home yesterday? I try to remember if anything odd happened the night before, but I can't. It was an evening just like any other. A lonely evening at home in the apartment with Sigge as my only company, an autumn storm raging outside the black windows.

The painting was the only truly valuable thing I owned. And all the money I had, I've lent to Jesper. What will I do now? The bills lie in a pile in the rusty bread bin, like mouldy slices of bread. True, there's only a week left until payday, but that money won't last long.

What if someone came into the apartment and stole the painting? And what if that someone broke in during the night, leaned over my sleeping body and lifted the painting from the wall? Listened to my breathing, while I lay there unaware of what was happening.

Suddenly I remember the dream. The silhouette in the moonlight. The paralysing horror when I realised I couldn't move or scream.

Nausea explodes in my stomach. I stagger to the toilet, sink down on my knees and vomit up a bitter yellow liquid. As soon as I try to stand up, there's more. I lie on the cold bathroom floor, roll over on my back with my arms and legs spread out like a starfish.

Dust hangs in long strands from the ceiling. They flutter in the faint rush of air coming from the ventilation grille. Somewhere in the building someone flushes a toilet; it gurgles and whispers through the pipes running along the wall, as if speaking to me in a foreign language.

Sigge comes over to me, seems surprised. He's probably wondering what I'm doing on the floor. Then he turns around and walks out with his tail in the air.

If only you could speak, I think. Then you could tell me what happened while I was sleeping.

Hanne

It's Owe's fault that I'm standing at the entrance to the police station. Last night after the concert at Hedvig Eleonora Church, we had a terrible fight. The kind that's like an insane explosion. No, he was insane. Explained to me how irresponsible and childish it was to even consider meeting with the police to talk about work, when our kitchen is full of Post-its, when I can't even remember which bread he wanted from the shops (the one with spelt and pumpkin seeds, which I remembered; I just bought the other kind to annoy him).

I wanted to tell him to buy his own fucking bread, but I didn't, of course. Instead, I took Frida with me and went to sleep in the narrow bed in the spare room. Tried to figure out why I have such a hard time saying no to Owe, why I let him treat me this way.

I couldn't find any good answers.

The next morning, after Owe had gone to work, I called that detective and explained that I'd be more than happy to come in and talk for a bit; would tomorrow work?

He said that would be perfect.

The young woman showing me up to the conference room on the second floor is babbling on about the weather. She asks if I had any trouble getting here through all the snow. I respond politely that the metro worked just fine, and that my clothes are so warm I could sleep outdoors.

She smiles pityingly, glancing at my baggy coat.

We arrive at a door. The woman taps on it and after a few seconds it opens. I don't know what I expected, but not this.

In the middle of the room, by the window, there he sits.

Peter.

And it's as if all the blood suddenly rushes down to my legs. As if the air is in some mysterious way sucked out through the cracks in the window, leaving behind a vacuum. My fingertips tingle and my heart jumps in my chest, as if it wants to get out, as if it wants to escape from the seemingly innocent, middle-aged man sitting in the blue chair.

He looks just as I remember him. Maybe more tired and a little rounder about the belly. Light, greying, short hair and deep-set green eyes. A sharp hooked nose, reminiscent of something from a Mafia movie in the sixties. Slender hands, so delicate they might belong to a woman.

I know exactly what those hands are capable of.

The thought comes from nowhere and it makes me ill. Once again I have to fight the impulse to turn around and flee the room. But I force myself to stand still, even though my body wants to do something completely different.

'Hello,' I say.

'Welcome,' says a vigorous, flushed-looking man wearing a pink shirt with a yellow handkerchief.

He looks comical. Out of place inside the institutional grey interior of the police station. As if he were a long-lost friend from one of Owe's hunting parties who, for some inexplicable reason, had wandered in here.

A dark-haired woman in her thirties approaches and introduces herself. I smile, take her hand, but don't hear what she says. Then he's standing in front of me. There's still something boyish about his body, his way of moving. A gangliness that never really went away. He stretches out his hand, and I see clearly how uncomfortable he is with this situation.

I take his hand but avoid meeting his green eyes. Still my reaction is so palpable, so physical, that it scares me. It feels as though someone has kicked me hard in the stomach. Then the moment is over and we let go of each other. I shrug off my coat, slide down on a chair and say no when the woman offers me coffee. I don't trust my hands to be able to hold the cup steady.

I look down at the white table. Small scratches criss-cross its shiny surface. Out of the corner of my eye, I glimpse Peter. He seems to be looking through the window.

'As I said, thank you so much for coming in,' the heavy man says. 'We met briefly ten years ago in connection with the investigation into the murder of Miguel Calderón.'

I nod, meet his gaze. He takes out a thick folder and starts pulling out reports and photos. The paper is yellowed and the photos are dog-eared. He lays them on the table.

I lean forward, examining the black-and-white images. The memories gush forth unchecked: the smell of the morgue, the young man's head placed several feet from his body, intentionally put on its neck and turned towards the door. The victim's taped-open eyes had haunted my dreams for months.

'Miguel Calderón, twenty-five years old, a temp who held down all kinds of jobs,' continues the heavy police officer in a soft voice, who I remember now is named Manfred. 'Found dead by his sister, Lucia, in his apartment on Hornsbruksgatan near Zinkensdamm on the fifteenth of August ten years ago. She'd been trying to get hold of him for a week and was worried. She had a key to his apartment, so she went in and found him murdered on the floor of the hall. The cause of death was numerous blows to the neck with a sword-like object which was never found. The head had been removed from the body and placed next to it on the floor and the eyelids had been taped open with duct tape, as if the killer wanted everyone who came into the room to be forced to meet the victim's gaze.'

I nod, concentrating on the images, and feel my heart slowly calming down. Feel the oxygen return. Thinking how strange it is that a brutal, ten-year-old murder seems to work so well as a distraction.

Maybe I can pretend he's not actually sitting just a few feet away from me. Maybe I can imagine him gone, if I just try hard enough.

Concentrate on death instead.

Manfred Olsson drops the thick stacks of paper on the table with a bang and continues:

'The investigation was one of the most extensive in Swedish history, maybe the largest, apart from the Olof Palme murder, of course. We interviewed hundreds of witnesses and acquaintances, mapped and took samples from a hell of a lot of people. Yes, we found a cigarette butt outside the door, so we had DNA from what could have been the murderer. The case was covered extensively on TV. There was even a journalist who wrote a book about it, in which he argued that Calderón was the victim of a Chilean assassin who hunted down political refugees in Sweden with the permission of the Swedish intelligence agency. You surely remember all of this, Hanne?'

I nod.

'And now this,' Manfred Olsson continues and slowly adds what appear to be new photos to the table. 'On Sunday night a young woman was found murdered in the suburb of Djursholm. The cause of death was numerous blows to the neck, just as in the Calderón case. The head was removed from the body, placed standing on the floor, facing the front door.'

'Were the eyelids taped open?'

I'm almost surprised that I dare to ask the question, that I'm actually capable of speaking.

The dark-haired woman shakes her head.

'No, no tape. And in this case we found the murder weapon on site, too. A machete. It's been sent to the National Lab for analysis.'

I can't help glancing at Peter. He looks pale and has his arms crossed in front of his chest. He is visibly upset, and somehow that feels like a triumph: a small, dirty but enjoyable victory.

Manfred Olsson continues, 'I remember you had a lot of inter-esting theories about the killer at the time. I'd like to ask you if you believe it could be the same person?'

I look at the pictures of death and chaos spread out in front of me. As usual, I feel a kind of sadness, but also a fascination with the irrepressible urge of human beings to kill each other. And some-thing else: a tingling, maybe a longing to bury myself in the case, turning and twisting it from every angle. Slowly building an image of the murderer, turning him or her into a human being made of flesh and blood.

I love my research, but there's something about police work that offers a totally different kind of satisfaction. I spend my days work-ing on theories. It's incredibly cool to apply that knowledge.

Suddenly I realise how much I've missed this practical side of things.

'As you might imagine, I can't really say anything definitive with-out looking more closely at the investigations,' I say. 'But my first impression . . . The victims are obviously different – a man and a woman – as are the crime scenes. And in this new case the murder weapon was left at the scene, which also differs from the Calderón case. But despite that, I would say that the similarities in approach are too great to ignore. You should definitely take a closer look at this. But you've surely already realised that, or you wouldn't have asked me to come here?'

The heavy policeman nods.

'Who would do this?' the dark-haired woman asked. 'A lunatic?'

I smile faintly. The word 'lunatic' is so often misused in our society.

'It depends on what you mean by "lunatic". Of course, it could be argued that a person must be crazy in some sense to commit this kind of crime. But if we were dealing with a murderer who is severely mentally ill, then he would be unable to take care of himself, and he also wouldn't have been able to cover his tracks or keep hidden. Most likely, you'd already have apprehended him.'

'You say "him"?' The policewoman bends forward and meets my eyes.

'Yes, the vast majority of murderers are men. Especially with this kind of . . . violent murder. But of course you can't exclude the possibility that it's a woman. We're talking about probabilities here – it's not an exact science.'

'And chopping off the head and putting it on the floor – what does that mean?' she asks.

I shrug my shoulders, then say, 'Well, I remember we speculated that it might be a way to demean the victim – the killer probably knew Calderón and harboured a deep hatred towards him. Strong enough to want to demonstrate it to the world. The action itself, the beheading, is an indication of . . . rage. Historically, decapitation has been used worldwide for thousands of years as punishment for the most serious crimes. The term "capital punishment" actually comes from the Latin "*caput*", meaning "head". And it's still used today in some places, like Saudi Arabia, for example. Sweden had its last beheading in 1900, but in many European countries beheadings went on well into the twentieth century. It's estimated, for example, that more than fifteen thousand people were beheaded in Germany and Austria between 1933 and in 1945.

'In many European countries beheading was considered more honourable than, for example, hanging or burning, and it was the method of execution reserved for nobles or soldiers. But in some cultures, for example in China, it was considered a disgrace. The Celts decapitated their enemies and hung the heads on their horses. After a battle those heads were embalmed, saved, so they could be displayed later – something that angered the Romans, who thought the Celts were barbarians. But for the Celts, it was natural to behead their enemies because the head symbolised life, the soul itself.'

The room is silent, and I realise that my lecture might have shocked these hardened police officers.

'Is there any connection between the victims?' I ask.

'Not that we know of, but we're working on it,' Manfred Olsson says. 'We actually have a suspect for the murder last Sunday, so we're investigating whether or not he has any ties to Calderón.'

I look again at the photo of the severed female head. Trying to imagine what it would take to do that to another human being. What mechanisms must be set in play for a person to commit such a crime.

'Who was she?' I ask and slide my finger gently over the photo.

The room is silent. Outside the window, the snow continues to fall. Big, soft flakes flutter by in the strong wind, obscuring everything outside.

'We don't know,' Peter says suddenly and meets my gaze for the first time.

I sense the pain in his eyes before he looks down. The others don't seem to have noticed the tension between us, because the heavy police officer quickly adds:

'I wonder if you'd be interested in helping us a bit with the case. On a consultancy basis, of course. It wouldn't be a full-time job, just a few hours. If you have the time and the inclination, that is.'

Stockholm is wrapped in a white haze as I walk along Hantverkargatan towards City Hall. Snowflakes whip against my face and everything is quiet. It would have been quicker to take the metro, but I needed to clear my head, to clear away Peter who's crept into my life again. Traffic rolls by slowly through the dense snowfall, and my steps crunch as I head back towards the city.

Peter Lindgren.

Actually, it's odd I haven't run into him earlier. I continued working quite a bit for the police afterwards. Sometimes I used to think of him sitting there, somewhere in the police station, working on a case as though nothing had happened. At the time, it made me so upset I found it hard to breathe. But that's just how life is. People betray each other all the time, and life goes on, whether you like it or not. Life doesn't care about what we want.

City Hall's reddish tower disappears into the haze, as if it went on all the way to the sky and beyond into the blackness of space and into eternity. Maybe one day my memory will be so affected that he'll fade away, I think. Blurred away like the city in this snowy mist.

I hope so.

Or in the worst case, the opposite will happen – everything else will disappear, and the only thing left will be the memory of him, his body, his words.

We met when I was consulting on an investigation into the murder of two prostitutes in Märsta, just north of Stockholm. I remember that he didn't make a particularly strong impression on me at first. He was just one of many police officers who crossed my path. Perhaps I thought he was a bit weak. There was something almost insecure about him – not in the physical sense; something in his way of expressing himself was tentative, a little roundabout. I remember thinking that he was an odd police officer; police officers tend to be direct, clear and confident.

And then came the incident in the lift.

They were renovating the police station and managed to saw through a power cable while Peter and I were taking the lift between the ground and first floors. In an instant, it went pitch black and the lift stopped. A few seconds later a weak, bluish light at foot level was illuminated, presumably some sort of emergency lighting. We spent a long time talking to a confused guard over the small wall-mounted intercom, until we were told the only thing to do was sit down and wait for help, which might take a while.

It turned out that we had to sit for more than three hours before the fire brigade came to our rescue. And it was during those three hours that I got to know Peter.

At first, we talked about this and that. Mostly about work actually, about the case we were investigating, and how it was that two ordinary teenage girls could end up as prostitutes when on the surface it seemed as if they had everything they needed. But pretty soon we drifted into more personal territory. I told him about my relationship with Owe, and I remember surprising myself by how honest I was with Peter; I told him things about Owe and me that I wouldn't even say to my friends. But there was something about his manner, that gentle but persistent fumbling after the important things in life, that made me let him into my most private spaces.

Perhaps it was also because he dared to share his darkest, most forbidden thoughts.

He told me about the sister who died as a teenager and the love affair that fell apart. About his five-year-old son, whom he almost never saw, and his sadness at turning into a person he didn't like. What it felt like to come to the gruesome realisation that he wasn't a particularly good man. Those were the exact words he used to describe himself: 'I'm not a very good man.' He said it in a matter-of-fact tone, as if talking about a car or an apartment. And he seriously seemed to believe that Albin, his son, was better off without him.

I tried to explain to him that everyone has their faults but that children – especially little boys – need a father, even if he isn't perfect. Our society tricks us into believing that parenting is about perfection, when really just turning up is so much more important.

But what did I know anyway? I didn't have any children.

He said that the only thing he knew for sure that he was good at was being a police officer, and so he was determined to stick to that. Maybe I should have taken that as a warning, but instead I was curious. As usual when I met somebody who was a little broken, I felt an urge to try to heal them.

As if I could fix Peter.

Two weeks later I went home with him after work. I don't really know how; it just happened. I slept over in his small one-bedroom apartment in Farsta, and we made love the whole night. I remember I thought it was magical; he aroused something in me that had been dormant for many years. That feeling of complete connectedness: physical, emotional and, yes, almost spiritual.

I shudder when I think of it. It feels so horribly banal now, here in the midst of a snowstorm ten years later. What did we have in common really, apart from a kind of bitterness about how life hadn't turned out the way we'd imagined it? A loneliness that pushed us into each other's arms. How would we have been able to build a life together? He was ten years younger than me, and I was married. Very married. We didn't have the same background, interests or frames of reference.

And yet.

All night, all day. His arms greedily groped for my body. We made love in his bed, in his squad car and in the bathroom at work. As though we were teenagers. We could barely sit in the same room without looking at each other, blushing and giggling. Our colleagues exchanged meaningful glances and shook their heads.

I stop at Berzelii Park. Try to make out the contours of the Royal Dramatic Theatre through the snowstorm. Turn my face upwards, open my mouth and let the snowflakes land on my tongue. Tasting the sky as it falls down on me.

Owe noticed, of course, that I was in love. Things like that, people can just tell – even if you don't think so yourself. But he didn't comment on it. Not then.

After a year or so, Peter and I started talking about becoming a real couple, living together. I was actually the one who had doubts – for all the wrong reasons, I admit now. I thought too much about what people would think if I left my husband for a police officer ten years my junior and settled in the suburbs. I who had everything: a beautiful house, a brilliant career and a man everyone looked up to.

Except me, of course.

But Peter was stubborn. He wanted me, he explained. Even though we could never have any children, and would certainly have to pay a high price for our love. He wanted me because he loved me and couldn't live without me.

Blah blah blah.

Words, just words. Or maybe he truly did feel that way in the moment. Yes, that must have been how it was.

Anyway, he finally managed to persuade me in the end, and I decided to leave Owe. I went home to pack what I needed and Peter promised to pick me up at my door that evening at five.

I remember that I felt excited and also guilty, like a child stealing sweets, as I packed my bag. Just as I was leaving the apartment Owe came home, which was not part of the plan – he usually didn't come home before six. I told him how it was, that I'd met somebody else and was leaving him. That I didn't love him and our marriage felt like a prison. He got angry, started shouting that I would regret this, that it was only a matter of time before I came crawling home, begging him to take me back. I didn't answer, just left without even closing the front door behind me. All the way down to the entrance, I could hear him screaming up above. Long after the words were discernible, his furious voice echoed in the stairwell.

Outside it was dark and a light drizzle fell on the asphalt. I put my bag on the steps and sat down next to it, suddenly overcome by a numbing fatigue. It felt as if someone was pulling me down to the ground, and my legs couldn't carry me any more; I was that tired.

And there I sat.

The clock struck five and then five-thirty. At quarter to six I called Peter to ask where he was, but he didn't answer. At half past six, I started to realise he wasn't coming, but I didn't have the strength to move, couldn't leave the stone steps. It stopped raining and a cold wind that smelled of sea and exhaust blew in. It sneaked in under my thin jacket and made itself comfortable around my heart. Chilling me from the inside.

When Owe came downstairs and picked me up at nine o'clock I didn't protest, though his fierce grip on my upper arm hurt. I followed him up to the apartment without a word.

A letter arrived a week later. Peter explained that he couldn't live with me, that he would only hurt me – that that's who he was; that he 'wounded people' – and that it was best for everyone involved, myself included, if we didn't see each other any more.

I arrive at the Svenskt Tenn shop on Strandvägen, press my face against the snowy window and peek in. It looks almost like our apartment. Colourful, bourgeois elegance with ethnic touches. Exclusive without being ostentatious. Tasteful without being anxious. A tram passes by on the street and I close my eyes, trying to drive Peter from my consciousness. Trying to be in the here and now, in the middle of a snowstorm. On my way home to the man I still don't love. With oblivion as my only salvation.

Peter

A murder investigation is like a life: it has a beginning, middle and end. As in life, you never know what point you're at until it's over. Sometimes it ends when it's barely started, and sometimes it seems to go on forever, until it dies a natural death or is abandoned.

The only difference is that, unlike life, an investigation is about reaching the end of the shit and knowing that you have. Though sometimes I wonder if life might not be that way too.

I used to think it was part of the allure of the job – the unpredictable, the element of chance that couldn't be controlled. But now that too has become routine, just like everything else.

The woman sitting in front of us in the interrogation room is named Anja Staaf. Whether or not she'll be able help us get any closer to figuring out what happened at Jesper Orre's home on Sunday, I don't know, but she's certainly one of the women he's spent the most time with over the past year, according to his friends.

She has dark, almost black, hair, set in a way that is reminiscent of an old-fashioned pin-up girl. Her skin is pale and her make-up heavy: thick eyeliner and dark-red lips. She's wearing a dotted dress that accentuates her breasts, a small cardigan and black boots. And she seems calm, unusually calm for being in an interrogation room at a police station.

Manfred pours her some water and turns on the tape recorder, explains that she's being interviewed in connection with the murder that took place at Jesper Orre's house last Sunday. She nods seriously and fiddles with one of the small, gleaming mother-of-pearl buttons on her cardigan.

'Nice jacket,' she says, nodding towards Manfred's mustard-yellow wool blazer. Manfred retains his composure, but lightly strokes his hand down his right lapel. 'Thank you. One does one's best,' he mumbles. 'Can you tell us when and how you became acquainted with Jesper Orre?'

Her eyes turn up towards the ceiling, as if she's making an effort to remember.

'It was at the club,' she says. 'At Vertigo, where I work. He went there sometimes and, well, we started talking. Then we started getting together now and then. Sometimes we ate dinner, sometimes he just came over and spent the night.'

'When was this?'

She pauses. 'Maybe a year ago. Though I haven't seen him for months.'

'And the club, Vertigo. What kind of place is it?'

'Well, it's just a normal club, though most of our patrons are interested in various fetish or queer cultures and like to party. But not everyone is kinky. You do have to be dressed right to get in, though. Granny pants and Crocs need not apply.'

She wrinkles her nose a little as she says the last bit, as if granny pants are the most disgusting thing she could imagine, obscene in some way.

'And Jesper is one of the . . . kinky ones?'

I can't help but smile at Manfred, who's been noticeably put off balance despite his long experience interrogating all kinds of people. However, perhaps it's not so much the fetish talk that makes him uncomfortable, but the fact that she's young, beautiful and, on top of it all, praised his beloved jacket.

'Jesper's really not that kinky. I think he's just curious about testing the limits a little. A thrill-seeker, you might say. Though basically he's a very sweet and gentle guy.'

'"Sweet and gentle" are not exactly the words his colleagues use to describe him.'

The woman sighs. 'Well . . . I don't know what he's like at work. Just how he acts when we used to see each other.'

'And how was he then?'

Again her eyes wander towards the ceiling.

'Well. Happy, nice. He could seem a little stressed sometimes, obsessively checking his phone all the time and stuff like that. But I assumed it was part of his job to be available at all times. I remember that I felt sorry for him. And, of course, he didn't really want to be seen around town with me. Which was probably because the tabloids were always after him. Yeah, I really felt sorry for him.'

She falls silent. Her intense blue eyes meet mine.

'So where did you meet?' asks Manfred.

'Like I said, at the club or my apartment in Midsommarkransen.'

'And how long were you together? You said you met a year ago, and you haven't seen him for several months.'

The woman laughs softly.

'Oh my God. We weren't "together". We just met up. Hooked up. Had sex. You know.' Manfred looks as if he doesn't know. 'Sex with no strings attached? That's the best kind. Wouldn't you agree?'

Manfred nods hesitantly. 'Was he ever violent during sex? Did anything happen that frightened you?'

'Frightened?' She laughs. 'Nope. He was sweet, like I said. A little rough. He liked it rough. But I do too, so that wasn't a problem.'

'Rough? Like S and M?'

'Nothing like that. He was just . . . oh, you know. Liked to grab me hard and stuff.'

She looks committed now, as if it's important for her to explain in exactly what way Jesper Orre was rough. As if she wants to avoid any misunderstandings in her deposition at all costs.

'Did you ever meet at his home?'

She shakes her head. 'Never. He lives out in the suburbs.'

'And what did you talk about when you weren't having sex?'

'Pretty much everything. Politics, sport. He was really into sport. I think he worked out a lot too, because he was very fit for his age.

It was obvious that he took good care of himself. Never ate peanuts or chips or that sort of thing at the club. Drank mostly water with ice and lemon.'

'OK. So a really wholesome kind of guy?'

She knits her brows and leans back. Crosses her arms over her chest, and I sense that she doesn't like how this conversation is developing.

'Yes, actually,' she says.

Just as Manfred is about to show Anja out, she turns and meets my gaze. 'Well, there was one more thing.'

'Yes?' I say.

'He stole my underwear sometimes.'

'He stole your underwear?'

'Yes. I assumed he liked lingerie. I didn't really care, except that it was pretty expensive, so he could at least have replaced it, considering what he earns. Don't you think?'

After Jesper Orre's friend has left, Manfred and I go back up to the second floor again. Manfred is panting slightly. I'm guessing it's the stairs, but I've stopped nagging him about losing the weight. He's an adult and I assume he knows just how unhealthy those extra pounds are.

'Well, I'll be damned,' he says. 'He's a pervert.'

'It's not illegal to fuck ladies in latex or play rough in bed.'

'But stealing underwear is.'

'What a great fucking idea! Let's bring him in for theft.'

Manfred grins. Takes off his jacket and wipes the sweat from his forehead.

'Half the force is out looking for Orre. We don't need an excuse to bring him in.' Manfred seems to shift gears for a moment, then says, 'It never ceases to amaze me how different people are beneath their polished surfaces.'

I nod, but also think there are worse things to hide than having an exciting sex life. For example, having nothing at all under the surface. Being hollow inside, like an empty milk carton.

Like me.

'Outwardly, a respected and hard-working CEO, but really a latex peeper who can't handle a real relationship. Afraid of responsibility. Afraid of life,' Manfred says, as if he were a doctor with the authority to deliver a fatal diagnosis.

I'm still sitting at my desk long after Manfred has gone. Watching the sky over Stockholm darken. Changing from a dirty grey to a deep black. A few lonely snowflakes swirl by in a gust of wind. The windows in the apartment buildings across the street are lit a warm yellow, revealing that all the normal, responsible people – whatever that means – are at home preparing dinner or slumped in front of their TVs.

The image of Hanne pops into my mind. How she shook my hand in the conference room without really meeting my eyes. It was as if she was looking at the wall next to my head instead. And of course I felt something when we touched: a kind of grief for what never came to be, perhaps. Or a silly desire to explain, to clarify why I acted the way I did. To say all the things that I didn't dare to say back then.

As if that could make anything better.

Then I think about what Manfred said, that Jesper Orre was afraid of responsibility. If my mother were alive, sitting here today opposite me, she would probably say I was the one who was afraid of responsibility. Any responsibility. Responsibility for relationships, for money. Yes, for the whole fucking planet.

I imagine my mother sitting on the chair opposite me. Her long dark hair gathered in a thick plait down her back. Her dainty body with the slightly broad backside. Wearing eighties-style glasses too big for her lean, tanned face.

'Ulla Margareta Lindgren, I've asked you to come in to give a statement about your son, Peter Ernst Lindgren. Yes, me, that is.'

'Is that really necessary?'

'It won't take long.'

'Well then, in that case. But can we speed it up a little? I don't have all day.' Pause. Mum fiddles with her hair and gives me a stern look that can't be avoided.

'Would you describe me as a responsible person?'

A deep sigh.

'You know I've always loved you, Peter. You have a heart of gold, you really do – no one can deny it. But you have never taken responsibility. Just look at how you live. So sloppy. Eating food from plastic packages that are bad for the environment. And you don't recycle, either. You never see your son. Poor Janet has had to bear the burden alone. Well, I'm not saying you should live together – adults have to decide those sorts of things themselves. And to be completely honest, I never really thought you were that compatible. But, for God's sake, you could have helped. Albin is your flesh and blood.

'And you don't show any interest in the world around you either, even though you're a policeman. You barely read the papers. In Syria and Gaza children are dying like flies, and all you care about is watching bad movies and working. It's so . . . shabby, Peter. That's all I'm saying. When I was young, I was an activist. Worked for what I believed in. Even though I had a job and two children. You went with me to rallies. There was nothing strange about that. I don't understand why you can't do that, too. Take that opportunity now, you, who are in the middle of your life. Before you know it, it's over.'

I get up, go over to the window, rest my forehead against the cold black window frame. Close my eyes and let the memories wash over me.

My mother was involved in the anti-Vietnam War movement. She was a graphic designer and helped with the layout of the *Vietnam Bulletin* and with various posters and leaflets. Sometimes my sister Annika and I would help her paint placards or put together newspapers in the small house in Kronobergs Park where the group met. I remember that my father hated when we went along, because he thought we were too small to have any understanding of the Vietnam question, or any political issue for that matter. But we begged and finally Dad gave in, kissed Mum on the cheek and admonished her to take good care of us, protect us from the worst of the anti–imperialist propaganda.

I loved those meetings.

There were always other children and the atmosphere was jolly and permissive. Though everybody worked hard, nobody was in a hurry. Children had the run of the place, but were never in anybody's way.

Because I was so small, I got the easiest assignments – colouring the letters on signs like 'USA Out of Indochina' with red on a white background. Annika, who was older, got to paint the American rockets, which made me jealous.

When we were finished working, the adults drank wine and played the guitar, or they might discuss the situation in Indochina. I played with the other children. And sometimes I fell asleep on the floor in front of my mother's legs.

Sometimes the Freedom Singers sang for us, and what started as a routine evening of work culminated in – or perhaps descended into – a raucous party.

Sometimes one of the skinny young guys with corduroy jackets and sideburns would sit very close to my mother, offering her cigarettes and indignantly pushing up his horn-rimmed glasses while talking about the Swedish Vietnam Committee or the friendly but oh so naive radical pacifists. Sometimes one of those men would put an arm around my mother, touch her long dark hair. But she always smiled and pulled away a bit. And somehow I knew, despite my young age, that that move signified security and stability. My mother belonged with my father, even if she called him a 'reactionary' – which I could tell was a very ugly word – now and then.

Then, one day, the war was over. The freedom fighters had won, and the imperialists had gone home to the USA to eat hamburgers and drink Coca-Cola. Firebombs no longer fell on the jungles and rice paddies, on the unprotected children. Napalm no longer cut through flesh and bone as easily as a hot knife cutting through butter.

And I remember that somehow I knew it should make me happy. Mum said it was a good thing, and that I should be proud I had taken responsibility and helped stop the war, but instead I felt sad. Empty.

No more rallies. No more demonstrations. No placards to be coloured in.

I prayed to God to bring another war soon, but harboured no great hopes, because my mother had told me long ago that God was a capitalist fabrication created to keep the poor in their place.

I turn around. My mother is gone; in an instant she's been transported from the chair opposite me back to the cold ground of the Woodland Cemetery. In the hallway outside I can hear my colleagues leaving the office. Conversations punctuated by laughter disappear and die out.

It's time to go home.

To turn on the TV and aimlessly pass one more evening of my life.

Emma

Two months earlier

'Oh, you sick?'

Olga sounds uninterested. In the background, I can hear the wretched playlist, and it suddenly feels like a relief not to have to go to work today.

'It's nothing serious. I think I just ate something bad. I'll probably come in tomorrow. Can you talk to Björne?'

Pause. 'Sure.'

I can see her in front of me, the way the phone rests between her shoulder and chin while she gives all of her attention to her nails, holding them up to the light to check that there are no cracks or scratches, that the shimmering rhinestones remain fastened to the polish.

'See you tomorrow then,' I say, but she's already hung up.

I try calling Jesper again, even though I no longer expect him to answer. I mostly want to hear his voice, but I don't reach the recorded message. Instead I hear a voice explaining that this number is no longer in use.

I decide to try another method. I look up the phone number of the corporate office. With trembling fingers, I dial it. The woman who answers connects me without question when I say I want to talk to Jesper Orre, which surprises me a little. Is it really that easy to contact a company's CEO? Can just anyone call the switchboard and be put through to him?

But, of course, Jesper isn't the one who answers.

Jesper's assistant picks up, identifies herself and asks in her unplaceable accent how she can help me. I explain that I'm looking for Jesper and it's a private matter. She asks for my name and number so he can call me back. I hesitate. Surely this was why Jesper asked me not to call his office: so that no secretary or receptionist would take my name?

I ask her if she can't connect me directly instead, and she responds politely that he's in a meeting.

'So is he all right?' There's a pause.

'What do you mean?' she asks and I think I hear a hint of suspicion in her voice.

'It's just that he promised to call me … several days ago, and when I couldn't get hold of him I got worried that something had happened.'

'He's doing just fine. If you give me your name and number, I can ask him to call you when he comes out of his meeting,' she says in her pleasant, professional voice.

I say that I'll try to call back later instead and she says that's fine. Then we hang up and I'm left sitting at my kitchen table, the clock above ticking so loudly it feels as though its hands are inside my head.

Why is Jesper avoiding me? Did he get cold feet, regret the engagement? Or is he just a really sick bastard, a sadist who enjoys making me suffer?

Could there be some other explanation? Could something have happened that caused him to withdraw: a death in the family, a crisis at work? Sure, but what could be so serious that you can't make a phone call or send a text message?

Three weeks earlier, we were lying naked on my living room floor. The sepia-toned evening light crept through my blinds, outlining a soft grid of light and shadow on our bodies. The window was ajar, and the curtain billowed a little in the chilly air.

Jesper was smoking. It didn't happen often, only after we had a few glasses of wine, or sometimes after we made love. He looked up at the ceiling while his large hand rested on my stomach. With his fingers he drew small circles on my sweaty skin.

'What happened?' he asked.

'She got sick and died.'

Jesper inhaled deeply. 'Yes. I got that. But what did she die of?'

'Inflammation of the pancreas. They said it was because she drank too much.'

'Poor thing.'

'Yes and no. Sometimes I can't help thinking that she had only herself to blame. It was nobody's fault that she drank.'

Jesper turned his head towards me. Met my eyes. 'It wasn't her I was thinking of. It was you.'

'Me?'

He laughed and shook his head slightly, as if I'd said something silly. 'Yes. You.'

'There's nothing wrong with me.'

There was silence for a moment. Sirens blared in the distance. In the kitchen, the fridge shuddered into life.

'I'm so sorry I can't go with you to the funeral,' he said after a moment, as if it was something he'd been thinking about.

'I'll be fine.'

'No one should have to go to their mother's funeral alone.'

I didn't respond. What could I say? He was right, of course; we'd been seeing each other for months by now, and it was becoming increasingly difficult to keep our relationship secret.

'Will it always be like this?'

He stubbed out his cigarette in his wine glass and turned to me. Heaved himself up on his elbow, kissed me softly. A kiss that tasted like ashes and wine. I turned my head away, something he must have interpreted as a protest against our situation rather than his breath.

'Of course it won't always be like this.'

'How long, then?'

He sank back down. Sighed deeply, clearly frustrated.

'We've talked about this a thousand times. You know how the tabloids chase me. Just yesterday there were two journalists who used the term "slave contracts" when they wrote about our employees' conditions. If the media sniffed this out . . . You know well enough yourself what would happen. I'd be fired. We have to wait until things have calmed down.'

'And when exactly will it calm down?'

'How the hell should I know? Whenever the hyenas find another company to focus on. By the way, you should start looking for a new job. It would help if you weren't employed by the company.'

He leaned forward, grabbed the blanket and spread it over us. 'It's cold,' he said. 'Should I close the window?'

'It's just so hard. Everyone is wondering who you are, and I can't say anything. It feels a bit . . . adolescent.'

He turned his face towards me. The draught had died down. A smile played at the corner of his mouth.

'Adolescent?'

'Yes, I seem like a fucking teenager. With a secret boyfriend.'

He laughed. Kissed my neck and continued on down towards my stomach. 'Am I your secret boyfriend?'

'I guess you are.'

'And you, then? My little lamb chop?'

I giggled. His tongue ran over my chest, dug into my belly button, twirling around in circles as if he were eating some invisible dish from my body. Then he continued down, let his tongue run along the inside of my thigh. I froze. Uncomfortably aware of my body. All its cavities, smells and sounds. He must have felt me tense up, because he lifted his head a bit and looked me in the eyes.

'Relax, Emma. You have to learn to relax.'

He was always telling me to relax, and not just in bed. And I really tried, but there was something about him that put me on my guard. Something about our whole relationship. It felt too good to be true. Me and Jesper Orre. The poor shopgirl meets an older, wealthy, successful man.

What did he see in me anyway? Why did he decide to start a relationship with an employee who was twenty years his junior?

Maybe he was right. Maybe this was all about my low self-esteem. Why wouldn't I be interesting to him? Why was our relationship so difficult for me to accept? Why was his love so hard for me to believe in?

'Relax, Emma,' he said again. 'I want you, and you are worth loving. How can I make you understand that? What do I need to do to make you believe it?'

We fell asleep on the floor that night.

When I woke up it was dark, and my back ached. I groped beside me on the rug, but Jesper wasn't there. Slowly, I stood up. My body felt stiff and clumsy as I shuffled into the bedroom. The floor was cold; the window was still open.

Then I saw him.

He was standing perfectly still in the dark. His eyes were fastened on the Ragnar Sandberg painting that hung above my bed. His hair was dishevelled and hung low on his forehead, as if he'd just got up. He had a blanket around his shoulders.

'I think I love you, Emma,' he murmured.

I'm sitting in bed, trying to get my laptop to work, but something is wrong with the Internet connection. It takes me a while to realise it's probably because of an unpaid bill. Now neither the TV nor the Internet work, and it's all Jesper's fault.

I decide to go down to a cafe on Karlavägen; I can connect to the wireless network there. The nausea has eased a little, and for the first time today I feel a kind of vague hunger.

When I pull on my jeans, I realise there's something in the pocket. It's a business card. I look at it and remember the journalist who visited the shop. I hesitate a few seconds, then go to the kitchen, open the bread bin and lay the business card on top of the pile of unpaid bills.

I sit in a corner with a half-full latte. Not far away sits a young guy with dreadlocks and a MacBook in his lap. Two ladies are whispering to each other in another corner, as if discussing state secrets. The cafe is dim, almost dark. I watch the autumn rain fall outside the large windows. The trees burn in shades of yellow, orange and brown. Now and then a single leaf floats down from the trees, landing gently on the grass below.

I skim through articles about Jesper. They call him both the 'Fashion King' and the 'Slave Driver'. Then I find an article in a business magazine: 'Who is the Real Jesper Orre?' I read on. Jesper is originally from Bromma; both his parents were teachers. He studied business at Uppsala University, but dropped out after two years. What follows, according to the writer, is a string of question marks. Long periods of time that can't be accounted for 'satisfactorily'. Years of inexplicable holes in his résumé.

I read on. The journalist has amused himself by mapping out Jesper's social connections, claiming that he associates with criminals. Two of his close friends were convicted for economic crimes, another for drug possession. I don't recognise any of them. This isn't something Jesper has told me about.

I search for images instead.

Jesper in a suit. Jesper in gym clothes. Jesper in a tux. Jesper standing on a stage, his shirtsleeves rolled up, pointing towards numbers on a screen.

Another picture: Jesper close up, a smile playing around his mouth. But I see the deep frown on his forehead and I know he's uncomfortable. He doesn't like to be photographed; we've talked about it many times, how he hates seeing his picture in the newspapers and on television.

There are other pictures too: Jesper with a blonde woman on his arm. She's leaning back and laughing. Her dress is very low-cut. He looks tired. His shirt is wrinkled and unbuttoned at the neck. On his trouser leg is a big stain, as if someone has poured a glass of wine on it. I go on. There are more pictures of Jesper with women – always different women. Not once do I see the same woman at his side.

I close my eyes and sink back into the couch, trying to think clearly. Were there any signs the last time we were together? Something that might reveal he was tiring of me? I can't think of anything. Everything was as normal. He was just as loving as usual. We met, ate a good dinner, had sex. Giggled for hours in my narrow bed. Talked about the future, what we would do when we were together for real.

When we no longer had to sneak around.

Then I remember one of our last meetings. We were at his apartment on Kapellgränd. I was lying on my side in the bed, facing the wall, and he came out of the shower with a towel around his hips, sat down beside me and began to stroke my hair.

'Do you love me?'

It was a strange question. He'd never asked if I loved him before. We didn't actually use that word too often, perhaps because it felt so binding, so big, almost scary.

'Yes,' I said.

'I understand how difficult this must be for you. Sneaking around all the time.'

He crawled onto the bed, cupped his body around mine and held me from behind. I felt the warmth of his damp, freshly showered body against mine, breathed in the scent of soap and aftershave. Closed my eyes.

'Promise me you'll wait for me. That you won't give up.'

'I promise.'

'Promise you won't find anyone else.'

'You're so silly. You know there's nobody else.'

His grip on my body tightened. 'What about before me?'

I felt confused. 'What do you mean?'

'Before we met. Did you have somebody else?'

Before Jesper.

I thought about my life before we met: lonely evenings in front of the TV with my cat, endless days in the shop. Frozen dinners for one. There was absolutely nothing to tell. Nothing to be ashamed of or to hide either.

'You must have had someone before me?' he said.

I didn't respond at first. There had been someone before, but I didn't want to talk about him now.

'Of course.'

'Who was he?'

'You know, that guy I told you about. Woody.'

'Your DT teacher?'

I nodded and closed my eyes. As soon as I did, it all came back to me, despite how many years had passed. The long, cold corridors, the clatter of the cafeteria, the smell of burnt sawdust in the wood-work room. I'm lying on the bench. Woody standing in front of me in a flannel shirt with his jeans pulled down to his knees. His face grim as he penetrates me.

I was crazy about him. And at home, everything was in chaos. I was so vulnerable. Only now do I realise how vulnerable. He took advantage of that. I was a lost fifteen-year-old, and he seduced me.

'It makes me furious to think about that,' Jesper mumbles.

'Stop it – that was a long time ago.'

'You had sex in the classroom.'

'Yes, but—'

Suddenly his grip on me became almost painfully hard, until I found it difficult to breathe.

'Let go. That hurts.'

'Did you like it?'

'What?'

'Fucking him in the sawdust? Did you like it?'

Jesper held me like a vice. I couldn't move. But I felt him getting hard. 'You're sick,' I said.

He pulled off his towel, pressed himself closer. Then his mobile rang and his grip loosened for a moment, but I still lay there, frozen. I couldn't move.

'You liked it,' he whispered. 'Right?'

I didn't respond.

I leave the cafe and walk home in the rain. The wind's started to blow; leaves no longer fall quietly to the ground, but dance in the breeze until they settle on the grass in the middle of the avenue. Why was Jesper so jealous of my past? Even though I've hardly had any relationships that he could be jealous of. Despite the fact that I was the one who had reason to be jealous, he lay there accusing me.

And why did he get aroused when we talked about Woody? It was as if it turned Jesper on to talk about him.

The nausea returns. I don't understand it. There's so much I don't understand.

I cross Karlaplan. The fountain is empty. Leaves and rubbish have accumulated in piles in the far corner. The area is deserted.

When I get home, I'm struck by the fact that something smells different. There's a faint scent of wet wool and soap in the air, as if someone has just passed through on their way somewhere else.

I walk from room to room, examining every detail, but nothing looks strange. Everything is where I left it. Nothing is gone.

I walk into the bedroom, stare at the bright rectangle above my bed where the painting used to hang. It seems almost illuminated, vibrating, as if it's lifting up for a moment from the dirty yellow wallpaper and moving towards me, trying to tell me something. From the kitchen, I can hear the crunch of Sigge eating his daily ration of the sad dry cat food that makes up the whole of his diet.

Everything looks normal. The only thing that makes me uneasy is the smell.

Tomorrow I have to go to work, I think, and sit down on my bed. No matter how I feel, I have to work. I already have five days of absence this month, and I know that Björne will be furious if I take any more. Absences are marked with angry red stickers on the calendar in the kitchenette. All the employees can see how many days their colleagues have been sick or at home with a sick child – another one of those strategies that sends the union through the roof, and keeps the media spending so many column inches on Jesper's 'slave-driving' methods.

I move my hand over the wall. The yellowing, shabby wallpaper makes me think of another wall, in another life.

It was evening, and I lay in bed looking at a wall that had once been white, but was now stained with a rich patina of cigarette smoke, grease and dust. You could engrave letters on that dirty yellow surface if you had a sharp object, like a toothpick or a twig.

No matter how hard I tried, I couldn't sleep. In part because of the pale-blue, early summer light filtering in through the window – it seemed to penetrate even my closed eyelids – and in part because of the angry voices of my mum and dad coming from the kitchen.

I had no idea what it was about this time, and it didn't matter. They fought almost every night anyway. The trick was to try to fall asleep before they started; then you could sleep until the next morning. In the morning, they were always nice again, though tired, since they hadn't slept very much.

Finally their voices lowered until they eventually died out. I held my breath. After a few seconds I heard a clear tone, like someone singing. The tone rose and fell, turning into a protracted howl.

Mum was crying.

It was always Mum who cried. Not Dad. I didn't even know if Dad could cry. Maybe dads don't cry?

A dull thud was followed by a shrill scream, and suddenly I felt worried for real. Had one of them fallen and hurt themselves? Had a piece of furniture turned over? I jumped out of bed, grabbed the jar with the cocoon inside and started walking towards the door. The linoleum floor was slippery and cool under my feet. The only sounds I could hear as I entered the hall were my mother's low sobs and the indifferent ticking of the kitchen clock.

Dad was on the floor, his face buried in his hands, and Mum sat weeping on a wooden chair. For some reason I was much more worried by Dad's silence and strange hunched-over position than by my mother's tears. Dads shouldn't sit like that: shrunken and resigned, silent, with their face in their hands.

Then he moved. It was just a little twist, a few inches in my direction, as if somehow he'd spotted me through his hands. His voice was toneless as he spoke.

'Emma, sweetie. Go to bed. You should be sleeping.'

Mum jumped up out of her chair. Her eyes had that wild look they only got late at night after she and Dad had been sitting in the kitchen for a long time. She reminded me of some sort of animal. A wild, unhappy animal trapped inside a cage, and therefore very dangerous.

'Fucking kid,' she screamed. 'Have you been eavesdropping again, you freak?' Dad got up and stood between my mother and me.

'Stop,' he muttered. 'It's not her fault.'

'I know you were eavesdropping,' my mother slurred. 'What are you going to do? Call Aunt Agneta and tattle? Huh?'

'No,' I said, but Mum didn't hear me. Instead, she grabbed the table for support and stumbled towards me, keeping her hands clutched tightly on the tabletop. Her body was strangely clumsy and she overturned her chair as she tried to push past my father.

'Let her be,' Dad said.

'I've got to teach her to stop eavesdropping,' my mother slurred.

She forced her way past Dad and reached for me. But I was quicker and stepped aside. When Mum wasn't able to grab hold of me the way she'd intended, she fell headlong onto the floor instead.

'Dammit,' she mumbled, and crawled up on her haunches. A narrow stream of blood ran from one nostril into her mouth. 'Do you see what you did, Emma? Do you?' She stood up slowly.

'But I didn't—'

The slap came like a flash, and this time I didn't dare move for fear Mum would fall again and that the narrow stream of blood would turn into a torrent, or maybe even a sea.

'You shut your mouth.'

Mum swayed slightly and her hair stood straight up the way it did when she first woke in the mornings. Dad had sunk down again and was holding his hands to his face as if trying to shut out the whole scene. I wished he would stand up and tell Mum to stop, explain that it wasn't my fault. I wished it were morning already and they were tired and nice again. That they'd give me money to go and buy breakfast because they had a headache. I wished I were someone else, anywhere else. Just not Emma. Just not here. Just not now.

Mum grabbed the jar with the cocoon.

'Give me that stupid jar,' she growled. 'You take that with you everywhere. I guess it must be important to you. More important than your mother, maybe. Right?'

I didn't answer.

'I'll teach you what's important,' Mum said, then staggered over to the kitchen window, opened it and threw out the jar.

After about a second, I heard it shatter on the Tarmac below. 'No!' I screamed. 'No, no! No!'

'Yes,' Mum said. 'Yes. I have to teach you what's really important. That was a fucking jar. Do you understand? A dead thing.'

I wasn't listening any more. Instead I ran towards the front door, opened it, hurried down the stairs, and rushed out into the court-yard. Shards of glass sparkled like stars on the black Tarmac. I tip-toed carefully, trying not to cut my feet. Then I fumbled with my hands on the cold, damp ground. The only things I found there were a few dry leaves.

'Here, Emma.'

I turned around. Dad was squatting next to me with his hand outstretched. In his palm he had some thorny branches. The cocoon still hung from its branch. The moonlight made it look almost luminous.

'That sounds seriously sick.'

Olga shakes her head so that her heavy earrings rattle. We are standing by the jeans table, folding. Björne isn't in sight, but we both know he's in the shop. It's a bit like being alone on the savan-nah – you know the predators are out there somewhere.

'What should I do?'

Olga shakes her head slowly, as if she finds the situation too weird to even comment on. Then she pulls up her distressed jeans, which have dropped down to her hips.

'He proposes to you, then leaves. Who is this man? You can tell me now, can't you?' Of course I could tell Olga about Jesper, but something makes me hesitate. If I tell her, everyone else will know soon enough. And that could mean trouble for me, too, not just for Jesper. What would Björne say if he knew about my lover from the corporate office?

'He's . . . nobody. Just somebody you see in the tabloids some-times. It doesn't matter. Even if he wants to end it, I still want my money back.'

Olga doesn't answer, and instead stretches for a pair of jeans that are about to fall off the small table onto the floor. She grabs them just before they do.

'What money?' she says in an indifferent voice, and it occurs to me that I probably didn't tell her about the loan.

'He borrowed a hundred thousand kronor from me to pay some contractors.'

'Are you crazy? You gave him a hundred thousand? . . . And?'

I shrug my shoulders.

'Come.' Olga takes my arm and pulls me towards the staffroom.

Suddenly Björne is standing in front of us. He looks stern. He has his hands on his hips, stands a little too close to us for comfort. I can see he's working on growing a beard. Ruddy stubble covers his narrow, protruding chin.

'And where are you off to?'

'Break,' Olga says without further explanation, then pinches her lips into a thin line.

Just then Mahnoor comes out of the staffroom. She is pulling her long hair into a knot at the nape of her neck.

'Can you watch the register?' Olga asks at lightning speed.

'Sure.'

She looks at us curiously, but Björne seems satisfied with her response; he turns around and walks to the menswear department. Olga pulls me into the staffroom, then pushes me down onto one of the white chairs in the kitchenette.

'What a fucking arsehole,' I mumble. 'Did you know they fired a girl at the Ringen shop because she took off too much time to be with her sick three-year-old? She had like ten absences in a month. But they blamed it on a shortage of work, so the union couldn't do anything.'

But Olga isn't listening. Instead she's leafing through a stack of magazines located on the shelf in the corner.

'So you been trying to get hold of your guy?' she says quietly as she lifts up an inch-thick stack of magazines and puts them in her lap.

'I've called, texted. Everything. He's not answering.'

'You tried visiting him at home?'

I remember the visit to Kapellgränd: the man with the ponytail, the snap and hiss as he defiantly opened his beer can, the furniture I didn't recognise.

Olga has finished flipping through the first magazine. She's looking at me with genuine concern.

'I went to his house one night . . .'

'And?'

'Someone else was living there. His furniture was gone.'

She doesn't say anything more, instead again turning her attention towards the stack of magazines.

'What are you doing?'

'Looking for something. Why did you lend him money, anyway?'

'Because . . . I don't know. I happened to have money at home, and he needed it to pay his contractors.'

'You have a hundred thousand at home?'

'Yes.'

'I'm sorry, but that is crazy. He steal anything else from you?'

'No, I reply,' but think immediately about the Ragnar Sandberg painting. Jesper was the only one who knew I had it. Besides my mother, of course, but she's dead.

'Here,' Olga mutters, flipping through a magazine that seems to consist of more celebrity pictures than text. 'Here it is.'

She turns the pages more slowly. Examining each spread.

Then she stops. Her hand rests on an article, 'Do You Live with a Psychopath?'

'Fuck. Your man is definitely a psychopath,' she mumbles, and slides her thin index finger along the text as if it were Braille.

'What does it say?'

She clears her throat a little, drums her long nails on the magazine.

'"A psychopath is initially charming, but quickly becomes manipulative and egocentric. Lacking in empathy, he shows no regard for your feelings or needs. He cheats and deceives without hesitation. He steals and lies without feeling remorse or guilt."'

I wonder. To me Jesper is warm, loving and empathetic. But if he's actually dumped me; if he's the one who stole the painting; if he has no plans to pay back my money . . . then maybe Olga's right.

'Does it say what to do?'

Olga nods and moves her mouth silently as she reads the last paragraph.

'"You should get as far away from him as you can, because he won't change." Psychopaths don't change. It says that here.'

She leans towards me, resting a hand on my arm, saying nothing, just looking at me with concern in her large pale eyes. I feel my tears coming. But still there's something else, stronger than my despair – the urge to know.

'I don't understand,' I mumble. 'He has so much money. And he's . . . famous. Why would he risk everything in order to cheat me out of a hundred thousand?'

'Maybe it's not the money,' Olga says hesitantly.

'What do you mean?'

'Maybe he wants to humiliate you. Piss on you. You know?'

I stand in front of the mirror at home in the bathroom. My long, reddish-brown hair hangs in wet strips across my shoulders. My breasts, those loathsome udders, are bigger than ever and very tender.

Slowly I bend forward, wipe away a little of the fog and examine my reflection. My freckles are particularly noticeable like this, without make-up, under the cold fluorescent lights.

I wrap a green towel tightly around my body and go out into the hall. On the floor under the front door lie three more letters.

One is from my bank, one is from my credit card company and one has no return address on the outside of the envelope. I take the letters into the kitchen and put them in the bread bin without opening them. It's almost impossible to close now; that's how full it is.

Of course I realise that this situation is unsustainable; some day the bills will have to be paid. But I don't know what to do about it. I have no money in the bank, no stocks or mutual funds to sell. None of my friends have money to lend me.

And I no longer have any family.

Jesper is my family, I think. It sounds strange, but he's the person who's closest to me.

I remember our last evening. We fought like crazy. It was the usual: How long does it have to be this way? I wanted to go out among people, go to the movies, a restaurant. He was stressed and irritated, had a shitty day at work, apparently. We were walking in the rain and I remember clearly that I was thinking, Now, now I've had enough.

A fine drizzle fell over Stockholm, transforming Götgatan into a shiny black mirror, upon which the reflections from the streetlights and shopfronts glittered like jewels. I had an umbrella, but didn't share it with him. Jesper didn't seem to care. He walked beside me gesturing, and speaking in an indignant voice.

'. . . hardly my fault. Right? I told you more than a month ago you have to find another job. Have you? No. Why should that be so fucking hard? Why should it always be me taking care of everything?'

We turned on Högbergsgatan. I could see from his body language, from his whole being, that he was upset. Neither of us said anything until we were standing outside the front door to his building on Kapellgränd.

'I want a date,' I said and put my hand on the cold brass handle of the door. 'This is like being together with someone who's married. I want a date. I want to know when you'll acknowledge me.'

Jesper took out his keys, fumbled with the front door. 'What do you mean "acknowledge" you? You're not a fucking African country that needs to be acknowledged by the UN. And there's nobody else, you know that. All this is about is how long we should wait to tell people about our relationship.'

The hall was dark, but neither of us cared enough to turn on the light. I kicked off my boots. Threw my jacket in a corner on the floor.

'And when were you planning on doing that, then? You just evade everything. You lie and evade.'

'Are you completely fucking crazy? I have never lied to you. Never.'

Now he was screaming. He threw his jacket against the wall. It landed on the small sideboard, knocked over the vase that I knew his mother had made sometime in the seventies. It fell to the floor with a crash.

'Yes, you lie to me and you take advantage of me.'

'"Take advantage" of you? How?'

His voice suddenly sounded cold and condescending.

'Everything is always on your terms. You think you can come and take what you want from me, when you want. My body, my feelings. You think you own them.'

Now he stood completely still. His eyes were turned towards the window. The light from a neon sign on the house opposite painted blue and pink streaks through his dark hair. I could see tiny drops of rain on his forehead.

'Don't I, though?' he said quietly, as if it were the most obvious thing in the world. His response caught me off guard. I couldn't reply at first.

'What do you mean?' I said finally, in a voice that was so weak I could hardly hear myself.

He turned to me and his face suddenly looked as empty as a ghost's. As if he were just a shell. An uninhabited shell, without emotion. 'I mean you are mine, Emma.'

He walked towards me until we were standing right in front of each other in the dark room. From a distance you could hear sirens approaching. Otherwise, everything was silent. He pulled me close, but there was something strange in his embrace: a stiff, stilted closeness with no real warmth. He's marking his ownership, I thought. This isn't about love, this is about something else. Power, maybe.

'Sorry,' he murmured in my ear. 'Of course you're right. We can't go on like this.' I felt him release his grip and root around in his pocket.

'I love you, Emma. No matter what happens, never forget that. Can you promise me that?'

I suddenly felt uncomfortable. 'What do you mean? What could happen?'

He ignored my question. 'I want you to have this.'

He held out his hand and I could see something glittering in his palm. Slowly I reached out and closed my hand tentatively around the small cold metal object.

It was a ring.

I hold it up to the light now. A thin ring of white gold with one impressive stone – a big brilliant diamond. It sparkles and glitters in the light as if nothing has happened.

The nausea overtakes me again. I sit down on the bed. The room seems strangely empty without the painting on the wall above. Everything seems to be spinning; proportions appear distorted. The window transforms slowly into a high, narrow streak. The ceiling tilts dangerously.

Sigge seems to sense that I don't feel well, because suddenly he's there, stroking his small, soft body against my legs. I bury my head in my hands, but my breasts hurt so much when I lean forward that I immediately have to sit up again.

And suddenly I understand.

It's like climbing to the top of a very high mountain in the middle of a deep forest after walking for days in the dark under the trees. Suddenly, the light is bright, the view is clear. The realisation hits me like a kick in the stomach and I find it hard even to breathe.

With fear pulsing inside me, I take out my mobile, browse my calendar and start counting days. I count once, twice. Then I count again. Still, I can't take it in; it's too bizarre.

But there's no other explanation.

I'm pregnant.

Hanne

Manfred, the fat, ruddy police officer, starts the meeting. He gets up, ambles over to the whiteboard and pushes his old-fashioned horn-rimmed glasses further up his nose with his index finger. Around the table sit the head of the preliminary investigation – a young blonde prosecutor named Björn Hansson – and the head of the National Homicide Division, Greger Sävstam. Sanchez is here too, as is Peter, who is sitting behind me. I'm grateful he's sitting there today, rather than across from me. I don't know if I would have been able to look at him.

In my little notebook, I carefully write down the name of everyone present, their titles and what they look like. Just an extra safety precaution. Names are particularly difficult for me to remember.

I've agreed to participate in the investigation, provided that the workload doesn't become too heavy. Maybe it's naive to think I can manage the work despite my illness, but I keep telling myself it will be fine. I'm not that confused, actually. Not yet. It's mostly my short-term memory that's malfunctioning, and some words that have a tendency to just disappear (like the names of the prime minister and the king, which the doctor asked during my last visit).

I like to imagine memory as a web, and my web has holes in it here and there. Small, ugly holes that will grow and multiply over time. As if someone has used a cigarette to burn holes into my web at random. So far, I can compensate for them, hide them from the people around me. But eventually the disease will eat up the web, until only thin threads hold together whatever pieces remain.

Sometimes I wonder what I'll be left with then. I mean, a person consists of their accumulated experiences, thoughts, and memories. If those are gone – who am I? Someone else? Something else?

Manfred Olsson clears his throat and leans against the wall.

'I thought I'd start by going through the new facts that have emerged in the case. We've now interviewed nine of Jesper's colleagues, five of his friends, his mother and father, and two former girlfriends. None of them have heard from Jesper Orre since Friday. Nobody knew where he was headed for his days off, or where he might be right now. The picture that is emerging is of an extremely ambitious and driven man with few interests outside work, aside from sport and women. In the media there's been talk about Orre's criminal connections, but we haven't found any evidence to back that up, though he does have a peripheral acquaintance who was convicted on a minor drug charge. Then we talked to the neighbours. No one saw anything remarkable on the evening in question. None of the tip-offs we've received since Orre's disappearance went public have led to anything.

'We've also gone through his emails and text messages without finding anything remarkable, but that doesn't necessarily mean anything – he could have a private mobile we don't know about. We're investigating that possibility now. He's been flagged since yesterday, so he couldn't have left the country since then. All border controls have been informed. And if he tries to withdraw any money, we'll notice it immediately. Unfortunately, that's all we've got on Jesper Orre right now. Oh – we spoke to the National Forensic Lab, and they said the machete found in Orre's hall is a panga, a tool used in East Africa, which has a broader blade and a more angular tip than a typical machete.'

Manfred hangs a picture of the machete on the whiteboard, points to the weapon's handle and says:

'The handle is carved from ebony. A rather unusual object, they said – probably quite old, too. You can find similar specimens at special auctions. There were no fingerprints on the handle, which indicates that the killer wiped them off after the murder. However, Jesper Orre's print has been found on the blade.'

Sanchez lets out a low whistle. 'We've got him,' she says.

'Not really. We can only prove that he's touched the machete, nothing else. The National Lab and the forensic technicians are working on comparing the blows to our victim with those Miguel Calderón received ten years ago, and they've promised us a report tomorrow or the day after at the latest. The blood found in the hall came from the victim. The urine, however, came from a man. The National Lab hasn't managed to obtain a full DNA profile yet, but they're working on it. As you know, it's more difficult to obtain DNA from urine than from blood and tissue.'

'So the urine came from a man. What does that mean?' asks Sanchez.

'That a man pissed in the hall,' Manfred responds.

Stifled giggles can be heard in the room. 'Yes, I get that, but why?'

'We'll have to figure that out,' Manfred says.

'Was urine found at the crime scene in the Calderón case?' I ask.

Manfred shakes his head and continues:

'No. I also talked to the technicians who combed through the rest of Orre's house.

Nothing remarkable was found, except for a basket of used women's underwear hidden in a cupboard in the laundry room in the basement. Considering the interview Peter and I had with Anja Staaf, which I mentioned earlier, we can conclude that Orre collects used lingerie. He gets off on it, I guess.'

Scattered laughter. It dies quickly when the National Homicide Division chief, Greger Sävstam, looks sternly around the table.

'They found something else, too,' Manfred continues. 'A pair of bloody, used knickers that were tucked under Orre's bed upstairs.'

'That time of the month?' Sanchez suggests.

Manfred shakes his head. 'The bloodstains are old and, based on their location, the technicians think someone used the knickers to staunch the bleeding of a wound. For example by wrapping them around an arm or a hand. Whether this has any relevance to our investigation we don't know yet.'

Manfred flips through his leather-bound pad and continues:

'Oh, and one more thing. Peter talked to the insurance company that's investigating the fire in Orre's garage. They told me that in all likelihood it was arson. Traces of paint were found in their chemical analysis of the ashes. The local police are also involved, and we've been in contact with them. So far there are no suspects. The insurance company hinted that they would put their money on Orre.'

'How is his financial situation?' Greger Sävstam asks in a broad southern accent.

'It's good,' Peter answers from behind me.

I don't turn around, and again it occurs to me that it might not have been so wise to come here after all. But I tell myself I'm strong enough to get through a few meetings with the man who destroyed my life ten years ago. It would be letting him win if I refrained from doing what I'm passionate about for fear of confronting my past. And it's important to prioritise my future, because there's so little left of it.

'He has an annual income of over four million,' Peter continues. 'In addition, he owns shares whose value is about three million. And he has no debts that we can find.'

Greger Sävstam fidgets in his seat. 'How can a man like Jesper Orre just go up in smoke?'

Manfred clears his throat. 'The entire force is looking for him.'

'I have a really bad feeling about this,' Greger Sävstam says, then stands up and shoves his hands into the pockets of his wrinkled suit trousers. 'We don't have shit. An old machete with an ebony handle and a pair of bloody underpants isn't going to solve this case. It's been three days, journalists are calling non-stop, and we don't even know who the victim is, or where Jesper Orre is. I don't plan on looking like a fool when I meet with the commissioner just because you people haven't managed to get any further than that.'

'Tomorrow we're meeting with Clothes&More's internal auditor,' Manfred says. 'Apparently they'd launched some sort of investigation into Orre. Rumour has it that he let the company pay for his fortieth birthday party. Maybe that will lead somewhere.'

Greger Sävstam looks stern and tired. He rolls his eyes as if he finds Manfred's response annoying.

'Even if he were embezzling company money, that won't help us with the murder investigation. Can we do anything else? Something more radical? Go to the media and ask for help?'

'It's already public that Jesper Orre is missing and a woman was found dead in his home,' Manfred begins.

Greger Sävstam waves his hand in irritation.

'Yes, I know. That's not what I meant. Could we publish a picture of the victim? So at least we're able to identify her?'

'She's been badly damaged ... We don't usually—' Manfred begins.

'I don't give a shit about what we usually do. We have to take this case to the next level now. We can't just sit here twiddling our thumbs, navel-gazing, asking ourselves why he liked to sniff old underwear.'

'We could ask one of our artists to produce a reconstruction, an image of the face,' Sanchez suggests. 'It's not as sensitive as publishing a ... mutilated, severed head.'

Greger gives her an exhausted look.

'That's the best idea you've had in a long time, Sanchez. Do it!'

I'm sitting in the big leather armchair in front of the fireplace, reading the preliminary investigation reports from the Calderón murder. The fire crackles, and on the low marble coffee table next to me a candle is burning. It's an odd feeling to see old reports I co-authored. So many years ago, and still so little has happened, I think. I live in the same apartment with the same man. Only the dog is new.

I look down at Frida curled up on the rug at my feet. Her black body trembles and her paws jerk in the air, as if she's dreaming of some violent hunt.

I return to reading. Remember that we noted at the time that the victim's eyelids were taped open. I close my eyes, feel the heat radiating from the fire into my body, and think. Why tape open the eyelids of your already dead victim – which the coroner concluded was most likely when it was done. The eyelids had been taped post-mortem, after death. The theory was supported by the presence of bloodstains under the tape.

So, the killer tapes open the eyelids of his victim and places the head in such a way that the next person who comes into the apartment will meet the dead man's gaze. Why? Did the murderer know who would find Calderón? Was it a message to that person? Or did he just want to humiliate the victim? Like the Celts, who hung their enemies' heads from their horses and rode home with them like trophies.

I make it no further in my thinking before I hear a key in the lock. Frida freezes, then jumps up and runs into the hall with her tail wagging. I know I should hide the investigation reports – Owe will be furious if he finds them – but I can't. Instead, I remain sitting with the papers in my lap.

He stands in the doorway, his grey hair tousled, his cheeks dark red with cold. His burgundy pullover stretches over his stomach, and his posture is one of irritation. He's like that sometimes, grumpy as soon as he gets home. Usually it's because he's quarrelled with somebody at work. It tends to seep out after a while, his frustration with some incompetent colleague or an unpleasant patient who treated him badly.

'Hello,' he says.

'Hi.'

He remains in the doorway, shifting his weight from foot to foot, as if unsure where to go.

'How was your day?'

'Good,' I say. 'Yours?'

He shrugs.

'Well, what can I say? The county hospital doesn't exactly attract the brightest sparks. I'm so bloody tired of teaching all these foreign doctors who can't tell the difference between a schizophrenic and a bipolar patient. And who can't write a decent report, because their Swedish is so shitty.'

'Sounds tough.'

He grunts something, but I can't really hear what. It's one of those guttural sounds he sometimes makes. Maybe I should be able to read them by now, after all these years, like parents who instinctively understand what their babies want when they scream.

'By the way, did you buy wine for tomorrow?' he asks.

'No, I . . . There were some other . . .'

My voice dies away. I didn't forget to buy wine; I've just been too busy at the police station. But I can't very well tell him that.

He sighs and starts to turn, but stops halfway. 'What are you reading, anyway?'

I cover the papers with my hands, but it's too late. He's already registered my hesitation, seen my hands instinctively try to hide whatever it is I have in my lap.

'Nothing special,' I say, but he's already on his way over to me.

He stops right in front of me, a huge dark silhouette against the fire. Bends over and firmly lifts my hands.

'What the hell is this?'

His scent overwhelms me, that stale mixture of smoke and sweat and something else I can't put my finger on, reminiscent of boiled cabbage. 'It's a . . . preliminary investigation report.'

'I can see that,' he answers with a voice one octave higher than usual. 'I'm wondering what the hell they're doing here, in our home? You said you weren't going to take on any assignments for the police again.'

'No, I didn't say that. You said that.'

In a single movement he grabs the papers and throws them across the room. From the corner of my eye, I see Frida run out into the hall with her tail between her legs.

'Goddammit, Hanne. We've already discussed this and decided it wasn't appropriate. You're not well enough to work. And now you go behind my back and do it anyway.'

When he says that, with all his patronising solemnity, while I'm surrounded by his stink, something inside me bursts. Breaks like when a load-bearing wall collapses and the whole house crumbles. It's like a thousand small explosions inside, and all the anger I've collected wells up, needing to find some way out.

I spring from the chair and start hammering his big body with my fists. The blows make no real impact – they're aimless, springing from hopelessness and despair that I can't quite put into words – and they mostly seem to surprise him.

'You bastard!' I scream. 'We never decided anything of the sort. You said I couldn't work. You decided it. As usual. You, you, you. I'm so fucking tired of you telling me what to do.'

He catches my arms in the air, locking them in a tight grip.

'Calm down. Have you gone completely fucking crazy? This is part of your disease, don't you understand that? Aggressiveness, depression. It's the disease.'

It's nothing new for Owe to blame my moodiness on the depression. Several times he's told me to go on antidepressants – whose welcoming, prescribed embrace scares me more than the disease itself.

'Stop blaming the fucking disease. This is not about the disease. This is about me. About how tired I am of your never-ending bullying and need to control.'

I fall silent and we stand there in front of the fire. Everything is still. The only sound is the fire crackling and my heavy breathing. His grip on my arms is painfully hard.

'Let me go!' I say.

He does as I say and remains standing there in the middle of the floor as I rake up the papers and rush into the bedroom.

'Hanne. Honey. What happened?'

'I've left him,' I say and set down the heavy suitcase beside me on the stone floor of the stairwell.

'Oh, sweetie. Come in.' Gunilla picks up my suitcase. 'Jesus. What do you have in here?'

'Watch your back. It's books. About Greenland. Only the most important ones.' Gunilla shakes her head slowly.

Frida runs ahead of me into Gunilla's bright hallway and I follow. Stamp snow off my shoes and take off my coat, hang it on one of the colourful hooks, go into the living room and sink into Gunilla's white sofa.

'Tell me everything!' she says and I do. About the meeting with the police. About Peter. About the ten-year-old cold case that has become relevant again, and my longing to do something meaningful with the rest of my time. To be able to use all of the knowledge I've acquired in a full career. And then I tell her about Owe, explain how his controlling behaviour, his self-absorption and even the smell of him repel me. How I simmer with anger for months, until it flares up like a forest fire, leaving me empty and exhausted. How I can't cope with this emotional slash-and-burn any more.

'Well then it was about time you moved out,' is all she says when I'm done.

The question I've been waiting for doesn't come until later, after we've drunk several glasses of wine and eaten some of Gunilla's stinky cheese.

'Do you think it's wise to leave him right now, when you don't know how you'll feel in a month or a year?'

There is a short pause before I meet her eyes and answer. 'That's why it's so important. I don't want to spend the time I have left with him.'

When I wake up the next morning the sun is shining for the first time in weeks, and heavy drops of melted snow fall onto the window ledge. It feels like a sign, and both my elation and my relief swell inside. It's almost narcotic, a wave to surf and be carried away by, in the midst of all this misery.

From now on, things can only get better, I think, and pick up my Louis-Jacques Dorais book about Inuit language and culture. Flip through it at random.

Snow falls from the roof and lands with a dull thud on the window ledge outside.

The thing about the Inuit having so many words for snow is a myth, born out of Western civilisation's romantic passion for primitive people and their symbiotic relationship to the elements. Certainly, the Inuit have more than one word for snow – but so do we. Moreover, there isn't 'one' Inuit language. Rather there are many languages and dialects spoken across the Arctic, in parts of Alaska, Canada, Siberia and Greenland.

But, as usual, we humans need to simplify things in order to make reality more manageable. Actually, we do the same thing at the police station. Simplify, try to understand, make connections and see patterns in the complex materials of the investigation. And maybe we also make the same mistake: attributing characteristics to people and applying models to explain events because it fits our world view.

Again I think of the Calderón murder. Have we missed something? Have our preconceptions coloured our view of events?

Gunilla's timid knock at the door interrupts my thoughts. 'Breakfast?' she asks.

'Yes please. I'm starving,' I say, realising that I actually mean it. For the first time in months, I feel truly hungry.

Emma

One month earlier

I'm sitting on the metro on the way to work, trying to make sense of what has happened. Jesper's child, our child, is growing inside me. In some dark, secret place a small tadpole with a tail and gills is about to assume a human form.

It's unimaginable.

I can't really grasp the fact that I'm pregnant; this is not just about me and my relationship with Jesper any more. Now I need to decide if I should keep the baby or not. I no longer have the option of simply letting go of Jesper and moving on. The equation has changed, and he has the right to know I'm expecting his child, regardless of whether or not he's the arsehole of the century.

I have to track him down and tell him what's happened, face to face.

Mahnoor and Olga are both sitting in the staffroom with a cup of coffee when I get to work. We don't open for another twenty minutes and Björne is nowhere in sight, so we might as well take the opportunity to have coffee now.

'Coffee?' Mahnoor asks.

'Yes please.'

I shrug off my jacket and sit down on one of the white chairs around the table. Mahnoor gently puts a cup in front of me. Her hair falls down onto the table as she bends forward and I note how beautiful it is, the kind of hair many envy.

'Where's Björne?' I ask.

'No clue,' Olga says. 'Maybe he's late.'

'Late? But usually he's so early. Perhaps he's ill,' I suggest.

'I don't think so,' Mahnoor mumbles. 'He hasn't had a single black mark for six months.' It's quiet for a moment. I sip the hot coffee and try to think away the nausea. Try my best not to think about the stowaway somewhere deep inside my body.

'You have ten dots this month,' Olga says and turns her eyes towards me. There's no tact or compassion in her voice. She notes the fact as objectively as if she's told a customer the price of a pair of pants.

'I'm sure it's not going to be a problem,' Mahnoor says and lightly touches my hand.

'Of course it's a problem. If you're out too many times, they fire you,' Olga says.

'I was sick,' I say.

'Don't matter,' Olga continues, as if explaining the most obvious thing in the world to a very small or perhaps very stupid child. Her fingernails drum the table, as if they wanted to take off on their own. They're so long her hands make me think of deadly weapons.

'You got to be careful with your job and even if you're sick sometimes you got to work. Try harder,' Olga says, emphasising every word. She continues:

'You have to be careful with all relationships. Sometimes you do things you don't want to do, for the sake of making peace. For example, if I want Alexej to be happy, I give him a blow job when he gets home.'

'Oh come on,' Mahnoor protests. 'That's hardly the same thing.'

'Yes it is. You have to make the effort, both at home and at work.'

Mahnoor is clearly annoyed. She stands up and puts her coffee cup in the sink with a bang. Brown liquid splashes out.

'You're sick, you know that? This isn't Russia,' she says and leaves the kitchenette in a huff. The heavy scent of her perfume lingers in the room.

'What makes her so pissed off?' Olga murmurs.

'Don't know.'

'Maybe because she's Muslim.'

'Maybe.'

We ponder this for a moment. The phone rings, but Mahnoor beats us to it; she must have picked up the phone at the register, because I can hear her talking to someone out in the shop.

'Are you going to apologise to her?' I ask.

'Apologise? For what? She's the one who stops out.'

'I think you mean "stomped".'

'Whatever. She thinks she's special 'cause she studies at the university.' Olga pinches her mouth shut and crosses her arms over her chest.

Steps approach from outside. Mahnoor appears at the door again and I can see from her posture, even before she begins to speak, that something has happened.

'It's Björne,' she says and her voice sounds almost breathless. 'He's been hit by a bus. He's not gonna die or anything, but he'll be gone for a while. At least a month.'

Neither Olga nor I say anything. We all dislike Björne, but nobody wishes him bodily harm. The thought of his lean form underneath a big bus makes me feel sick again.

'Poor Björne,' Olga whispers.

'Yes, poor Björne,' Mahnoor says.

'What happens now?' I ask.

'We have to run the shop by ourselves,' Mahnoor says and straightens up a little. 'They asked me to take charge until further notice.'

I wonder if they decided to make Mahnoor responsible for the shop, or if they asked her because she happened to answer the phone.

'Oh, and there was one more thing,' Mahnoor says. 'There have been some articles about our dear CEO again. If any journalist tries to contact us, we're supposed to make no comment. All questions should be referred to head office.'

'He's been a naughty boy again?' Olga smiles slyly. Mahnoor shrugs.

'No clue.'

But Olga doesn't give up.

'Your friend, the one in the personnel department. She's investigating him, right?'

'She doesn't work in the personnel department, she works in the finance department, but yes, there was something about how Jesper Orre got the company to pay for his birthday party. But I don't know anything about that.'

Later, my lunch consists of a plastic-packed salad. The prawns are so tasteless and mushy that I find it difficult to imagine they ever lived in the sea. It feels more like they were moulded from flour and fish broth.

I'm sitting in front of the computer at the small desk in the staffroom. To my left is the kitchenette. The table is covered with magazines and a plastic container with a few lonely prawns left in it is standing on the counter.

I wipe my hands off with a napkin, pull the keyboard towards me, and look up Jesper Orre. After just a few seconds this article pops up: 'Jesper Orre Accused of Sexual Harassment'. I click on the magazine's website and scroll down. A woman who 'worked closely with Jesper' for a few years has accused him of sexual harassment. It doesn't say who she is or what she was working on, but I conclude it must be someone at head office, because they worked together. Maybe a secretary or someone in the marketing department. Neither Jesper nor the company will make any comment about the matter but 'reliable sources' claim that an internal investigation has been launched.

I wonder. For some reason the article doesn't upset me. Jesper often spoke about how vulnerable he was, how the people around him could be divided into two groups: yes-men, who tried hard to stay close to him all the time, and those who did their best to sabotage him at every opportunity. And often the yes-men slowly turned into saboteurs when they didn't get the response they hoped for.

I'm guessing this woman is a saboteur. Jesper is fair game now; the train has left the station. This is an easy way to get attention and perhaps avenge some old injustice. Jesper was right: it's tough at the top. You're exposed up there and can't trust anyone.

And yet. There is always the possibility that I'm wrong.

How well do I know Jesper, anyway?

I look at the article again, my eyes struck by the byline. Anders Jönsson. The name sounds familiar. Where have I heard it before?

Then I remember. That journalist who came into the shop, who wanted to talk to me about working here and gave me his card. It's in my overflowing bread bin now, along with all my bills.

Mahnoor enters the room, sits down on the chair opposite me. 'What are you doing?'

I quickly shut off the computer. 'Nothing special. My Internet isn't working at home.'

She nods slowly.

'Are you OK, by the way?' I say. 'It seemed like you were a little upset earlier.'

Mahnoor sighs and rolls her eyes.

'It's just that Olga has fucking awful ideas about being a woman. It bothers me. You'd think she came straight from the 1800s. Right?'

I wonder. Olga is different. I haven't actually thought about her attitudes towards women – more about her insensitivity, about how her comments, probably unintentionally, sometimes sting like a slap.

'I haven't thought about it before,' I say.

'Well, I have,' Mahnoor states.

'By the way, is it OK if I leave a little bit earlier today?' I ask.

She looks searchingly at me and crosses one leg over the other. 'Sure. That's fine. I should probably close anyway. Now that I'm . . .

responsible or whatever.' She adopts a frown that is annoying and comical at the same time.

'Thank you,' I say. 'There's something I need to do.'

As Mahnoor and I are closing the shop, a heavyset woman with blonde hair and a far too small coat passes by, and without being able to stop it, I start thinking about Mum again. I remember one day when we were lying in bed, just her and me. It was one of those rare and precious moments of intimacy and love that usually occurred after Mum and Dad had been tired and angry for a long time. Mum was stroking my hair. Her face was serious.

'Sweet, darling Emma.'

I didn't answer, just closed my eyes and let the warmth of the blanket and her affection envelop me.

'Sorry that . . . that . . . I'm so grumpy and mean sometimes,' she said suddenly.

I opened my eyes and met her gaze. She looked pained, as if she had a stomach ache again and needed one of those small white tablets she kept high up in the cabinet.

'It doesn't matter,' I replied.

She relaxed. 'It's just that . . . sometimes it's so stressful . . . and I'm so tired. And then I . . . lose my temper.'

I guess a person could lose their temper in the same way you might drop a bag or a bottle onto the floor. Then again, if you dropped it, why couldn't you pick it up? But I didn't say that, because I didn't want to ruin this delicate, perfect moment. I realised it was my responsibility to manage it.

'It's OK.'

'No, sweetie, it's actually not OK. I just want you to know that. When I get that angry it's my fault. It's wrong and stupid, and as an adult, I should be able to control my temper better.'

There were tears in her voice now, but I absolutely didn't want her to start crying. Suddenly it felt like the most important mission in the world to keep her from getting sad. Because if she started to cry she wouldn't be able to stop, and the day would be destroyed and everything would be my fault.

'I don't think you're angry. I think you're nice.'

'Oh, you're Mummy's little darling,' she mumbled and kissed me on the mouth.

Her breath smelled of sour coffee and old milk, but I didn't pull aside. Instead I was careful to lie completely still, so that she could kiss me properly. At that very moment the phone rang in the hall.

'I'll be right back,' she murmured. Then she stood up and wrapped the pink dressing gown around her big body.

Outside, the sun was shining and the children from surrounding buildings were on their way to school. I had been coughing for several days, and Mum had insisted on keeping me at home which angered Dad. He didn't think you should 'act like a baby'. And lying in bed because of a cough with no temperature was definitely acting like a baby.

I enjoyed those days at home alone with Mum. I spent so little time around her when she was happy and energetic. In the evenings she always sat in the kitchen with Dad drinking beer, and in the mornings she was always tired and worn out and needed her rest.

'No, we have no pets at home. Why?'

I could hear Mum clearly from the hall. She had that sharp little voice, the one that meant she was getting annoyed with someone. It was the voice she usually had in the evenings, just before she got angry for real and beer cans and plates started flying across the kitchen at Dad.

'I don't understand. What do you mean, can't relate to other children? My daughter has no problem playing with other children. She has lots of friends here in the area.'

There was silence again.

'I don't believe that. I'll ask her, but my impression is that she has a lot of friends in school too.'

I got up to close the door. My chest suddenly got tight even though I didn't need to cough. 'Special needs? You have to be joking. And why would it be any better if she spent time with animals? That sounds like complete nonsense to me. How does grooming a horse or petting a puppy make you any less shy? And yes, I think it's shyness, nothing else, because . . .'

I shut the door and went back to bed.

Outside my window early summer had exploded. Trees and bushes dazzled in shades of green. The perennials in the flower bed bloomed elegant and high; the rosehip bushes by the swings were dotted with pink flowers that would soon turn into hard fruit filled with first-class itching powder.

I lay on the bed, hoping that Mum would stop talking soon. That she would come back and crawl into bed and be soft and kind.

I longed to be babied by her again.

My chest still felt strangely tight. As if someone had wrapped a skipping rope round and round my body.

Then I saw something. A motion on the floor beside the bed. I carefully lifted the glass jar. On one of those bare, jagged branches sat a large blue butterfly. Its actual body was black and round and a little hairy. Its wings were an intense cobalt blue with black markings at the edges. It gracefully brought its wings up and down, as if learning to move again after spending such a long time in its little cocoon.

It's dark as I walk from the square at Sergels torg down Hamngatan. My umbrella only partially protects me – gusts of wind keep sweeping rain underneath it. The streets are strangely empty and only the occasional pedestrian hurries past in the darkness. By the time I arrive at Regeringsgatan it's five o'clock. The big C&M shop is illuminated like a cruise ship, shouting out its message, promising a better, more exciting life on the other side of the window. A few women with wet hair wander aimlessly between the shelves, searching through the garments.

I turn to the left onto Norrlandsgatan and continue another hundred yards. I see the entrance to the Clothes&More head office across the street. The wooden door is dimly lit. It almost seems to glow in the dark.

Next to me is a doorway. I glide into the darkness, glad to have protection from the rain. Here I can wait without being seen. The question is whether I'll be able to determine who's going in and out of the door on the other side of the street. It's not that close, and it's dark.

I put on my gloves and prepare to wait. After maybe five minutes the door opens and two women around my age come out. They laugh loudly and cross the street while putting up their respective umbrellas. The wind takes hold of one and turns it inside out. They laugh even louder. I'm pretty sure they can't see me huddling in the darkness.

Several times I catch myself thinking, Am I losing my mind?

I'm standing in the rain, spying on Jesper. Like a stalker. If someone had told me a month ago I'd be doing this, I'd have thought that person was crazy.

Still. Given the situation, I don't know what else to do. I have to talk to him. I realise there's so much I don't know about Jesper, endless gaps to be filled in. So many holes and so little solid matter to lean on. I'm starting to wonder if I ever knew him.

The rain falls unabated for the next hour. Periodically the door on the other side opens and people come out and disappear into the darkness. Not once does anyone glance in my direction. It is as if I'm invisible, as if I've turned into a rock on the ground.

Despite the fact that I'm standing under a roof the occasional raindrop finds its way in. Settles into my hairline, my neck, along my wrists. I take a few small steps to try to warm up. Discreetly slapping my arms in the darkness.

At exactly ten past six, he walks out.

I recognise him immediately. He has a black, unbuttoned coat on over his suit and it flutters behind him in the wind as he hurries across the street. Suddenly I can't move; it's as if my body won't obey me, as if I've turned into a piece of uncooperative meat, frozen solid on the wet street.

Just a week or so since we met last, I think. Yet it feels like months. All those calls, text messages and there he is, the man I love, a shadow in front of me in the rain.

Then the paralysis releases its grip on me. I take a few steps out of the doorway and start hurrying after him. The rain lashes my face, but I don't have time to stop and open my umbrella, don't risk losing him in the darkness.

His stride is confident and somehow graceful, as if he's almost dancing in the rain. Then he's suddenly gone, swallowed up by the black Tarmac of Regeringsgatan. I pick up the pace and when I reach the place where he disappeared, I see an entrance to a parking garage.

Of course.

Why didn't I think of that? Of course he drives to work. How can I follow him now?

I look around. No cars or taxis in sight. I see a door opening twenty yards ahead. Headlights are visible from inside the building. He drives a black Lexus. For a few seconds I see his silhouette against the lights of the parking garage. Then he drives out and disappears into the darkness towards Stureplan.

I don't care about the rain any more, don't even feel it. I walk Hamngatan down towards Nybroplan. If I hurry, I'll be home in fifteen minutes, but what does it matter? There's nobody waiting for me there and I have nothing I need to do.

Kungsträdgården lies silent and deserted, and I have the sudden urge to cross the street, walk into the park and find somewhere to lie down, maybe under a huge tree. Let the wet grass accept me, go completely numb. Become one with the plants and gravel and wet late-autumn leaves. Disappear. Forget. Die, maybe.

Then I think of Woody.

It's hard not to think about him now that everything has turned out the way it has.

At first glance, his appearance was rather unremarkable. Dark shoulder-length hair, worn-out jeans that were always a little too big. Check shirts. And he was old, too, of course.

At least twenty-five.

There was a lot of talk about Woody that term. All the girls in class gossiped about him. I can't say that I was a part of that really. I was kind of an outsider, observing the social games without really participating. Maybe I was a little shy, or maybe I just wasn't interested.

Maybe I remember wrong.

That autumn we made butter knives and bowls and other unnecessary items that could be given away to family members or friends. I couldn't make a proper butter knife. At first it was awkwardly shaped and too large, and when I tried to correct the proportions it shrank more and more, turning into something that resembled a fat toothpick.

'Watch out that it doesn't disappear completely,' Woody said one day and winked at me.

I didn't know what to say, but I felt myself blushing. Do you think he's handsome? Elin had asked me earlier that day. I don't know, I had answered truthfully, because I had actually never thought of him that way. He was just one of my teachers, albeit a little younger and less dull than the others.

But still. Super old.

'I can help you later,' Woody said and ran his big finger over the scratchy surface of the wood, pushing bits of sawdust onto the table. I felt him looking at me, but didn't dare to meet his eyes, just nodded silently.

It was the same year Dad fell down into his dark hole. The one that only he could see, and that for some reason was so deep he couldn't climb out again. Trapped by hopelessness and fear, he spent his days in self-imposed isolation in our apartment on Kapellgränd. They called it depression. Outside our kitchen window spring woke up, but Dad lay in his bed becoming more and more tired, staring at the seaweed wallpaper as if those long blades might give him some kind of answer. Mum tried to talk to him. They had long mumbling conversations inside their bedroom. I tried to hear what they were saying but never succeeded. Whatever it was, though, it was terrible enough to require whispering.

The beer cans and wine bottles disappeared from the kitchen at about the same rate that Dad got worse. Now Mum would be cooking dinner when I got home: meatballs or sausages with slices of tomato and onion inserted into them. I wasn't used to seeing her playing house and it made me nervous. Mum's little projects often ended in disaster. Like when she tried to sew curtains. Having failed to make the curtains symmetrical, she ripped the fabric into long strips and tossed them out the window. The strips hung there fluttering in the bushes for months, a reminder of the curtains that never were and Mum's dangerously explosive temper. She tossed the sewing machine at Dad's shins and he ended up with a big dark-blue bruise.

I looked at my butter knife again. Sighed.

'What is it?' Elin said when she saw my critical gaze.

'It's ugly.'

Elin didn't answer. Instead, she returned to the sleek little wooden box she was working on. Everything Elin made in woodwork class was good. It was as if her hands possessed some kind of mystical knowledge, as if they intuitively knew what to do when they came into contact with wood or fabric or paper. Not like my hands. They refused to do what I told them to; they destroyed everything they touched. Or at least it felt that way.

Elin moved the sandpaper gently over the already perfect lid to polish away some invisible unevenness, at the same time blowing a big bubble with her Hubba Bubba gum. Marie, who was sitting at the table in front us, leaned back in her chair and turned to Elin.

'Are you going to Micke's party?'

Elin shrugged. 'Haven't decided. Petra is having a party the same night.'

'Petra is a freak.'

Elin fired off a crooked smile. 'And Micke is pathetic.'

Marie laughed delightedly at Elin's analysis of Friday's events, flipped her long hair and turned around. Meanwhile, I looked down at my deformed butter knife. No one ever asked me if I'd like to go to a party. But I wasn't bullied either. No one in my class had ever been mean to me. On the whole, it was as if I didn't exist to them. I might as well have been one of the chairs in the room.

I didn't really know how to feel about it. Maybe I ought to be sad, feel ostracised, insulted. But the truth was that I thought it was nice to not have to participate in that game. I didn't need to go to Micke's party and get drunk and puke in the flower bed or pass out in the bathroom. I didn't want to listen to Marie's never-ending complaints about her boyfriend or hang out with Elin outside the kiosk. I preferred staying at home and watching television.

The bell rang.

The room began to empty out, but Woody signalled for me to stay. 'You don't say much,' he said.

I didn't know how to answer that. My grip on the butter knife tightened and I felt my hand become damp with sweat. My cheeks flushed.

'You're pretty, you know that?'

Woody pulled out a chair and sat down next to me. Bent forward so that our faces were close.

'Thanks,' I said.

For the first time I met his gaze. His eyes were close-set, warm brown and bordered by long black lashes. He had a few grey hairs sticking up here and there in his thick black hair, like dead trees in an otherwise lush forest.

'Sorry, I don't want to seem pushy, but I wanted to ask you something.'

He fell silent, chuckled and shook his head slowly, almost as if he was embarrassed. Out in the hallway the sound of laughter and footsteps was replaced by silence.

'Yes?'

He closed his eyes.

'Do you have a boyfriend, Emma?'

When I get home, I find the familiar smell of cooking and stale cigarette smoke in the stairwell strangely soothing. I look at my hands. They are wet and pale but have stopped shaking. Somewhere in the darkness outside, Jesper Orre has parked his big black Lexus and entered whatever he calls home. I try not to think about it, but the realisation that he's probably sitting on a sofa somewhere, maybe with a glass of wine in his hand, hurts.

As I climb the stairs, my boots leave wet prints on the worn stone steps. It's starting to dawn on me that Jesper was hiding something. Why did we always meet only at his pied-à-terre or at my place? Why was it so enormously important for him that we were never seen together? It couldn't have just been his job. Could it?

I stand in front of my door, breathless from the exertion of climbing five flights of stairs. My body has started to relax, finally begun to get warm.

As soon as I put the key in the lock, I realise something is wrong. The door is unlocked, and when I open it there's a bang from inside the apartment. I always lock up when I leave, and no one else has the key to my apartment, not even Jesper.

I look around. The stairwell lies dark and silent behind me. If someone is hiding down in the darkness, I can't see them. The thought makes my stomach knot.

I carefully crack open the front door. The hall is quiet and empty. There's no sign that anyone has been here. I stretch out my hand, grope for the switch. Seconds later the hall is bathed in light and I take a cautious step inside.

Nothing seems to have been touched, but I feel something else. A draught of cold air flows through the apartment, sneaking past my ankles. I shut the door behind me and the air grows still once more, but it's cold, too cold, and I wonder if something is open. Without taking off my shoes, I go to the living room and turn on the overhead light. Everything looks the same: the slender green Malmsten armchairs, the small desk with physics textbooks piled up on it. I haven't even had time to think about school for the last week. For a moment I wonder if I should put my physics textbooks in the bread bin too, so I don't see them.

As I continue towards the kitchen, I realise that something is wrong. I can hear the rain and the noise of the city too clearly, almost as if I were standing outside in the storm again. I turn on the light and stand in the doorway.

The window is open.

I almost never open it and yet there it is, wide open, inviting the night into the apartment. I walk over to close it, but as I do, it hits me.

Sigge.

I call his name and search through every room. Under the bed and the sofa, inside closed cupboards, on the hat rack, in the bath. Sigge is nowhere to be found. He's not in the habit of hiding, so I become increasingly convinced that he's disappeared out the window.

As I go back to the kitchen, I try to remember whether or not I forgot to lock up when I went to work, but the morning is a blank and I can't recall a single image from it. Just hours ago, I think, and yet so far away.

I lean out the kitchen window, as far as I dare, and shout Sigge's name. The rain whips against my neck. Five floors below, the court-yard is just a dark rectangle. The trees and bushes dance in the wind, but there's no Sigge in sight. I quickly pull on my coat, open the front door, half-run down the stairs and out into the courtyard.

The smell of decomposing leaves and wet soil is overwhelming. I walk over the cobblestones to a spot that I guess is right beneath my kitchen window, turn my face upwards and squint into the rain. Far above, I glimpse the open window. It's at least a thirty-foot drop, maybe more.

Could a cat survive that?

The cobblestones are empty. I squat down. Close to the wall, where the stone is almost dry, there's a dark stain. I touch it gently and then look at my fingers.

It's blood.

I find faint traces of blood going in the direction of the wall facing the street. Follow them while still crouching to see where they lead, but the rain has washed them away.

Between the wall and the building is a narrow opening, big enough for a cat to sneak out onto Valhallavägen. I lean forward and peer out into the rain; I can see nothing but indifferent cars passing by in the dark.

Peter

These last few days have been damn difficult. In part it's because the investigation has stalled, and in part because Hanne's presence at the meetings makes me nervous. She just sits there without saying anything, which is the idea, of course; she's studying the case. But it bothers me. And there's something accusatory in her eyes.

Sometimes I get the indefinable feeling that she expects me to take some kind of initiative. Talk to her. Maybe explain why I did what I did. Or is that just my guilty conscience playing tricks on me?

I guess that's how life is. It itches and stings like a boil on your bum, and the only way to put an end to your misery is to put an end to it.

But I'm not quite there yet.

The car stops and Morrissey goes silent. 'Umm, Lindgren. Are you asleep?'

I turn to Manfred, smile apologetically and jump out of the car he's just parked in the garage at the NK department store.

'Just wanted to make sure I hadn't lost you.'

'Sure, I'm fine.'

We go down the stairs of the parking garage and out onto Hamngatan.

Christmas shopping is in full swing, and the pavement is packed with people. Water drips from every roof and windowsill; almost all the snow is gone, just small, dirty mounds here and there pressed up against building facades. The sky is blue and the air feels damp, clean and crisp, like newly hung washing. Sunshine streams down between the tall buildings, playing on the road in front of us as we cross the street. I squint in the bright light and search for the entrance to the Clothes&More headquarters.

Agnieszka Lindén meets us at the reception. She's in her forties and wears a very proper dark-blue suit. Her blonde, slightly thin hair is worn in a neat bob and her cheeks are plump and rosy. She looks healthy and reminds me vaguely of one of my old gym teachers in high school – Sirkka, who used to advocate an ice-cold shower on an empty stomach every morning (after a run, also to be undertaken before breakfast).

'Welcome,' she says and shakes our hands, looks at me briefly, then gestures towards the corridor where the walls are filled with gigantic fashion posters.

'The spring collection,' she mumbles and shows us into a small room whose windows face Regeringsgatan.

We sit down in the black visitors' chairs across from her desk and take out our notebooks. Agnieszka's desk is completely empty, her pens placed neatly in a small grey plastic desk organiser. She clasps her hands and smiles.

'So, how can I help you? This is concerning Jesper, I suppose? The journalists are apparently calling non-stop.'

Manfred nods.

'We're investigating the murder that took place at Jesper Orre's home. And we were told by some of your colleagues that you were investigating him. Could you tell us more about that?'

'Of course. In June Jesper arranged a party. It was a combination of a fortieth birthday party and an official dinner for selected upper management and retailers. Half of the cost was paid by the company and half by Jesper. In September, we received an anonymous complaint from a person claiming that Jesper had abused his position and allowed the company to pay for his private birthday party. I work as an internal auditor here, and my job includes investigating these kinds of events and reporting them to the board, so I looked into it.'

'And what did you conclude?' I ask.

'You can have a copy of my memo if you like. My conclusion was, briefly, that it was reasonable for the company to pay for some of the costs because so many of the guests had a direct or indirect link to the business.'

'So he did nothing wrong?' Manfred asks.

Agnieszka Lindén smiles guardedly and runs her hand across her clean desk.

'Yes and no. It would have been better if he'd run it by our finance department before the party. In addition, he authorised the bill himself which is, of course, unacceptable and goes against regulations.'

'So what did the board think about it?' Manfred asks.

'I don't know. I'm not privy to their meetings. But I heard they were annoyed. Jesper has been at the centre of a lot of controversy over the past year – I'm sure you've seen the papers. And now this . . . I would think he's hanging on by a thread here, but don't pass that on.'

Manfred nods and says:

'You mention that there have been controversies. Have there been other problems besides the party?'

Agnieszka stretches and sighs.

'Yes. Well, you'll probably find out about it anyway. One of our project managers in the marketing department accused Jesper of some kind of sexual harassment. I don't really know the particulars, but I've heard rumours.'

'Could we get her name?' I ask.

'Of course. Her name is Denise Sjöholm and she's on sick leave. I can give you her contact information.'

By the time we exit onto Regeringsgatan, the sun has disappeared behind clouds and the sky has darkened.

'Shit,' Manfred says. 'I really thought that would give us more of a lead.'

'Well, we'll talk to that Denise woman. I wonder why none of Orre's other colleagues said anything about her?'

Manfred shrugs and holds the door to the parking garage open for me as I squeeze past his large body.

'Maybe they didn't dare. Orre is their boss, after all,' I answer my own question.

Manfred hums in response.

We sit in silence in the car for a while. Traffic is heavy on our way back to the police station and I note that Manfred looks at me a bit strangely as we creep forward on the Klarabergs viaduct. There's concern in his eyes and it bothers me.

'Is everything OK?' he asks finally.

'Of course,' I respond.

He doesn't say anything more. Instead, he turns on the music again. Another thing I appreciate about Manfred: he doesn't feel the need to dig so bloody hard into your emotions (apart from when it's job-related, of course). Not like women, who always ask what you're thinking and are never content with a straightforward answer like 'Nothing really.' Even Sanchez is like that, despite being a police officer. Always asking how I feel, though I've told her a thousand times that I'm fine.

I wonder if it's genetic.

After we get to the police station I sit in the small conference room reading through the Calderón case again. Page after page of interrogations, excerpts from technical reports, analyses of blood spatter, fibres, shoe prints and pictures from the crime scene.

Outside it's starting to get dark and I hear the wind pick up. Small hard snowflakes whip against the window.

We still haven't found any connection between our victims. Even though it seems as if an invisible thread runs through time and space from Calderón to the unidentified woman in Orre's home. When I lay the picture of Calderón's head next to the picture of the woman's head, you can't ignore the resemblance. Is it really possible that two different murderers committed such identical crimes? What is the likelihood, really?

There's a knock on the door and when I look up Hanne is standing there. 'Oh, sorry,' she says and turns around.

It's pure impulse, maybe because she looks like a sad puppy, but I ask her to come in. She does as I say, closing the door gently behind her and sinking into one of the chairs opposite me.

'What are you doing?' she asks.

I look down at the papers scattered across half of the conference table. At the pictures of violent death, at reports that say so much and explain so little.

'Reading the case.'

'Ah.'

She looks a little confused. Runs her hand through her hair as if she wants to make sure it's neat. (It's not. Her thick grey-brown hair spreads out in every direction, like a plant with sharp needles.)

'I've been thinking,' she begins.

'Yes?'

'That maybe we should talk. If we're going to work together.'

'OK. About what?'

She meets my gaze, and those beautiful grey eyes of hers, which I know so well, are suddenly filled with sorrow. And I know I'm about to do it again: hurt her, even though I don't want to.

'Listen. I'm sorry,' I say. 'I didn't mean it like that. Of course we can talk.'

She relaxes, exhales and rests her dainty hands in her lap.

'You're a real bastard, Peter. Do you know that?'

I nod. 'That's never my intention. I never meant to hurt you, Hanne. Believe me. You are the last person on earth I would want to hurt.'

'And yet you did. And you continue to do so by pretending that nothing happened. Do you understand?'

I look down at the table. Try in vain to bring some order to the thoughts and words swirling around inside my skull. Searching in vain for a way to explain it to her. But words have never come easily to me. It's as if there's some disconnect between my head and my mouth – the words end up in disarray, come out in a completely different way than I imagined.'

'It's so hard to . . . explain. That's all I can say. I thought I was doing what was best for you.'

I immediately feel ashamed. What a stupid thing to say. What a fucking embarrassing explanation to a woman who was left on the doorstep of a new life. But Hanne doesn't seem to react; instead she stares through the window at the dusk that's falling over the city and the thick mix of snow and rain running down the windowpane.

I have the urge to touch her face, to run my hand through her thick unruly hair. The thought is so tempting, I almost have to restrain myself. Force myself to keep still on that uncomfortable chair.

'Do you regret it sometimes?' she asks in a voice that is so quiet I can barely hear what she says.

'Every day,' I answer without thinking and realise immediately that it's true.

After Hanne has left, I remain there alone in the room. Wondering how this started, when the first time was that I betrayed someone. But I already know the answer.

Annika. My sister. That summer out on the island of Rönnskär.

The summer had begun like every other summer, but ended with a disaster that changed my family's lives for ever.

I was heading down the steps towards the dock at our summer house outside Dalarö. I think I was searching for small treasures on the rocks. I was holding a 'Left Party' button that I'd found by the house. Maybe I was hoping that one of the neighbouring children would be down by the water so we could play Baader-Meinhof on the dock.

The waves were beating against the rocks; the sea breeze blew the hair from my face and made the skin on my arms turn to goosebumps. I remember I noticed the slight smell of cigarette smoke and for a moment I was surprised: Dad was back by the house. And then I saw her: my sister Annika, three years my elder, sitting on the cliff to the right of the dock in a bikini.

She was smoking.

She had one leg lazily stretched out in front of her and the second one drawn up so that the arm that held the cigarette rested on it. Her reddish-tan skin shone and her blonde hair was gathered in a bun on the top of her head. Her pointed breasts were covered by a tiny triangle bikini.

At that very moment she turned her face towards me, caught my eye and let out a little sound. No words; more like a small whine.

I stood completely still. This was explosive, of course: Annika was secretly smoking on the rocks. It was sensational information, and like all information, it was valuable. It could be exchanged for benefits or confidences, disclosed in retaliation or perhaps hinted at in small pieces at sensitive times.

I remember I could see it in her eyes, despite the distance: the horror.

'You wouldn't.'

Her voice was quiet. Outwardly controlled, but I sensed the panic underneath. Such privilege: to have the upper hand over her. It didn't happen often.

She stood up, wrapped a towel around her shoulders. I was closer now, could see her goosebumps and her nipples standing out in her minimal bikini top.

'You wouldn't,' she repeated. 'This is our secret. OK? And a secret is a responsibility. Can you take responsibility?'

But all I could do was smile. And the more I smiled, the stronger I felt. It was as if the situation filled me with a heady recklessness, a narcotic sense of power. And though it hadn't been my plan, I began to jog back up the steps leading from the dock to the house. Slowly at first, but then faster and faster.

Annika was behind me, still with the cigarette in her mouth. I could hear her feet on the rickety wooden steps.

'You stupid little brat, come back here!'

But I ran. And if there was one thing I could do, it was run fast. My legs beat like drumsticks over the rocks and steps. Over heather and pine needles that perforated the thin, delicate skin between my toes.

Annika ran after me, breathless. Helpless.

I wasn't really going to tell, but for some reason Mum was standing on the porch when I got up there. Resting her broad hips against the railing and staring out over the sea with an inscrutable expression. She pushed a dark, slightly greasy strand of hair from her face and tucked it behind her ear.

'Annika was smoking on the cliffs!' I spluttered. Mum looked at me blankly in disbelief.

'What did you say?'

'Annika was smoking. On the cliffs.'

Then she was all over me. Her sinewy arms groped for my head, trying to silence me. Forcing my face down onto the dry, pink heather, the needles that covered the ground.

'You shut your mouth. Brat.'

She was strong for a girl. Holding on to me hard, so hard that it was impossible to move. So close that I could smell the scent of her sweat.

'Annika was . . . smoking—'

'Stop that immediately.'

Mum's voice was shrill. In two seconds she was beside us. She grabbed Annika roughly by the arm and forced her up, away from me. Then she drew a deep breath and gave Annika a slap across the cheek.

Mum's reaction shocked me. That she, who was always so kind and empathetic, could get angry enough to actually hit one of us was incomprehensible.

Annika stood stock-still, her face down and her hand on her cheek, on the spot Mum had just slapped.

'Don't you dare!' Mum's voice was a hiss when she met Annika's gaze. 'You know how bad I feel when . . . you behave that way.'

'You're ruining my life.'

Annika's voice was thin and brittle, and I could see a red spot on her cheek. 'Don't be so dramatic,' my mother said and snorted.

Annika started to cry. She sobbed until her body shook and the towel fell from her shoulders down onto the ground.

'Shut up. Shut up, all of you,' she screamed. 'It's your fault. Everything is your fault. You're all crazy. I hate you.'

And suddenly Dad was standing there, the sun at his back, his hair glowing like a halo around him.

'Annika, you come here. Do you hear what I'm saying?' His voice was deceptively calm, as it always was when he was truly angry.

And Mum clutched her chest as she always did when she was upset.

Annika trembled, then let out a single short roar, stood up, turned around and ran back towards the dock.

Dad shrugged.

'She'll calm down,' he sighed and returned to the radio. I followed Dad up onto the terrace while watching for Annika down near the dock. Then I saw her. Walking all the way out and bending over and . . . What? Was she taking off her bikini? Why?

Annika threw her bikini onto the rotting dock and without turning around dived into the water.

It was a beautiful dive. The kind that leaves no ripple on the surface. Though of course I wouldn't see them from the house.

Then she surfaced again, a long way from the dock now. She was swimming purposefully out. Away from the dock. Away from

Rönnskär. And suddenly, it's impossible to say exactly when, it crept up on me: the suffocating feeling that something was wrong. Maybe it was because she swam beyond the boat, maybe it was her determination or the power of her strokes. Maybe it was because the air suddenly felt cooler.

'Dad!'

But Dad raised his hand to me and turned up the volume on the radio.

'Dad!'

He looked up at me with a tired expression and wiped the sweat from his wrinkled brow with his big hand.

'What?'

I didn't answer, just pointed to Annika who was swimming straight out into the bay and channel.

Dad stood up slowly and shaded his eyes against the sun.

'What the hell.'

In seconds he'd tossed the radio onto the wooden terrace and rushed down the stairs. The flimsy wooden structure sagged under his weight.

Then Dad was down at the dock.

I could hear him shouting something to Annika, but if she heard him she didn't react, just kept swimming straight out into the cold water. Her head bobbed up and down in the waves.

I suddenly saw something approaching from the corner of my eye. It was the ferry, which went from Utö to Ornö then on to Dalarö. Every afternoon it made the same trip. Dad used to praise the new boat and call her 'our rugged workhorse'. She was fitted with cold storage to bring fresh produce to the little shops in the archipelago.

I remember wondering whether Dad understood the danger. He was still standing on the dock, shouting for Annika. Then he made a decision: he untied the rowing boat and hopped in.

It all happened very slowly. Annika swam slowly. Dad seemed to row even more slowly. The ferry, on the other hand, ploughed along over the bay at a good clip. I suddenly felt a hand clutching my shoulder and turned around. It was Mum.

'Oh my God. Damn that girl. What's she up to now?'

Dad was closing in on Annika, but at least a hundred feet still separated them. And again I felt that suffocating sense of impending danger. Like a mild nausea, an inner chill.

'Why is she doing that?' Mum asked, as if the important thing right now was to sort out the causal relationship that made Annika dive gracefully from the dock and swim out to the channel.

'You don't swim straight out into . . .'

Now Dad was standing up in the rowing boat. He waved his oars in the air, signalling danger to the approaching boat. After a few seconds we heard the prolonged roar of a horn blowing from the boat.

They'd seen him, at least.

But the ferry continued straight ahead with undiminished speed, and what at first seemed to be happening in slow motion was suddenly happening very fast. My father was still standing in the small rowing boat, now with his head lowered and his oars hanging at his sides. The ferry ploughed through the water.

Time stopped.

Those final moments are engraved, excruciatingly, into my memory forever. The ferry letting out another roar. Annika's head disappearing somewhere behind or under the white hull. The dark outlines of passengers gathering on the deck, leaning over the railing to witness the drama. The sun going behind a cloud. Mum dropping her water glass onto the rock. The pin from the Left Party digging deeper and deeper into my palm.

Then silence. A silence as if time itself had stopped. And somehow I knew already. Knew that she was gone.

Emma

One month earlier

I lie awake in bed, listening to the storm outside. No matter how many blankets I pile on top of myself, I can't get warm. The cold has taken possession of me, I think. Like a squatter that's moved into my body and refuses to leave.

I searched for a long time, thinking that Sigge might be injured and hiding somewhere. Animals do that, right? But he was nowhere to be found. It's as if he's been erased, has dissolved into thin air, swallowed up by the black, oily soil under the bushes in the yard. Or worse – has mindlessly disappeared into the traffic on Valhallavägen like the silly indoor cat he is.

Is Jesper behind this? He took my money, my painting and now Sigge too, the only thing I had left that meant something to me. Now there is nothing left to take, nothing more he can rob me of, I think.

I'm shaking with cold. My fingers are still numb. Small wounds cover my hands, traces of prickly bushes that scratched me while I searched the courtyard. My mouth tastes like iron and the tears burn my eyes. Meanwhile, a strange listlessness has taken root in me. Is this what it feels like to have nothing left to lose? At the centre of these emotions – the eye of the hurricane, so to speak – is a kind of peace. A remarkable confidence that comes from the fact that the worst has already happened. I think I recognise the feeling, have actually experienced it before, because what has just happened is uncomfortably reminiscent of what happened with Woody.

Jesper has opened up the abyss of my past again, an abyss I fought so hard to avoid all these years.

Finally I realise that I won't be able to sleep. I get up, put on my thickest jumper and socks, and sit by my desk. I gently push the textbooks aside, take some paper from the top drawer and start writing.

I explain how I feel: that I still love him, even though he's disappeared without explanation, but that something has happened and we have to meet.

I think for a moment, then continue. I tell him about the child, that I haven't decided if I'm going to keep it or not. I write that I don't expect him to take on any sort of fatherly role, but that I really need a sounding board and he needs to take some responsibility for what's happened.

I address the letter to the office, but label it with both his name and the word 'PRIVATE'.

Then I go back to bed. Pull the covers over my head.

But the memories of Woody have been unleashed again.

It was ten days after my father died. Ten days I spent alone with my mother in our small, dusty, overfurnished apartment before I finally returned to school. I didn't really know what I felt yet. It was as if all of the emotions still tumbling around inside me hadn't yet settled, like paper cranes caught in the autumn wind.

I tried to think about it, to truly understand and accept the fact that Dad would never be coming back, but I couldn't. The thought was just too huge to fit inside my head. Of course I knew he was gone, but it felt as if he'd come back sometime. In the winter, maybe. Or for my birthday.

Dead. Buried. Gone. For ever and ever.

I couldn't imagine it and maybe it was just as well.

Mum spent most of her time on the bathroom floor. I went in to her with food and she ate obediently without saying anything. Like an animal at the zoo.

Aunt Agneta called in almost every day. She'd hug me hard, so hard that my head got caught in the gap between her huge breasts when she asked if I was OK. I always said I was – Aunt Agneta had a tendency to worry too much. Or at least that was what Mum used to say. Agneta would pack individual portions of the solid home cooking she'd bring with her into our small freezer, then go into the bathroom to see Mum. There they'd sit on the cold tiled floor, smoking and talking for hours. I heard Aunt Agneta ask Mum several times if maybe I should come and stay with her for a few weeks, until things calmed down, but Mum wouldn't budge. She said it would be harmful for me to change environments now. Said Agneta knew very well how 'sensitive' I was.

I never really understood what Mum meant by that. I had always thought of myself as the opposite. I wasn't sensitive; actually, there was something blunt about me. What other people thought of me didn't bother me much, and I had no need to hang out with the girls in my class, or the guys either for that matter.

Insensitive. Maybe even uninterested. That's how I probably would have described myself.

'Emma, can you come with me to the storage room?'

The question sounded innocent enough and no one in the class reacted. Steffe and Rob were deeply absorbed in some sort of model of a guillotine. Another stupid thing to build in woodwork class. Beside them lay a tube of wood glue that I suspected they were planning on stealing at the end of class. The girls were standing around the carpenter's bench giggling in a forced way. Only Elin saw me. She gave me a long, inscrutable look when I stood up.

'Sure,' I said. 'Great.'

Woody touched my arm and went ahead of me towards the door of the storage room. I stood up on unsteady legs and followed him. He had a special way of walking, a sort of swaying.

'What?' Elin mimed to me, but I just shrugged as if I had no idea why Woody needed my help in the storage room.

The rattle of keys mingled with his whistling. He seemed to be in a good mood today. The door creaked as it slid open. He stretched out his arm and waved for me to go in ahead of him. There was something impatient about the gesture, as if he were in a hurry to get me into the storeroom. As if something important were waiting inside.

For a second, I hesitated.

On some level I knew that if I went into the crowded storage space with Woody, nothing would ever be the same again. I'd walk out of there a different person, the world changed, the old Emma gone. Maybe I should have stopped there, turned around and gone back to my dwindling butter knife, but my curiosity was too strong. My longing for another place, for a new Emma, won over my fear.

The door swung shut with a bang. Woody locked it and walked towards me slowly. I stood there, unsure of what to do, looking around at the planks and tools hanging neatly on hooks on the walls. Smelled the scent of fresh wood. Crossed my arms across my chest.

Woody looked at me intently, and for a moment I was overcome by a paralysing fear. Not of what would happen, but of my own inability to handle the situation. I wished I had more experience. That I was cooler.

He put his hands on my shoulders, pulled me gently and slowly towards him.

I didn't protest when he kissed me and held me closer. Kissing him was unlike anything I'd ever done before. His tongue was slippery and a bit rough and moved like a floundering fish inside my mouth. And the whole time I felt so unsure of what I was expected to do. Should I kiss him back, wrestle with his tongue? Should I press myself against him as hard as he was pressing himself against me?

'Emma,' he murmured.

But that was all he said. He fumbled under my shirt. Along my back, across my breasts. Squeezed them roughly and kneaded them. Then he pulled up my skirt, found his way in under my knickers, investigating my body. Groping along my thighs. He put a finger inside me, then two. I fidgeted, not sure where I should draw the line, if I should draw a line. But my resistance was already shattered. I knew we had already broken all taboos. That it was impossible to go back now.

He pushed me in front of him. I backed up, succumbing to him, letting him steer me, until I hit a small bench in the back. With a determined grip on my backside, he lifted me up onto it and began fumbling with his belt, unbuttoned his trousers and pressed himself against me.

'What if somebody comes . . .'

'Shh,' he said as he pressed his hand against my mouth. Then he kissed me again. His tongue slipped into my mouth, whipping around as if looking for something.

I pulled my head back. 'I don't know . . .'

'Emma,' he said. Then he pressed himself inside me.

Jesper. Woody. Jesper. Woody. Their names and faces seem to flow together. Places, bodies, words and promises jumbled together like pick-and-mix. Jesper's face on Woody's body. Sawdust from the woodworking room on the floor of a pied-à-terre on Kapellgränd. The eyes of my classmates still burning into my back, even today.

The time is half past two and I've made up my mind. Tomorrow I'll find out where Jesper lives. I have to confront him, can't stand to wait any longer. I reach for the mobile lying on the bedside table, find Olga's number.

Can I borrow your car tomorrow after work? I write.

There's something wrong with the metro this morning. It's moving unbelievably slowly between stations and the rising irritation in the train is unmistakable. Rain-soaked commuters pace back and forth impatiently, mobiles are taken out so passengers can text their colleagues that they'll be late today, something's wrong and no, they have no idea what.

Finally the conductor informs us that the reason for the delay is a technical error and that it will take time, a long time, for the train to reach its final station.

I'm lucky. I have a seat and if it weren't for the smell of sweat and wet wool, which brings my nausea back to life, I wouldn't have anything against just sitting for a while. Outside the window the black tunnel wall passes by slowly. The outlines of blasted rock loom behind my own tired reflection in the glass. My hair falls down over my freckled cheeks and my eyes are dark holes staring back at me.

Two teenage girls are having a hushed conversation. They giggle and whisper and then giggle some more. They seem totally unconcerned by the delay. The smell of cigarette smoke is noticeable, even though they are a few yards away from me. Suddenly it strikes me that my own adolescence seems infinitely distant. It's not actually been that many years since I was their age, but it feels like an eternity.

Those formative years of secondary school. That cut-throat hierarchy and the power struggle between the girls in my class, which I somehow managed to keep out of, probably because everyone knew I was different, didn't participate in the game. Those long corridors with their cinder-block walls. The spot where kids smoked at the back. Mopeds parked in a row outside.

Woody.

I never understood why he chose me. There were so many girls in my class who were prettier, cooler. Had enough confidence to act provocatively towards him. Flicking their hair and sticking out their chests when he helped them with the lathe. I mostly sat quietly in a corner. Many teachers thought I was angry and defiant. Other people, like my mother, had decided I was shy.

It took me a while to realise that Woody wasn't looking for a pretty, lively girl who stuck out her chest in the classroom. That he chose me precisely because I was different, a little bit broken. I think he sniffed me out as effectively as a predator finds wounded prey. Certainly it was no coincidence that he approached me right after my father died. He must have sensed my grief, my vulnerability. Decided to use it to get what he wanted.

Jesper, Woody. Woody, Jesper.

The nausea returns. Stronger this time. My body reminds me of what's happening inside. Jesper and I never talked about children, but for some reason I assumed it was part of the package. That our shared future, the one that we planned for, contained a couple of kids and a house in a good suburb.

How wrong I was.

I remember that night in August, when we had a picnic in the Djurgården Park.

Jesper had had a tough day. A particularly malicious journalist from a business magazine had turned up at Reception in head office demanding an interview immediately.

'So what did you do?' I asked him.

He gave me a surprised look, as if he couldn't understand why I'd asked such a question, and poured more wine into my plastic cup. Despite his suntan, he looked more tired than usual. His thin skin seemed stretched over his cheekbones and chin and the wrinkles around his eyes looked like deep grooves carved with a sharp knife. 'I gave him his fucking interview.'

'But why, when he behaved . . . like that?'

'You can't win with them. You're totally fucking powerless. If I hadn't talked to him, he would have made a big deal out of it. Punished me. That's what this is all about, you know. That's why I don't want us to be seen together. They would love to butcher me in the media for having a relationship with an employee.'

He took out a pack of cigarettes, shook one out and put it in his mouth – a sure sign that he was more stressed and frustrated than usual.

We were sitting on a blanket on the grass under a large oak tree, near the path that leads to the Rosendal garden. Despite the beautiful weather, we were almost alone. Now and then a cyclist or dog owner passed by. Above the treetops, in the east, the sky was beginning to darken.

Jesper lit the cigarette, inhaled deeply and coughed.

'You shouldn't,' I mumbled.

'Please.'

'Sorry. I just don't want—'

He raised his hand. 'No. It's my fault. You meant well and I took my irritation out on you. Sorry, Emma.'

We fell silent. In the distance, birds were singing. The moisture from the ground soaked through our thin blanket and I suddenly felt cold.

'It's OK,' I said.

He took my hand, squeezed it hard, locked me in his gaze. 'Are you sure?'

'What?'

'That you forgive me.'

His grip tightened on my wrist and he twisted a little. The pain came unexpectedly, like a whip; it spread up towards my shoulder and my fingers went numb.

'Let go. That hurts.'

He released me immediately, smiled almost as if in embarrassment.

'Whoops,' he said as if he'd knocked over a glass of water rather than practically dislocated my arm.

I sighed. Rubbed my arm.

'Do you always have to be so fucking rough?'

'Forgive me. Please.'

'I forgive you. For everything.'

When I said that, he immediately looked relieved, almost happy, but I glimpsed something mischievous in his eyes as well. He got up on his haunches, brushed off his jeans.

'Come here,' he whispered.

'Why?'

He motioned to me with his hand, craned his neck and looked around. 'I want to show you something.'

I stood up, my body aching from sitting on that cold blanket. All around us, it was starting to get dark. August twilight had crept up without us even noticing. The smell of damp earth hung heavy in the air. He took my hand and pulled me into the woods, behind a big oak tree.

'What. . . ?'

He didn't answer, just turned towards me, took my face in his hands and kissed me. His palms were cold as ice on my cheeks. I kissed him back and put my arms around his waist. A branch snapped as I leaned towards him, startling us, and we giggled. Somewhere in the distance we heard a boat departing for the archipelago.

He put his icy hands under my shirt, caressing my back with slow, circular motions, and then moved down to my waistband, under my jeans and to my buttocks.

'I want to fuck you here, in the woods.'

'People can see.'

'Don't be such a prude.'

He sounded a little annoyed, as he could be when I didn't show the same enthusiasm for his little antics as he did. His hands remained on my buttocks, like two ice packs. Then he let go, started to unbutton my jeans and kissed me again. His tongue was cold, too, and tasted like white wine and cigarette smoke. I pushed him away from me with a gentle nudge.

'You have to be careful. I forgot to take my pill several times this week.'

He shrugged. 'Does it matter?'

'Of course it matters. What if I got pregnant?'

He leaned back a little, so he could meet my eyes. His features almost flowed together with the bark of the ancient oak in the dim evening light. 'That's what I mean, Emma. Does it matter?'

Hanne

Two things happened this morning that knocked me completely off balance. First, I woke up in a cold sweat and with my heart racing, which usually only happens if I've drunk too much wine at one of Owe's and my dinner parties. And when I woke up I didn't know where I was. It was as if Gunilla's spare room had suddenly became unrecognisable to me. The white walls, the colourful pillows, the neglected geraniums slouching over in the window – everything looked foreign. And for a moment it felt as if I was in free fall. The fear literally made me dizzy. I understood clearly that my memory had failed me.

It took maybe a minute or two before I remembered where I was. But during that minute the fear made me sob, and Gunilla came running in from the kitchen to comfort me.

I didn't tell her why I was crying. Didn't want to scare her. And maybe it wasn't the disease making itself felt, just stress. She didn't ask, either. She probably thought I was upset about leaving Owe.

The second thing that happened was that Owe was standing outside Gunilla's front door when I went to take Frida for a walk. As soon as I stepped outside, he jumped from behind a parked car and started shouting about how I needed to go home with him, that I couldn't take care of myself, and that if I didn't come with him he'd make sure I was taken into custody in accordance with the law for compulsory psychiatric care. (It was just nonsense, of course; I googled it at length as soon as I got home.)

Again Gunilla came to my aid. She was on her way to work and came out while we stood there arguing. She raised her eyebrows with studied surprise, in that way that only she can, and stood wide-legged with her arms crossed, facing Owe.

It was almost comical. Gunilla was two heads shorter than Owe, despite her high-heeled boots, but still radiated a commanding presence and had a calm that visibly annoyed him.

'Owe, what are you doing here?' she asked in her slow drawl.

'I'm here to take Hanne home. She doesn't understand what's in her best interests.'

'She doesn't?'

Gunilla met my eyes and carried on:

'Do you understand what's in your own best interests, Hanne?'

I was so upset that I couldn't speak, so I just nodded.

'Well then,' Gunilla continued. 'I think it's best that you go home now, Owe.'

'I'm not going anywhere.'

Gunilla sighed loudly. 'Well, I guess I'll have to call the police then.'

'Stay out of this,' Owe growled. 'This is family business.'

'What the hell, Owe. Give up. She doesn't want to live with you. She's so fucking tired of you she wants to smash something whenever I mention your name. Leave her alone. Give her some time. Maybe then she'll come back.'

'As I said,' Owe repeated. 'This is a family matter.'

Gunilla took her mobile out of her bag and looked at both of us with an exhausted expression.

'I'm calling the police now.'

Owe took two steps towards me, grabbed Frida's lead and whipped around.

'Fucking bitches,' he muttered. 'You won't neglect Frida, at least – I'll see to that. She's coming with me.'

Then he disappeared down the street with Frida in tow, the dog casting anxious glances back at me all the way down the hill.

And that was that.

More tears. Gunilla awkwardly tried to comfort me for the second time that morning. 'Hanne. You'll figure this out,' she said. 'Just be glad you don't have children – then it would have been truly complicated.'

And then, of course, I thought about the children who'd never come, and that just made me cry more.

But I couldn't say that to Gunilla. Instead, I went back up to her apartment, showered and put on make-up with care. My face was red and swollen, and the skin seemed to sag more than usual under my chin, on my arms and in all the other places where age had taken its toll. I noted objectively that it was repulsive – that my body had actually become ugly. Female ripeness (or whatever you want to call it; I'm not so fond of the term 'ripe' because it reminds me of decaying fruit) is not attractive. It's just terribly unattractive, and you'd better hide it under make-up and as many layers of clothing as possible.

So. There I was, fifty-nine years old with early-onset dementia, newly separated, and on top of all that I was flabby and had bingo wings. The realisation started to sink in, and I wondered if I'd really done the right thing packing up my things and leaving the relative security of our apartment. At the same time, I knew with a crushing certainty that a life with Owe was not an option. Because even though the future I'd just chosen was unpredictable and intimidating, it felt impossible to return to him.

It would have been easy to just lie down on the sofa and pull the covers over my head, but I didn't. Mostly to spite Owe. I was determined to prove that I could make it on my own, without his care. Once again, I reminded myself of all the reasons I couldn't stand him:

Self-righteous. Egocentric. Narcissistic. Domineering. Smells bad.

Then I went to work.

The first person I see when I enter the bright premises of the police station is Peter. He's sitting in front of his computer. His long body is bent into an uncomfortable posture and he seems to be staring at something on the screen. When he sees me he jumps up, runs over and grabs my arm as if we're best friends, as if our little conversation the night before somehow spirited away the fact that he's the man who ruined my life.

His hand is warm and dry. And it feels strangely good to have it there – on my forearm.

Like the most natural thing in the world.

'Come,' he says. 'I'm about to talk to one of Jesper Orre's employees. The one who accused him of sexual harassment. Come with me!'

'OK,' I say, because I have nothing else I have to do.

Denise Sjöholm is twenty-eight years old and has an MBA. I find myself thinking that she looks too young to buy booze without showing ID. But that's just a sign of my own age – yet another example of how even my frames of reference have slowly shifted over the years without me noticing it. I have to remind myself that Owe and I had already been married for several years when I was her age.

So hardly a child then.

She looks a little lost in the interrogation room, exposed somehow. She's wearing a bulky sweater, ripped jeans and no make-up. Her big brown eyes are filled with fear, which isn't really that strange. I imagine it must have meant a lot of trouble for her when she accused her highest superior of sexual harassment.

Peter also seems to have noticed her fear, because he explains that she's not accused of anything and that we just want to interview her in connection with the murder that took place at Orre's home and his subsequent disappearance.

She nods silently and fiddles with a loose thread hanging from her jeans.

'How long have you worked at Clothes&More?' Peter asks.

'One year.'

'And what's your job description?'

'I was . . . am . . . a project manager in the marketing department. I'm in charge of various advertising campaigns. For example, I'm responsible for the Christmas campaign running on TV right now. Until I went on sick leave, that is.'

Her gaze wanders back and forth between Peter and me, like a troubled bird who doesn't dare land anywhere.

'And when did you get to know Jesper Orre?'

'Pretty much as soon as I started. There aren't that many of us in headquarters. And he always stopped by the marketing department to see what we were up to. I remember that I thought he was great. Relaxed, you know. Though there was a lot of talk about how nasty he could be. About how he was firing people left and right.'

'And then what happened?'

Denise looks down at the floor and her thin brown hair falls in front of her face.

'He asked me if I wanted to go to a party with him. That was in the spring.'

'OK. What kind of party?'

'Well. He didn't say more about the party, but we decided that he'd pick me up at Stureplan on Saturday night. And he did. But then he drove me to his house instead. And there were no other people there. Just him and me. Anyway . . . we ate dinner – he'd bought some lobster and champagne. I was very impressed that he wanted to have dinner with me, alone. I mean, Jesper Orre could get a date with whoever he wants . . .'

Her voice dies out and she shakes her head slowly.

'I was so fucking naive,' she continues. 'As soon as we'd finished eating he wanted to sleep with me. Of course.'

'And what did you do then?'

Denise seems a bit confused, as if she doesn't quite understand the question.

'We had sex. And then we continued hooking up every now and then. I realised quite quickly that he didn't want a real relationship with me. So after about two months, I broke up with him, or whatever you want to call it. We were never really together.'

'How did he react?'

'He was furious. Said *he'd* decide when it was over. And that I'd regret it if I didn't understand that.'

Denise pulls on the thread from her jeans so hard that it snaps with a small pop.

'And what did you do then?'

She shakes her head and laughs quietly.

'I should have known I couldn't win against him. I should have played along, but instead I got angry, told him to go to hell, that I decided who I slept with and when. He left without saying anything. And then, at work, he started being mean to me. Asking me impossible questions at meetings. Dissing all my suggestions. Making sure I didn't get any exciting projects. Punishing me, I guess. But it was after I went to HR and complained that the real circus began. I was questioned by HR with him present. As you can imagine, it wasn't fun to sit there and talk about our . . . relationship while he listened. In the end, I felt so terrible thatI took sick leave.'

'When was this?'

'I've been on sick leave for . . .' Denise counts on her fingers. 'Eight weeks. No, nine tomorrow.'

Peter nods and makes a note in his notebook, then says, 'I know this may sound a bit strange, but was he rough in bed?'

Denise looks embarrassed, crosses her arms in front of her chest. 'No. Not particularly.'

'Did he ever steal any lingerie from you?'

'Steal lingerie?'

'Yes, did he ever take your underwear?'

'Not that I know of.'

'Have you heard anything from him since you went on sick leave?'

She shakes her head. 'Not a word.'

'Do you know if he did this to any of the other women at your office?'

'No. But it wouldn't surprise me. He's a sick fucker.'

'Do you know if he was seeing any other women during this time?'

'No. But like I said, he's a sick fucker.'

As we walk Denise out, I can't stop myself. I put a hand on her arm and look into her eyes.

'You do understand that you didn't do anything wrong?' I say. 'He took advantage of you because he could, because his position allowed him to.'

She looks at me for a long time, then shrugs. 'Maybe. But I still regret going to HR. He would have grown tired of me eventually.' She hurries out with her head lowered.

'What a fucking arsehole,' I say to Peter as she disappears into the fog.

Peter shrugs slightly, looks at me, and I can't help but think:

Like you, Peter. A real arsehole, like you.

It almost seems as if he senses what I'm thinking, because he suddenly seems self-conscious. He looks away and starts walking towards the lifts, mumbling, 'Last time I checked that wasn't illegal.'

As I walk back to Gunilla's apartment three hours later, it's already getting dark. A cold wind tears at my clothes and the temperature has dropped. The wet road has acquired a hard, slippery layer of ice and I have to walk slowly so as not to slip.

I already miss Frida, but I don't know how I can get her back. I can't file a police report. Frida is Owe's dog too and you can't steal something that you already own. Right?

Owe was never particularly fond of Frida. Mostly he thought she barked too much and smelled bad (as if he didn't). He didn't take Frida to protect her from me; he took her to hurt me. Just the way

Jesper punished that poor girl, because she didn't want to be his sex slave.

Power, I think. It's always about power.

Every time I pass a news stand, I stop and read the headlines. The drawing of the woman who was murdered in Orre's home is on the front page of every newspaper in the city with this bold headline underneath: 'Who Did the Fashion King Murder?'

If we don't find out who she is now, I don't know if we ever will.

When I get to Slussen it starts snowing again. Small hard flakes whip against my face and sting. My mobile rings and I instinctively turn my back to the wind, take the phone out to answer it.

It's Peter.

'Hanne,' he says. 'I've just talked to the National Lab. The machete used at Orre's house is the same one used in the Calderón murder. They've found marks on the vertebrae of both victims that can be linked to the weapon. The marks match the machete's blade exactly. You know what this means, right?'

Emma

One month earlier

'But why kill your cat? I don't get it.'

Olga frowns and twists her heavy rhinestone-studded bracelets. I look out over the empty boutique and reflect for a moment. Music flows from the speakers. Mahnoor is nowhere in sight. She's probably busy with one of her crucial new administrative tasks.

'If it's like you said before and he's a psychopath, maybe he wants to harm me in some way. Maybe he gets pleasure from ruining my life.'

Olga looks doubtful. As expected, she finds it easier to believe Jesper is looking for money or sex than that he's a real sadist. And on some level, I agree with her; I have a hard time myself believing he'd get anything out of ruining my life. But I can't see any other explanation for his behaviour.

'But a cat – what do cats have to do with anything?'

'Sigge is important to me. If he hurts Sigge, then he hurts me too, right?'

'If that's so,' Olga begins, handing me a new roll of receipt paper to replace the old, 'then he's really fucked up.'

'That's what I'm saying.'

'Did you look him up? Maybe he's done this before. Maybe he's been to prison or a mental hospital.'

The idea seems almost ridiculous and the images immediately pop into my head. Jesper Orre, CEO of the company where we both work, wearing a straitjacket, locked up in an institution. Or dressed in striped overalls, like a cartoon character, standing behind thick iron bars.

'Maybe he killed somebody,' Olga whispers, as if she's afraid somebody might hear her in the empty room.

I meet her eyes without saying anything. She looks regretful.

'Sorry, sweetie. Of course he didn't kill anybody. All I'm saying is sometimes you don't know people, even when you think you do.'

'That's probably true,' I say, thinking that she has no idea how right she is.

'What are you going to do? Report him to the police?'

I turn around, close the till and pull out a bit of the receipt tape. 'I want to talk to him first.'

'You gonna try to find him?'

I nod and look out over the shop. A couple of teenage boys are loitering around in a corner by the jeans table; they give me a long look and I get the feeling they might try to shoplift. It's usually obvious, at least when it's kids who haven't yet learned to control their faces and who almost invariably steal in groups, as if shoplifting were a team sport.

'I know what you do,' Olga says and suddenly looks enthusiastic and a little sly at the same time. 'You get revenge. Take back the power. I'm good at it. I keep the upper hand. Not to play my horn, but it's true.'

'"Toot", you mean. 'What?'

Olga looks confused.

'You say, "toot your own horn".'

'Who cares – we practise spelling later. Pull yourself together and get your revenge back from that arsehole. Find out where he is and go to him and demand answers. Don't let him get away. Show him who's in charge!'

The boys by the jeans counter have started moving towards the exit. One of them is carrying a suspiciously large gym bag. Olga sees them too, but doesn't seem to feel like doing anything about it.

'So, you think I should get revenge?'

She nods. At that very moment a man comes through the door and heads towards the checkout counter. He looks purposeful, as if he knows exactly what he wants. That tends to be the case with older men. They rarely stroll around the shop browsing. Instead, they come directly to us and ask for socks or shirts or underwear. Then they buy five packs of each, pay and leave the shop immediately.

'Welcome! How can I help you?' Olga asks in accordance with regulations and smiles mechanically as she spins her rhinestone bracelets one more turn.

'I'm looking for Emma Bohman,' says the man without answering her smile.

When I tell him I'm Emma Bohman, he introduces himself as Sven Ohlsson, Head of Human Resources for the Eastern Region, then takes me aside and says, 'Can we sit in the staff room?'

His face is expressionless. He has very short, reddish-blonde hair and round cheeks, even though his body is slender, almost skinny. He lifts up his bag, an old leather briefcase with grease stains on it, and takes out a stack of papers.

The moment he says his name, I know what this is about.

'You've been with us for three years, Emma.'

I nod, suddenly unsure if it's a question or if he's stating facts, reading aloud from his stack of paper. Then he picks up a pair of tortoiseshell glasses. Takes out a small blue handkerchief and polishes his glasses thoroughly, in silence.

'Do you want some coffee?' I ask. Mostly because I don't know what else to say.

'Thank you, yes,' he says without lifting his eyes from his glasses.

The sound of the clock ticking in the corner suddenly seems deafening and the smell of coffee overwhelming, impossible to defend myself against. I set a cup in front of him, sink into the chair opposite, overcome by my powerlessness.

I never thought a moment like this would come my way; this is something that happens to other people, not me. I've always been good, followed the rules. Except for lately, when letters from collection agencies started piling up and rows of absences started to fill the attendance sheet on the wall.

'We are facing some serious economic challenges,' he says and puts on his glasses. For the first time, he meets my eyes. His eyes are a pale grey and completely emotionless. He's a polite bureaucrat with a deadly mission, sent by head office. Slowly he puts his cleaning cloth into his briefcase and continues:

'Profits are down. We're going to be forced to close two shops in the coming months.'

I still don't know what to say. I just nod. He falls silent. Suddenly looks tired. Maybe he really is tired. Maybe he's actually a nice person in real life.

'Poor profits?' I say as if wanting to help him along.

He meets my eyes again. Still not revealing the slightest emotion.

'Poor profits, yes. Thank you. You've done a fine job here, Emma, according to Björne Franzén, but unfortunately management has decided to reduce staff costs in order to ensure our long-term survival.'

'I understand.'

'This isn't personal, Emma. This is simply about dealing with new economic realities.'

I want him to stop using my name. I don't know him, don't want to be 'Emma' to him. 'Sure,' I say.

'It's just economics.'

'I understand. So it has nothing to do with . . .' I gesture towards the absence report that hangs on the wall. The angry red stickers shine like nasty pimples on pale skin.

He smiles for the first time during our meeting. It's a pale, almost sad smile.

'Everyone has the right to be ill,' he says. 'Or to stay at home with sick children. That's not grounds for termination. Those are just malicious rumours. You know how the media writes about us.'

He slurps the coffee and I find myself wishing he'd burn himself. But it's a wish that won't come true. The coffee from the machine only gets lukewarm at best. It's been that way for a year now, since Björne kicked the machine one time when he lost his temper.

Then the man sets down the stack of paper on the table, pushes it slowly towards me with one finger.

'We have to talk a little bit about practical matters now, Emma.'

'Who was that?' Mahnoor asks as he's leaving, gazing after the funny man with the short red hair and tortoiseshell glasses who looks like a grown-up version of Tintin on the run from the comic-book world.

'He was from HR. Where is Olga, anyway?'

I have no desire to talk about the conversation I've just had, about the pile of paper that summarises the terms of my dismissal: that my job terminates immediately, that I get two months' severance, and that my building access card must be sent back to head office in a stamped envelope.

'Olga?' Mahnoor says absently.

'Yes, where is she?'

'No idea.' She shrugs. 'She's probably Googling make-up or underwear, the little misogynist.'

'What?'

Mahnoor waves away my question. 'Nothing.'

'Last time I saw her she was actually reading a book,' I say, remembering Olga at the table in the kitchenette with a paperback in her hand shortly after the man from HR left.

Mahnoor raises her well-shaped eyebrows.

'Probably just some shit she found at the supermarket.' Mahnoor's ill-concealed contempt makes me uneasy.

'Maybe it was a perfectly normal, good book,' I suggest.

'Are you kidding? I don't think she'd recognise a good book if it sat down spread-eagled on her face.'

Mahnoor is picking around among the hairclips and necklaces displayed next to the till. She fixes some that are hanging awry and then asks in a neutral tone:

'So, what did he want, the guy from head office?'

I hesitate for a moment. 'Nothing special. He just wondered how it was going for us now that Björne was sick.'

'And what did you say?'

'I told him the truth. That we get on just fine without him.'

I'm sitting in Olga's car. The rain patters against the roof and the cramped car is damp. Periodically I have to wipe the front window in order to see out.

It's just after six and I've been parked here for a little over an hour. If I'm unlucky, he won't be in the office today. Maybe he's on a business trip or at a meeting somewhere.

I take a sip of lemon-flavoured mineral water that tastes like detergent and think about the red-haired man from head office. About his unfashionable glasses and shabby briefcase. I would never have guessed he was employed by a fashion company.

Was this also Jesper's work? Yet another piece of the puzzle in his diabolical plan? If so, it was genius, because he actually managed to deprive me of something else that was important to me: my job. I didn't think about it before, when I was feeling sorry for myself earlier; I thought he'd already taken everything I cared about from me. Maybe there's more he can take, something else I haven't thought of, that I take for granted. My home? My health?

My life?

The thought makes me shudder.

I think about the apartment on Kapellgränd. About the rag rug in the hall and the red wooden chairs, arranged neatly along the hall like horses from the Spanish riding school. In my mind I see Jesper lying naked on that colourful rug. The yellow flowers of the carpet surround him so it almost looks like he's lying in a field of sunflowers. His body is relaxed, his face soft like a child's. His mouth is slightly open and his chest falls and rises. I'm sitting in a car in the rain, but at the same time I'm standing in the apartment on Kapellgränd looking at Jesper. Trying to understand why this man, this boy, this human being who lies there looking so innocent would want to harm me.

A man hurries across the street just a few yards ahead of the car. I bend forward, wipe the moisture away from the windscreen to see better. It's not Jesper. The man's too short, and he's blonde. With quick steps he disappears into the darkness.

If I were able to see myself now, the way I've just seen Jesper, what would I see? A madwoman sneaking up on her lover in the darkness outside his office? Am I going crazy?

Is that his final goal, to deprive me of my sanity? The ultimate violation: to drive a person to madness.

The nausea comes again and I take a sip of the disgusting mineral water.

If this is a play, carefully directed by him, then does he know I'm here? Has he already thought out his next step? Will I find the truth if I follow him, or just what he wants to show me?

The questions never end; every answer leads to a new one. It's like looking into a mirror reflected in a mirror. Reflected in another mirror. I get dizzy just trying to figure out what's happening and why. And I haven't even started thinking about how to solve my most immediate problems: the baby, the bills, the job I've lost, whisked away by the red-haired man from head office.

Maybe Olga's right. Maybe I should get revenge?

Maybe that's exactly what he wants?

A sense of unreality overcomes me. It's like I'm in a movie, like I only think I'm in control of my own behaviour, but actually somebody else is directing it. I feel as though I'm in free fall with no control over my life. I look at the ring shining on my finger. Think, This is real, proof that I'm not actually crazy.

Then I see him.

He's hunched over in the rain, his coat flapping behind him like a broken sail, just like the last time I stood here in the dark. His steps are vigorous and determined. I have the impulse to jump out of the car, run over and ask him what the hell he's up to, but something stops me. I want to know what he's hiding, see where he lives.

I want to know more before I reveal myself as completely vulnerable to him.

A few minutes later, a big black SUV turns out of the parking garage. I start the car and follow him, careful not to get too close. At every other red light, the engine stalls; I'm not used to driving with gears. I swear and start the car again, terrified to lose him now that I've finally found him.

At Roslagstull the traffic increases considerably. I pull up directly behind Jesper in the sea of cars on their way home in the dark. He takes E18 north and exits at Djursholm. When he slows down I do the same, letting the distance between us increase. There are no other cars in sight. We pass by large villas with lit-up, park-like lawns. We pass by a small central area. A food shop, a bookshop, a small square with a few leafless trees. Again that feeling: I'm in a movie, passing through desolate scenery on my way to some sort of resolution. But what kind of film is it? A drama, a thriller? A tragedy?

We arrive at the water, black and shiny like a piece of silk spread out in front of me in the night. Jesper turns to the right and I follow. My curiosity is awakened and the feeling of being close to some sort of resolution gets stronger. We drive along the water for a while. Here the villas are even bigger, almost castle-like, and I wonder if ordinary people really live here or if the houses are used only by companies or maybe embassies.

I don't notice when he slows down and I almost rear-end his black car. He turns up a small street to the right and I wait a few seconds before I follow. The small road is lined with evergreen hedges: boxwood, yews and white cedar. There are piles of wet leaves on the narrow pavement. The houses here are smaller, look like more ordinary houses. I turn off my headlights, creep along slowly behind him. He turns again and I follow. Our little game is almost starting to amuse me. I've never tailed anybody before.

He stops in front of a white modern house. Warm light streams out of the windows, painting the lawn and the wet autumn leaves outside golden. I turn off the engine. Wait. Watch him as he takes out his black briefcase, walks up to the wrought-iron gate and raises his hand to open it. But then he stops himself, takes a step back and walks a few yards towards me on the pavement.

At first I'm worried he's going to discover me, but then I see where he's going.

Beside the fence lie piles of wet wood. A green tarpaulin covers one of the piles. Jesper sidesteps it and goes over to a newly built building, maybe a garage, to the right of the gate.

It hasn't been painted yet and where the door should be there's plastic flapping in the wind. He drops down on his haunches, inspecting something on the siding. Then he stands up, turns round and walks back to the house.

It occurs to me immediately – am I looking at my lost money? Did I pay for the building in front of me? Were my entire savings turned into a garage for his big black car?

Then he is standing outside the front door. When he rings the bell instead of opening the door himself, I suddenly feel uncertain. Does he live here or is he visiting? Then he takes out a key, puts it in the lock and, at the same time, someone opens it. A woman stands in the doorway. She's dark-haired and tall and beautiful. I can see that clearly, even though I'm a good distance away. She has that confident charisma that only beautiful women have, as if her posture communicates her worth.

The woman bends forward and Jesper kisses her. It's no quick kiss on the cheek, reserved for friends and family, but a long and intimate kiss.

Then I see no more. The house fades away, the rain stops drumming against the car roof. Everything goes mercifully black and silent.

I'm running through the darkness. Someone is screaming. It's a long, heart-wrenching roar, and after several seconds, I realise the person screaming is me. Branches whip into my face. Ice-cold water runs down my neck. Out of nowhere a garden chair pops up in front of me. I take a step aside but still knock into it, and it falls over with a bang. I increase my speed, feel like a hunted animal. Can't remember why I'm out here in the dark, just know I'm running for my life. Away from something terrible, something that threatens my whole existence.

My boots sink into the mud and I slip, but regain my balance, keep running forward with my hands stretched out in front of me as though I'm blind.

A fence emerges from the darkness. It's not particularly high, just three or four feet. Without thinking I climb it, throw myself over the edge. But I get stuck on something; the fence has caught hold of my jacket. I fall headlong and hit my side hard. The pain is unimaginable. I can't breathe, can't think, and everything goes black.

Something touches my cheek. I open my eyes. Trying to think. Remember.

It's dark. I'm lying on the ground of someone's lawn. Just a few feet in front of me is a sandpit. Buckets and spades and small yellow trucks are scattered in the sand and on the grass, like mushrooms in a forest.

How long have I been here? I sit up but stop halfway. My whole stomach clenches in a painful cramp. I bend forward, curl up in a ball, but the pain in my stomach won't stop. It's just after nine, so I must have been here for an hour.

I'm shaking with cold as I rise up on my haunches. Grope with my hands over my face, brushing mud and branches from my cheeks. Trying to understand.

Slowly but inexorably, the memories come back to me. I'm in Djursholm, somewhere near Jesper Orre's house – the house he seems to share with a beautiful dark-haired woman. I've been deceived more completely than I ever could have imagined. I've been doubly betrayed and violated. Robbed of both money and love. By the person I loved.

Jesper has someone else, as he probably did when we were seeing each other. That was obviously why he wanted to keep our relationship secret. That was why it was so important to meet only in the small apartment on Kapellgränd or at my home.

But I still don't understand. If all he wanted was a little adventure, some sex, why propose to me?

Why take Sigge, the money and the painting? And why was I fired? There's something else chafing at me. I remember Olga's words, *Your man is definitely a psychopath.*

Does he want to humiliate me? Destroy me? Was this also part of the plan, that I would see how happy he was with this other girlfriend?

I find an opening in the fence and push through. Good thing too, because I'm not sure I could climb over it again. The pain in my stomach forces me to crouch, walk hunched over through the next garden. In the darkness in front of me I see the overturned deck chair and know I'm heading in the right direction.

Just before I reach the street, I walk past a yellow house. Through the window I see a couple and two children sitting on a beautiful sofa in front of a flat-screen TV. They're eating popcorn. They look happy. Happy and successful.

Everything I'm not.

The door to the car is unlocked, the keys still in the ignition. I sink down in the driver's seat and close the door. The sight of my muddy, swollen face scares me. I look crazy. Dangerous. I dry off my face with a scarf, but it only smears the mud more.

I drive slowly back to the city. Avoid any sudden braking or acceleration for fear of exacerbating the pain in my stomach. I park the car and walk towards my front door in the rain, praying to God that I won't run into any of my neighbours; I don't have the energy to explain why I look like this. But I meet no one. The musty smell of my building is still there. The staircase is dark and quiet. The house could just as well be uninhabited, a haunted house.

The lift stops with a whine on the fourth floor and I get out. I unlock my door and step into the warmth. Fumble with the buttons of my coat, wriggle it off, let it fall to the floor. I look around for Sigge before I remember he's gone. I step out of my boots and trudge into the bathroom. My jeans are wet and muddy, but something else catches my eye as I take them off. A large stain in the crotch. I bend forward to get a better look, but I already know what's happened.

It's blood.

I've lost the baby.

Peter

The investigation is heading in another direction, shifting focus from one day to the next as investigations do sometimes. The news that the National Lab have linked the machete to both murders – the unnamed victim at Jesper Orre's home and Miguel Calderón – has hit the police station like a bomb. The activity is as frenetic as before, but some of the resignation has lifted and been replaced by expectation. The large evidence wall in the conference room, papered with pictures from Orre's house, maps and pictures of Orre's colleagues and acquaintances, has now been joined by another evidence wall with similar images from the old case.

Sanchez apparently spent half the night reading through the Calderón case and is already searching for points of contact between Calderón and Orre. I suspect that may be difficult; on the surface their lives seem to be completely unrelated.

Calderón was twenty-five years old when he was found dead in his rented apartment on Södermalm in September ten years ago. He had multiple odd jobs. He worked as a cook, a home-care giver, a newspaper distributor and a substitute hospital orderly. In his free time he studied karate and played bass in a jazz band. He had no girlfriend, and his sister hinted that she thought he was probably gay. Five years before he was murdered, he was convicted of assault and theft, but according to the preliminary investigation there was nothing to suggest he had any criminal connections at the time of his death. There is also no evidence that he socialised at the same places as Orre: Sandhamn, Verbier, Marbella or the nightclubs around Stureplan.

The fact that Orre is still missing increasingly suggests he murdered the unidentified woman – and thus also ended Calderón's life.

But a few stolen thongs and ruthlessness in business hardly suffice as proof. We need to find a connection between all of them – and if there is one, we will find it. Even if we have to sift through every miserable inch of their lives.

It's at this point that the familiar feelings of boredom and resignation start to sneak up on me. I've grown tired of these plodding murder investigations. If someone had asked me ten years ago, I would have said this was the most exciting and challenging task a skilled investigator could sink his teeth into, but all I feel now is paralysing fatigue. What I want more than anything is to buy a six-pack, go home, collapse on the couch and watch sport. I don't think anyone who's not a police officer could understand how much work it takes to map out a person's life. How many hundreds of hours of interrogations, research and paperwork have to be trudged through before the picture becomes clearer and the essentials start to emerge.

And then there's Hanne.

In a way, it was good we had a chance to talk, even though I didn't say much. But nothing has changed between us since. I feel it clearly, though I can't quite put my finger on it. Like a deep, vibrating tone that's always present when she's here. Almost like tinnitus. And I don't have a fucking clue how to get rid of it.

Sometimes I find myself looking at her when she's sitting at her desk in her wrinkled shirt, her greying hair pushed up in a sloppy ponytail. Sometimes my thoughts escape to that forbidden place where we're together again. Yesterday, when I put my hand on her forearm, I found myself thinking that she's still the most beautiful woman I've ever met. And the only one I could ever really talk to.

I don't know why, but I find it so damn hard to talk about important things to anyone, and especially to women. Maybe I'm too scared to let anyone in, as Janet always claimed. Or maybe I don't have much to say because I'm basically uninteresting.

But with Hanne I always had things to talk about. Back then, when we were together. We could lie for hours in bed talking about politics or love or silly things, like why a certain kind of cheese slicer only exists in Sweden. And sometimes she'd tell me about Greenland and about the Inuit who'd lived there for thousands of years in perfect balance with nature. She dreamed of travelling there, kayaking between drift ice and hunting seals.

The Inuit apparently didn't have special wedding ceremonies. They just got together and that was that. We used to joke that we'd probably be considered married from an Inuit perspective.

I remember I thought she was so positive and, well, mischievous, especially being as old as she was.

Ten years older than me.

It never bothered me, even though she didn't seem to believe me when I said so. Instead, she told me I had to think about how we could never have a child together, how she'd get old long before me. Did I really want to be with an old lady?

Yes, I did. And I said so, too.

And yet I couldn't go through with it. I left her waiting on the street that night. I sat frozen on my bed, clutching my car keys with a vodka bottle between my knees. Petrified and covered in a cold sweat. And when she called me, I couldn't even answer. Couldn't pick up the fucking phone and tell her what was going on. Tell her I wasn't ready for the commitment.

Not ready to commit.

What a fucking expression, by the way. What an indescribably lame excuse for what was chafing and twisting and pulsating inside me. The monster and the fear that could not be named.

Afraid. I was, quite simply, afraid.

I just wish I'd been able to say it. To explain in simple words and without euphemism what was eating at me.

Then maybe my life would be different today.

Manfred turns up at my desk and frowns at me. 'You look like shit, Lindgren.'

'Thank you, thank you very much. And you're heading out on a fox hunt, I see.'

He grins and adjusts his checked vest. As usual, he's impeccably dressed – a living anachronism on the second floor of the police station in a three-piece tweed suit with a silk scarf in his breast pocket.

'I do what I can.'

'Anything new?' I ask.

'We received a ton of tip-offs from that drawing of the victim – Bergdahl's team is helping us sort through them. But Orre is still missing without a trace. Oh, another thing. A guy who works as a glazier in the Mörby shopping centre called us. Apparently he fixed a basement window at Orre's house recently. According to Orre, he'd had a break-in but nothing was stolen. Which is probably why he never reported it.'

'We'll have to look into that. Ask Sanchez to meet with him,' I say.

'My God, what would we do without Sanchez?'

Manfred sings her name with a heavy vibrato, like an opera singer, and raises his right arm above his head theatrically.

Sanchez throws us a surly glance from her desk, but refrains from saying anything.

I leave the police station around eight o'clock. There are limits to how much overtime I am willing to put in, even though we're in the middle of a major investigation. Nobody thanks a police officer for sacrificing his life to the job.

When I park outside the apartment building where I live, I get the strange feeling that something's wrong. The lights in the stairwell are lit and the door is slightly ajar, as if someone didn't shut it firmly behind them. I take out the pizza I picked up on the way home, go in and start walking up the stairs.

The building was built in the fifties and has glaring pistachio-green walls and a speckled floor. It looks as though someone has scattered small black-and-white stones at random over the cement. Each floor has three apartment doors and the mandatory rubbish chute. I live on the top floor, which seemed like an advantage until I broke my foot three years ago and had to jump all the way up with crutches.

Outside my door Albin is sitting with skateboard in hand. He's wearing a far too thin hoodie and jeans that hang low on his hips. He's holding a torn plastic carrier bag in his hand. His thin blonde hair hangs down in front of his face, and his ears, which he inherited from Janet, protrude slightly.

'Hi,' he says.

'Hi,' I say. 'What are you doing here?'

'Had a fight with Mum. Can I crash at your place?'

I'm disconcerted. Albin has never slept at my place before.

'I don't know. Maybe I'd better call your mum,' I say as I take out my keys and unlock the door. On the floor inside is a pile of dirty laundry: underwear and T-shirts I planned to wash this evening. I shut the door again.

'Aren't you gonna let me in?'

Albin stands up and meets my eyes. He looks confused and anxious. Understandably unsure of whether or not he can trust his father.

'Yes. Of course. It's just that . . . it's messy.'

'Like I care.'

'No, of course.'

I open the door and we go in. Albin's slim figure glides past me into the living room like a shadow and sinks down into the sofa.

'Albin,' I say. 'It's nice to see you, but I don't know if it's such a good idea for you to stay over.'

'Why not?'

'Because . . .'

'What is it?'

'I don't have a bed for you.'

'I can sleep here,' Albin says, patting the couch. Then he lies down, pulls off his trainers and puts his feet up on the armrest.

I note how skinny he is and wonder if I should ask him if he's eating properly. Isn't that something parents do?

'I have to get up early tomorrow, so the timing isn't great,' I say instead.

'So what? I can just stay here when you leave. Mum's totally lost it – I can't go home.'

'Besides, I have to work tonight.'

'I won't bother you.'

I pace back and forth across the room, not knowing what to do with myself. Then I put the pizza down on the coffee table.

'And Janet? Does she know you're here?'

Albin puts his arm over his eyes, as if he can't cope with any more questions. 'Nah.'

'Then I bet she's worried sick. I'm going to call her.'

Janet turns up an hour later. She's in a better mood than I've seen her for a long time, chirpy even. She seems to love studying to be a nail technician. She shows me her new long hot-pink nails, and I say that they look good even though I don't think so.

Janet and Albin whisper to each other for a while. Then she gives him a tight hug and I assume they've reconciled.

It wasn't difficult to persuade her to come over. All I had to do was explain that I didn't have room for Albin, not tonight. She sounded neither surprised nor upset. Why would she be? I've never had room in my life for Albin before.

I stand at the window and watch them head over to her little red VW Golf. Just before Albin gets in, he turns and meets my gaze. Without really understanding why, I take a step back behind the curtain. Shut my eyes tight until I hear the car drive away.

Sometimes, when Albin was younger, I played around with the idea of actually spending time with him. Maybe taking him to an amusement park or a football game. But as soon as I tried to imagine us together, something inside me knotted up. I didn't know how to act when I was with him.

I told myself it was probably better to wait until he was older and understood more. At least I know how to talk to adults.

But with each passing year it became more and more difficult. How do you even start to spend time with your child, whom you don't really know, after so many years? What the hell are you supposed to say to a stranger who happens to be your flesh and blood and who might hate you because you've never been around? Not even football felt like an option any more. Would we stand there with some forced feeling of solidarity, a beer in our hands, pretending that we're mates or something? Or was I expected to break down sobbing and explain why I never wanted to have him in my life?

There never was any football game, of course.

The following morning I drive out to Jesper Orre's house with Manfred. It's still cordoned off with police tape, which flutters and rustles in the heavy wind as we walk the short distance from the gate to the front door. Manfred finds the right key from the pile we got from the technicians, opens the door and turns on the hall light.

The blood is gone; it appears as an ordinary hallway. Only if you look carefully can you make out the faint traces of rust brown in the seams between the stone tiles on the floor and between the moulding and the walls. Death has a tendency to soak into things, I think. As if it doesn't want to let go of anywhere it's visited. It bores its way into walls and floors, leaving behind the distinct whiff of transience which cannot be washed away. Most people actually choose to renovate a house after something like this has happened.

'What are we looking for?' I ask.

'No fucking clue. Anything the technicians might have missed.'

We start searching the house methodically. Going from room to room, taking pictures, rooting around in clothes and china and old medications. We take pictures for our own use – the official crime scene photos have already been taken by the technicians.

It's a neat and orderly home, bordering on sterile, and contains very few personal items. The only photo we find – of Orre and a few women on a beach – is standing on a shelf in the living room.

Manfred nods at it:

'They've got that in their report. You don't need to take a photo.'

'Why is the glass broken?' I ask and run a finger across the few shards that still sit in the frame.

Manfred shrugs. 'No fucking clue.'

'Maybe one of the women in the photo is the victim.'

'Maybe. It's impossible to say – the photo's too blurry.'

As usual during our house searches, I feel weirdly ill at ease. Like I'm an intruder. There's nothing like rooting around in somebody's old underwear and groceries to make you feel like a vulture, even though I know it's necessary.

Manfred goes through the bookshelf, which contains only a few books, some decorations and a lot of business magazines. He lifts out a stack of books and reaches into the shelf.

'Look what I've found behind the books, Lindgren!'

I go over to him. He's got a DVD in his hand. On the cover a naked, bound woman lies in a car park, on her back with her legs splayed. A man with a whip in his hand stands next to her, facing away from the photographer.

'Damn . . .'

'I told you he was disturbed,' Manfred mumbles.

'You gonna take that home with you?'

He smiles at me crookedly. 'To tell you the truth, Afsaneh would castrate me if she found this in my stuff. Maybe you should take it instead? You seem like you need some cheering up.'

'Sure. Violent porn always puts me in a good mood.'

We put the movie back and go into the kitchen. The glossy black cabinets and stainless-steel counters remind me of the autopsy rooms in Solna. Even the sink and tap with adjustable shower-like nozzle feel institutional.

'Not exactly cosy,' Manfred says and frowns.

I agree with him but I'm grateful that, even after working together for so long, he's never seen my apartment. I can guess how depressing he'd find my home. Manfred and Afsaneh live in a beautiful turn-of-the-century apartment with tiled stoves and art on the walls. They have curtains, cushions, colourful carpets, books and all that other stuff I've never managed to acquire. Pie dishes, baby bottles, ice cream makers and juicers are crowded into their kitchen cupboards. Invitations to various events hang on the mirror in the hall, screaming out how popular they are.

'Should we check out the basement?' Manfred asks and starts walking towards the hall without waiting for an answer. I follow him down stairs that creak under our weight.

A faint scent of mildew and detergent. A humming sound coming from the boiler room. For some reason I start to feel dizzy and weak, have a sudden urge to sit down. But I follow Manfred obediently into the laundry room. He turns on the lights and opens the cabinets. Towels and sheets are folded neatly beside the basket of women's underwear that the technicians found hidden in a cupboard. He carefully empties the garments onto the counter next to the washing machine. Black lace and red silk, roses and glittering rhinestones. Here they are – Jesper's hunting trophies.

'Look,' Manfred says, holding up a pair of tiny knickers with pearls sewn into the crotch. 'These look fucking uncomfortable. Are you supposed to have this . . . pearl necklace in your . . . arse? Between your bum cheeks or something?'

I don't respond. I think about how I've never seen Hanne in anything like that, and how I probably never will.

We put back the underwear and go over to Jesper's dirty laundry baskets. Identical white shirts and pants are crammed in with towels and workout gear. I pull out a pair of jeans and hold them in front of me. They appear to be of normal size, with no weird damage or stains that speak of anything suspicious. Just as I'm replacing them, I feel something in the back pocket. A small bulge, as if someone has forgotten some cash or a receipt.

I take out a handwritten note and unfold it. It's about half a normal page, and the handwriting is soft and tilts backwards a little. It looks almost childish.

Jesper,

I'm writing to you because I think you owe me an explanation. I understand that love can end, I truly do. But abandoning me the night of our engagement dinner, without any explanation, is not OK. And then to pretend I don't exist when I try to get hold of you – how do you think that makes me feel? If you wanted to hurt me, you've certainly succeeded.

What you don't know is that I'm pregnant with our child. And no matter how you feel about me, we have to talk about the baby. I don't expect you to be a father, but I have to discuss the situation with you. I think you owe me that much at least.

Emma

Emma

One month earlier

I lie in bed with my aching stomach, thinking about Woody. About the day Elin walked in on us.

He and I were standing in the storage room when I asked Woody:

'Have you ever felt like none of this is real? Like your life is just a movie?'

'That's a strange question. What do you mean?'

He hung his hammer on a hook on the wall. The hall outside was empty; it was half past twelve and all the other students were either in the cafeteria or outside in the schoolyard.

'I just mean that life feels sort of unreal sometimes. You never feel that way?'

'No.'

He gave me a long, searching look.

'Maybe that's because you've just lost your dad,' he said more softly.

I didn't respond. Didn't want to think about Dad. About the men who came and carried him out or about Mum, who'd been sleeping on the bathroom floor since he disappeared.

Woody took out the broom, started sweeping the floor in silence. His keyring rattled slightly as he leaned forward. I took a step back until I was standing against the wall, trying my best to take up as little space as possible, feeling the cold concrete on my shoulder blades. Then he put the broom against the wall, leaned back against the bench, looked at me and gently shrugged his shoulders.

'It'll get easier.'

'How do you know that? Everybody says that, but how do they know?'

Woody brushed a little sawdust from his jeans. 'I know. My dad died when I was your age. He survived a dictatorship, but died of a heart attack when we got to Sweden. Stupid, right?'

I didn't know what to say.

'I thought I was so strong,' he continued. 'Thought I could handle it, but I ended up in a really bad place. I wish I'd had someone to talk to. Someone who'd have listened to me and understood.'

'What happened?'

Woody looked at his hands. Inspecting them as if he wanted to make sure they were clean. He had an ugly gash on one thumb which had started to heal. There was a dirty plaster on the little finger of the other hand.

'I messed up.'

'How?'

'I hung out with the wrong people. And it almost destroyed my future. It took me a long time to . . . repair the damage I caused during those years.'

'Did you hurt somebody?'

He responded with a short laugh, as if I'd said something stupid. Ran his hand through his black hair.

'Myself, mostly. But that won't happen to you, Emma. You're . . . a good girl. Do you understand? You live in a good area, and you have family and friends who care about you. You'll be fine.'

Disappointment washed over me like a wave. I didn't want to be a 'good girl'. I wanted to be more important, grander and perhaps more dangerous than that. I wanted to be somebody. I wanted it to be like last time in the storage room. My name in his mouth, his hands on my bare skin.

I took a careful step towards him.

'Emma?' He looked puzzled.

I took another step, put my arms around him and clung to his warm body. He smelled like cigarette smoke and sweat; he stood completely still, then put one hand on my shoulder, patted it gently the way you might pet an obedient dog.

'It'll be OK, Emma. I promise.'

His words provoked me. Who said I wanted it to be OK? I leaned back, but only a little so I could look at him, catch his eyes. I wasn't sure but I almost thought he looked frightened, and I glimpsed something in those eyes, a question perhaps, or worry.

So I stood up on tiptoe, leaned forward and kissed him. His lips were hard and small, didn't feel at all like last time. He jumped back, his whole body trembling, and pushed me away with the force.

'Emma. What . . . ?'

There was a scrape and a small bang from outside. I turned around and saw a shadow in the doorway.

It was Elin. She was leaning forward as if balanced on the edge of a pool, ready to dive into the water. Her mouth was half-open and she had a can of fizzy drink in her hand.

'Elin,' Woody called. 'Come in. I want to talk to you.'

Elin didn't move, but the can slid slowly from her hand. It seemed to take an eternity for it to hit the floor and for the liquid to spurt out all over the linoleum.

'Elin,' he cried again, but she had already turned round and started running out of the room. Her worn leather jacket and red knitted cap disappeared through the door as the sound of her steps died away.

At three o'clock I take a painkiller. My stomach aches and I'm bleeding. Eventually I slip into a kind of stupor. I don't know if I'm dreaming or if I just lie there until it's time to get up.

My stomach feels better now, much better. Maybe I'm going numb. I feel as though I'm slowly turning to stone: cold, hard, indifferent to how the world treats me. The windows are black and the room is freezing. It's tempting to stay in bed, but I know I have to get up and do something about my situation. I can no longer be a pawn in Jesper's game.

When I decide to go to work, even though I'm no longer wanted there, I tell myself it's because I have to return the car to Olga.

'Hi.'

She greets me without lifting her eyes from the tabloid she's reading. 'Hello.'

I slide down on the chair opposite her as Olga slowly turns the pages, flattening the paper with one hand. In the other she's holding an unlit cigarette. I take out her car keys, put them in the middle of the newspaper.

'Thanks for letting me borrow your car.'

'This Eurovision is crazy.'

I don't respond.

'You wanna join me?' She holds up her cigarette.

I shrug. 'Sure.'

We walk into the hallway behind the kitchen, the one that leads to the refuse room. You're not supposed to smoke there but everyone does anyway. Bundles of compressed cardboard boxes are crammed along the wall.

'Want one?' Olga takes a pack of cigarettes out of her pocket.

I shake my head. 'No thanks.'

She looks at me with eyes as big and shiny as marbles as she lights her cigarette. Then she leans forward, runs her finger across my cheek. 'Jesus Christ, Emma, what happened?'

'I fell into a bush.'

She looks doubtful. 'Was it him? Your guy? He hit you? If he did, you report him.'

'No one hit me. But I followed him yesterday. I know where he lives now. I . . .'

I hesitate, tears pricking at my eyes. Olga squeezes my arm gently and I feel those long nails through my cardigan.

'What happened, Emma? Tell me. Things seem better when you talk.'

'He . . . he lives in a big house in Djursholm, and he had another woman there. He tricked me from the beginning. He said we couldn't tell anyone about our relationship because of his job, and that was why we could never be seen together. But really, it wasn't about that. He already had a girlfriend. Can you believe it? It's just so . . . sick. And then I thought about that other stuff you said, that maybe he was trying to hurt me. Maybe he *is* a psychopath. But now I don't know what to do about it. He's ruined my life, and I don't know what to do.'

Olga sighs and leans back against the concrete wall. Stares up at the bare bulb on the ceiling. A muffled rumble comes from a metro train passing deep below us. The smell of damp concrete and mould clings inside my nostrils.

'Emma,' she says, blowing smoke out slowly. A long trail rises to the ceiling before finally dissolving. 'You need to let go of him. You are . . . obsessed. If that is what he wanted, he has succeeded.'

'Let go of him?'

'Yes. You know. Keep moving forward. Before you've completely soaped yourself into a corner?'

' "Painted" myself into a corner.'

Olga ignores my comment. 'Forget him. Go out with somebody else. He's not worth it. You've got to move on.'

'I can't do that.'

My voice is thin and weak. I hear a bang, and a puff of cold air sneaks past my ankles. Someone is coming. Olga stubs out her cigarette against the wall, adding yet another black spot to the hundreds already there.

'Why not?'

She sounds accusatory.

'Because . . . he didn't just dump me. He took my money and my cat and . . .'

'You're sure he took your cat?'

'No, but . . .'

'When he borrowed the money, did you write any contract?'

'Of course not. You don't write a contract with your boyfriend.'

'Then you'll never prove it. So you have nobody but yourself to blame.'

I suddenly feel annoyed. Olga can be so crass, so completely lacking in compassion. She doesn't seem to notice my annoyance and instead looks lost in thought. From the corridor outside, steps are approaching. Nonetheless, she lights up again.

'Maybe you can pursue him.'

' "Pursue" him?'

'Yeah, in court.'

'You mean "sue" him? For what?'

'You come up with something.'

The door opens and Mahnoor peeks in. Her dark hair is set in a knot on her head and her eyes are surrounded by thick lines of kohl. She reminds me of a geisha.

'You know you can't smoke in here?'

'You gonna tell on us?' Olga mumbles.

'Come on. You can't both leave me alone in the shop.'

She turns around without waiting for an answer and the heavy steel door slides closed with a sigh.

'Just like Björne,' Olga says with a snort.

Jesper and I were walking along the water south of Tantolunden Park. It was one of the rare occasions when we went out together. The heat was so oppressive and the sun so alluring that we couldn't bring ourselves to stay inside the small apartment on Kapellgränd that afternoon.

'So what happened to your dad?'

'He died.'

'Yes, I got that, but what happened? How old were you?'

'Fifteen.'

'A sensitive age.'

I thought about it. Was it actually any harder to be fifteen than twelve, or eighteen? Or was it just something he said, out of courtesy, to show empathy?

'Maybe.'

'Was he sick?'

Jesper stopped next to one of the little garden cottages that lined our path. Geraniums of many colours and porcelain animals filled the little garden. A small dog appeared, ran over to us and started barking loudly.

'He hanged himself.'

'Oh my God, Emma. Why didn't you tell me before?'

'You never asked.'

'You should have said something.'

He pulled me close, hugging me tightly.

'Would it have made any difference?' I mumbled into his neck.

'No, of course not. But I could have helped you. Offered some support.'

'Support?'

I didn't mean it to sound ironic, but it did. The thought that he – who didn't even want us to be seen together – would suddenly be so eager to support me seemed absurd. Jesper didn't seem to perceive the irony. Instead he kissed me lightly and stretched out his hand.

'Come.'

We walked along the water in silence. There were scantily clad Stockholmers everywhere: on foot, on bikes, in canoes. A short distance away, two Asian men were fishing. Their floats bobbing quietly in the calm water near the dock testified to their lack of interest – maybe they were on holiday, too.

Jesper braided his fingers together with mine. Squeezed my hand so hard it hurt my knuckles. But I said nothing, thinking instead about my family disappearing. About Dad and Mum and the apartment and all the things we had in there: broken furniture, pieces of discarded towels and rugs, empty bottles, glass jars of various sizes with or without lids. Why did we have so much stuff anyway? Who collected it? It must have been Mum, because I don't remember it getting any better after Dad died. I also thought about all the little things we argued about: washing the dishes, if I could stay out until eleven, the right way to slice a hunk of cheese, and why my mum needed a few beers to relax and feel like a human being again.

Now nothing remained. Only fragmentary memories of a lost time, of people who died and withered away. Of places and things. Dreams, promises, plans, love and grief.

'Why did he kill himself?'

'I don't really know. He drank a lot – so did Mum – but I don't know if that was why. It's so strange. It's like I can't really remember, as if there are holes in my memory. Several years just went up in smoke.'

'Isn't that just how it is? We forget.'

'Is it?'

He didn't answer. We had arrived at a small dock. As if by tacit agreement, we walked to the edge, sat down on rotten wood that smelled faintly of tar. Just a few inches beneath our feet the sun danced on water that was ruffled by a light breeze. On the other side of the channel, the apartment buildings of Årsta spied through lush greenery, like children playing peekaboo.

'You don't have to answer if you don't want to, but who found him?'

I leaned back so my elbows rested on the rough wood of the dock. I lay staring straight up at the sky. Small postcard-perfect white clouds slowly floated by above us. Seagulls circled over the water, screeching in the way seagulls do.

'Mum found him. He hanged himself in our living room. She took a kitchen knife and cut him down. When I came home, he was still lying on the rug in the living room with the rope around his neck.'

'You saw him?'

'Yes.'

'Holy shit. You should have told me, Emma.'

I didn't answer, but when I closed my eyes I saw Dad in front me – lying on his side on the rug with yellow sunflowers, the one my aunt had made. The blue plastic rope was wrapped like a lead around his neck. His face was a strange colour, and his tongue was pushed out of his half-open mouth. My mother was squatting beside him, rocking back and forth, mumbling incoherently.

Jesper lay down beside me, his eyes closed against the sun, and placed his hand on one of my breasts.

'Poor little Emma,' he mumbled. 'I'll take care of you.'

And in that moment, with the sun on my face, surrounded by the perfect, ravishing beauty of Stockholm, I believed him.

I truly believed what he said.

'Don't forget the hats and scarves.'

Mahnoor points to the rack by the checkout counter. I nod, but don't answer. All day long I've been waiting for Mahnoor or Olga to tell me to go home, remind me I've been laid off.

But no one says anything and as the hours tick by I become more and more convinced that they don't know I've been fired, that maybe there's no contact between HR and our staff. In some strange way, I feel as though I could stay here in my bubble for as long as I want, that it's up to me to decide when my employment ends.

I slowly start to pull the stand with hats and mittens from the checkout towards the entrance. This constant rearrangement of clothing and furnishings is exhausting. Sure, I know it's so we'll sell more, but there are few things that feel as useless as moving mountains of jeans from one end of the room to the other.

Olga helps me. She grabs the scarves, puts them next to the hats and mittens. I look at the instructions from head office and then at our shop. 'I think they're in the right place now.'

Olga reaches for the diagram. 'Let me see.'

She looks back and forth between the paper and what's in front of her, then nods.

'It needs to be like this,' she says and moves the hats a bit. Sometimes we get unannounced inspections from head office. They look at everything – from how our signs are set up to whether or not the staff bathroom is clean. If they aren't satisfied the shop gets a mark against them, which affects staff bonuses. And we're the staff. No matter what you think of Management, you have to admit that their methods of control are quite effective.

'Olga, that thing you said about revenge. What do you think I should do?'

Olga crosses her arms and frowns. 'I don't know. Meet with him. Tell him off.'

'And if he doesn't listen to me?'

Olga picks up some mittens that have fallen on the floor. When she looks at me again, I can see the irritation in her face.

'How should I know?'

The sharpness in her voice surprises me.

'No, of course. But you were the one who suggested it. I thought you might have some good ideas.'

She doesn't answer. Pretends to be busy hanging up a pair of red leather gloves. From the checkout, I hear Mahnoor's soft laughter as she talks to a customer. I hesitate a second but ask anyway.

'He owes me a hundred thousand. Does that mean I have the right to . . . steal that from him?'

Olga squirms but doesn't meet my gaze. 'Why not?'

I lock the wheels of the rack and rearrange some of the clothes and hats. Make sure they hang neatly on the narrow metal bars.

'Suppose he has a dog,' I say. 'Could I take it? Drop it off in a forest somewhere far away?'

Olga freezes and finally looks at me. Her eyes are filled with disgust. 'Why you want to take his dog? That's sick.'

'But he took my cat.'

'You don't know that was him. Maybe the cat just ran away.'

No, I know it was him, I think. But I don't have the strength to argue with Olga about it. She can think whatever she wants.

I catch a whiff of perfume and Mahnoor pops up at my side. Puts her hand lightly on my shoulder.

'What are you talking about?'

'Oh, nothing special,' Olga lies and hands her the plan from head office. 'Is it right?'

Mahnoor compares the diagram and our set-up in silence.

'Very good,' she says, and Olga turns and trips away towards the kitchenette in her sky-high heels.

I think that no matter what kind of revenge is fair, I have to do something. I know I'll fall apart if I don't. My whole body knows it.

But what can I do to a man like Jesper Orre? A man who has everything: success, money, women. The logical course would be to retaliate in kind – an eye for an eye, a tooth for a tooth. He sneaked into my home, stole my things, my pet. He took my job, my money, my child. But maybe Olga was right and I couldn't really do the same thing to him.

Could I?

As I adjust another hat, I see the ring sparkling on my finger and suddenly I know exactly what I have to do.

Watches, jewellery and silver objects cover the shop from floor to ceiling. The room is dim, but several bright lamps stand on the counter in front of me. There's a worn burgundy leather sofa behind me. A dark-haired woman in a red coat sits in the middle of the sofa, a bag in her lap. When I turn around she looks away.

I turn back towards the woman behind the counter. She's in her sixties, has short blonde hair and is wearing a twinset and pleated wool skirt. She looks like a woman in a newsreel from the fifties or an ageing Doris Day who moonlights at a pawnshop. She lifts up the ring, examining it through something that looks like a tiny telescope.

'Very nice,' she says. 'A lovely stone.'

'We've broken up,' I tell her.

She lowers her magnifying glass and raises her hand almost imperceptibly, as if wanting to put the words back into my mouth, letting me know that there's no need to tell her why I'm selling the ring, that this information isn't relevant here.

'We get a lot of engagement rings,' she mumbles and returns to her magnifying glass. When she bends forward, her head is so close I can see the grey hairs sprouting like weeds at her hairline. Without looking up from the ring, she continues:

'You can get twenty thousand for this.'

'No more? It cost much more than that.'

She suddenly looks tired, puts the magnifier on the glass counter. Then places the ring on a small blue velvet cushion.

'We can't give you more than that. I'm sorry.'

It's quiet for a moment. I look around the shop one more time. A Gibson guitar is hanging on one wall. I wonder if it's for sale. On a shelf to my right are several gold rings; they look like engagement rings. Hundreds of broken dreams on view under a glass case. The woman on the leather sofa is still there. She looks away again.

'Fine,' I say.

Doris Day nods guardedly and fixes her hair with one hand.

'Then we'll arrange a pawn ticket for you. I'll need some information.' She takes out a form and puts it in front of me. Puts a tick in front of some of the boxes. 'You should fill in your information here and here and here. And I need your ID.'

I give it to her and think, No, I'm not ashamed to be here. It's not my fault I've ended up in this fucking mess, and I'm not ashamed to be finally doing something to get myself out of it. Suddenly it feels important to highlight this fact – I have nothing to be ashamed of.

'Great, then I can pay my bills. I can get my phone turned back on. And my cable too, of course. And the rent, I almost forgot that. What if they'd evicted me? That would have been awful.'

Doris Day doesn't answer, just nods, her head bowed. She's heard it all, I guess. The woman on the couch is blushing, looking like she wants to run away with her plastic bag.

'Goodbye,' I say to her. 'Hope you get a lot for that.' She squeezes the bag in her lap without answering me.

Hanne

Gunilla drives me to Skeppargatan. It's already dark, though it's only four o'clock in the afternoon, and it's treacherously slippery. She parks on Kaptensgatan, shuts off the engine and turns to me. Her blonde hair shines like a halo around her head under the glow of the streetlight.

'You want me to come with you?'

I consider it. 'Yes please. If you don't mind. He's not usually home at this time, but you never know . . .'

'Of course. Let's go and get Frida.'

We walk the short distance to the door.

Strange. It's only been a few days since I left, but the building already feels altered in some way. Darker, less hospitable, as if it doesn't really want to be my home any more. As if it's terminated our contract and kicked me out. Though the opposite is the case, I think. I'm the one who's leaving Skeppargatan.

I punch in the code and the door opens with a muffled hum.

As we take the lift up, I root around for the keys in my bag, feel my fingers shaking as I finally grab hold of them, and when Gunilla opens the lift door I drop them on the floor. She picks them up and puts her hand tentatively on my cheek, as if wondering whether I have a temperature.

'Oh, sweetie. You're shaking.'

'It's just—'

She nods quickly, grabs my arm and leads me to the apartment. Takes the keys from me and unlocks the door. Frida immediately rushes out, jumping around my legs. I squat down. Bury my face in her black coat and let the tears flow. Frida licks my face and whimpers slightly.

All this unconditional canine love, I think. What have I done to deserve it? And why does human love always require us to submit and adapt? Why can't we just love each other without needing to own each other?

We go into the hall and turn on the light. It looks exactly the same. My clothes and shoes are hanging neatly on hooks in the hall. The post lies in a small pile on the bureau under the mirror. Gunilla goes to it, rifling slowly through the stack and taking out a few pieces which I suppose are for me.

I look into the kitchen. My little yellow Post-it notes are still hanging on the cabinets. Fluttering gently in the draught from the window.

Reminders.

The sound of the clock ticking in the kitchen is annoyingly loud, penetrating my ears. I turn around and go into the living room. Run my eyes over the bookcase. Think a few seconds, then grab Halvorsen's memoirs about his move to Greenland at the beginning of the last century and a collection of essays about the Inuit that my father gave me when I started at the university. Then I look at all the objects: masks and statues and the rest. But the only thing I feel is disgust, a kind of nausea almost, when I think about why we got them. I can't bring myself to take even one of them to Gunilla's.

'Don't you have enough books? Shouldn't you bring some clothes instead?' Gunilla asks.

I shake my head. 'I need to buy new ones anyway.'

We fall silent and the sound of the kitchen clock creeps into my head once more, bouncing between my temples and drilling small, distinct, painful holes into my consciousness. Suddenly I feel the whole room start to warp, as if it's swinging, and I feel sick. Take a few steps forward to Gunilla and take her hand.

She seems concerned. A deep wrinkle has appeared between her eyebrows and she squeezes my hand.

'Toiletries? Is there anything you need?'

I shake my head. 'Nothing,' I say. 'I don't need anything from here.'

When we get back to Gunilla's apartment, she boils tea for me while she packs. She's going on a twenty-four-hour cruise with her new lover. The man who makes her feel young again.

Randy. In a way her former husband hadn't done in years.

Frida lies on a blanket on the sofa, sleeping. Happily oblivious to human problems. Gunilla is singing softly; I can't make out what, but it's comforting. It reminds me of something long ago – a time I've forgotten, or perhaps buried because it's too painful to think about.

Imagine being that ridiculously happy again. In love and randy and passionate, even though you're close to retirement and your children are grown up. Going on a cruise, eating good food and having sex with someone you actually want to make love to. Because of lust, rather than habit or loyalty or maybe just submission.

Was it ever like that for Owe and me? Back when we were both young?

Though actually, only I was young when we met. Nineteen. He was almost thirty, had already been married once, and was finished with his residency. You can't escape the fact that I went from one parent to another, from one kind of submission to another.

But surely we had passion?

I'm trying to remember. But as usual when I think back on my relationship with Owe, there's so much missing, so many holes in the brittle fabric of my memory that I can't really evoke how things felt. Maybe because of everything that's come between it: the shame in Owe's face when he looks at my notes on the kitchen doors, the weak but still perceptible smell of boiled cabbage around his body, the ugly cardigan that he insists on wearing even when we have dinner parties. And his way of silencing guests with his haughty drivel about philosophy or the theatre – even when he doesn't really know what he's talking about.

'Will you be OK?' Gunilla says as she sets her weekend bag down in the hall and puts on her fur jacket.

'Absolutely.'

'And you'll call if you need me?'

I go out into the hall and give her a long hug. Breathe in the scent of her perfume and rest my cheek for a second on the coat's soft lapel.

'Have a wonderful time,' I say and hope it sounds as though I truly mean it.

She lets go of me, a little hesitantly. Raises her hand in a small wave, smiles faintly, takes the bag in her hand and leaves.

I pour water into a glass and take my medicine, one yellow pill and two white. Think, Here I am, living on borrowed time. In Gunilla's kitchen, far from Owe on the other side of the city.

Life is strange and doesn't become any less so as you get older. But you get used to strangeness, learn to accept it. The trick is to reconcile yourself to the fact that life never turns out the way you expect it to.

It's nine-twenty in the evening, and the storm beats against the kitchen window and whistles around the building. But inside it's warm and cosy. Floral cushions, colourful curtains with ruffles – everything Gunilla's husband loathed – crowded into the room. Jörn was a builder, though he fancied himself as something of an architect. Their home was all in white and various shades of grey, as minimalistic and asexual as a medical laboratory. And every one of Gunilla's attempts to lighten up their strict home with colourful cushions or hand-painted porcelain was ruthlessly rejected.

I look out through the black window, wonder how Gunilla is doing out on the Baltic Sea in this storm.

Owe has texted me three times today. The first time he apologised for his behaviour yesterday outside Gunilla's apartment. Explained that he loves me, that Frida's being well cared for and that they both miss me. The second message was more urgent. He'd discovered that Frida was gone and wrote that I 'could at least have warned' him. I could sense his frustration between the lines of the short message at losing control of me, like a dull, menacing undertone in a piece of music.

The third message arrived an hour ago and was filled with a barely suppressed fury:

Suggest we meet at 20.00 at KB to discuss our options. I assume you'll be there. Owe

I can almost see him at the bar, a glass of Chablis in hand. Furious that I haven't turned up, his grey hair sticking on end.

My mobile buzzes, and I pick it up. Feel only exhaustion when I read his message:

Do not expect ANY support from me. I have put up with you for the LAST time. Your behaviour is INEXCUSABLE. You're on your own now.

I look down at the kitchen table which is covered with papers. I browse aimlessly through the reports about Calderón's murder. Looking once more at the severed head and its taped-open eyes. Reading my own words:

The head has been deliberately placed so it is visible from the entrance door, the eyelids taped open. Probably so potential visitors will be forced to meet the victim's gaze. Possible reasons for this are . . .

Somewhere deep in my mind a thought is forming, so vague it almost slips away. I reach for the technician's report from Jesper

Orre's house and search through it. My eyes stop on the list of objects found on the floor of the hall, and there it is: two broken matchsticks found next to the dead woman's head.

I reach for my mobile and call Peter's number. He answers almost immediately, as if he were waiting for my call out there in the storm.

'Hanne?' he says.

'I've found something.'

'Found something?'

'Yes, in the technician's report from Orre's house.'

Pause. I hear music in the background.

'Ah, OK. Shall we take a look at it tomorrow morning? I'm on my way home.'

'I think it's important.'

Another pause. 'Where are you?'

Fifteen minutes later the doorbell rings. Peter has snow in his hair and on his hooked nose, and I have the impulse to lean forward and brush it off. I stop myself at the last moment. 'Come in.'

He stomps off his shoes and hangs his jacket on the hook next to mine. Glances around the bright hall. His thin cheeks are red with cold and drops of water glisten in his blonde eyebrows.

'Nice apartment. Yours?'

I shake my head. 'No. I'm staying with a friend right now.'

I lead the way into the kitchen and gesture towards one of the chairs. 'Sit down. Would you like a cup of tea?'

He shakes his head. 'No thanks. I'm fine.'

I sit down next to him and flip through the technical report from Orre's home. 'That neighbour,' I say. 'Did she touch the victim?'

Peter looks confused.

'The old lady? The one who found her?'

'Yes.'

Peter runs his hand through his hair and looks up at the ceiling.

'Yeah. She did. If I remember correctly, she said she checked to see if she was really dead. As if there could be any doubt about that.'

'So she touched the head?'

'She could have, yes.'

'Did she move it?'

He meets my eyes again. His green eyes are bloodshot, as if he's been crying or maybe partied too hard. I lean towards the latter option.

'Did she move it? No, I don't think so. She might have touched it.'

'Then something may have been . . . dislodged at the crime scene.'

'Absolutely. The way she trudged around.'

'Because it says here . . .' I slide my finger along the text, looking for the passage that caught my interest, and continue, 'It says here that two broken matchsticks were found on the floor next to the head.'

Peter leans forward. Reading the report.

'Yeah. Two matches, a one-krona coin, a cigarette lighter and a Chanel lipgloss. Probably things that the victim had in her pockets and that fell on the floor while they fought.'

'What if the matches didn't end up there by chance?' I say.

'What do you mean?'

'What if the killer had put them in the victim's eyes, to hold them open?'

Peter examines the technical sketch.

'The matches were found here,' I say, pointing to the sketch. 'Adjacent to the head. If the killer placed them in the victim's eyes, they may have fallen out and onto the floor when the neighbour moved the head.'

Peter sighs and puts his forehead against his hand.

'So what you're saying is that the murderer might have wanted to keep this victim's eyes open, like in the Calderón case?'

'Exactly.'

'So the person who came through the door would have to meet the victim's gaze.'

'That's the other thing I've been thinking about. What if it's the opposite?'

'The opposite?'

'Yes, what if it's the victim who's being forced to see?'

'But the victim is dead.'

'Well, of course. But think symbolically. The killer murders and mutilates the victim. But that's not enough. After the murder, he tapes or braces the victim's eyes open so that he or she will have to watch him leave. The ultimate humiliation. I take your life and then I leave, as if nothing has happened. And I force you to watch me do it.'

Peter looks doubtful.

'What's the difference?' he asks finally.

'Well, there's a huge difference. Keeping the eyes open to ensure that the next visitor meets the victim's gaze is an aggressive act directed at the outside world, or against the visitor. Keeping the eyes open so that the victim is forced to watch the murderer leave is an act directed at the victim. The ultimate revenge. For some reason it was important to the killer that the victim watched as he walked away. Think of it as a kind of liberation from the victim.'

'And what does that mean on a practical level?'

'It's likely that the victim and the murderer had a close relationship.'

'What kind of relationship?'

'I don't know. A love affair, perhaps.'

We're still sitting in Gunilla's kitchen a few hours later, talking about the case. Peter isn't completely convinced by my theory. He seems to accept that the matches might have been deliberately placed in the victim's eyes, but even though I explain it to him over and over again, he doesn't seem to understand why it's so important that the victim, rather than anyone else, should be forced to see.

After a while we start to talk about other things. A tentative conversation about the weather and his colleagues at the police station. About politics and how the town has changed over the past ten years.

Cautious questions about our lives – neither of us mentions the strange fact that we're sitting here, alone, in a kitchen at night. That after so many years we're actually talking to each other again, for real.

I allow myself to feel a kind of sadness over what will never be. The life we could have had together.

At half past ten he says he has to go. He has to be up early to sift through all the tip-offs that have come in as to the identity of the unknown woman. There's something restless in his gangly body as he gets up, goes out into the hall and pulls on his jacket. He bends forward, puts on his trainers which are too thin for winter.

He always dressed too lightly, I think, and remember the old black leather jacket he wore no matter what the weather. In the end it was so worn out it literally fell apart. Maybe I should have bought him a warmer jacket, but that's not something you do, not for your lover. That kind of care is reserved for a husband.

'Well,' he says. 'See you tomorrow?'

'Yes, see you then,' I say.

Then we stand opposite each other in Gunilla's hall. Actually, much too close for comfort. So close that I catch a whiff of his scent – sweat and cigarette smoke – and see the wrinkles that mark the passage of time on his face, like rings on a tree.

For a second I think he wants to kiss me: he leans forward slightly, over me. But then he extends his hand.

I take it quickly and for a moment that desperate feeling of out-rage and sorrow over his betrayal comes back again, that desperate feeling of outrage and sorrow over his betrayal. And anger. Anger that his touch still makes my body remember how it was back then.

Then he's gone. And all I can think is, He shook my hand. What a bizarre way to say goodbye to someone you've once been so close to. Couldn't he just have hugged me, like normal people do?

He shook my hand.

Emma

One month earlier

I'm thinking about the night Mum killed the butterfly – this time really killing it.

From the outset, several things made that evening different from most. First, there was Mum slamming the china in the kitchen. Plates, glasses and cutlery clanging against each other. And then wine glasses. I could definitely tell they were wine glasses. The sound is different from a water glass – a deeper, rounder and more sinister ring. The scent of chicken and fresh herbs spread through the apartment.

It all added up to something bad. An ordinary evening was merely monotonous, but an evening with wine and fancy food was completely unpredictable. In the best-case scenario, Dad would fall asleep while Mum watched TV on the sofa, but it was more likely that tense discussions would turn into arguments and then, as a kind of finale, the china would end up crashing against the floor and walls.

Once the police even knocked on the door because the neighbours had complained. I felt so ashamed I hid under the bed. But the two people who should have been ashamed, Mum and Dad, seemed completely unmoved by the visit. They'd pulled themselves together enough to almost seem sober and in low, remorseful voices swore they'd calm down and be quiet. Yes, they'd had a fight, been a little too loud, but it wouldn't happen again. And no, they hadn't been drinking, at least not very much. A couple of glasses of wine at most.

'Come and eat now, Emma,' Mum called from the kitchen.

I took my jar and blue butterfly with me. Dad was already sitting at the dining table with a glass of wine and a beer beside it. Mum stood by the stove, wearing an apron and stirring a big red pot. She looked just like a real mother, one on TV. It made me nervous – this feigned domesticity always ended badly.

'Sit down,' Mum mumbled and pointed to a chair.

I sat down, relieved that she sounded angry and irritated. Maybe everything was normal after all? I placed the jar gently beside me on the table so I could look at it while I ate. It had been just over a day since it hatched, and the large blue butterfly did nothing but sit on a stick and occasionally gently move its perfect deep-blue wings.

'Have you decided what to do with it yet?' Dad asked.

I shook my head. Both Mum and Dad said I had to let it go, so it could return to nature and live freely. I understood their reasoning, but as soon as I thought of never seeing that small black body or those tissue-paper wings again, something knotted up inside me. It was like asking a toddler to give up her favourite doll. And that was the problem in a nutshell – I was no longer a little kid. I was supposed to rise above wanting to own the butterfly and do the right thing, because the other option was to kill it or wait until it died. Then we could pin it to the wall with a needle, and I could keep it as long as I wanted. But the thought of sticking a long needle through its small body felt so barbaric it made me sick.

'I don't know what I'm gonna do.'

Dad emptied his beer glass with a single gulp.

'You'd better decide soon. It won't last long in there.'

I leaned forward and peered into the jar. My breath fogged up the glass, making it impossible to see much. The butterfly turned into a diffuse blue cloud, afloat in the jar.

'Do you have to have it on the table?' Mum said in the sharp, surly tone of voice she used when she was getting angry. At the same time she put the chicken stew down with a bang so hard that the hot liquid slopped out over the edges.

'What does it matter?' Dad snorted and emptied his wine glass too. Mum opened a second bottle of wine. Even the plop from the cork sounded disgruntled and bitter.

'It's an insect.'

'It's in a jar,' Dad said.

'I don't want insects on my dinner table.'

'Come on, let it be,' Dad said.

Outside a blue August twilight descended over Stockholm. Through the half-open window warm evening air flowed into the room. It smelled of damp earth and dog poo.

'Please, Emma. Take the jar into your room,' Mum said.

I looked at Dad, trying to figure out if I should obey or not.

'Leave the jar on the table,' he said in an ominously muffled voice, and I got the feeling that he was speaking directly to Mum, even though he was looking at me.

Mum sat down at the table. Her mouth was a thin line and she was rubbing one temple. Her skin wrinkled as if it were made of thin cardboard under her fingers. Dad ate without saying a word. I held my breath and counted. If I inhaled a lot of air, I could hold my breath until fifty. Dragan could hold his breath for two and a half minutes, and Marie, in Special Ed, could hold her breath until she fainted, though Elin said it was because she had cerebral palsy.

'What are you doing?' Mum asked. She put down her fork and looked disapprovingly at me.

'Nothing. I just . . .'

'Stop it now. It looks like you have some kind of . . . tic.'

I didn't know what a tic was and I didn't dare ask either. Mum turned towards Dad, her cheeks flushed, and I could see that her left hand, the one in her lap, was in a fist, as if she were holding something small and valuable.

'Did you pay the rent today?'

Dad stirred the chicken stew with a fork and didn't answer.

'You promised,' Mum whispered. 'I don't know why I trusted you. You're just as out of it and confused as . . . as . . . the kid.'

I looked down at my plate where a few lonely pieces of chicken swam in a clear broth. If I wanted to I could make Mum really upset now. The only thing I needed to do was to remind her she could pay the bills herself, even though she couldn't read that well. But of course I didn't say anything.

'Don't drag Emma into this,' Dad mumbled.

'You are exactly alike. Equally hopeless,' she clarified.

'You know what? You're acting like a real cunt.' Dad sounded both triumphant and relieved, as if he were delivering a long-awaited truth.

'Cunt,' he said again, stressing every consonant.

'You'd better watch yourself,' Mum screamed. 'I don't have to take this shit. You know that. There are plenty of men who'd be happy to have me. There are plenty of candidates—'

'Candidates? In your dreams. Who wants a drunken bitch with tits down to her knees who does nothing but nag?'

'That's enough, goddammit. If you don't like it, I'll leave. And I mean it.'

'You say that every time.'

'Emma, go to your room,' Mum said.

I stood up and hurried out of the kitchen.

'And take that fucking insect with you,' she added.

I turned round just as Mum threw the jar across the room. It flew in a high arc over my head, and even though I tried to catch it there was no chance. It smashed against the kitchen wall.

I sank down on my knees.

Shards of glass were scattered across the floor. The nest of old dry branches lay next to the wall, and beside it was the butterfly.

One wing was in two pieces and its body looked strangely flat. I stretched out a finger and touched it gently.

The blue butterfly was dead.

It's raining as I walk home. The trees on the Karlavägen road esplanade stretch their naked branches upwards, as if trying to reach the sky. A thick layer of wet leaves covers the ground. Is Sigge somewhere out here? I wonder. He's not in the courtyard, that's for sure. I've searched for him there several times, and there's no trace of a cat. I couldn't find him on Valhallavägen, either. Did he disappear into the rain-soaked maze of streets and alleys that make up Stockholm? Is he lying somewhere, injured and unable to find his way home? Did somebody take him in?

I don't think so.

I think Jesper killed him. I stop for a moment, close my eyes, turn my face up to the rain, trying to see it in front of me: Jesper closing his big hands around Sigge's neck. Throwing him out the window.

But I can't.

I can't conjure up such an image. The only thing I see is Jesper sleeping peacefully on a colourful rug. The field of sunflowers. His chest moving up and down in time as he breathes. His mouth half-open.

I continue walking home. Karlaplan lies deserted in the darkness in front of me. The leaves have filled up the bottom of the empty fountain. A part of me wants to lie on the edge, rest my cheek on those wet leaves. But something stops me. Something bold, efficient and relentless has come alive inside me. Maybe because I took the ring to the pawnshop, thus buying myself some time. Maybe because the pain in my stomach has disappeared.

Or maybe I've just had enough.

As I pass by the entrance to the metro, I hear something behind me – a small thud, as if someone has dropped a book or a bag of flour onto the ground. I turn around but can't make out anything under the dark shadows of the trees. For some reason I don't get scared, just angry. I'm convinced he's standing in the dark, waiting for me. And it just pisses me off.

'Hello?' I shout, but there's no response. The only thing I hear is the sound of endless rain and a car disappearing in the distance. A window stands open in one of the buildings on the short side street, and music and voices stream out into the darkness.

I turn around, walk towards the shadows. The light from a street-lamp almost blinds me and I look down, staring at the rain-soaked Tarmac.

'Come out, you coward. I know you're there.'

Then a shadow detaches itself from the darkness and glides down the side street in the direction of Valhallavägen. The sound of somebody running echoes between the walls of the apartment buildings and dies away.

My legs suddenly feel feeble and numb. I look down at my high-heeled boots, realise I have little chance of catching up with the shadow which has already disappeared. 'Fucking coward! I'll get you!' I bellow.

Just as I decide to give up, I feel a hand on my shoulder. I turn around. An old lady in a raincoat is looking at me anxiously. Her two dachshunds are also staring at me with their unfathomable dog faces.

'Have you been robbed, my dear?'

'No, it was just . . .'

'Should I call the police?'

Her eyes are big as saucers, and I sense that this is the most exciting thing to have happened to her for a long time, maybe for years. One of the dachshunds growls softly.

'No,' I say. 'It's nothing serious. I can take care of it myself.'

Peter

All the way down Brännkyrkagatan, I feel ashamed. Why on earth did I shake her hand, as though we barely knew each other? But there's just something about Hanne that makes me feel so unbelievably insecure. I wonder if she knows it and, if so, if she uses it to her advantage, the way Janet did.

You can't trust women.

They're no more intelligent than men, but they put more energy into figuring us out. And so we men find ourselves at a constant, self-inflicted disadvantage.

The car is illegally parked on Hornsgatan, and when I put the key in the lock I feel a sudden uncertainty. Maybe I should go back and apologise. But what would I be apologising for? For taking her by the hand when I wanted to do something else entirely? For never turning up on that evening ten years ago, or for never contacting her over the many years that have passed since?

That's a lot to apologise for all at once.

I sit in the car, start the engine and think for a while. I take out my phone and punch in Manfred's number before I can change my mind.

It rings seven times before he responds.

'Jesus Christ, Lindgren. It's almost midnight. I hope this is important.'

'Good evening to you too, sir.'

Manfred isn't that angry, not really. But you never know about the fathers of young children. They defend their sleep with the same intensity with which other men protect their balls. But what do I know? I've never changed a nappy in my life.

'Do you have the coroner's report there?'

'Which one?'

'The autopsy of the woman in Orre's house.'

He sighs loudly. 'Yeah. On my computer. Wait a minute.'

He comes back a few minutes later. In the background I hear a baby crying, a piercing cry that rises and falls rhythmically like a broken fire alarm. 'Sorry if I woke you,' I say.

'You should have thought of that before you called,' he mumbles. 'What do you want to know?'

'Did the victim have any marks or damage in or around the eyes? On the eyelids, for example?'

There's silence on the other end of the line, and I look out over Hornsgatan. Some night wanderers disappear into the wind down towards Södermalmstorg Square. At Mariatorget Square a man struggles against the wind with a dog in tow. A lone car glides by in the direction of Hornstull.

'The eyes, you said? Yes, actually. Thank your lucky stars that Fatima Ali did the autopsy, and not that sloppy arsehole from Borås. She found . . . two small puncture wounds on the inside of each of the upper eyelids and a small wound eighteen millimetres below the right eye. The wounds were between one and two millimetres in diameter and did not penetrate the skin. Superficial, in other words. She declined to speculate on what caused them. Why? What's this about, anyway?'

It takes a while for Hanne to open the door. She's dressed in sweatpants and a faded T-shirt and has a toothbrush in one hand. Her eyes are quizzical and perhaps a little scared, which isn't strange. You should be suspicious of strange men who come knocking on your door in the middle of the night.

And even more suspicious if they're not strangers.

'You were right,' I say.

She doesn't answer, just slowly takes a step backwards. Letting me into the warm apartment.

I wake up at seven. The only sound is Hanne breathing evenly in the darkness, and the heater humming next to the bed. I move myself closer to her as gently as I can until my body is touching her skin and her warmth belongs to me. I put my hand on her skinny hips and breathe in her scent: cinnamon and sweat. It's a moment that's so perfect, so pure. Like spring water or clear, cool autumn air on a cliff by the sea after a rainstorm. A gleaming moment to save for ever, right beside all the bullshit that's crowded into the meandering paths of my memory. And because I know myself, I'm desperately afraid to dirty it. Soil it in the same way I always soil and destroy what's beautiful and clean.

Love and beauty are transient.

The shit is eternal.

But sometimes these small, clear moments of happiness appear, and the only thing you can do when that happens is nothing.

So I lie completely still under the warm blanket, breathing as quietly as I can. Touch the soft skin of her groin near her curly pubic hair.

Back when she was mine for real, when I had both her body and her trust, I was never this gentle. I guess that's also one of life's lessons – you don't realise what you have until it's gone. A cliché, I know, but true. Longing is an excellent way to measure the value of what you've lost – a currency as reliable as any other.

At half past seven I creep out of bed, get dressed, write a note and put it on the kitchen table. Explain that I have to be at the police station by eight and tell her we'll meet later. I consider for a while whether or not I should sign it 'xo' or maybe write 'Thank you for yesterday' but without really knowing why, I decide not to do it.

Sanchez and Manfred are already at work. They're both sitting in front of the main evidence wall, each holding a cup of coffee. Manfred looks tired, and I wonder if he got any sleep after we talked. After a minute we're joined by Bergdahl, the investigator helping us sort through the public tip-offs. He has a stack of paper in one hand and a pack of cigarettes in the other.

Manfred rises laboriously from his chair and puffs.

'Maybe it's best if you start,' he says and gestures to me. 'You discovered something last night, right?'

I nod and tell them about the matches, the small wounds around the victim's eyes, and Hanne's theory that the killer wanted to force the victim to see, not the other way around.

'Interesting,' Sanchez says and actually looks as if she means it. Her usual irony is gone.

'I told you the witch knew her shit,' Manfred mumbles.

'If I understand her correctly, that means that the motive is some kind of revenge?'

Sanchez asks.

'That's how I understood it,' I say. 'But it's probably best if she explains how she's thinking.'

'Do you know when she's coming in?' Sanchez asks.

I shrug. 'No clue.'

'All right,' says Bergdahl, who's in his fifties and seems to be ashamed of his baldness; he insists on wearing either a cap or a hat even indoors – today it's a saggy black knitted beanie. He continues, 'I thought I'd go through some of the tip-offs we've received since that sketch was plastered across every paper and TV station. We've received hundreds of calls – the majority, about eighty, we've been able to dismiss by tracking down and contacting the person named in the tip-off. That leaves us eighteen people. We've divided those eighteen into two groups – interesting and less interesting, especially in terms of their physical resemblance to the victim. We'll continue to examine them over the next few days.'

There is the sound of steps coming down the hall and then Hanne walks in, takes off her coat and sits down on a chair next to Sanchez without meeting my eyes. I can't help but stare at her. Her finely cut face, the hair hanging damp over her shoulder, as if she's come here straight from the shower, and the pilled, much too big sweater. It makes my stomach clench.

'So how many interesting candidates do we have?' asks Sanchez.

'Three,' Bergdahl says, and puts three blurred images on the evidence wall, then points to the first. 'Wilhelmina Andrén, twenty-two years old, Stockholm resident. Ran away from Department 140 at Danderyd Hospital two weeks ago and hasn't been heard from since. She suffers from schizophrenia and is under compulsory psychiatric care. But according to her relatives, she's never been violent. She has delusions. Apparently believes she can communicate with birds. She's disappeared before and has most often been found in a park, where she hangs out with her friends.'

'Birds?' Manfred asks.

'Exactly. The problem with her is that she's a little on the short side to be our victim, but we'll continue investigating her. Then we have Angelica Wennerlind, a twenty-six-year-old preschool teacher from Bromma. She was heading out on holiday with her five-year-old daughter on the day of the murder and hasn't been heard from since. Her parents say she rented a cottage somewhere, but they don't know where. It could be that she has no mobile coverage wherever she is and she just hasn't checked in. But she's quite similar in appearance to the victim. Unfortunately the body is in too bad a condition for the parents to be able to identify her, so we'll have to wait for the dental records.'

'And the third?' Sanchez asks.

Bergdahl readjusts his silly hat and points to the last image.

'Emma Bohman, twenty-five. Until a few weeks ago she was employed as a salesperson by Clothes&More, the company Jesper Orre is CEO of. Though a couple of thousand other people are too, so that doesn't necessarily mean anything. She lives alone on Värtavägen in central Stockholm. Her mother and father are dead. An aunt reported her missing three days ago and got in touch with us again when she saw the sketch in the headlines. The aunt has been trying to contact her for a week, with no luck, but says she doesn't really resemble the woman in the picture. For example, she has much longer hair. But she might have cut her hair, so we'll continue investigating her, too. We've ordered dental records for all three women, and will hopefully have them by later today. Based on that, the forensic odontologist should be able to determine fairly quickly if any of them are identical to our victim.'

'Emma,' Manfred says.

'Like the woman who wrote that letter,' I say and look at the handwritten note which is now hanging from the evidence wall next to the other pictures and documents.

'What?' Bergdahl asks and looks confused.

'We found a letter at Orre's house,' I say, 'from someone named Emma who apparently had a relationship with Orre and got pregnant.'

Bergdahl nods slowly.

'OK. Was it written recently?'

'We don't know. We didn't find an envelope, just the letter itself. It was in the pocket of his jeans.'

'Can we compare the handwriting to that of the missing woman, Emma Bohman?' Manfred asks.

'Sure,' I say. 'But probably dental records will be faster.'

Sanchez puts her notebook on the table and says, 'Fatima said that the victim had either given birth or been pregnant. Angelica Wennerlind had a child, but what about the other women?'

'Only Angelica had any children,' Manfred says. 'But we don't know, of course, if either of the other two have been pregnant. If Emma Bohman is the Emma who wrote the letter, she was pregnant.'

There is silence for a moment, then Manfred continues:

'Well, I talked to the glazier. He replaced the glass in one of the basement windows on the west side of Jesper Orre's house two weeks ago. Orre told him he'd had a break-in, but nothing had been stolen. Beyond that the glazier had nothing interesting to say. Thought Orre seemed a bit pompous and stressed-out, but that's hardly illegal.'

From the corner of my eye, I see Hanne writing in the notebook she always carries with her. She seems to have become more diligent over the years; she takes notes constantly, as if she's anxious not to miss a single word of what's being said. It's a bit odd – when we were seeing each other ten years ago, I perceived her as more careless and unstructured. Bohemian, almost. She never wrote anything down, but she seemed to remember everything anyway.

Sanchez stands up. Tugs at her silk blouse.

'We got a call from the County Police, too. They're investigating the fire in Orre's garage. The crime is classified as second-degree arson, since the building was situated in a residential area. They confirmed the insurance company's assessment that the fire was arson. The National Lab found traces of petrol on site, and there were a number of burnt petrol cans in the garage. Apparently Orre was away on that particular evening. He was in Riga to meet some Baltic shop managers. So he couldn't have set the fire himself, if it was insurance money he was after.'

'He could have hired someone,' I suggest.

Sanchez nods and stretches so the silk blouse slips up again, exposing a flat, tattooed belly.

'Sure. But there's nothing to suggest that Orre needed the money. Plus there's new witness testimony from a neighbour who says she saw a woman standing on the street watching the fire. She couldn't describe what the woman looked like, but she was sure it was a woman and that she left while it was still burning.'

'A passer-by?' Manfred asks.

'It's possible. Or the person who set fire to Orre's garage. It's impossible to say at present. The only thing we know is that a woman stood there watching the garage burn for a while. Like it was a damn bonfire. Those were the neighbour's words.'

Emma

Three weeks earlier

'I have a doctor's appointment. I need to leave at four. I'm sorry, but I can't change it,' I say and make an effort to look anxious.

Mahnoor raises her well-plucked eyebrows and nods slowly, as if pondering what I've said.

'Sure. But you'll get a bad mark.' She nods towards the calendar.

'I know, but I still have to go.'

Olga, who is sitting at the table with a cup of tea, rolls her eyes.

Mahnoor turns instantly on her. 'I saw that.'

'Saw what?' Olga retorts and looks at her innocently: widens her pale-blue eyes and cocks her head to the side so her bleached hair falls over one shoulder.

'Stop it. I'm not stupid. I'd be a little more cooperative if I were you. You have . . .' Mahnoor turns to the calendar, sliding her finger slowly across the line with Olga's name on it, counting. 'Five bad marks this month,' she says contentedly, turns around and exits the staffroom without another word. Her steps fade away, blending with the familiar music pumping out of the speakers.

'What did she eat for breakfast?' Olga murmurs, biting her fingernail.

'Be careful,' I say. 'It's not the world's most fun job. But it's a job.'

She shrugs. 'So what? I could always work for Alexej's cleaning company if I want. He invariably needs help.'

'Do you want to clean ferries?'

Olga fidgets. 'Better than eating her shit with a knife and fork every day.'

'Come on. This is an OK job. Do you have any education? Any work experience besides this? Do you seriously think you could get another job tomorrow if you get fired from here?'

Olga slumps into the chair opposite me, suddenly looking older than she is. 'Well aren't you a little bitch?'

'Come on. I'm not being a bitch. I'm just trying to help you. I don't want you to lose your job just because Mahnoor has gone over to the dark side. It's not worth it. Try to be a little tactical instead. Ignore her when she says that kind of stuff. Move on, put it behind you. Don't be so proud.'

'Like you?'

Her voice is a whisper, but I sense the sharpness in it.

'What do I have to do with any of this?'

'Like you and that guy. The one you never stop going on and on about. Sometimes moving on is not so easy. But you know what? I don't want to hear more about you and that guy. It's not fun any more. Go and harass somebody else with your boring life.'

I'm speechless. Jesper has robbed me of my life. Just days ago, I lost my child and now this little Eastern European cunt says that it's not fun any more. How does she think it feels for me?

'It's not the same thing,' I say.

'You're obsessed with him. You do nothing but talk about him. Love ends – accept it. Get a hobby. Hang out with friends. Get a life.' Olga stands up. Stretches like a cat. 'I need a smoke.'

Then she disappears into the corridor without turning around.

It's four o'clock when I get to the car hire company. All the employees seem to be boys under the age of eighteen and members of the same basketball team. They're tall, lanky and beardless.

'I just need to hire a car for one day,' I explain to an assistant named Sean, according to his name tag, 'and I don't need a big car, just a spacious boot.'

'Maybe an estate car,' he suggests and runs his hand over his pimply chin.

'That's fine.'

I hand him my credit card and driving licence while he goes through the conditions. The car has to be returned by no later than 6 p.m. the next day. The fuel tank should be full and the keys should be posted through the letterbox. Do I have any questions?

I shake my head.

'Then have a pleasant trip.'

'Who said I was going on a trip?'

'Oh. OK. Well, drive carefully then.'

'I will,' I say and try to smile. 'Was it number six, you said?'

He nods without saying anything more, and when I leave the shop he has already started helping the next customer.

The paint shop is crowded with people.

'Terrible weather we're having,' says a fat lady wearing a Loden coat and holding a dachshund on a leash.

It strikes me that she looks a lot like the woman I met the other night, when Jesper was stalking me in the shadows around Karlaplan. Or maybe all the old ladies in this area have dachshunds? Loden coats, dachshunds and tweed hats. They all look like they live on some country estate, the lot of them.

I put my tins on the counter. My palms sting and my muscles are trembling from exertion. The man standing at the checkout looks incredulously at the tins. Then he looks at me again, as if he wants to make sure I'm not crazy.

'There are smaller containers,' he says hesitantly. 'We have one-litre bottles.'

'I want these. Thank you.'

He shrugs, decides it's my problem if I buy too much. The door to the shop opens again and the dachshund barks.

'OK then.'

He tips the tin to the side to scan the barcode and nods at me. 'How many are you buying?'

I look down at the floor where two tins sit between my feet. 'A total of four,' I say.

I drive carefully. The temperature's dropped to just below freezing, and I'm afraid that the shiny black road has become deceptively slippery. Strangely, it's not hard to find my way to the house again. It's as if my body remembers, as if every twist and turn in this exclusive suburb is imprinted on my spinal cord. I don't even need to think, just follow where my body takes me.

Big cars are parked on neat driveways. Palatial homes tower over manicured lawns. Then the houses start getting smaller again and I know I'm almost there.

I see his house in front of me in the dark. There are no lights on inside and no car parked outside. The piles of wood are still on the pavement next to the newly built garage.

I park a short distance away, careful not to get too close.

The tins are heavy and awkward to carry. I have to make two trips. On my way towards Jesper's gate I look around, but there are no signs of life. Though lights are on in the surrounding houses, I see no people.

I inspect the new building next to the gate. A real door has now replaced the gaping hole that was covered by plastic last time I was here, but the small window to the left of the entrance gapes open. I stand on my toes, bend forward and look inside. After a few seconds my eyes adjust. There are two cars in the garage – a small red sports car and an older-model Porsche. So you like vintage cars, I think. Another secret you never shared with me.

I back away from the window, open the lid of the first tin and pour the contents along one wall. After a bit the tin becomes lighter and easier to handle. I try to splash the liquid as high up on the wall as I can. Then I repeat the procedure with the remaining three tins. How much is needed? I couldn't exactly ask the guy at the paint shop for advice.

The work is heavy and I'm sweating under my thick jacket. A light rain has started to fall, small, soundless, almost imperceptible drops. Still, moisture soon starts to cover my face and hands.

When I'm finished, I push the empty tins, one by one, through the small window. They fall to the garage floor with a hollow sound. I step back, make sure I have the car keys ready. The last thing I want is to get stuck here, or to be forced to make a run for it without the car.

Then I take out the matches, lean forward in order to protect them from the rain and the wind, and light one.

The flame flickers in the darkness.

This is for the money you stole, you bastard.

That night I sleep better than I have in a long time, even though the smell of smoke has penetrated my skin and hair and won't wash out, even after showering twice. When I wake up, the image of those flames is burnt into my retinas. I remember how they lit up the late-autumn night, how the heat scorched my skin, even from a distance. It felt cleansing somehow. I don't know if it was the fire or the fact that I was taking back what was mine, something he'd robbed from me.

I get up, shower again, dress and eat some cornflakes while doing my hair and putting on my make-up. Maybe it's my imagination, but I think I look more alert somehow. Stronger. And maybe that's true; maybe the woman staring back at me from the mirror is someone else. Maybe yesterday changed me in some essential way.

Before I leave, I dig the journalist's business card out of the pile of bills in the bread bin and put it in my pocket. I decide it's time to call him.

On my way to the metro, I realise something else feels different. At first I can't quite put my finger on what, but then it comes to me. The sun is shining for the first time in weeks. I stop, close my eyes and turn my face to the sky. Soaking in heat and light. I stand like that until my skin is hot and my eyelids are glowing. Thinking life might not be so bad, after all.

For some reason the image of my father the night before he died pops into my mind. How he lay motionless on the bed in his dark room.

Outside, Mum paced back and forth worriedly. I couldn't understand why she, who seemed to hate Dad so much, would be so worried now that he was sick. It was as if she had only two states of mind, angry or worried, and that now she was very worried.

She'd spent most of the morning on the phone with various aunts. I had been working on my physics homework while listening to her long, whispered conversation about Dad's health. Words like 'totally passive' and 'lost the will to live' were interwoven with theatrical sobs and the usual talk about the lack of money and her boring job and egocentric boss. Everything culminated in the assertion that she deserved better, something that the aunts seemed to agree with, because there was never any argument after she said it.

I thought about what she meant by 'deserved better'. Was Mum dissatisfied with her life? Did she want another one? Another apartment, another husband? Another child, perhaps? And was that something you earned, which you were entitled to if you were a better person? Was Mum really better than Dad and me? And if I was so bad, what did I deserve?

I sat down gently on the bed beside Dad. The dim room smelled like sweat and cigarette smoke and something else, something that reminded me of old dandruff, and I realised I didn't have to worry that he'd notice I'd been sneaking cigarettes with Elin earlier.

I couldn't understand why he insisted on keeping the blinds down, why he wanted to be in the dark all day. The bed sagged when I sat down on it, even though I tried to be as careful and light as I could.

'Little Emma,' he mumbled and turned to me.

Then he took my hand in his. That was all. He didn't say anything else, just lay still, breathing heavily, as if every breath was painful. I thought for a moment about what might make Dad happier. Normally, I'd suggest that we do something together, maybe go for a walk or cook some food. But I sensed that wasn't going to work this time.

'Are you feeling better now?' I asked.

'Yes,' he said after a long, worrying pause. Even his voice sounded different. Hollow, toneless. As if it came from inside a can.

'Little Emma,' he repeated, and pressed my hand harder. 'I just want you to know how much I love you. You're a wonderful girl.'

I didn't know what to say. The situation made me uncomfortable. I wasn't used to seeing Dad so weak. He could be tired and indifferent or angry and disorderly or even drunk and reckless. But not weak. The man who had been my idol from the time I learned to walk wasn't weak. It was as simple as that.

'Please, Daddy—'

'Emma,' he interrupted me, 'remember that caterpillar you kept in a jar when you were small?'

'Yes?'

I wondered where he was heading with this.

'I'm so sorry I let Mum smash that jar. I knew how that night would end, and I did nothing to stop her.'

'Stop it – it was just a silly insect. And besides, that was a long time ago.'

'Yes, an "insect", that's what she called it. But it was more than just a butterfly. It was your special project that you'd been working on all summer. It was the only thing you cared about at that time, and despite that, or maybe because of that, she destroyed it. And I let it happen, so I'm just as guilty.'

I thought I heard a sob in the darkness, but wasn't sure.

'Do you remember how beautiful it was?' he continued. 'Remember its metamorphosis from an ordinary caterpillar to a beautiful butterfly? It was so blue it almost glowed. Do you remember?'

I nodded, although he couldn't see me in the dark. This conversation had given me a lump in my throat and I no longer trusted my voice to carry.

'I just want you to know ... you're just like that little caterpillar, Emma. One day you'll also turn into a beautiful butterfly. Never forget that. No matter what people say about you, you have to promise me that.'

'Oh, Dad.' I let out a giggle, the situation suddenly seemed so absurd. As if I were trapped in a melodrama. 'Stop talking like that. You're scaring me. OK?'

He didn't say anything. The only sound in the room was his laboured breathing.

'If someone says you're different, I want you to think about that butterfly. Different doesn't mean worse. Different can just as well mean better. Promise never to forget that.'

'Of course, but ...'

The lump in my throat grew. I'd never heard Dad talk like this before. This was something I wasn't prepared for. No special dinner or impromptu walk along the waterfront was going to fix this problem.

'I want you to be . . . like before,' I whispered, trying to avoid the word 'healthy', because that would mean he was sick now, and that just wasn't something we said to Dad, neither me nor Mum. We said it about him, but not to him.

'Everything's gone to shit for me,' he said with an unexpectedly cheerful voice, as if he'd made a joke. 'Complete shit.'

And those were the last words my father said before Mum found him hanging in the apartment the next day.

Hanne

Long before I became interested in behavioural science, I studied social anthropology. I ploughed through Franz Boas and Bronislaw Malinowski and dreamed about conducting a year-long field study of the Inuit in northern Greenland, perhaps because I watched that old documentary *Nanook of the North* as a child. But this was in the seventies, so in the wake of increasingly loud demands for a more activist anthropology, interest in picturesque indigenous peoples with no geopolitical importance decreased.

The Eskimos weren't 'in' any more.

Despite that, I've maintained my interest in anthropology. And perhaps this was why Owe occasionally brought back small presents from indigenous people after his travels.

Or so I thought.

After a medical conference in Miami in the eighties, he gave me a braided mesh mask made by the Huichol people in western Mexico. Another time, when he'd been at a psychiatry conference in South Africa, he gave me an antique tobacco pouch from the Xhosa people. And so on. In the end, almost the entire bookshelf was full of Owe's souvenirs.

It must have taken me ten years to realise those gifts were compensation for something else altogether. I don't really remember how I caught him. Maybe the phone rang in the middle of the night now and then, and there was only silence on the other end when I answered. Maybe a letter arrived with the word 'Private' written on it. But mostly it was due to Evelyn.

Evelyn, an American in her forties, was Owe's therapist, which in and of itself wasn't remarkable. In our social circles everyone had at least one therapist. Visiting your psychoanalyst several times a week was considered perfectly normal. I think it was even a bit of a status symbol. So Owe spent a considerable amount of his free time talking about his childhood on Evelyn's chaise longue.

I remember he often seemed exhausted when he got home. Sweaty, absent-minded and with a glazed look in his eyes, he'd sink down on the sofa in the living room and demand to be left alone. On those occasions, I was always a little extra-loving towards him, because I assumed he'd been discussing some difficult topic. His father's illness maybe, or his mother's partiality for painkillers and tranquillisers. But one December evening, when we'd been married for about ten years, I caught him. I remember that I'd woken up because I was cold. The radiators weren't working so well at the time, and the duvet had slipped off. I realised Owe wasn't lying next to me and went out into the hall to see what he was doing. I could hear a whispered conversation in the kitchen, and I stayed silent and crept closer without giving myself away.

He was speaking English. And it wasn't about work. It didn't take me long to figure out it was Evelyn on the phone and that their relationship wasn't at all what I'd been led to believe.

I considered rushing into the kitchen and ripping the phone from his ear, slapping him, or maybe throwing something to the floor, but instead I turned around and went back to the bedroom and pulled the duvet over my head, filled with an intense, inexpressible contempt. Because contempt is what I felt, not sadness or anger or jealousy. I couldn't respect his disgusting hypocrisy – the fact that he never told me about Evelyn or any of the others, yet constantly reproached me for my indiscretions.

Because yes, I'd been unfaithful as well. More than once. And especially in the beginning of our relationship. But it was another time then – people had 'open' relationships and practised polygamy and God knows what else, and I never lied or hid my affairs. Now and then I ended up in bed with another man after some boozy party, and Owe's reaction was always the same: he took me home – carried me if need be – and talked some sense into me. Treated me like I was a child who'd missed her curfew or perhaps got caught shoplifting. And it put me at a moral disadvantage – which he'd used, I now realised, to sleep with Evelyn three times a week on her therapist's couch.

I think that was when I started to hate him.

When I met Peter, I felt that there was no reason to deny myself real love. Why should I? Owe had allowed himself to fall in love with that American bitch.

In a way, it felt like a rebellion to initiate a relationship with a man like Peter. He wasn't an intellectual; he lived in a tiny apartment in the suburbs and he loved watching sport. In short, he was the kind of man our friends would refer to, with slight condescension, as an average guy. Someone whose dreams didn't go beyond his next holiday or a new car and who thought Chekhov was a brand of vodka.

I never really learned that much about Peter's background. He told me his mother had been politically active and engaged in the anti-war movement, that he used to go with her to meetings and demonstrations as a child. On those occasions I would think he very well could have been brought up among my friends. But despite his background, he wasn't at all interested in politics. I suppose that happens often – we deliberately choose a different life from the one our parents lived.

In any case, Owe's inflated self-esteem took a severe blow when he realised I was seriously considering leaving him – even after Peter left me to my fate on the pavement on Skeppargatan that night.

But all my frustrations with Owe, which culminated that night, eventually turned to resignation and a kind of passivity. Falling in love again, learning to trust another man the way I did Peter – only to be let down again – seemed unthinkable.

So I stayed, for lack of any better alternatives. That's the way life works. And now he's crept into my life again.

Peter.

The only man who's meant anything to me in the last fifteen years. A haggard policeman with low self-esteem and a pathological fear of commitment. Just a few hours ago he was lying in bed next to me. On me. In me. And all I can think about is when I'll see him again.

Maybe I'm turning into Gunilla, I think, and remember her words.

We're so incredibly . . . attracted to each other. Horny, to be vulgar about it. Is that allowed, at our age?

Starting our relationship again is, of course, out of the question. Not only because I'm afraid of being left again, but also because I'm sliding into an incurable disease. A dark tunnel of oblivion and decay. It feels as if I'm an explorer about to enter a mountain through a crack, and I know it will only get narrower and narrower, until I'm firmly inside the bedrock with no way of getting myself out.

And in there, not even Peter could help me.

When I arrive at the police station, his colleagues are sorting through tip-offs received about the drawing of the dead woman. I look through the pictures of the girls, hoping that none is identical to the victim in Orre's house. But whether one of these particular pictures does or doesn't match up, eventually one will, of course. There's no way to escape that. Someone is lying in a refrigerated compartment waiting to get her name and history back. Albeit posthumously.

I avoid looking at Peter. Not because I regret what happened last night, but just because I don't really know what to say or do. It's been a long time since I found myself in a situation like this. Like a teenager. *So, we had, like, sex yesterday, but I don't really know if he 'likes me' likes me or if we'll do it again, or whatever.*

It's actually laughable. Maybe the funniest thing that's happened to me in years.

How long has it been since I had sex, anyway? I don't know exactly – maybe five years?

I remember I used to tell Owe I had a headache. Not because it was a good excuse, but because it was such a terrible excuse that it would make it clear to him that I didn't want to sleep with him any more.

And it did.

Eventually he stopped touching me that way at all. Just went quietly to bed every evening and turned off the light without even giving me a kiss. I knew it was meant as a punishment. But it suited me just fine. I was tired of him, even though I never seriously considered trying to leave him again.

And then came the disease. It started with forgetting names. It could be the name of a friend we'd socialised with for years. Or – even more common – the name of a place.

Sundsvall, Soderhamn, Sollefteå. Örebro, Örkelljunga, Örgryte. Arboga, Abisko, Arvika.

Who the hell can keep track of all of that? If it had stopped there, I doubt Owe would have noticed anything. But then I started missing appointments, forgetting to call friends back like I promised, and losing my credit card and my mobile.

One day I forgot Frida outside the supermarket and when I got home, I couldn't remember where I'd left her. I called Owe in a panic. A week later he forced me to go to the doctor, who wrote me a referral to a memory clinic.

The memory clinic.

I linger on the words. It sounds so poetic and absurd at the same time. Like a play by Kristina Lugn or a book by Kurt Vonnegut.

Not that it was particularly poetic or absurd at the clinic itself. It was mostly just a lot of tests and questions, and after a few months the doctors came to the conclusion that I have emergent dementia, but what form they couldn't say. Nor how quickly it would develop or whether or not the pills could help me.

I look at my colleagues sitting at their desks. I wonder what they'd think if they knew that they have a colleague with 'mild cognitive impairment'. That the experienced behaviourist who charges nine hundred kronor per hour to consult is slipping into the great oblivion. In a few months I may not be able to distinguish a banana from a baton.

Manfred comes over to me. He's as stylish as usual, like a peacock, and he squats down beside my chair.

'Good fucking work on those matches,' he says.

'Thanks.'

'So do you think the murderer and the victims knew each other?'

'Based on the mode of killing, yes. I think they had some kind of relationship, and that the murderer was seeking revenge on the victims. Punishing them.'

'And if you had to guess, what kind of relationship did they have?'

'Strong emotions must have been involved. On the other side of that hatred there must have been something else. Something equally strong. Hate doesn't occur in a vacuum.'

'Like what?'

I think for a moment. 'Love, for example.'

At lunch, I get a text message from Owe. He writes that he wants to apologise for his behaviour and his threats. That he's doing well, that he loves me, and that he doesn't think he can live without me.

That's surely true. But I don't respond. Instead I buy a salad and sit down in the conference room with Sanchez and Manfred, who are about to brief the investigators in sorting through tip-offs. It's not really that important for me to be here. I could go home to Gunilla's apartment and read a book on the sofa instead, but I don't want to.

A younger investigator, Simone, who has dreadlocks down to her waist, cocks her head to one side and says:

'We can remove Wilhelmina Andrén from the investigation, the woman who escaped from the psychiatric ward at Danderyd

Hospital. A dog owner found her frozen to death near the sound in Solna this morning. Her parents have identified her, so there's no doubt about who she is.'

'Poor thing,' Manfred mumbles and strokes his red stubble. Simone nods and continues:

'So that leaves Angelica Wennerlind and Emma Bohman. Dental records have been sent to Solna, and we should get our answers no later than tomorrow.'

'I thought we'd hear back tonight,' Manfred says.

'The forensic dentist is in Skövde and needs a few hours to get here,' Simone says.

At that moment the door opens and Peter walks in. His cheeks are red and he has snow on his new leather jacket. He doesn't bother to take it off or sit down. Instead, he points to Manfred and me.

'Come with me. We have a colleague here who says she met Emma Bohman two weeks ago. Apparently she and Jesper Orre did have a relationship.'

Emma

Three weeks earlier

'I have to pay some bills. Can I borrow the computer in the office for a bit?'

Mahnoor shrugs her shoulders, puts a little lipgloss on her index finger. She's going with the baggy look today. Her jeans hang dangerously low on her hips, exposing the edge of her lace knickers.

'Sure.'

I'm surprised she doesn't object. I have several more excuses ready to explain why I need to do this right now, when we're just about to open. But Mahnoor just smiles sweetly and disappears into the shop. I hear her and Olga talking in the distance; it sounds as if they're laughing, and it makes me stop and think.

It feels different. Everything feels different. The shop seems brighter. Olga and Mahnoor are in a better mood. It's even sunny outside. But nothing has really changed, except that I have taken back the power over my own life again.

Maybe that was all I needed?

It's easier than I expected to find what I'm looking for online, though I have to spend a little time researching. I have no idea which model is best or how many volts I need. After twenty minutes I order the small device that looks like a mobile. The website promises delivery within twenty-four hours, but as long as it arrives within three days, it's fine by me. Then I take the business card out of my jeans pocket.

Anders Jönsson, freelance journalist.

Before I call, I go over to the door, crack it open and peek out into the shop. Olga is helping a customer at the till, and Mahnoor is folding jeans, swaying a little in time to the music.

Anders Jönsson answers after the third ring. At first he doesn't seem to remember me, so I explain: that he found me in the shop, that I didn't want to talk to him then, but I would be willing to now. He's silent for a moment. Then excitedly says he'd love to meet me. As soon as possible. Maybe even today?

So easy, I think. That was so easy.

Summer was exploding in shades of green outside the windows of the hallway we were walking down. The echo of our steps bounced like ping-pong balls between the concrete walls. I did my best to keep up with him, but he was walking so fast. Hurrying towards the entrance where the sun streamed down through the large glass doors, making the dirt-brown floors glow.

'You know we can't see each other, Emma. You understand that, right?'

He turned to me and we stood there, outside the physics class-room. The drab walls seemed to be getting closer, as if the hallway were narrowing, and I started having trouble breathing. The ceiling was tilting ominously. It was white, with black stains here and there.

Woody put his hand on my forearm. Patted it gently, which once again made me feel like a little child. Didn't he understand how that felt, how demeaning and destructive his gesture was?

My cheeks turned hot. From shame, but also from something else. Rage. He'd taken advantage of me, played with me. Sucked and licked and penetrated and kissed and caressed and all the rest. But then he didn't want me any more. Then he was finished with me. He had taken what he wanted and that was enough for him.

And here I was.

'What do you mean, "can't" see each other?' I said and regretted it immediately, because the last thing I wanted was for him to see me as a clingy little kid.

He looked at me blankly, took a step backwards as if he'd suddenly discovered I smelled bad.

'You had no problem with it before,' I added.

'I don't understand,' he said, as the bell rang and all the doors opened into the hallway. And he looked genuinely worried, he really did.

Students poured out of classrooms, rushing past us, a river of teenage flesh, but his gaze stayed firmly on me.

'I want to help you, Emma, but not in that way.'

And at that moment I fell apart.

The corridor collapsed around me and the stained ceiling cracked. I died. In a cloud of concrete dust I'd ceased to exist. My body was crushed. The pain clawed and pounded in every cell. My atoms were torn asunder, annihilated, had disappeared. The only thing that remained was the pulsating pain and shame.

On Lützengatan I trudge through drifts of yellow maple leaves. It feels like walking through deep snow. The scent of decomposing vegetation tingles inside my nostrils. A gust of wind catches a few leaves, which swirl above me like swallows. I stop in the middle of the street with my eyes on the leaves, as if hypnotised by the scene.

I'd forgotten that life could be so beautiful. So perfect.

He's standing outside the bakery on Valhallavägen, just as he promised. I recognise him immediately. He's wearing the same old parka. The wind flutters his thin yellow hair above his head so comically that I have to force myself not to stare. We greet each other and enter into the warmth. It's as cramped and dark as usual. There are a few seats along the wall and we settle in, each with a coffee and cardamom bun.

'So, how are things at work?'

He makes the question sound innocent. As if we're two old friends grabbing a coffee together, talking about what we've been up to for the past few months.

'It's OK.'

'Really?'

He raises his pale eyebrows. Looks surprised. But I've decided not to tell him I got fired. It would smack of revenge – which it is.

Your job for my job, Jesper.

'Oh well, you know how it is for us.'

He nods, swallowing half the cardamom bun in one bite. 'It's awful.' He stresses every syllable, as if to emphasise just how horrible he thinks it is.

'Umm-hmm.'

'How do you handle it?'

'It's a job. And I need the money.'

'Long live capitalism,' he mumbles, his expression suddenly bitter.

'I have no choice.'

He nods slowly. 'I understand. That's why it's so brave of you to come here today. What was it you wanted to tell me?'

He seems very curious suddenly. The troubled expression is gone. I lower my voice and lean over the small table, so that the woman behind the counter doesn't hear me.

'Jesper Orre. I know things about him.'

'I'm listening,' he says and leans in closer, so close I see the sugar granules in the corners of his mouth and smell the coffee on his breath.

I try to look worried, shrink a little on my chair. 'But it doesn't really feel right telling you all this.' He widens his pale eyes, touches my arm lightly.

'Your loyalty is admirable, but you have to think about your colleagues now. You have to think about them, because he won't. The only thing Jesper Orre cares about is money. He doesn't give a damn about any of you. Never forget that. Jesper Orre doesn't give a shit about you, Emma.'

I sigh. Nod slowly. He doesn't know how right he is.

'OK. I'll tell you. Everyone's talking about it anyway. His house burnt down yesterday, or maybe it was his garage. And apparently the police think he started it himself.'

There's a twitch in the corner of his eye as he leans closer towards me. Something has sprung to life in his gaze. He's very animated now, seems to have forgotten about his bun. He's placed it back on his plate and pushed it aside. He still has his hand on my forearm and I gently twist out of his grip.

'Sorry,' he mumbles when he realises that he's been holding on to me. 'Do you know why he did it?'

I shrug and look at him with what I hope is an innocent expression. 'No clue. But the garage was apparently full of expensive cars.'

'So an insurance thing, then?'

I shake my head slowly. 'I don't know. It sounds a little weird that he would have done it himself. Especially if he had his cars in there.'

He smiles indulgently, and I realise he's buying my naive act – hook, line and sinker. 'Do you know if anyone can confirm this?'

'No, but the police surely know about the fire.'

He nods silently.

'Emma, this is important. If you know anything else about Jesper you should tell me now.'

'What do you mean?'

'Like, does he have any other problems?'

I try to look like I'm thinking hard, searching every corner of my memory. Then I nod. 'Well, maybe the investigation.'

'The investigation?'

'Yeah, C&M's finance department is investigating him.'

'Do you know why?'

I tilt my head to one side. Widen my eyes and twist a long strand of hair between my fingers.

'They say he let the company pay for his private birthday party. But that's probably just BS. I mean, he could surely afford to pay for it himself?'

I treat myself to wine and takeaway pizza that night. Light the candles – the same candles I lit for our engagement dinner. I put on music, too, and suddenly everything feels easier. More manageable, maybe. I have a clear mission now: seeking justice. Like I've become a kind of instrument. There's something liberating about that. Surrendering to something larger and more important than yourself is liberating. To live for only one thing means you no longer have to make decisions – the road ahead is already mapped out.

I can't drink too much, I think. Can't risk being hungover, slow and stupid. Not now. Every hour, every minute, even every second is important if I'm going to be able to carry through on what I need to do.

Discipline. Restraint. Self-control.

Justice.

I press the cork back into the wine bottle after the second glass. Lean over the kitchen sink and drink cold water from the tap. My hair falls down into the sink. It glistens under the overhead light. What beautiful hair I have, I think.

I go into the bathroom. Meet my reflection and almost lose my breath. My hair glows; my skin is so pale it almost shimmers. And I see it: I'm beautiful. I am truly beautiful. Why have I always thought I was chubby and boring and childish when I looked at myself in the mirror? Why have I never seen myself clearly? It didn't matter how many times Jesper said it to me, I never believed him. But now I can see it for myself.

I'm strong. Beautiful. And I don't need anyone. Not even Jesper. Especially not Jesper.

The metro is running late, but I barely notice. Instead I sit on the platform with my nose buried in a newspaper, tracing the text with my index finger, as if afraid to miss a single word. 'Controversial CEO Suspected of Arson and Breach of Faith', I read. The story describes a number of abuses that the journalist believes have been committed by Orre and discovered by the company. 'The controversy surrounding the fashion king intensifies,' he writes, before concluding the article by speculating on how long the shareholders and board will allow Jesper Orre to remain in charge. A graph next to the text shows how the company's stock prices have plummeted in recent months. At the bottom of the story is a small picture of the man I met yesterday – the journalist with the crumbs around his mouth who listened so intently to my story.

It was almost too easy, I think. He ate it up, wanting so desperately to believe every word I said. Or?

Cosmic balance?

Maybe there is some kind of higher power at work after all.

As I cross the square, my steps grow lighter. An almost warm breeze caresses my hair. The clouds chase one another above my head, and between them I catch glimpses of blue. Outside the shop, the bums are already in place, sharing the day's first bottle of something strong. When I look at them, I see people who never took control of their lives, who surrendered to their fate rather than standing up and fighting back. If I hadn't taken my revenge on Jesper, I might have become one of them: downtrodden, crushed. A human wreck with no goals or purpose, swirling as aimlessly as leaves in the wind.

Olga is standing outside smoking. There's something odd about her posture, the way she moves her cigarette to and from her mouth. Something jerky and stiff. She looks nervous. Also, she almost never smokes outside the entrance; she always goes to the back room. According to the manual from head office, we're not allowed to stand outside the shop smoking. Apparently it looks bad.

When she sees me, she waves her arms over her head as if she's been waiting for me. She flicks away her cigarette and the wind catches it immediately, carrying it past the vodka-drinking men in their ratty jackets and towards the broken fountain in the centre of the square.

'Hello,' I say.

'The police are here,' she stage-whispers to me as her light-blue eyes widen. A gust of wind catches her thin hair, exposing the dark roots.

'The police?'

'They want to talk to you.'

'Me?'

'Yes. You.'

'About what?'

'No clue. I thought you knew.'

I shrug, trying to look unconcerned, but as I enter the shop my pulse starts to race and a drop of sweat slides down between my shoulder blades. I can feel Olga's eyes burning into my back. It wasn't nervousness that made her stand outside waiting for me, I realise now, but impatient curiosity.

They're standing with Mahnoor at the till. A man and woman in their forties, wearing normal clothes. They could be customers, that's how normal they look. The man is short, stocky, with close-cropped, greying blonde hair. He's haggard in a handsome way. Like a villain in an action movie. The woman is tall, thin and stooped over. Her hair is ash blonde, ratty and long. It lifts from her shoulders as she turns and examines me with a critical eye.

'Emma Bohman?' she says and extends a bony hand that squeezes mine with surprising strength. 'My name is Helena Berg and I'm with the police. We'd like to talk to you.'

Her colleague has crept up on my left side without me noticing it.

'Johnny Lappalainen,' he says. Then silence. Nothing else. No title, no further explanation.

Behind Johnny's shoulder I glimpse Mahnoor. Her eyes are big and black and I can see she's curious as to what this is all about. I shake my head slowly at her: no, I don't know what they want.

'We'd like you to come with us down to the police station for questioning,' the skinny woman says, looking at me with an expressionless stare. I've already forgotten her name. There's no room for her name in my consciousness right now; every nook and cranny is occupied. I desperately try to sort out the events of this last week. To go through every critical moment. Did someone see me outside Jesper's garage that night? Could the man in the paint shop have contacted the police? Did Olga say something? But she doesn't know what I've done. She only knows what Jesper did to me. Hardly that even, because I didn't tell her everything.

'Do I have to?' I ask.

'Yes,' says the man abruptly, 'but it won't take long.'

I look at Mahnoor again. She says nothing, but nods to me as if she's anxious for me to do what they say.

The policewoman with straggly hair sits opposite me in a small white room with white furniture. There's a laptop on the table between us, but nothing else. Up close, she looks older. Deep lines run from the corners of her mouth down to her chin, and there are streaks of grey at the roots of her hair.

The man sits silently beside her. He strokes his short hair, as if wanting to ensure that every sparse strand is in place, and stares out the window. I follow his gaze. A pale late-autumn sun shines down onto the square and the empty fountain. Dead leaves fly around in the small whirlwinds over the pavement.

'Do you recognise this?' the policewoman asks, opening a brown envelope. Something falls onto the white table with a bang: a tiny plastic bag with a small object that looks like a metal button. I pick up the bag, weighing it in my hand, and open it.

It's the ring.

My engagement ring.

'Yes,' I say. 'This is my engagement ring.'

'Are you sure?' the man asks.

I nod.

'Pretty sure. We never engraved it, but it looks like my ring, yes.'

'When did you see it last?' he asks and leans back until the chair makes a squeaking sound, as if protesting against his weight.

'When I left it at the pawnshop on Storgatan. I needed the money.' The man and woman opposite me exchange a quick glance.

'When and where did you buy it?' asks the woman, leaning over the table.

'It's an engagement ring, like I said. I didn't buy it, it was given to me.'

'OK, just so we understand. When and where did you get it? And from whom?'

I sigh. I don't understand what they're getting it. I look through the window, suddenly wishing I was sitting on that park bench outside in a dirty padded jacket with a bottle of alcohol in my hand. Like the bums outside the shop this morning. Anything would be better than this.

'I got it from my boyfriend, or fiancé. Two weeks ago. But then he broke up with me. I needed the money, so I left it at the pawnshop. That's not illegal, is it?'

The man shakes his head. 'Of course not. But this ring was stolen from a jewellery shop on Linnégatan just over two weeks ago. Do you know anything about that?'

'Stolen?'

'Yes. It was stolen from the shop. Pawnbrokers check every object they acquire against our list of stolen goods, so the ring was identified pretty quickly. And the pawnshop had your personal information. So now here we are.'

A cold sensation starts to spread through my body. It creeps up from my feet, to my chest and then to my head, until my whole body is in its iron grip. Did Jesper steal the ring? And if so, why? Did he simply not want to spend money on me, or is this also part of some sort of sick plan I couldn't foresee?

The woman leans over the table, fixing me with her eyes, and looks even more forbidding than before. I can see tiny, tiny hairs on her upper lip. I want to tell her to back off, don't get any closer. Every inch that she moves closer to me, the lump in my stomach grows. The whole situation is too close to the bone for me. I need distance. Space. I can't take this intrusive closeness.

'We think you stole the ring from the shop, Emma.'

I can't answer. My mouth is so dry, like it's full of sand. My tongue grates against the roof of my mouth. All I can do is shake my head. The man with the Finnish last name sighs deeply. I guess he's heard every excuse imaginable in his career. He doesn't believe me, I think. Neither of them believes me.

'Emma. Look at this.'

He turns the computer standing between us on the table towards me, and I see a grainy black-and-white picture. At first I don't know what it's from, but then I recognise the interior of the jewellery shop. Small white text in the right-hand corner displays the date and time. The policewoman presses play, and the image comes to life. A female assistant is talking while standing with her back to the camera. Her movements are jerky as she gestures and lifts up a small box. Then she points to a table with two chairs and sits down at one of them with her back to the camera. The other person, the customer, follows her, sits down on the other chair and takes off her gloves and hat.

It's me. The customer is me.

The woman sitting opposite the assistant is me.

Then the one that's me touches the rings. Tries them on one after the other. I seem to smile, as if I'm enjoying the situation.

'I'm trying on rings,' I say. 'Jesper and I are trying rings.'

'We see that,' the man replies. 'But from what I can see, you're the only one in the shop.'

I don't understand. It doesn't make sense. 'Wait, stop,' I say.

He shrugs. Stops the video. 'We've looked at this several times.'

'Rewind a few seconds.'

He does as I say and starts the video again. 'There,' I say. 'Stop.'

Behind me I see a grainy shadow moving towards the centre of the picture. 'There he is,' I say. 'That's him.'

The police officers look at each other. Exchange a long, expressionless stare. When the woman begins to speak, I sense weariness in her voice.

'You claim there was someone else with you at the shop?'

'Of course. You don't try on engagement rings by yourself.'

'And this other person was . . . ?'

'Jesper Orre. My fiancé.'

'The Jesper Orre?'

'Yes. The Jesper Orre.'

Peter

Hanne and Manfred follow me into the small conference room and say hello to a female police officer. She introduces herself as Helena Berg and tells them she works at the Östermalm police station. There's something vaguely familiar about her skinny body, her sharp features and her thin light-brown hair. I wonder if we might have met before, but she doesn't seem to recognise me.

I sometimes think there must be something about the way I look that makes people fail to notice me. Maybe I'm just too ordinary to make an impression on the people I meet. One of those guys you sit opposite on the bus for a week without remembering. Not like Manfred who everyone in the building knows, which I guess is exactly why he dresses the way he does.

Hanne and Manfred sit down next to Helena, and I sit opposite. I glance at Hanne. She looks just the same as always: calm and collected, with a notepad in her lap. Her facial expression is impassive. No trace of yesterday's intimacy is left – she could be a fellow passenger on the bus, one of those who doesn't see me.

Janet did that sometimes – ignored me, as if I weren't there. Mostly when she wanted to punish me for something, like forgetting her birthday or not wanting to spend the whole weekend going to look at houses.

But Hanne's not Janet.

In fact, Janet and Hanne are just about as different as two people can be. There's really no reason to compare Hanne's behaviour with Janet's. At least not if I actually want to understand what Hanne is thinking.

I turn towards Helena, who's here to tell us about her meeting with Emma Bohman.

'Thanks for coming,' I say.

She shrugs her shoulders and smiles wryly.

'Of course. I just wish I'd put two and two together earlier. But you know how it is – we meet so many people. So many nutcases . . .'

I nod. The others at this table know exactly what it's like to be a community police officer – we've all been there. Except Hanne.

'Go ahead and tell them yourself,' I say. 'Hanne and Manfred are participating in the investigation, and they haven't heard anything about your interview with Emma Bohman.'

'OK,' Helena begins; she nods thoughtfully and says, 'A little more than two weeks ago, we were contacted by a pawnshop in central Stockholm. Someone had brought in a pretty valuable diamond ring. An engagement ring. And when they checked it against our catalogue of stolen items, they discovered the ring was taken from a jewellery shop on Linnégatan a few weeks earlier. The ring had been left at the pawnshop by an Emma Bohman, who lives on Värtavägen, which is right next to Karlaplan and the jewellery shop. My colleague Johnny Lappalainen and I interrogated Emma Bohman two weeks ago, and during our interrogation we also showed her a surveillance tape that places her at the jewellery shop at the time of the theft.'

'And what did she say to that?' I ask.

'She said she'd been in the shop, but she wasn't there alone. According to her, she visited the shop with her boyfriend, Jesper Orre, to look at engagement rings. And then she said that she'd neither stolen nor bought the ring – Orre had given it to her later.'

'Could she prove it?'

Helena shrugs slightly. 'Not really. She pointed out a glimpse of someone else on the surveillance video and said it was Orre. But it was impossible to determine whether or not that was true. The film was poor quality and the person she pointed out could only be seen on the edge of the image. Anyway, we contacted Orre by phone to check her details, and he said he'd never heard of her and certainly hadn't bought a ring for her. He told us weirdos accuse him of things all the time, and said he was so tired of being a public figure. And so . . . I guess that was all. Our workload is heavy, so the investigation hasn't progressed any further. But when I saw the pictures of the murdered girl on TV and heard Orre was missing, I thought I'd better contact you. I've emailed you the interrogation report and surveillance video, in case you want to see them.'

I take out the drawing of the dead woman. Put it on the table and flatten it with my hand.

'So you've seen this?'

'Absolutely,' she says, frowning. 'Hard to avoid. Is it true that she was decapitated?'

I nod.

'Jesus. There are some sick people out there. Yes. I've seen the picture, and I don't think that they look much alike. If I remember correctly, Emma Bohman had longer hair. But who knows, maybe she cut it?'

After we escort Helena Berg out, we sit back down at the table. Sanchez is excited in that way she gets whenever an investigation takes a major leap forward. She drums her fingers on the table and asks:

'So, what do you think?'

Manfred clears his throat and takes off his glasses.

'The logical conclusion is of course that Jesper Orre had a relationship with Emma Bohman that he didn't want to admit to, right? It's conceivable that she visited him in his home, maybe to confront him, and that he killed her and fled.'

Hanne leans forward and meets Manfred's gaze. 'But what about the other guy?'

'What other guy?'

Hanne suddenly looks confused and her cheeks turn red.

'The guy who was killed . . . ten years ago. Surely that's how it was? I don't remember . . . What was his name again? The Chinese guy.'

'Chinese?' Sanchez asks.

'Yes, you know. The one . . . the other one without a head.'

'Do you mean Calderón?' Sanchez says.

Hanne exhales, but is clearly embarrassed. Tugs at her hair with one hand and blinks quickly, as if near tears.

'Exactly. Calderón.'

'He wasn't Chinese. He was Chilean.'

'Sorry, I misspoke. But why would Jesper Orre murder and decapitate him?'

'We don't know,' Manfred says. 'Not yet. But if we root around long enough in Orre's past, there has to be a connection somewhere.'

I turn towards Sanchez and decide to take advantage of all her puppy-like energy. I recognise it well from my early years as a police officer, though I haven't felt it myself in years. 'Emma Bohman's parents are both dead,' I say. 'But her aunt reported her missing. Can you get hold of her and see if she knows anything about Emma's relationship with Orre? And talk to her colleagues at Clothes&More, too. We don't know how close she was to her aunt.'

Sanchez nods and departs, with Manfred in tow. Leaving me alone with Hanne. 'Shall we take a walk?' I say.

We traipse through the snow along the square, towards the water. The wind sneaks in under my thin jacket and the newly fallen snow creeps up along my ankles, a cold reminder of the winter boots I still haven't bought. Hanne walks beside me, a silent shadow in shapeless coat and heavy boots. At the water, we take the left towards City Hall. The snow whirls over the bay, covering the water with a white haze, blurring the outlines of the buildings on Södermalm.

'Are you OK?' I ask.

Hanne turns her head towards me, looks at me with an inscrutable gaze. 'Why wouldn't I be?'

There's something reserved in her voice, as if she's eager to highlight a distance from me.

'I was thinking about what . . . happened yesterday.'

She stops, turns her back to the wind and pulls up her hood. Looks at me with a sad expression. Snowflakes melt on her cheek and I want to stretch out my hand, wipe them away, but I know I'm not allowed. She hasn't given me permission to do such a thing.

'What happened yesterday . . .' she begins. 'It was nice. I liked it. But I have to be completely honest with you, Peter. There can never be anything between us again. Not really. Maybe we can see each other again if you want, but we can never be together. Do you understand?'

For some reason her words make me feel desperately disappointed. Even though I can't really say why. I mean, what did I expect? That we'd be a couple again after one night together? That what I did ten years ago could be forgiven and forgotten?

'May I ask why?'

She turns and starts walking towards the pier. Stops and looks out over the water. I follow and stand beside her. Big black birds circle above us. Maybe some kind of jackdaw or crow.

'Do you think they're freezing?' she asks.

'I bet they're cold as hell,' I say.

'I'm ill,' she says and turns to me. 'For real. And I can't make that your problem. It wouldn't be right.'

When she says she's ill, I think of my mother. How she sat on the terrace smoking in one of the old garden chairs with a thick jumper on, despite the heat, and a silk scarf wrapped tightly around her head.

Something inside me softens at the memory of that thin woman who was my mother, or what remained of her anyway. And the scents return: soap, cigarette smoke and the other. The smell of the disease: disinfectant and open wounds. A smell I know well. Hospital corridors, dirty sheets, boiled potatoes and sweaty cheese sandwiches wrapped in plastic.

The smell of institutions.

'Do you have cancer?' I ask.

I don't know why, it just slips out of me.

Hanne laughs. 'No,' she says. 'Why would you think I have cancer?'

'I don't know. A lot of people . . . get it.'

She doesn't comment on my strange statement. Instead she looks quizzically at me with a smile in the corner of her mouth.

I think about Janet again. A few years ago she was convinced she had a tumour in her breast. Called me crying and begging me to take care of Albin if she died. I wasn't even worried. The thought of the mother of my child fighting a life-threatening disease left me completely unmoved.

I wonder what that says about me.

'So what is it?' I ask.

'I don't want to talk about it,' Hanne says and turns around. Disappears into the snowstorm towards the police station with steps so deliberate that I don't dare follow her.

Just as I'm about to return there myself, the phone rings. It's Janet. Her voice is even more forced than usual, and I can tell immediately that something has happened.

'You have to talk to Albin,' she says on an inhalation.

I walk towards a covered entrance to get out of the wind. 'About what?'

'About . . . He's started skipping school. And he's hanging out with that awful gang in Skogås. You know, the ones I told you about.'

I step into the entranceway where I'm protected from snow, and warm one hand against my neck. My fingers feel like icicles.

'OK. He's hanging out in Skogås. And why should I talk to him about it?'

I hear how I sound and regret it immediately. It's not my intention to put her down, but it's always like this. Janet calls me as soon as there's a problem with Albin. Even though we decided long before he was born that she'd bring him up by herself. Since she had him against my wishes.

'Because you're a police officer. You know things. About drugs and that kind of stuff. And you know what happens to boys who flip out. And because . . . you're his father,' she adds quickly and almost silently, as if she's uttered a forbidden word.

I look out into the snow. Trying to figure out how to make her understand without being rude. Wondering what argument might stop her nagging.

'I'm sure he's fine,' I say, perhaps a little too feebly.

'It is not fine,' she shouts. 'It's always like this. You won't take any responsibility for Albin. You never help me. Even when I beg you to. Do you have any idea how fucking hard it is for me to ask you for something like this? Do you know how long I hesitated before I picked up the phone and dialled your fucking number? Do you understand?'

I squirm. I decide this is probably not the right time to remind her of our agreement, which we entered into more than fifteen years ago.

'OK,' I say, and warm my other hand on my neck.

'Good. When?'

'What do you mean, "when"? Not today, anyway. I'm in the middle of a murder investigation.'

'Tomorrow, then?'

'Tomorrow . . . no. I don't have time tomorrow. Maybe next week.'

'You know what, Peter? This is so fucking typical. I don't even know why I called you. You can take your fucking job and go to hell, because Albin and I never want to see you again. You hear me? Go to hell!'

I stand there for a long time, watching the snow fall. Looking at those black birds flying above me. Thinking about my mother and sister resting in the Woodland Cemetery, wondering if they're cold lying six feet under the ground. I think about how fucking unfair it is to lose Hanne when I've finally got her back. Then I remind myself: I haven't got her back. But somehow it still feels that way.

Then I remember all that I've lost, even those who are still alive, like Albin and Janet. Everyone I've pushed away, lied to or run from. And when I consider that for a moment, I realise I deserve this. This is probably a fair punishment – Hanne will never be mine.

Emma

Two weeks earlier

It's absurd. I've never even shoplifted a chocolate bar, and here I am being accused of stealing an expensive piece of jewellery. I'm sitting in one of my green armchairs with my feet up on the table. And suddenly I realise how much I miss Sigge. True, he was just a cat, but he was my companion, and somehow his presence transformed this apartment into a home. Without him, it feels so empty and bare and cold. Maybe I should buy a new cat, but that doesn't feel right either, somehow. It feels as though I should mourn Sigge a little while before bringing home a new pet.

My physics textbooks are lying untouched, gathering dust. I've lost several weeks of studying because of Jesper. And he was the one who was so anxious for me to finish school, get my qualifications. And to go to college, too, if I wanted to. I close my eyes. Lean back.

Try to remember.

'But why did you drop out of secondary school?'

'Jesus, do we really have to talk about that now?'

Jesper pulled out of me, rolled sideways and lay down beside me in bed. Then he bunched up a pillow as support for his head. His expression was amused, almost annoyed. Once the weight of his body had disappeared, it became easier to breathe. I inhaled deeply and met his eyes.

'You don't like to talk about that, huh?'

'Honestly, I have no problem talking about it. But it's not very romantic, is it?'

'But I want to know. I love you, and I want to understand why you did what you did.'

'Do we have to know everything about each other?'

'Of course not.'

For a moment he looked so serious it almost scared me. As if he'd suddenly turned his gaze inwards, towards some dark secret brooding inside. Then the moment was gone, and he looked the same as usual. I sighed, aware that I couldn't get myself out of this situation without some kind of explanation.

'Why did you drop out?' he asked again, stressing every syllable.

'I didn't drop out. I never started. When Dad died . . .' I paused.

'Yes?'

He leaned over me, cupped his left hand gently around my breast and kissed me. I could feel the humid warmth radiating from his body.

'Basically, my life got too messy. First Dad died, then that thing happened with Woody, my DT teacher, in the spring of ninth grade. And I just wasn't able to keep going to school after that. So I left that summer, took a six-month break. Then I started working.'

He released my breast suddenly, as if he'd burnt himself on it. 'So all of this was that damn Woody's fault?'

'I don't know. I guess it was both of our faults.'

He laughed drily. 'Oh, please. You were just a kid, and he was a grown man. What he did to you was sick and disgusting and . . . repulsive. Fucking paedophile.'

'But I went along with it.'

Jesper sat up, suddenly looking angry, and wrapped the blanket around his hips. 'You don't mean that after all these years, you still blame yourself for what happened?'

'I don't want to talk about this.'

He sighed. 'I'm sorry. I just get so fucking upset when I think about how he used you. You were a minor, under his care, and he violated you.'

'Come on. It wasn't exactly an assault.'

'Call it what you will. It was wrong and he should have understood that.'

'What do you call this, then?'

He froze. 'I'm not sure I follow you.'

'Well, I'm your inferior too, right? You're the CEO of the company I work for. But you have no problem fucking me.'

'That's hardly the same thing. We're two adults who love each other. Neither one of us is using the other. This might be . . . I don't know. It might be unprofessional of me.'

He sounded convincing, but I sensed that I'd hit a nerve. He edged a few inches away. Groped for the pack of cigarettes lying on the bedside table.

'Be honest now, Jesper. Do you think this is a completely normal relationship between two equals?'

He didn't answer.

I'm lying in bed, fully dressed, staring up at the ceiling. In one corner a spider's web flutters in the draught coming through the window. A long crack runs diagonally across the ceiling, from one corner of the room to the other. Some day this apartment has to be renovated, I realise, but how am I going to pay for that now?

Jesper's fault.

All of this is Jesper's fault. I feel weak again. The excitement and energy that came from burning down Jesper's garage are gone. It feels as if I'm falling into a deep black hole again. And outside, the rain keeps falling over Stockholm. Even the sky is crying.

I'm suddenly gripped by a strong desire to confront Jesper. Corner him and force him to tell me why he's doing this to me. If

I do, if I'm strong enough to meet him as an equal, maybe I can regain control of my life again and reclaim my dignity.

It has to work, I think. It worked with Woody.

The principal's office consisted of two rooms: a small waiting room with two worn plush armchairs in it and another room behind a frosted-glass door. I sat in one chair in the waiting room and Mum sat in the other. There was a birch-veneered coffee table in front of us, piled with newspapers. I browsed through them: *Today's School, Pedagogical Journal*. Nothing interesting. On the other side of the frosted glass I could see some movement, but it was impossible to make out who was in there.

Mum fiddled with her new cornflower-blue bag and let out a hissing sound, which I knew meant she was annoyed.

'I don't understand why they won't say what this is about. I have a job to do and can't just sit here all day if this isn't very important – I told the principal as much on the phone. This'd better be very urgent, because I have my job and my husband's funeral to think about. And besides that—'

'Mum. Please stop. They might hear you.'

She shot me an icy stare. 'You'd better hope you haven't been up to anything. Have you?'

'How should I know? I don't know why we're here either.'

I looked at the clock on the wall. The thin black second hand looked like a spider moving across the clock face. When it reached twelve, the minute hand made a little shaky leap forward.

'Have you been shoplifting?'

'Come on. Of course not.'

'Have you been skipping school?'

'Stop it! I haven't been skipping.'

'Then can you explain to me why I'm sitting here instead of at work?'

Mum was always pointing out to anyone who would listen that she had a job. She'd been unemployed for several years after developing back problems, so the job meant a lot to her.

She glanced at the clock on the wall, which now showed ten past eleven. 'I have thirty minutes. No more.'

She folded her fat hands in her lap. Then she was silent. I didn't know what to say. On the other side of the frosted glass I heard the sound of chairs scraping against the floor.

'Emma,' Mum said.

'Yes?'

'You haven't been smoking weed, have you?'

At that very moment the frosted door opened, and Britt Henriksson, the school principal, stuck her sunburnt head out. Her thin brightly coloured summer dress hung like a sack on her skinny body.

'So good you could come. Welcome!'

She took a step back and opened the door. Mum stepped forward, said hello, and I followed hesitantly behind her. Principal Britt's smile was strained as she took me by the hand.

In a swivel chair opposite the desk sat Sigmund, also known as Dr Freud, the school psychologist. Despite his nickname, his close-cropped dark hair, bushy beard and generous proportions made him look more like Pippi Longstocking's father than he did the stern German psychologist. Next to Sigmund sat Elin. Her cheeks were red and she was staring down at the floor.

'Thank you, Elin. You can go now. We'll let you know if there's anything else,' said Principal Britt.

Elin stood up and, without taking her eyes off the linoleum floor, left the room.

'It's so stuffy in here,' Britt said. 'Sigmund, could you please open the window?'

The principal was right. The air in the room was thick and smelled like sweaty old socks. Sigmund heaved himself up from the chair with some effort, waddled over to the window and opened it. Letting summer into the small room.

'That's better,' Britt chirped. 'Would you like some lemonade?'

I nodded, but Mum raised her hand. 'None for me, thanks. I'm in a hurry to get back to work.'

Britt nodded, poured the lemonade into a white plastic cup and handed it to me. It was the same as the cups in the school cafeteria, I noticed. For some reason that surprised me. I'd imagined that the teachers and principal used real dishes, that everything was nicer and more grown-up in the staffroom and the principal's office.

Britt readjusted her sack-like dress and sat down carefully on the edge of her chair, as if she were afraid it would break otherwise.

'Emma. Maybe you already know why you're here today?'

I shook my head.

Britt cleared her throat and looked down. Obviously, she was embarrassed by the situation. Sigmund said nothing, just stroked his beard and looked longingly out the window.

'What has she done?' Mum asked.

'No, no,' Britt began. 'Emma hasn't done anything wrong. It's come to our attention that one of our teachers . . . that a certain teacher has made advances towards Emma.'

'What?' Mum said and lost her grip on the cornflower-blue bag. It fell to the floor with a thud.

'One of our supply teachers, in DT. He's actually quite good, but . . . according to our information he's also . . . Emma, maybe you'd like to tell us yourself? Am I correct? Has he made advances towards you?'

I couldn't answer. It felt as though my mouth was full of sand and a hard lump had parked itself in my throat.

'Emma,' Sigmund said in his nasal German accent. 'It's very impor-tant that you tell us what happened. Both for your own sake and for the other young people in this school. Has he ever approached you?'

I hesitated for a second and then nodded. Mum emitted a hissing sound and picked up her bag from the floor.

'What did he do?' Britt asked in a softer tone, and put her bony hand on mine. I pulled my hand away without answering. A tiny ladybird with two dots was crawling on the table beside my lemonade. What was it again ... Could I wish for something, or did the ladybird need to have more spots?

'I'm sorry, Emma, but we need to know. Has he kissed you?'

The ladybird crawled towards the edge of the table. It was so close now I could touch it. I stretched out my hand to see if it might want to climb up on my finger.

'Emma.'

Britt's voice was insistent.

'Has he kissed you, or touched you in any way?'

I nodded without lifting my eyes from the ladybird. The room fell silent. So silent I could hear the cars passing by on the busy street outside and the sound of children laughing in the schoolyard.

'Have you ...' Britt hesitated. 'Have you had ... intercourse?'

Intercourse. I shuddered. The word sounded like a contagious disease. I poked at the little red insect with my fingertip.

'Yes,' I said. Yes.

The ladybird changed direction and headed towards the glass of lemonade again.

My mother pulled on her blazer. Every breath she took was followed by a loud hissing.

Her face was red and she pressed her bag tightly against her chest as she turned to me.

I don't know what I was expecting. A comment about how hard all this was for her, maybe. Or irritation that she'd lost valuable time coming to school in the middle of the day.

The slap came without warning and almost knocked me off balance. For a second the room spun, and then a burning pain spread across my cheek.

'Slut,' Mum said, and walked out of the room with heavy steps.

Hanne

I get lost on my way back to the police station. I don't know if it's because I'm upset after talking to Peter or if it's the fault of the disease.

Maybe it's just the weather. The snow makes it hard to see more than a few yards in front of my face, and all the buildings are wrapped in a white haze. The street names are visible, but I can't seem to remember where the streets lead, as if the whole map of Kungsholmen has been erased from my memory.

The snow is creeping in around my neck, melting, running down my chest. My hands are frozen, and panic lurks somewhere behind my ribs, like a fist in my chest. It would be easy enough to ask the people I pass on the street: the young woman with the pushchair, the man with a tennis racket slung over his shoulder, or even the couple kissing unabashedly in front of an apartment building. But I can't; I'm not able to admit even to myself that I can't find my way back to the police station.

The wind tears at my hood, and the hard little flakes whip against my cheek. Everything is white. Everything is snow and ice. I might as well be with the Inuit in Greenland, it's that cold.

I think of the men who tried to conquer the polar regions, often with disastrous results: Amundsen, Andrée, Strindberg and Nansen. But most of all of Claus Paarss, the Danish-Norwegian military man who travelled to Greenland in 1728 to find the Norwegian settlers no one had heard from in two hundred years.

When they'd planned the expedition, they figured young Norwegian men on skis would be able to explore the unknown continent in all directions without much trouble.

Paarss crossed the North Atlantic with about twenty soldiers, twelve convicts, a group of prostitutes and twelve horses. Once they arrived, his struggle against the elements – and his own men – began. Paarss's men committed mutiny, and no sooner had he suppressed their insurrection than the crew began to die of scurvy and smallpox. The horses died, too. And twice Paarss failed to cross the continent on foot over the sharp blocks of ice. Eventually, even the native Greenlanders abandoned the colony, and Paarss's dream of populating the continent with Danish aristocrats and their families was dashed.

Where does the human urge to tame the world come from? This urge is by no means limited to nature – we humans want to rule over each other as well, both in our societies and in our close relationships.

Like Owe, I think. He's spent his life trying to tame me. But he won't succeed. Because I'll do as the polar ice does: tire him out with my stubborn cold until he gives up and finds someone else to dominate.

I blink against the snowflakes. Try again to find something to fix my gaze on, a landmark in all that white. It's almost tempting to call Owe, because I know that he'd drop everything, jump into the car and come and pick me up. Save me, just like he always has when I mess up.

A few seconds later the snowfall lessens, and the familiar contours of St Eriks Hospital emerge. I draw a deep breath. Now I know exactly where I am, and how to get back to the warmth of the police station. But that terrible, paralysing feeling of helplessness has taken hold. Doesn't want to let go of me even once I'm back at my desk again, looking out the window towards Kungsholmsgatan. And even though I drink three cups of hot tea in a row, I'm still so cold I'm shaking.

I glance at Peter. He's sitting a few yards away, his back turned to me, his eyes fixed on his computer. His grey-blonde hair is damp and on the floor beneath him small puddles have formed around his ridiculously thin trainers.

I wish I did have cancer – then I could tell him. But you can't tell people you have emergent dementia. Especially not if it's a person you've just fallen into bed with. It's a thousand times worse than a sexually transmitted disease. More shameful, in some way. Losing your mind, getting lost inside yourself, is disgusting. Repulsive. I'm slowly turning into a vegetable, and nobody wants a vegetable.

Except Owe.

Maybe that *is* love. Being there for each other no matter what happens. It reminds me of that verse from Corinthians: 'Love bears all things, believes all things, hopes all things, endures all things.'

But I don't want Owe to 'bear' and 'endure' me. I just want to be left alone.

Maybe I should go to Greenland. Make the trip that never happened. Now, while I still have time. But instead I'm sitting here, in the police station, the place where it all began and where it might all end.

Gunilla keeps saying I shouldn't give up hope.

There you go, something that is even more shameful: giving up hope. No one who is seriously ill should ever give up hope; it's an unforgivable betrayal of your family and doctors. Yes, of your whole society, which believes that all problems can be solved, all diseases cured.

Gunilla says that as long as there's life there's hope. Who knows – maybe the scientists will find a cure tomorrow.

But if you don't have the strength to hope, what then?

Hope is just an overrated life raft that sick people are expected to cling to with a brave and grateful smile. Letting go is apparently not only foolhardy, but disloyal.

But I'm just so tired of being loyal.

After lunch I go through the local police's interrogation of Emma Bohman. I can't quite put my finger on it, but something about it bothers me – something that's not consistent with our theory. Suppose the woman in Jesper Orre's house really is Emma Bohman.

There remains the question of why Orre would murder her. If they had an affair and he wanted to get rid of her, then he couldn't have been that emotionally involved. So why kill her in such a way? The placement of the head, the braced-open eyelids – all of it points to a murderer who harboured a very intense hatred of the victim. And I really can't make out why Orre would hate Emma Bohman that much. At least not with the very limited knowledge I have of the two of them.

Also, if Orre really wanted to kill Emma Bohman, why did he do it in his own home and not even bother hiding the body afterwards? He must have realised he would be exposed as soon as she was found.

Finally, if he did kill her – out of rage or perhaps affected by a temporary psychotic attack – why leave home without a wallet or mobile? Where do you go with no money and no phone in the middle of winter?

It's starting to get dark outside, and the yellow glow of the Advent candles reflect off the window. A calm has descended over the office. Only scattered quiet conversations and the clicking from Sanchez's desk as she types something on her computer can be heard.

I keep skimming through the investigation. Reading testimony of Jesper's colleagues and friends. Nothing indicates any kind of psychiatric problems. No mention of violent behaviour. This is also a problem. These types of crimes aren't committed by healthy people with normal personal histories. Serious violent crime is also a kind of career, or whatever you want to call it. Usually there are signs from a young age that something is wrong – deviant behaviour, early criminality, or perhaps violence against animals or young children. Jesper Orre's partiality for rough sex and pilfering women's underwear must be considered normal enough. Most of us have dirty little secrets, but very few people murder or chop off other people's heads. That behaviour is so deviant it requires completely different explanatory models.

And then there is Calderón. Who is not Chinese. Where the hell did I get that from, anyway? Just one of those stupid things I say nowadays. Maybe, when I'm seriously ill, I'll end up being really funny for the first time in my life. One of those patients who doubles their carers over with laughter and has the other patients choking on their baby food.

Oh well.

And even though Sanchez has gone through the Calderón investigation with a magnifying glass and interviewed his family again, she's found no connection between him and Orre.

I'm roused from my thoughts by a commotion at Sanchez's desk. Manfred is talking loudly, waving his arms, and a few seconds later Peter goes over to them. Manfred pulls on his coat. Sanchez does the same, puts her mobile in her pocket and turns off the light on her desk with a quick movement.

Peter turns around and walks over to me. There's some nervous energy in his body, and I understand immediately that something has happened.

'They've found a dead man near Orre's house. Are you coming, Hanne?'

We're in a small wooded area just quarter of a mile from Jesper Orre's house. The snow has almost stopped falling as police lights sweep across the white landscape, turning it blue in the twilight. The branches groan under the weight of fallen snow, which crunches beneath me as I walk. Manfred holds up the blue-and-white police tape and waves me beneath it. Sanchez and Peter are already at the front of a group of people gathered about thirty feet away. Outside the police tape some curious onlookers jostle about. One is jumping in place to stay warm; another takes photos with his mobile. Uniformed police officers hold them at bay, telling them there's nothing to see and urging them to go home.

As I get closer to the group of officers and forensic technicians standing under a big tree, I see a familiar green box with the word 'SAND' sticking up out of the snow, a storage container for the kind of sand they put on roads in the winter.

'Some kids found him,' Manfred says and meets my eyes. 'Why do children always have to find the corpses? They were playing hide-and-seek when they found the body. As frozen as a fucking ice lolly.'

I reach the group gathered around the box. Nod to some familiar faces and try to see what's hidden inside. On the bottom of the container, I can just make out the outline of a man. He's lying in a foetal position and is dressed in jeans and a light sweater. His face, which is covered with blackened blood and frost, looks strangely familiar.

It's Jesper Orre.

Emma

Two weeks earlier

I root around in my makeshift toolbox. Decide on a hammer and chisel and stow them in my bag. The temperature is close to freezing, so I put on my thick jacket and winter boots, then leave the apartment and walk out to Valhallavägen to find a taxi.

I'm freezing, even though I have on both hat and gloves. A few dog owners walk past in fur coats and down jackets, hunched over in the gusty wind. There aren't many cars in sight. It would obviously have been better to order a cab, but I don't want to leave any trace in the taxi company's booking system.

After maybe ten minutes, I manage to flag down a cab. The windscreen is covered with small ice crystals. I give the taxi driver an address a few blocks away from Jesper's – might as well be cautious. The driver is named Jorge and he's very chatty. I answer his questions curtly and hope he'll take the hint, which he does, falling silent after a while. Then there's only the sound of the engine and the classical music on the radio.

How could he do it? How could he live a double life for months, maybe years? How could Jesper be with me at the same time he was with another woman? Was it a game, a sport; was he trying to fool everybody – or just me – for as long as possible? Did he want to hurt me, ruin my life?

I still have no answers, but the questions abound.

And who's to say I'm the only one? Maybe there are more women out there that he's fooled. I rest my cheek against the cold window of the car and close my eyes. Trying to imagine others like me scattered across Stockholm in lonely apartments, but I can't. I neither can nor want to believe that's the case. How would he have the time, anyway?

The taxi slows down in front of a red wooden house. I pay cash and step out into the cold. Jorge disappears into the night, and everything is still and quiet. In the distance, a dog is barking.

I start walking along the narrow street. Almost immediately, I step in a puddle. A thin film of ice cracks with a brittle crunch. On both sides of me stand big, turn-of-the-century houses. Their windows are lit, and I think about how in every house there's a family with its own, unique story. I catch myself assuming that the people who live in those big beautiful houses are happy, but of course that's ridiculous. Because money and power are no guarantee of happiness, right?

The street is so small I almost miss it. Here the houses are newer, maybe from the fifties, and a bit smaller. The pavement is covered with drifts of leaves which frost has transformed into a treacherously slippery patchwork. A full moon floats above the houses on the right, perfectly round and shimmering gold, like a ripe piece of fruit.

I recognise the house immediately. Blackened stumps stick up out of the ground where the garage once stood, and a faint odour of burnt wood speaks to what happened. Blue-and-white police tape is wrapped around the burnt-down building like ribbon around a giant gift. It flutters a little in the wind. My heart leaps in my chest. At least I've had some impact on his life, reached him, even if it's not in the way I had imagined.

You brought this on yourself, I think. It didn't have to turn out like this.

There's a light shining from the window in the front door, but otherwise the house lies dark on its woody slope. I hesitate for a second before opening the gate and approaching the entrance.

Drooping, frostbitten plants line the narrow gravel path and beyond them lies a wide lawn. A few scattered junipers and pine trees stick out like on a barren mountainside. It's not a very nice garden. Gardening must not be one of Jesper's interests. But then again, what do I actually know about his interests, about who he really is?

The brass button of the doorbell is cold under my finger. For a moment it feels as if something very important is about to happen, as if by pressing this button I'm making an irreversible decision. I push away the thought as ridiculous. This started a long time ago. That I'm standing here today is a natural consequence of what Jesper did to me.

But maybe this is exactly what he wants?

The thought bothers me, and I do what I can to avoid following it to its inevitable conclusion. Instead I press the doorbell. Immediately I hear an angry buzzing sound inside the house. My heart is racing now and my stomach cramps up. I'm not sure what I'll do if he opens the door and we end up face to face. Maybe I should have prepared more, written some notes, because I don't trust myself to remember everything I need to say.

I stand for a while on the front steps with my finger on the doorbell, watching my breath turn into small white clouds that the wind dissolves, but nothing happens. I press the doorbell again. It buzzes. Drilling a deep, ugly hole into the silence.

I look around.

I see the house across the street which is completely dark, and further away, down towards the water, more houses. There are lights in some windows and smoke rising from one chimney, but besides that all is still, no people or cars in sight.

After a few minutes, I go down the stone steps and walk around to the short side of the white stucco house, where two basement windows sit low to the ground. I crouch down and peer inside. It's dark, except for a faint light streaming through an open door at the far end of the space.

After a while, the contours of a washing machine emerge from the gloom. I continue around the building, inspecting windows. The house seems empty. I consider the risks – the house could have an alarm. But surely I'll hear it if it goes off? Also, I haven't seen any signs or stickers warning of an alarm system.

When I go back to the basement windows on the short side, I note that they're completely hidden from view. This side of the house is obscured behind a hillock of sprawling pines. The full moon shines between the branches. It provides just enough light for me to see what I'm doing. I look through the glass again. The washing machine is conveniently placed beneath the window; it should work as a landing surface. Cautiously, I take the chisel and hammer from my bag and realise I don't have the faintest idea how to break in through a window. I try using the chisel and hammer to pry it open.

It doesn't work. All I do is make an ugly gash in the wood.

I wipe the sweat from my brow. Then lift up the hammer and hesitantly pound it into the middle of the glass. The glass tumbles down onto the ground and into the basement. I lift up my hammer again and again. Knocking away every single piece of glass from the window frame. Then I sink down on my haunches and hold my breath, listening for approaching steps or angry voices.

Nothing.

It's just as quiet and still as before. The full moon is reflected in the shards of glass scattered on the ground in front of me, as if the sky has broken into a thousand little pieces and fallen down at my feet.

I sit next to the window and peer into the dark room. All I have to do is step in and jump down onto the washing machine. After some hesitation, I put the chisel and hammer back in my bag and throw it into the basement. It lands with a dull thud on the floor. Then I crawl inside, sit on the ledge, bracing myself against the window frame, and jump down.

It goes much more smoothly than I expected. Standing in Jesper's basement, I regret not coming here earlier. It smells faintly of detergent and mildew. A dryer sits next to the washing machine and a pile of dirty laundry lies in a corner.

Not especially glamorous.

When I open the door, I see I'm bleeding from a wound on my hand. I must have cut myself without noticing it as I climbed in through the window. It doesn't drip, it flows, and I see a deep gash between my thumb and forefinger.

I go over to the cabinet next to the washing machine, open it and see a basket inside. It seems to be filled with washing. I choose a small white item. It's only when I wrap it around my injured hand that I realise what it is: a pair of women's knickers. I shudder, but decide they'll have to do. Then I head into the house.

I'm a bit surprised. The house seems a little the worse for wear. The white walls are discoloured and the hardwood flooring is scratched, and here and there missing a piece. But the decor is typical of Jesper: severe Danish furniture and lamps that I recognise from interior design magazines. The shiny chrome and lacquered surfaces reflect the moonlight. Large black-and-white photos of animals and naked women illuminated in backlight hang on the walls. It's like a stab to the heart. This could have been our home.

I'm suddenly overpowered by the tears that have been lodged somewhere in my throat since I climbed into this house. I sink down into a black leather sofa and let them flow. The moon's soft light spills across the floor. A damp scent of stale cigarette smoke hovers in the air. Maybe it wasn't such a good idea to come here, after all. Everything feels so much more pronounced here, in his home. His betrayal feels so much bigger and so impossible to understand.

I look around the room. A photograph stands in the bookcase: Jesper and a group of women on a beach. The women, all in bikinis, are slim and beautiful and have small, shapely breasts – completely unlike my udders. A dark-haired woman stands very close to Jesper. Too close. So close I know she has to be more than a friend.

I turn away and my stomach cramps up again.

Does she know – that dark-haired woman – that he's cheating on her, or was she also deluded into thinking she's the only one? Maybe I should tell her? Then it strikes me: she might know about me; Jesper might have even left me for her. Maybe she knew exactly what she was doing when she got together with Jesper. She might even have knowingly manoeuvred me out.

The other woman.

This could also account for the hasty break-up and lack of explanation. Suddenly I know it had to be so. The beautiful dark-haired woman must have taken Jesper from me; whether she knows it or not, she's the reason I've lost him. I feel a sudden fury towards her. I knock the picture down from the shelf and it falls to the floor. As the sound of breaking glass echoes through the room, I walk away without turning around.

Everything in the kitchen is new and glossy. The black lac-quered kitchen cabinets have no handles, and it takes me a while to figure out that you open them by giving them a light nudge. The dishes are black, too, and the slender wine glasses are pushed in between plates and bowls. Two black trays with small white elephants on them lean behind the chrome tap, which resembles a shower hose.

I run my hand over the stainless-steel counter. Not a crumb, not a speck of dust. Just that cold, clinically clean metal sheet. The only thing that distinguishes this kitchen from an autopsy room is the black dining table and the drawing hanging on the wall above it. My guess is that it's of a snowman, but I'm not sure. It's not very good. You'd have to be a parent to love a drawing like that. 'For Jesper' is scrawled above the snowman in straggly blue letters.

Of course. That's how it is. The other woman has a child, but Jesper's not the father. They must have met later, when Jesper and I were together. And then he left me for her.

For them.

A fridge is hidden behind one of the glossy cabinet doors. I inspect its contents: milk, juice, butter, eggs and half a bottle of white wine with the cork pressed down. Nothing particularly exciting. On the bottom shelf stands a plastic container of leftovers. I gently lift off the lid: meatballs and macaroni, with a dry lump of ketchup in the corner.

I put the plastic container on the table, go back to the fridge and take out the bottle of wine. I set it down next to the macaroni and think for a moment. In the window, next to a drooping ivy tied up in a bow, is a small stereo with an iPod on it. I turn it on and scroll through the playlists, select a song at random and push play. Then I sit down at the table.

Frank Sinatra sings Christmas carols for me while I eat cold meatballs and drink Jesper's Chardonnay. When he sings about 'happy holidays', I feel the rage inside me come to life again. I have never seen it so clearly before, how much his glossy, prosperous life differs from my hermit-like existence in my small apartment. It's not fair, and someone has to make him understand that. And that someone is me.

His bed is wide and soft and feels luxurious. I try it out and find that it's wide enough to lie on both lengthwise and crosswise. The sheets smell faintly of soap or some sort of perfume. On the bedside table lie a few paperback mystery novels and a couple of business journals. I gently pull out the bedside drawer and look inside: a mobile charger, lip balm and some lube.

Once again, I feel something cramp inside. My stomach contracts and that familiar lump parks itself in my throat. I've got too close to the truth I was searching for, and now I have to pay the price for my curiosity. The knowledge is more painful than I ever imagined. Of course I wanted to know where Jesper was and why he didn't get hold of me. But I didn't want to see the pictures of him and the other woman, didn't want to smell their sheets or rummage in their dirty laundry.

The tears press behind my eyelids and I let them come. I bury my face in a down pillow and sob. Unleashing the despair I've carried for so long.

When I wake up it's light outside. At first I don't know where I am, then I see my hand. The white knickers wrapped around my wound are almost completely soaked with dried blood.

I sit up, gently unwind the makeshift bandage. At least I'm no longer bleeding. I poke the bloody pants down behind the headboard with a vague feeling of revulsion, but also with sadness – they remind me of the baby I've lost.

When I stand up, I feel how stiff I am. It's as if my body doesn't really want to obey me as I walk over to the window. I have no idea what the time it is or how long I've slept, but the sun is up and the world outside is a shimmering white. A thin layer of snow covers everything in sight. In the distance I see a car approaching.

I stand there a few seconds before I understand what's about to happen. The car, now less than a block away, is a black SUV that I recognise as Jesper's. I panic, looking around the room, scrambling for my bag and coat, and run down the stairs and back into the basement. I don't know how much time I have. One minute? Thirty seconds? Without turning around I throw my bag out the window, then jump out myself. Maybe I imagine it, but at the moment I stand up, I think I hear a door slam.

I turn and run between the pine trees and houses down towards the water. After a minute, I see a shed on a small hill, with an unobstructed view of Jesper's house. I run to it and look in through the dirty windows. Garden furniture is piled up. A broken barbecue stands in a corner while an old sofa is alone in the middle of the floor. I turn around, looking at the house the shed belongs to. It seems abandoned. The windows on the lower floor are boarded up, and under the snow I see what I take to be the outline of a gutter that's fallen off the side of the house onto the overgrown grass.

As I leave the abandoned house behind me, I know I've just made an important discovery.

There are new bills. I sit at the kitchen table, looking at a pile that in just a few days has grown almost twice as big as it was. I don't know what to do. I have no jewellery or any other valuables left to sell. Even the painting that used to hang above my bed, which for some reason was valuable, is gone. I think of those childish football players in pastel colours gathered around the ball. If what I was told when I inherited it is right, it was worth at least three hundred thousand kronor. But that doesn't matter now, since Jesper's taken it. It strikes me that I should have been searching Jesper's house for it while I was there, instead of eating comfort food and crying myself to sleep in his bed.

Outside my window snow is falling. Christmas will be here soon. This will be the first Christmas without Mum, and I still have no idea how to celebrate. Christmas isn't really that important to me: as far as I'm concerned bringing home pizza and renting a movie works just as well as a traditional celebration. Maybe even better, because there's something about Christmas that induces a slight, but still perceptible, anxiety. I think I felt it as a child too, but then the anxiety was about other things: how to appreciate my presents enough to keep Mum and Dad from getting upset and, even more important, how to become invisible by the time they got drunk, loud and erratic.

I weigh the bills in my hand, thinking for a moment, then put them back in the bread bin. The lid closes with a screech that sounds like a sob.

I go into the bathroom, pull the brush through my long hair, and realise I don't recognise the woman staring back at me from the mirror. She looks older than me. Bitter. Weak, in a feminine, subservient way. Like a woman in a costume drama who has to be saved and protected. It pisses me off, because the last thing I want to be is weak. I close my eyes and remember the feeling of control and power I had after the fire and I know I have to get it back: strength, focus, fearlessness. I have to change, on the inside and maybe on the outside too.

There's a pair of nail scissors under the mirror, old and warped and so dull that your nails just fold when you use it. But I pick them up anyway, grab hold of my hair, and start to saw my way through it. It falls onto the floor like the snow outside my window. I cut through one lock after another. Hair slowly covers the floor and the woman in the mirror changes before my eyes.

At first I don't like it. It starts out as a pageboy cut that I think makes me look like an old lady librarian. I decide it has to be shorter. Carefully, I work my way around my head again with those little scissors. My thumb and forefinger burn from the effort. But in the end I'm satisfied.

I have finally become someone else.

Peter

Darkness falls quickly over Stockholm, and the traffic gets worse as I drive from the Djursholm suburb towards the police station on Kungsholmen. I'm thinking about Jesper Orre's frozen body in the green grit container. About that bloody face covered with frost. And as usual when I run into death, the image of my sister Annika appears before my eyes: Annika basking on the rocks that summer so many years ago. Her lean body that had just started to curve, the smell of cigarette smoke hovering over dry heather, and the feel of sharp needles under my thin-skinned feet.

What would have happened if I hadn't told my mother about Annika's sneaking a cigarette down by the cliffs? Would she be alive today?

I think my mother suspected I felt guilty for Annika's death, because she told me again and again that it was an accident no one could be blamed for. She repeated it almost like a mantra. Though maybe that was because it was too painful to admit that Annika swam to death of her own free will.

Annika was the first. She taught me life was not for ever. Others followed: Petter, the red-haired boy in 7B, drove his moped into a tree and was brain-dead for four weeks until his father turned off the respirator, packed a bag, left for Thailand and never came back. Marie, who was at the police academy with me, got cancer at twenty-five. She promised everyone she'd be back soon, even when she was lying in the hospice.

And then my mother, of course.

After her, I stopped counting. It seemed as though everyone around me died – a terrible feeling. It made me feel as if my turn was next. And as if everything that I spent my time on – murder investigations, takeaway pizza in front of the TV or dreary Internet porn – was meaningless. And as if I might as well jump off the West Bridge, because no one would miss me anyway – as soon as the ripples on the water ceased, I'd be forgotten.

It's true: no one on earth depends on me. No one really needs me. Not my colleagues, not Janet. Not Albin.

Not really.

Still. You could kill yourself, or you could have a beer. And when the choice was between the bridge or the pub, I always chose the pub.

Sanchez stands in front of the evidence wall, pulls her hair into a ponytail and says:

'We got the call just after three from someone named Amelie Hökberg, who lives on Strandvägen in Djursholm. She's the mother of Alexander Hökberg, ten years old, who, along with his friend Pontus Gerloff, found Orre's body in the grit container. Apparently the boys had been playing all afternoon and Alexander was about to hide in the box when he found Orre.'

Sanchez points at the map pinned to the board. 'The grit container is four hundred yards west of Orre's house and stands in a wooded area. It takes about seven minutes to walk there from Orre's home.'

'How long had he been lying there?' Manfred asks.

'The coroner can't say yet. There has to be an autopsy first, and the body has to thaw before she can do that. It will take at least a day.'

'What can she say?' I ask.

'He had injuries on his head and forehead. He received a blow or suffered some other form of trauma. And he probably froze to death.'

I look at Hanne. She seems strangely calm, almost serene, sitting next to the small window with its Advent candles. She doesn't seem at all ill, I think, and remember my mother's emaciated, cancer-ravaged body.

'OK. Orre murders Emma Bohman,' Manfred says, and stretches his huge body so that his waistcoat tightens precariously over his stomach. 'So how the hell did he end up in the grit container?'

The room is silent for a moment.

'Maybe he was hiding?' Sanchez suggests. 'He was on the run from a crime scene, injured and confused. Maybe he ran into someone and hid in the grit container. And then . . .'

She falls silent. The only sound is the hum of the ventilation system. It's eight o'clock and most of our colleagues have already gone home. A lone detective is sitting at the far end of the room in front of his computer, seemingly engrossed in something. Outside, the lights of Kungsholmen glitter against the black winter sky.

'So Orre kills Emma Bohman, that's our theory,' Manfred continues. 'He chops off her head. Props open her eyes with matches and flees without a wallet, phone or coat. Doesn't even take a pair of used lady's knickers to sniff on. Then he climbs into a grit container and dies. Glad we have the sequence of events cleared up. Who wants to call the prosecutor?'

Sanchez sighs loudly. 'Do you have to be so . . . fucking critical all the time? I didn't say that's the way it happened. I'm just trying to find an explanation that fits the evidence . . .'

'The problem is that we don't have any evidence. We don't even know the identity of the woman in Orre's house. How the hell can we say what really happened? Can you answer that?'

Sanchez crosses her arms and pinches her lips. Looks up at the ceiling. Blinks. For a moment it seems as though she might start crying. I know how much pressure we're all under and I feel sorry for her. She's doing her best. She always does her best; that's who she is. A dog can't be anything apart from a dog. And Sanchez can only be Sanchez. One day she'll be a brilliant detective, and maybe that's what irritates Manfred.

'You know what? I don't need to take this shit from you, Manfred. I'm going to drive to Forensic Medicine in Solna right now and find that odontologist. Call me if you need anything.'

She turns around and disappears down the hall. The sound of her sharp heels fades away.

'Was that necessary?' I ask and meet Manfred's eyes.

'Jesus Christ, Lindgren. Don't tell me you buy that theory?'

'She's doing the best she can.'

Manfred shakes his head slowly. 'I'm sorry, but that's not enough.'

He stands up, reaches for the coat hanging on the back of his chair and says:

'I have to go home for a few hours and relieve Afsaneh. Call me if anything happens. Otherwise, I'll be back in two or three hours.'

He lumbers away, leaving me alone with Hanne. Her grey eyes rest heavily on me. 'What?' I ask.

'Nothing. I'm just wondering . . . Are you always like this . . . so hard on each other?'

I shrug. 'This isn't a course in personal development.' I glimpse a faint smile on her thin face.

The room is silent for a moment. The lamps flickers and Hanne closes her eyes, as if trying to keep the cold light outside. She suddenly looks older. No less beautiful, just older and more tired, once you get past the years.

'How are you?' I ask.

She opens her eyes. Starts to giggle. And she resembles a teenager again – something about her impish laugh, or maybe her way of rolling her eyes.

'You're funny. I'm fine.'

'Because I've been thinking about what you said—' I say quickly.

'Don't worry. I'll survive this investigation.'

I can no longer control myself. As if it's finally hitting me how important she is to me. She's the first and only person I've ever truly wanted, and it makes her more important than anything else – I just never realised it before. Perhaps it's because she told me she was ill, and I know now our time together isn't infinite. Instead, it has been reduced to a number of brief moments, assembled into days and weeks, which could be over much too soon.

'I love you, Hanne,' I say. And the moment I say the words, I know I mean them, maybe for the first time in my life.

Hanne's eyes become shiny.

'Oh, Peter. You don't know that. We haven't even seen each other for ten years.'

'No. I do know. And I loved you then too, I was just too stupid to understand it.'

A few tears wind down her cheeks, but she ignores them. 'It doesn't matter any more,' she whispers and looks down at her hands, resting quietly in her lap. 'I'm ill and we can't be together.'

'But I don't care if you're ill. I can take care of you. I want to take care of you.'

She meets my eyes. 'Believe me. You don't.'

The rattling of the detective on the other side of the room has ceased. He stands up, pulls on his leather jacket, turns off his desk lamp and leaves the room.

'Yes. I do.'

Hanne sighs and stares up at the overhead lamp. In the bright light the skin beneath her eyes seems thin and has a bluish iridescence. Like the belly of a fish.

'Jesus, Peter. You're like a stubborn kid. I'm ... losing my memory. Soon I may not know my own name. You can't be my carer – surely you can understand that.'

'Losing your memory? How so? Like Alzheimer's?'

Hanne buries her head in her hands. 'I have to go,' she says and stands up without looking at me.

'Wait! Can I come with you?'

She turns around. Puts her hands on her waist and shakes her head slowly. 'No. Give up! I've told you it won't work.'

I can't tell if she's angry or just thinks I'm too persistent.

Before she leaves the room, she stops in front of the evidence wall. Stares for a long time at the picture of Emma Bohman before finally turning around and waving goodbye to me.

The darkness outside looks even blacker and denser than before. I stand at the window searching for Hanne, but all I see is a snow-plough approaching on a deserted street.

I wonder if it's true, that she's really losing her memory. But why would she lie about that kind of thing?

I am suddenly filled with sadness. Thinking of her slender body in bed, the freckles on her shoulders glowing in the dawn light. About her greedy desire when we make love, and her loud, uncontrollable laughter afterwards, when we lie next to each other talking in the narrow bed. I can almost still hear her light snoring – it reminded me of a creaking boat, anchored in a calm sea.

A safe sound.

But most of all I think about how I felt when I was with her. How fantastically wide open, vulnerable and light I became.

Like a feather.

Who says it can't be like that again? Who decided it can't happen?

Life is about loss, my mother used to say when she stood smoking under the fan. Loss of the innocence we're all born with, of the people we love, of our health and our physical abilities, and ultimately – of course – the loss of our own lives.

As usual, she was right.

Manfred calls around nine. His voice is excited, and something else: there's a sense of purpose there that I know well.

'Are you in the office?' he asks.

'Yes. Why? I was heading out soon.'

'Bergdahl's spoken to one of Angelica Wennerlind's girlfriends.'

I look over to the evidence wall where the image of Angelica Wennerlind hangs next to a photo of Emma Bohman.

'And?'

'You'll never guess what she told him. She's on her way to the police station now, with a colleague. We can talk to her in twenty minutes.'

Annie Bertrand is short and blonde and wearing workout clothes, as if she's come straight from the gym. We meet with her in a small interrogation room on the ground floor; it smells like mould and cleaning products. Manfred has brought some coffee and buns from 7-Eleven but she declines the latter politely, explaining that she doesn't eat bread.

Avoiding gluten – or sugar or milk – seems to be all the rage nowadays. Sanchez has also stopped eating it, claiming her stomach swells up like a balloon as soon as she even glances at a pastry.

'Thank you for coming,' Manfred says. 'We don't usually ask people to come in at this time of day, but the investigation into the murder at Jesper Orre's house is at a critical stage and we don't want to lose any time. Can you tell us how you know Angelica Wennerlind?'

'We've been friends since school. We hung out quite a bit back then, but nowadays we meet maybe once a month. She still lives out in Bromma, works at a preschool in Ålsten, and I live in the city. Also, she has Wilma, so she doesn't get much time . . .'

Her voice dies out.

'Wilma, that's her daughter?' Manfred asks.

'Yes. She's the cutest thing ever. But really intense too. She's only five.'

'And Angelica doesn't live with Wilma's father?'

'No. He's American. Lives in New York. Wilma was kind of a mistake, I guess you'd say. Angelica met Chris on holiday and they never really had a real relationship. But when she got pregnant, she decided to keep Wilma. She loves kids.'

Manfred writes something in his notebook.

'Can you tell us about Angelica Wennerlind's new boyfriend?'

Annie Bertrand nods and takes a sip of coffee.

'Yes. It was top secret, of course – I might have been the only one who knew. She was seeing Jesper Orre and I think it was pretty serious. He'd even met Wilma. But they wanted to lie low, considering how the media chased Jesper. I don't even think Angelica had told her mum and dad about him. You know, they say he's a huge womaniser. It probably wasn't much fun for Angelica to read about him in the tabloids all the time. But I think they were pretty happy, actually. She said so, in any case. Told me it was serious and that Jesper had said he was in love for the first time in his life. He wanted to move in with her, build a life together. Start again. He even thought about resigning. Was tired of being under so much pressure and scrutiny. They were going to go away this week. They'd rented a cottage somewhere, I think, but she didn't say where. They probably wanted to get away from everything. Be left alone.'

Manfred meets my eyes in silence and slams his notebook shut with a small bang.

Emma

Eight days earlier

I sweep up my hair and weep. Not because I've cut it off, but because I've finally completed the transformation that I always knew deep down inside would happen. It feels fated, melancholy and magnificent at the same time, and it makes me think of the caterpillar I carried around in the glass jar, which finally turned into a butterfly.

I asked my father why the caterpillar couldn't stay a caterpillar, and he told me it had no choice: change or die; that's how nature is. And here I am, changed and reinvented. No longer Emma but someone else instead, someone stronger, who refuses to be a victim. Someone who has power over her own life, and who will take revenge against those who have betrayed her.

I throw the hair into the rubbish, and then I take all the bills and put them in the sink. I find matches in the bottom drawer of the bathroom cabinet. I hesitate for a moment before setting fire to the bills. The fire quickly takes hold and for a moment the flames are worryingly high, then they die out and all that's left are the charred remains of my debts. The feathery paper remnants remind me of black petals.

The bathroom is warm and humid. I paint thick black lines around my eyes with kohl and inspect my new face in the mirror. Emma is gone. She died or vanished, or just got tired of being a loser. The girl in the mirror is someone else. Suddenly I realise how hilarious it is: in some way Jesper actually created the person I am now. His betrayal is what has forced me to transform. He has been the nature to my caterpillar.

And now here I am.

I pack. Only the bare essentials go down into the backpack: woollen underclothing, the warm socks I got from Aunt Agneta the last Christmas she was alive, binoculars that were once Dad's, and the big knife with the carved handle Dad got from his grandfather who was a sailor. Then I listen to my phone messages. There's only one. It's from the police. They'd like to see me again and talk some more about the engagement ring. The word 'talk' annoys me, because it sounds like we're going to sit around chatting about something nice – our latest holiday, for example, or housing prices in the inner city. If it's an interrogation, can't they just say that instead?

Change or die.

I go over to the kitchen window, open it and look down. The cold air is filled with small, sparkling ice crystals which swirl into the kitchen. The snow settles like a thin film on my skin and immediately melts. Somewhere down there Sigge disappeared, I think. No – I know it's true, even though I never found him. I grab the phone and hold it out the window.

I let go and it falls to the ground. After a few seconds I hear a smash beneath me in the courtyard.

I have no need for a phone any more.

'What kind of sleeping bag? How low will the temperatures be?' says the shop girl.

I don't know how to answer. I can't exactly explain how I intend to use it. For a second I think she's looking at me strangely, maybe because of my DIY hairstyle or my harsh make-up. But it must be my imagination – doesn't half of the Swedish population look like this? She's obviously not looking at me any differently than she would anybody else. She's just doing her job.

'It needs to withstand outdoor temperatures at this time of year,' I say in a moment of quick thinking, and pick a little at the wound I got when I climbed through Jesper's basement window.

'OK,' the girl with the light-blonde ponytail says. She nods and goes over to a shelf by the window. Next to the backpacks and ice picks, a wide range of sleeping bags is lined up.

'I'd recommend this,' she says, pointing to a yellow one. 'It's synthetic, which makes it good even in humid environments. It can handle as low as fifteen degrees, but then you have to be wearing insulated underwear and a hat.'

I nod as if I know exactly what she's talking about. 'I'll take it.'

'Anything else?'

'Yeah, wait a minute. Let me check.'

I take out the list and read the other things aloud. Ten minutes later and several thousand kronor poorer, I go out onto the street. All my money is gone. I have only a few hundred left for food and a hire car.

The snowfall has changed – instead of sharp tiny crystals, now large feathery flakes fall silently to the ground. It's getting dark too; a grey-blue haze covers the city and the streetlights turn on.

Despite the lack of funds, I feel strong and light. Knowing exactly what to do is such a relief. I go to the mini supermarket on the square and gather what I need. It occurs to me that I must look like a bag lady now: I'm dragging two large plastic bags and my hair is standing on end. But no one seems to see me. Maybe I've become invisible for real, like Frodo when he wears the ring.

Today none of the pimply guys behind the counter at the car hire company say hello. They clearly don't recognise me, which is good. Very good. Without a glance at my big bags, Peter – it says so on the name tag, as if that would make us friends – inputs my name and address into the computer.

'How long do you want it?'

'One day,' I answer, though I really have no idea. But I only have enough money in my bank account for a day and know they'll run a security check on my card now.

He hands me the keys.

'Can you find your way to the car park?'

'I'll find it.'

It almost feels like I'm on my way home. Every junction, every side road is familiar. Despite the darkness, I know exactly where I'm going. I park three blocks away. It would be stupid to park too close to Jesper's house. It might attract undue attention.

But it's not Jesper's house I'm on my way to. Instead I walk to the abandoned house situated further up the hill, lying dark and gloomy in the snow like a grounded shipwreck. Cautiously I creep over the white carpet of newly fallen snow towards the little shed in the garden. I leave clear footprints behind me, but the snow is still falling. Soon my tracks will disappear, as if I never passed this way.

It's not difficult to get into the shed. The key, lying under a plastic geranium on the wooden steps, takes less than a minute to find, even though I don't use a torch. It looks odd, a blooming geranium covered by snow. Even if the flower is artificial, it just doesn't fit. The brain doesn't want to accept it. The image of delicate pink flowers and inches of thick snow contradict each other.

Like Jesper kissing the dark-haired woman.

Inside, the shed is dim and smells of mildew. I have to rearrange a pair of teak chairs in order to fit all my bags. My arms ache from the effort of carrying those packs, and I'm sweating even though it's below freezing.

I spread the yellow sleeping bag with care on an old worn sofa, then stand in the middle of the small space. I put the food on the garden table in the corner and the rest of my pack I stow under the barbecue. Then I sit down on my provisional bed with binoculars in hand and look out the window, but the falling snow makes it difficult to see anything.

I lean back and close my eyes. Something is lurking just below the surface of my consciousness, struggling to rise up, make itself known. Something important.

Then I remember.

Jesper was standing beside me on the crowded bus. We weren't looking at each other, but from the corner of my eye I sensed that he was smiling. It was a kind of game. We stood there as if we were strangers, but after a while he'd sneak his hand down and gently stroke my thigh. And now the important part: I couldn't react, couldn't reveal that I felt his touch.

Then his hand would find its way into my trousers or under my skirt or jumper and brush against my skin. No groping, just a light touch, as if it were all happening by accident. And here maybe I might stretch a little, spread my legs, let him reach me more easily. Then he'd press against me, so I knew he was hard. Yes. That's how it was supposed to be: in the middle of a crowded bus, bumping and lurching along, we remained bound by our desire.

And maybe I'd throw him a glance, as if in passing. As if I were actually just looking out the window, checking to see where we were. And our eyes would meet, and his face would be as expressionless and uninterested as mine.

But now it didn't go as planned. Not this time. Just as I felt his hand against my bum, I heard a voice somewhere in front of us on the bus. 'Jesper. Well, what a surprise. Long time no see.'

He froze behind me. His hand disappeared instantly. 'Hey! How's it going?'

A man in his forties wearing a suit was heading towards us. Winding his way through the sea of humanity until he was standing next to Jesper.

I felt Jesper slip away, and knew immediately I shouldn't say a word to reveal that we knew each other. This was his other life. His real life – which included jobs and friends and a past and future.

For Jesper and me there was only the present.

'. . . Great. And sure, compared to Austria, it's expensive, but it's fucking worth it. I don't know about you, but that whole charter thing makes me feel sick. What you're after is quality and something genuine. You won't find that in St Anton. That's just how it is. And then there's the food. The French can really cook . . .'

Jesper's acquaintance continued to babble on about the skiing and stellar restaurants and après-ski with masseuses circulating between the tables dressed in tiny rabbit-fur skirts.

'And what about you? What did you guys do over the holidays?'

I freeze. My legs start shaking uncontrollably, and I reach for the Thermos, the one that holds a litre of scalding-hot coffee. Dusty streaks of moonlight cut through the dirty window, but it's so dark in the narrow space that I knock over a carton of soup while I'm groping for my steel Thermos.

He said 'you guys'.

Jesper's friend didn't ask what he had done, but what they had done on their holiday. Why didn't I think of that earlier? Probably because I didn't realise how important it was. 'You guys' could have been Jesper and his friends or maybe even his colleagues. 'You guys' could have been anyone. But it wasn't.

'You guys' was the woman with the dark hair.

'You guys' was the reason that Jesper left me, and why everything else went to hell.

After a few seconds of hesitation I stand up, go over to the window and rub off the bottom two panes with my sleeve. It has stopped snowing. The garden spreads out, an innocent white in the moonlight. The snow rests inches thick on bushes and trees. Directly below stands Jesper's house. Light pours invitingly from the windows. It looks very cosy. Like an advertisement for one of those ski trips Jesper and his friend on the bus were talking about.

I see them instantly. They're sitting in the kitchen, eating, and the binoculars take me so close to their family idyll that I shudder. Jesper sits with his back towards me, and the woman with the dark hair sits opposite. She has a T-shirt on, and it looks like she's in the midst of some sort of discussion with Jesper; she gestures excitedly, leaning forward towards him while stabbing something that looks like a piece of meat with a fork.

A blonde girl who's probably around six or so is sitting next to the woman. That must be her daughter, I think.

Suddenly I feel ill and the heaviness in my chest returns.

Hanne

Gunilla wraps me in a blanket and puts on some tea. All the while telling me about the responsibility she says I have to myself.

'If he likes you and you like him, I don't understand why you persist in pushing him away.'

'But I'm ill,' I insist.

'Oh, please. Stop that. You might not get any worse for several years. Are you going to sit here alone until then? With me and Frida? Do something with your life instead. Otherwise, you might as well move back in with Owe.'

The thought of Owe and our dreary apartment on Skeppargatan makes my stomach turn.

'I will never move back in with Owe.'

Gunilla sighs and sinks down on the chair opposite me, massaging her bad back with one hand while lighting a candle and yawning.

'This is exactly what Owe wants. You're trapped in your own self-pity. Taking no initiative and acting like you're still with him. Enjoy your life instead of punishing yourself.'

I ponder her words. That I might be too strict with myself is a completely new thought. I've always been the one who revolted, at least until Owe forced me into submission. Owe is the rigid one, not me. He's the father to my defiant teenager. But maybe there's something to what Gunilla says: I don't allow myself anything. I use my illness as an excuse not to participate in life – which is flowing like sand from a fist, with me unable to stop it.

'I just mean that I can't burden him with my disease. I can't expect him to be my caretaker.'

'Oh my God. Listen to yourself. He's a grown man. He can decide for himself if he wants to be with you. You were honest and told him about the disease.'

I sip the hot tea without answering. Maybe she's right.

'So what do you think I should do?' I ask after a while.

'You don't need to make any life-changing decisions right now. Go out together a little. Allow yourself to feel what you want. Don't take everything so seriously. You're not going to get married and have kids, right? You're two middle-aged people who like each other and want to spend time together. That's all.'

'But that's also a problem. I'm far too old for him. He should meet a younger woman. Start a family. You know, all that stuff.'

'It doesn't seem as though he wants a family. Maybe that's not his thing. Besides, he already has a son, right?'

I think about Albin, the boy he never sees and never wants to talk about. There's so much about Peter I don't understand, so much that's strange. But maybe that's just how life is. People make strange choices, and it's impossible to ever fully understand anyone else. Sometimes you just have to accept them as they are. Actually, the same is true of Owe. I don't really know why he is the way he is, even though we've lived together for so many years. The only thing I know for certain is that I can't stand him any more. That I've had enough.

'Maybe,' I say. 'We'll see.'

'Maybe is good,' Gunilla says and nods slowly.

Gunilla leaves to hang up washing in the basement, and I remain in the kitchen. Staring into the warm flickering flame of the candle and thinking about the children who never came. The children who never grew up in our big apartment, who never started school or joined the scouts. Never came home with skinned knees, never played video games or asked for more pocket money. Never graduated or had girlfriends or boyfriends, never moved away from home.

I didn't miss them until it was too late. But afterwards, when I was too old, the sadness of what never was suddenly hit me. Sometimes it almost felt as if it took physical shape, materialised between Owe and me at the dinner table, keeping us from reaching each other.

I open the notebook lying on the kitchen table. Tear out a sheet and pick up a pen. Begin a list entitled 'Continue Seeing Peter'.

In the plus column, I write:

Company.
Good sex (finally!). True love (?).
Something I've chosen, for my own sake.

I think for a moment and continue with the minus column:

Becomes complicated if/when I get worse.
Becomes unbearable if/when he betrays me again.

I look at the list for a while without getting any wiser. Then I move it over to the candle and let it catch on fire. The flame flares up and a wave of heat slams into my face as my fears and hopes are turned to ashes.

I'm about to blow out the candle when my mobile rings. It's Manfred. He sounds out of breath, as if he's just run up a flight of stairs. But when I hear what he says, I realise that something else is making him sound that way: excitement and maybe a hint of stress.

'Jesper Orre had a relationship with Angelica Wennerlind, and it can't be ruled out that she's dead too. The investigation team is meeting in half an hour. Can you come?'

On my way to the police station, I think of Peter. How strange it is that he's never explained why he didn't turn up on that night ten years ago. I'd like to ask him about it someday. Not because I'm still angry, but because I need to understand what happened. What he was thinking when he left me on that porch, alone with my shame and my two old suitcases plastered with stickers from my childhood holidays.

The event was so life-altering for me, so self-defining, and he'd never given me an explanation. All I got was that silly letter, in which he wrote that he couldn't live with me because he'd only end up hurting me.

Hurt me how? I want to ask him. As if his betrayal didn't hurt enough, I think as I look out the car window and the taxi stops in front of the police station entrance.

I exit into darkness so black and dense, it's almost possible to touch it. I think about the Inuit. They're not afraid of the polar night. They lie on the ice, waiting next to the seals' breathing holes until one of the fat, spool-shaped animals surfaces. Waiting for the right moment to throw their harpoons.

Or rather, they did until the Danes came. Now I've heard it's all about movies and beer, even in the remotest corners of Greenland. Sitting inertly in front of a TV has replaced waiting alertly on top of pack ice even in the smallest villages.

Seven years ago, I actually managed to convince Owe we should go there. The flight to Nuuk was booked, as well as our transport to Ittoqqortoormiit, via Kulusuk. We had a sitter for Charlie, our dog at the time, and Owe had taken two weeks off. But then the Edith incident happened.

Owe was Edith's advisor for the psychiatric portion, and Edith was a doctor doing her residency. I soon realised she was more than that. There was something about the way Owe talked about her, how he mentioned her name all the time, and how he lingered on that first syllable when he said it.

Eeedith.

I knew he'd soon tire of her. He always did. Especially with the younger women, who didn't offer sufficient mental stimulation. Even if he was a dirty old man, his vanity needed someone who could reflect his intellect and confirm it – and usually those younger women couldn't do that for him.

It turned out just as I had predicted. After a few weeks he stopped talking about Edith. But then one night, two days before we were going to leave for Greenland, he came into the bedroom and stood behind me. I was packing and had my back to him when he put his hands lightly on my shoulders:

'I can't go, Hanne.'

I carefully folded my thermal underwear and put it in the suitcase on the bed. Turned around and met his eyes.

He released me and looked out the window. 'It's Edith. She's had a miscarriage.'

The difficult thing about Edith wasn't that she'd fucked my husband – many had. The difficult thing was that she got pregnant when I couldn't. That her young body was actually willing to bear Owe's children.

But Edith didn't really change anything between Owe and me. Our relationship was what it was. We just never went to Greenland. And after that episode I no longer felt like going anywhere with him. Now I'm starting to suspect that my obsession with Greenland is about something else. That Greenland is a kind of symbol for all the things in my life that have never turned out. That the country embodies all the hopes and desires I once had.

The office is lit up like a Christmas tree, far out into the corridor, and the atmosphere is animated but also nervous, as if everyone is aware that something crucial has occurred. Manfred and Peter are talking to each other, and Bergdahl, the investigator who helped sort the tip-offs, is pacing around the room in large circles with his hands in his pockets.

Peter raises his hand and I nod back. I try to avoid looking at him too much. Maybe I'm afraid he'll see what I feel.

Owe always claimed he could see what I was thinking and feeling just by looking at me. And as the years went by, I started to believe that was true, because he was almost always right. Though in hindsight, I think it was probably just another way for him to exercise power over me. He was so obsessed with controlling me – he wanted me to believe I couldn't think an independent thought without his approval.

'Angelica Wennerlind and Emma Bohman both had relationships with Jesper Orre,'

Manfred says, pouring fresh coffee into flimsy paper cups, 'We have to assume that there may be at least one more victim that we haven't found yet. The area around Orre's house will be searched again tomorrow morning and the radius will be extended. Bergdahl is in charge of that. We'll keep our fingers crossed that we don't find any more bodies on that block; we'd never live that down. Sanchez is working on trying to connect Orre to the Calderón murder, and apart from that we're waiting for confirmation from the odontologist as to the identity of the woman in Orre's house. We should get that in the next few hours.'

'What a fucking psychopath,' Bergdahl mumbles.

Manfred catches my eye. 'What do you say, Hanne? Was Orre a psychopath?'

I shrug my shoulders. I'm both flattered and worried that Manfred seems to think I can determine such a thing without ever having met Jesper Orre. Lay people often make that mistake – they think that psychologists and behavioural scientists can diagnose people just by reading a report about them. As if evaluating a person's mental health is something you can learn through a correspondence course.

'"Psychopath" is a misused word. We call everyone a psycho these days.'

'Fuck psychological subtleties for now,' Manfred says.

'Psychological subtleties are my profession,' I say. 'And I'm not going to abandon that just because you want me to make a premature statement. Based on what we know about him, there's actually nothing to suggest he was a psychopath. Sleeping around and preferring your sex kinky doesn't mean you also like to kill people. And being an arsehole at work isn't particularly damning either. Sure, he *may* have killed those girls, but there's not much in his past to suggest he's capable of such a thing. That's all I can say.'

'OK,' Manfred says. 'But what do you think?'

I ponder for a moment, go over to the wall and stare at the information hanging there about Orre, Calderón and the missing women. There's something bothering me here, something lurking beneath the surface that doesn't want to reveal itself, and it frustrates me.

'Something is off,' I say.

'Oh, you don't say,' Manfred responds acidly.

I ignore him. Run my finger over the papers. Stop in front of the document about Emma Bohman's background. Raised on Kapellgränd on Södermalm. Went to primary school at the Katarina Norra School. Started working at Clothes&More three years ago. Her mother died in September of this year, her father in May exactly ten years ago.

'Here,' I say. 'Here it is!'

But just as I'm formulating my thoughts, I'm interrupted by the ringing of a mobile.

Manfred raises his hand to me and answers.

'Yes,' he says. 'OK. And he's sure? Thanks. See you soon.'

He hangs up and puts the phone on his desk, clasps his hands behind his neck.

'That was Sanchez. The murdered woman has been identified as Angelica Wennerlind.'

Emma

One week earlier

First night in the shed. I close my eyes and hope the sleeping bag is as good as they claimed. So far it feels fine, but I'm wearing both my hat and coat as I lie motionless in my yellow polyester cocoon.

I'm just like the butterfly, I think. I'm biding my time, waiting for my transformation to happen, so I can do what I'm destined to do. I fiddle with the short tufts of my hair, thinking about Olga and Mahnoor walking back and forth across the shop, listening to that hopelessly repetitive soundtrack day in and day out. I feel sorry for them. They're no more than animals in a cage. I am infinitely freer. I'm broke and I've been dumped, but I'm free. And soon, very soon, I'll finish what I started.

The plan is simple. I'll wait until the dark-haired woman and child leave the house, and then I'll go and speak to Jesper. I'll force him to listen, even if I have to threaten him. And this time he won't get away. I deserve to know the truth.

What happens after that I don't really know. But I won't hurt him, because I'm not a monster.

A monster is a person who lies and deceives. Someone who wrecks and destroys things for their own amusement. Who leaves another person's life in ruins like a bombed-out city or a burnt-down forest.

A monster is someone who does all that and enjoys it.

Like Jesper.

Mum said I should be cautious about men, that they're always after something. She made it sound as though they wanted to steal something from me: my dignity, or maybe my independence. I wish she'd told me the truth instead. The opposite is true. You never get rid of the men you let in close. It is as if they're stuck fast to your life.

Jesper. Woody.

I carry them with me wherever I go. They're in my thoughts and in my dreams. Even my body remembers them: their scent, the feeling of their soft, warm skin against mine, the sound of muffled groans and heavy breathing next to my ear.

I wish I could wash them off like dirt. Wish soap and water could take away what I can't erase from my consciousness. I wish in some mysterious way I could be transported back in time to before I met them. Back to when I was still full of hope and had a clear, naive vision of how my life would turn out.

I wake up to something tickling my cheek. Grey light filters in through the dirty windows, over which hoarfrost has spread during the night. Even though it must be below freezing in the shed, I'm not cold. But my neck and back ache after a night spent on that hard, too-short sofa.

I sit up wearily, reach for the Thermos and pour the hot liquid into a tin cup. The floor is freezing cold and I immediately pull on a pair of ski pants. Then I go to the window with my binoculars. Only now do I see that the hoarfrost is on the inside of the window. I rub off a bit with my sleeve. The sky is a dull steel grey, as if it's carrying more snow. The slope down towards Jesper's house is untouched under a thick layer of new-fallen snow. No one – no sledging children, not even a dog – has been anywhere near my hiding place during the night.

It's almost funny.

They're sitting at their kitchen table eating breakfast, in exactly the same places as yesterday. As if they've been sitting there all night and just exchanged their meat for cereal. The little blonde girl is there too. She's wearing striped pyjamas, and the woman is wearing a thick white robe, like something out of a spa ad. Jesper is still sitting with his back to me, as if he knows where I am and wants to demonstrate by his indifference how little he cares about me.

You can turn your back to me, but you can't escape, I think. I'm close now. Can almost reach out and touch you and your perfect life. Poke at it and make it collapse like the flimsy house of cards that it is.

The thought puts me in a better mood and I take out bread and ham from the bag tucked under the old rusty barbecue and we all eat breakfast together, or whatever you want to call it with me eating my breakfast while watching them eat theirs. A moment later Jesper leaves the kitchen. The woman and child remain. Five minutes later he comes back in, dressed in some sort of workout clothes. The dark-haired woman, who's still sitting at the table, leans back so that the dressing gown gapes open, and Jesper bends forward and kisses her while putting his hand under her robe against her breast.

I put the binoculars in my lap, clench my eyes shut. Pick at the scab on my hand so hard that it falls off and warm blood starts to drip onto the floor. It's strange that it hurts just as much every time. I know that he deceived me. That's not news. I've been in their house, seen them together. So why does it still hurt so fucking much? Why haven't I learned to defend myself against the pain?

I pick up the binoculars again and catch a glimpse of Jesper jogging away from the house towards the water. Then he disappears out of sight. And now the kitchen is empty. Just a solitary cup remains sitting on the table.

I follow the side of the house with my binoculars and up towards the upstairs windows. The curtains are pulled in Jesper's bedroom, but in the window next to it I see the little girl again. It's impossible to make out what she's doing, but her little blonde head is moving up and down in the room, as if she's jumping or running around. Then she disappears too. The house seems empty, abandoned, but I know they're in there somewhere.

I decide to take a break. I pee in the old red plastic bucket standing in a corner, brush my teeth and run my fingers through my short hair. Then I settle back into the sofa and wait, staring out the small window. After maybe a half hour Jesper returns. I see him come jogging cautiously back, as if it's slippery and he's afraid of falling. He stops and stretches a bit against a tree before heading towards the entrance.

It's Sunday. What does a happy little family in a nice suburb do on a Sunday? Go to the museum? Invite some successful friends over for an ambitious brunch of omelettes, smoothies and freshly baked sourdough bread? Build a snowman in the freshly fallen snow?

That should have been me.

That should have been me sitting there instead of that dark-haired woman. Only now do I realise how much I hate her.

The whole day goes by without anything happening. I eat my sandwiches and try to move around to stay warm. The coffee's run out and I've switched to the fizzy drink, which fortunately didn't freeze during the night.

Suddenly Mum pops up in my mind, like one of those old-fashioned hand puppets. I don't really know, but I think it's because, like Jesper, she lived a lie.

I remember when the call came from the hospital one morning while I was getting ready to leave for work. At first I was unsure if I should answer, because I was already running late and a late arrival meant a black mark. At least if Björne was in a bad mood.

The woman introduced herself as a doctor and told me that my mother was ill. She'd gone to accident and emergency last night and had been hospitalised for further tests.

'How is she?' I asked with the mobile wedged between my shoulder and ear, while pulling back the front door and starting down the stairs.

'We don't really know what's wrong with her yet, but she's stable. There is no immediate danger to her life, but she's very worried and she keeps asking for you.'

'She's asking for me?'

It had been months since Mum had called me, and I had a hard time believing she'd missed me. Not even when she was sick and alone.

'Yes. She'd like you to come and visit her.'

I was quiet.

'We have visiting hours between two and six,' the doctor continued. 'Should I tell her you'll be coming?'

'Yes. I'll be there,' I heard myself say, while I exited onto the street.

We hung up and I hurried to the metro. Winding past patches of ice and squinting against the crisp spring sunshine. Breathing in the scent of damp earth and last year's rotting leaves.

She's very worried and she keeps asking for you.

I was confused. Knew I had to go to the hospital at once. If for no other reason than to find out why Mum was suddenly so anxious to see me.

She had a room at the end of a bright hallway. It looked like every other hospital room I'd ever seen: a bed with a small table on wheels and a chrome stool beside it, a television mounted on the wall, a couple of cabinets and next to them a sink. The obligatory bottles of soap and hand disinfectant hung on the wall next to the tap.

I found her sitting up in bed reading. I don't really know what I was expecting, but I thought that she would be more seriously ill. Not that she'd be sitting in a tracksuit and reading a tabloid.

'Emma, sweetheart!'

She took off her reading glasses and pushed her bleached hair from her forehead. The scent of coffee arrived from the hallway. Afternoon tea was on its way.

'Hi. How are you doing?'

I shrugged off my bag and jacket and sat down on the stool next to the bed. Mum put down her tabloid on the yellow hospital blanket draped over her legs and turned her deep-set eyes to me.

'It's terrible what you have to put up with in this place.'

I noted she'd avoided answering the question I had asked. 'Really?'

She coughed and put her hand on her stomach, as if in pain.

'They wake us up at six in the morning. Six. Can you imagine? And they're running in and out of here constantly. Different people all the time. It's like trying to sleep at a train station. And they're all immigrants. Not that they can help it, but they can't speak Swedish, you understand? How are you supposed to take care of someone you can't communicate with? And last night there was another woman in this room. She snored so loudly I couldn't sleep a wink. I told the night staff, explained how sensitive I am to sounds, but they claim they don't have any other rooms. In the end I had to ask for a sleeping pill, but they refused to give me one. Treated me like I was a junkie asking for heroin. It's crazy. You work and pay taxes your whole life and then you get treated like this when you finally need help.'

I don't remind Mum that she hasn't worked until recently but was actually on disability for most of her adult life. She moves her thick hand to the corner of her eye, wipes away an invisible tear.

'Oh, Emma. Getting old and sick is no fun. I can tell you that.'

She looked expectantly at me, as if she wanted me to back her up, but I didn't say anything. I didn't know what to say.

A nursing assistant came into the room carrying a tray. Her uniform was dazzlingly white against her black skin.

'What did I tell you?' Mum whispered and nodded to the woman.

'It's a liquid diet for you today,' the nurse said, smiling as she set the tray down on the table beside the bed. Then she left.

Mum didn't answer. Just looked with disgust at the light-brown soup. 'This isn't fit for human consumption. Do they expect me to eat this?' She stirred the soup with her spoon, then set it aside on the tray.

'What happened?' I tried again.

Mum waved her hand as though it were unimportant.

'They can't really say. Something about my stomach. You'd think they'd be able to diagnose me more quickly considering how many people they have running around here.' She gave me a crooked smile.

'But . . . when can you go home?'

Mum shrugged. 'The only positive thing about this is, it makes you grateful for what you have.'

She looked at me. Her eyes were set so deep that it was impossible to determine their colour. Her cheeks were red and seemed swollen, as if she had a mouthful of cotton.

'We have each other, Emma,' she said and grabbed my hand.

If she had told me she was heading for the moon, I would have been less surprised. In the last five years we'd seen each other maybe twice. What did she mean, we had each other?

Mum sighed deeply and wiped away another invisible tear with her free hand, while squeezing mine so hard it felt as though it was going numb.

'Remember, Emma? We had it so good. Your dad, you and me. And then when Dad . . . disappeared, we comforted each other. I thought we were a strong little family, even without him. We helped each other as best we could. Maybe our troubles made us even stronger. They say that kind of thing brings people closer. Right?'

I sat stock-still on my stool. Couldn't believe my ears. When had we ever been a happy family? And the idea that we somehow got closer after Dad's suicide was absolute bullshit. The only times I got closer to Mum – at least closer physically – was when I had to lead her to bed after she'd passed out at the dinner table or in the bathroom. The only time I helped her was when I went and bought cigarettes and antacids for her hangovers. And as for her helping me, I couldn't recall that she ever did.

'I don't regret anything,' she sobbed, and now I saw real tears. They rolled like glass beads down her fat cheeks. 'But I wish we'd had your dad with us a little longer. He was such an incredible person, and we loved each other so much.'

She said the last bit in a barely audible voice.

Memories of Mum and Dad's fights flashed before me like shadows on the edge of my visual field. Barely discernible, but still there. Fragments of a life that no longer existed. Dishes flying across the kitchen. Screaming. Police knocking on the door in the middle of the night because the neighbours had complained. The broken blue butterfly lying in shards of glass on the kitchen floor.

For a second, I wondered if I should protest. Remind Mum what it was really like in that cramped apartment. But I knew it would be pointless, that the story she'd so carefully crafted couldn't be changed. Her world view stood there between us like an elephant, preventing us from reaching any real mutual understanding.

I suddenly felt tired. Longed to just go home and rest. Not think any more about the fat woman in the hospital bed, lying to me and to herself, and probably to anyone else who would listen.

'I should probably go now.' My voice was a whisper.

'Already?' She stopped sobbing instantly, almost as if someone had pressed a button. I nodded and stood up.

'We have a meeting at work,' I lied.

As I walked down the corridor, it occurred to me that Mum hadn't asked how I was doing. She hadn't shown the least bit of interest in me.

I'm shivering from the cold. Now and then I catch a glimpse of Jesper, the woman or the child just beyond the edge of a room. It's harder than I'd thought to keep watching the house without losing my concentration. And the binoculars are heavy. After a few hours my arms ache and my fingers are stiff with cold. I've tried keeping my mittens on, but then I couldn't hold on to the binoculars, so I have no choice but to leave them in my bag.

I almost miss the moment when the woman and little girl leave the house. Twilight has started to descend. The sky is still light, but the landscape has darkened and windows are starting to glow. The woman and girl climb into a red Volvo and drive away in the direction of the city.

I stand up slowly on legs that are stiff from hours in the cold. They're gone. That must mean that Jesper is alone in the house. I take a few steps towards the window and train my binoculars on the house. And suddenly a wave of heat washes over me. My hands feel soft and warm. My cheeks flush and my heart starts to pound so hard, it's as if it wants to escape from my chest.

He's sitting at the table with a laptop in front of him. Beside him on the counter is a glass of wine. A sandwich lies on a plate.

It's time.

I stand on his front steps with my finger on the doorbell. The time has come. There's nothing I can do to stop the inevitable now. Maybe this was settled long ago. Maybe it's the logical conclusion of the chain of events Jesper set off the night he disappeared. Yes, that has to be so, I tell myself. That's how this started. I was standing in the kitchen, making canapés for our engagement dinner. That's when it started.

He started it.

The thought gives me strength. I press the doorbell and hear a buzzing sound coming through the door. It's not a pretty sound. No ding-dong or fragile ringing – more of an aggressive snarl. A sound that would drive you mad if you had to listen to it often enough.

At first I don't think he's heard – nothing happens. Then the door opens and there he is.

The king himself. The mighty man who crushed my life, turned it to shit without the slightest tinge of regret. He doesn't look like much today. His hair is greyer than I remember it, his face sunken and tired, as if he's suffering from some debilitating disease or hasn't slept for a long time.

'Hello,' I say.

Peter

Manfred stands in the middle of the floor, immovable, like a monolith. Resting his eyes on us, one by one. There's something cunning in his face. Something primitive that makes you think of a predator on the trail of its prey.

'Well I never,' Bergdahl mumbles. 'It wasn't Emma Bohman after all. We'd better focus on that other girl, that Angelica Wennerlind, now.'

'No,' Manfred says. 'No. Something's not right. Two women had an affair with Orre. Both disappeared, but we have only one murder victim. And Orre is thawing out in Solna like a pack of frozen prawns as we speak.'

Hanne stands up. Walks slowly over to the evidence wall and points to one of the papers. She looks comically small next to Manfred, but her voice is deep and sonorous as she begins to speak:

'Emma Bohman's mother died three months before the woman in Orre's house was murdered. And her father died in May, ten years ago, four months before Miguel Calderón was murdered.'

The room falls silent for a moment. A security guard passes in the corridor, looks in through the door and says hello. The rattle of his keys disappears down the stairs.

'What are you getting at?' Manfred asks.

'For a mentally fragile person, the death of a loved one can trigger mental health problems, even psychoses. And I find it odd that her parents' deaths happened so closely in time to the murders. Maybe it's not a coincidence.'

I'm struck by how confident Hanne seems as she stands in front of the evidence wall. How her entire being exudes calm and authority. If she does have memory problems, they're not obvious.

'This investigation is full of strange coincidences,' Manfred says and sinks down on a chair. 'For example, both Emma Bohman and Angelica Wennerlind had a relationship with Orre.'

'We don't know that,' Hanne says quietly. 'They both claimed they were seeing him, but no witness has confirmed their relationships. Angelica Wennerlind's friend says that Angelica told her about her relationship with Orre. And Emma Bohman claimed that Orre was her fiancé and that he bought her an engagement ring. But in the surveillance video from the jewellery shop only Emma appears. No one else. And, of course, he denied the relationship.'

'That in itself isn't surprising,' Sanchez says. 'He was very secretive about his girls.'

'We should talk to Emma Bohman's aunt again,' Manfred chimes in. 'The one who reported her missing. Bergdahl, can you get hold of her? And bring her here if she's awake.'

Bergdahl nods and leaves the room with mobile in hand. Manfred turns towards Hanne again.

'Could Emma Bohman be involved in this crime?'

Hanne shrugs. 'I guess it's possible. Though there's nothing specific that points to it, besides the fact that her parents died just before the murders. Do we know if there's any connection between Emma and Calderón? Apart from the timing of the murders, that is?'

Manfred crosses his arms over his chest. Closes his eyes. 'We haven't been looking for that kind of a connection.'

'Maybe we should have been,' Hanne says.

'There's a lot we should have done,' Manfred mutters under his breath.

Steps approach from the stairs and a few seconds later Bergdahl enters. 'The aunt was awake. I've sent a car to pick her up. She'll be here in twenty minutes.'

While waiting for Emma Bohman's aunt to arrive, I go outside with Manfred to smoke a cigarette. He asks Hanne to come too, and she hangs her coat over her shoulders and takes her little notebook along, as if she's going to take notes outside.

When the police station became smoke-free, it forced us inveterate nicotine addicts out onto the balconies or into the street in order to practise our harmful habit. We go to the small terrace on the first floor, which overlooks the courtyard. Two snow-covered terracotta pots with long-dead plants function as ashtrays, but there are butts lying in droves next to them, like fallen fruit next to an old fruit tree. The sky is black and starless above the city and the cold stings your cheeks.

'That thing you said about Emma Bohman and Angelica Wennerlind,' Manfred begins and turns to Hanne. 'That they claimed to have relationships with Jesper Orre. What exactly did you mean by that?'

Hanne's eyes look away, across the buildings and into the city. She fiddles with her notepad and says:

'I meant exactly what I said. We can't know if they were telling the truth or lying.'

'Why would they lie about something like that?'

Hanne shrugs, squeezes out a wry smile.

'Why do people lie? Maybe to seem more exciting or interesting. Or maybe they believe it themselves.'

'Now I'm not following,' Manfred says and lights a cigarette.

'You could be suffering from a delusion. They're not unusual among psychotic patients. There are many examples of people who've believed they had a relationship with someone without ever meeting them in real life. There's even a medical term for the phenomenon – erotomania. Often people suffering from these delusions fall headlong in love with a celebrity or some authority figure, and sometimes they're convinced they've lived together for many years. Maybe even married them and had children together.'

'A celebrity or authority figure. Like the CEO of the company you work for?' I ask.

'Exactly,' Hanne says and meets my gaze. 'And they believe that love is reciprocated, even though it's not.'

It feels as though Hanne is speaking directly to me, and something inside me breaks. Cracks like a dry branch under a boot. For a second I wonder if I might have imagined everything that has happened over the past few days: our calls, the night at her house, the walk in the snow on Södermälarstrand. The palpable feeling of closeness might just be something that my brain has conjured up in the absence of any other close relationships in my life, or maybe to lessen the weight of the debt I will never be able to repay.

Manfred stubs his cigarette out against the wall and looks at his watch.

'It's quarter past. The aunt will be here any minute. We should go back in.'

Lena Brogren is in her sixties and extremely overweight. She's wearing a tent-like floral-patterned tunic that reaches to her knees and a pair of pilled leggings. Her feet are wedged into fur boots, which look like two small dogs crowding around her legs. When she says hello to us, I'm struck by how scared she seems. Her eyes flicker between us and she fiddles with the cigarette packet she holds in her hand.

'I guess you can't smoke in here?' she asks.

Her voice is strangely bright and clear – she'd make a positive contribution to any choir – and contrasts sharply with her large body and haggard, shiny face.

'Sorry,' Manfred says.

The woman nods and looks at me.

'Little Emma. What has she done now?' she asks in a quiet voice, shaking her head slowly so that her double chins start to swing.

'We're not sure she's done anything at all,' Manfred says and explains to Lena Brogren why she's been called in after ten in the evening. 'We're investigating the murder of a young woman and Emma's name has come up.

'Can you tell us a little about Emma?' I add.

'Emma is . . . sweet and well behaved. Doesn't make much noise. Never has, actually. We've spent plenty of time together since she was a little girl, so I know her well. But she's always had a hard time with her social life, our little Emma. And since Gun's death – Emma's mother, my sister – she's become very introverted. Difficult to connect with in some way. I usually visit her up there on Värtavägen, make sure she's taken care of – I promised Gun I would. But the last two times I was there, she didn't open the door. Even though I heard someone inside. When I saw that picture of the dead girl, I called your hotline immediately.'

The woman struggles for breath and continues, 'She's not dead, is she?'

'No, no,' I say. 'The woman found in Jesper Orre's house has been identified and it isn't Emma.'

Lena Brogren's relief is palpable. She sinks deeper into her chair. Nods and wipes the sweat from her forehead.

'Why did Emma drop out of school?' Hanne asks.

The woman looks confused. 'She didn't drop out of school. She never started. That horrible thing happened with her DT teacher and it pushed her off balance.'

'What happened with her DT teacher?' I ask.

'That supply teacher. He assaulted Emma. They fired him, of course, but what good did that do? The damage was already done. Can you imagine taking advantage of a fifteen-year-old who you're also responsible for? What kind of monster does such a thing? But the Lord works in mysterious ways, doesn't He? That man ended up dead anyway. Murdered. A horrible story, but I couldn't feel too sorry for him. We coddle criminals nowadays, don't you think? You work with this kind of thing all day, you must think—'

Manfred interrupts her gently:

'This supply teacher. What was his name?'

She hesitates for a moment, seems to be searching her memory. 'They called him Woody.'

Hanne bends forward and puts her hand lightly on Lena Brogren's arm. A gesture that's empathetic but also expectant and curious.

'Woody? That sounds like a nickname, Lena. Do you remember what his real name was?'

The woman blinks several times, and for a second I think she's going to start crying. 'No,' she says. 'Something foreign, of course. Yes, he was an immigrant. Did I mention that?'

'Miguel Calderón?' Hanne proposes.

The woman's face clears and she shudders. Nods slowly with her jaw clenched. 'Calderón. Yes, that was it.'

Emma

One week earlier

Jesper quickly pulls the front door shut but I'm faster, wedging my ergonomically correct boot – the one that can withstand both rain and falling rocks – into the gap before he can close it. I take out the small plastic gizmo I bought on the Internet, the one that looks like a mobile, and hold it against his hand while pressing the red button.

He lets out a shrill scream, releases the door and collapses on the floor inside. I look around quickly before slipping into the warmth of the hall and closing the door behind me.

The stun gun isn't dangerous; it said so clearly in the instruction manual. It just incapacitates the victim for a few minutes. It's unpleasant but in no way harmful to healthy people. And Jesper is healthy. He's healthy and successful, and like most healthy, successful people, he has no idea how lucky he is. And he needs to be reminded.

I put the stun gun back in my pocket and drop down on my haunches beside him. I take out the plastic ties and fasten his wrists together behind his back. He snorts and spits and wriggles a bit, but puts up no real resistance, which almost disappoints me. It's a little too easy. I've played countless scenarios in my head in which Jesper and I roll around on the hall floor in a fight to the death. But instead he just lies there, as helpless as a child.

It strikes me he's no longer sexy or attractive. Just a pale middle-aged man whose delusions of grandeur have finally caught up with him.

'It's not dangerous,' I say. 'I had to. We need to talk. You owe me an explanation.' His legs jerk a little and he drools on the floor which makes me uncomfortable because it reminds me of a bedridden old man. Then he coughs. 'Let me go, for fuck's sake. It hurts.'

'I'm sorry,' I say, 'but I need you to be still and listen to me. Then you can do what you want.'

He doesn't answer. Just lies there on his side on the floor, looking pathetic. His chest is heaving up and down and his eyes are closed, as if he's trying to shut me out. I take off my coat. Fold it, bend over and put it under his head. Then I sit down beside him on the floor and gently stroke his hair.

'What do you want?' His voice is a whisper.

'I want to know why.'

'What do you mean "why"?'

He sounds confused. I guess due to the lingering effect of the electric shock.

'Why you left me. Why you took my money and my painting. Why you got me fired. Why you killed my cat. Why. Why. *Why.*'

'I don't know what you're talking about.'

His voice is as harsh and unfriendly as the frozen ground outside. As if I were a mere burglar pushing my way into his home instead of his girlfriend. I take out the stun gun and give him a shock, mostly to show him it's not OK to talk to me like that. He jerks as if he's been kicked in the groin, moans and then lies still.

'Don't you dare mock me. You toyed with for me as long as it suited you, and then you threw me away. And all I want to know is why. Is that too much to ask?'

He doesn't answer but I can see him breathing. Around his hips a wet spot has formed; it spreads across the hall floor towards the door.

'You killed our child,' I say in a low voice.

He makes a little noise. It sounds like a cough, or maybe a dry, unhappy little laugh that he's attempting to mask.

'I don't know what you're talking about,' he repeats.

I consider giving him another shock but decide that's not a good idea. I don't want to hurt him, just force him to listen. And give me an explanation.

'Why didn't you contact me?'

Jesper draws a deep breath and looks at me for the first time since collapsing on the floor. His eyes are bloodshot. His gaze flits anxiously between me and the ceiling.

'Are you the one who wrote that letter?' he asks.

'Yes.'

'I . . . thought it was best not to contact you.'

He sighs and curls up on the floor like a shrimp. There's a short pause, then he starts speaking again:

'What's your name?'

'Come on. You know that. My name is Emma.'

'Please, Emma . . .'

Tears run down his hollow cheeks as he continues:

'Listen to me. Can you do that?'

'Sure.'

I lean against the wall, cross my arms over my chest, simultaneously curious and disturbed by this sudden initiative.

'I know you believe we know each other. That we . . . are close to each other. But it's not true. I've never met you before. What you remember . . . never happened. I haven't betrayed or deceived you or . . . killed your cat or whatever it was. All of that . . . is in your head. Do you understand? It's something you've imagined. We have never . . . you and me. We have never met before. I don't know how to make you believe me, but . . . Emma. I don't think you're a bad person. Really, I don't.'

I lie down beside him on the floor, rest my cheek against the cool stone tiles. My face is just inches from his. I wonder if everything he says is purely a lie or if he actually believes it himself. Maybe this is some form of repression.

'You left me the day we got engaged. I don't know why you disappeared so suddenly, but my guess is that it has something to do with that dark-haired girl. What you didn't know is that I was pregnant.'

He doesn't answer, just lies there with tears streaming down. I continue:

'Leaving me . . . I can understand that. People do that. I get it. What I don't get is why you did all those other things, why you had to . . . destroy me.'

His face contorts in a grimace and he looks so miserable that I take my hand and rest it across his cheek.

We lie there for a moment in complete silence on the cold floor. His breathing calms down a little bit and his sobs peter out.

'Listen, Jesper. Everything will be all right again.'

He nods, and a string of drool runs from the corner of his mouth to the floor. 'Everything will be all right again,' he says quietly.

'Because we love each other,' I say and kiss his tear-and-snot-smeared cheek.

'We love each other,' he repeats.

Suddenly I hear someone coming up the front steps, and then a click as the door opens.

I turn around and there she stands.

The dark-haired woman puts her hands over her mouth, as if trying to stifle a scream.

She backs slowly towards the front door without saying a word, while I jump up and run over to her. The scent of perfume hovers around her, and I'm suddenly aware of how I must appear: unshowered, smelly, my hair on end.

I grab her wrists and she loses balance. She's wearing slender high-heeled black leather boots more suitable for shopping than hand-to-hand combat.

'What the hell?' Her voice is shrill and surprised, and I reckon I'm the last thing she expected to find here in the hall. She must have assumed she'd already outmanoeuvred me. We pull in opposite directions while spinning around in the hall. I let go of her wrist at just the right moment, when she's just at the top of the stairs leading down to the basement. She flies away like a child jumping out of a swing. Her scream as she tumbles down the stairs is horrendous, like a dying animal's.

She's lying halfway down the stairs and I take a few paces towards her. Her dark hair is spread out like a fan around her head and a red spot is growing fast. I squat down beside her and watch. It's impossible to see if she's still breathing, but the blood continues to flow from her head. A sea of blood is forming and a little river has broken free. It flows down the stairs like a waterfall.

I stand up. Everything is rocking back and forth. This wasn't part of the plan. No one was supposed to get hurt. I was going to talk to Jesper, nothing else. I close my eyes in an attempt to force the dizziness away.

Jesper screams. 'Stop! She has nothing to do with this. Hit me instead. I should have answered your letter, your text messages. Do what you want to me, but don't touch Angelica. Please, Emma. Please.'

The room is spinning faster and faster, and I'm overcome by a sudden nausea. The smell of blood and urine closes in on me. I throw another glance at the woman. She lies as motionless as before. Beside her feet something metallic glitters: a pair of car keys. I pick them up and pull the woman's body up onto the hall floor. Kick her in the face to see if she's alive. She whimpers slightly.

'Please. Let me go. Please . . . I'm sorry. I should have called. Please. Forgive me!'

Jesper's voice sounds distant, as if it's coming from inside a tube. I see no reason to answer him and frankly I don't know what to say. Everything has gone wrong and the only thing I want is to get out of here. To escape the sight of Jesper's lean body on the floor and the smell of fear and death.

But I can't. Not yet.

I have to show this woman, this woman who took Jesper away from me, that she hasn't won. She has to see who he loves and belongs to, even if I have to force her to.

'Watch,' I whisper. 'Watch closely now.'

Hanne

Owe's text message arrives at five o'clock in the morning. It wakes me from a troubled sleep. I pick up my mobile from the floor and read it.

I love you.

That's all. No threats, no begging for me to come home. I stare at the display, which glows in the dark. Marvel at how trite that sentence sounds. It's as if the words have lost their meaning – they feel doctored and tasteless, like processed food.

I sit up. My back aches after hours on an uncomfortable sofa in the waiting room. The group has been working all night, but I needed to lie down for a while. I've always been like that. Owe thought it was funny. Teased me because I was like a child who needed to eat and sleep at specific times.

But the fact is, it's true. I can't go for an extended period of time without sleep. It's not that I get grumpy and surly – no, it's that I lose the ability to think clearly, to make the simplest connections.

And I can't allow that to happen right now.

Where could she have gone, the woman who murdered Jesper Orre and his girlfriend? The woman who . . .

I realise with growing frustration that I actually don't remember her name any more. It is as if it has disappeared during sleep, gone up in smoke while I was on that hard sofa, dissolved into the stuffy air of the waiting room.

I sit up and pull on my cardigan. The floor is cold under my bare feet as I walk to the window. In the darkness outside lonely snowflakes whirl past. The surrounding buildings are dark, with only a few windows here or there dimly lit, gleaming like beacons in the night.

In the room on the second floor there's feverish activity. Manfred, Sanchez and Bergdahl are here, as well as a dozen other people I don't recognise. Peter walks over to me as soon as I enter the room. Puts his hand gently on my shoulder.

'How's it going?'

His gangly body, his open, boyish face. The light touch of his hand. It all affects me and I can't defend myself. Makes me weak and impatient at the same time, as if my body is signalling some-thing urgent. Something important and inevitable is about to hap-pen, a sort of natural disaster. My whole body feels it.

I tremble and take an involuntary step backwards. 'Good. A little tired. Have you found anything?'

Peter nods towards his colleagues.

'We've gone through Emma Bohman's bank statement. Two days before the murder of Angelica Wennerlind, she spent three thousand kronor at a camping shop. Furthermore, she hired a car which she never returned. We've found it a few hundred yards from Orre's house. And a few weeks earlier, on the night Orre's garage burnt down, she spent fifteen hundred kronor in a paint shop.'

'Petrol?'

'We think so. And then we put out an APB for Angelica Wen-nerlind's car. A red Volvo 740 estate. We believe Emma Bohman may have used it to flee the crime scene.'

'Have you been in . . . Emma Bohman's apartment?'

'Yes, but it was empty. We got a search warrant and searched it a couple of hours ago. It was a fucking mess. Full of empty ice cream packages and cut-up pieces of paper. There was dry spaghetti on the kitchen floor and ketchup stains on the mirror. Cushions all over the floor. The technicians are still there. Do you have any theories about where she is now?'

I look out across the room. Observe our colleagues' concentration.

'Somewhere where she feels safe. Let me go through her background information again. Maybe there's something there.'

The hours pass as I work my way through a stack of papers. It starts to get light outside, a dawn as cold and hard as granite. The corridors are crowded and the smell of freshly brewed coffee spreads through the room. The noise level rises. Someone places a cup in front of me and I nod in thanks without looking up.

Around ten, I take a walk. I trudge around the block through newly fallen snow, letting the icy wind open my coat and snowflakes melt on my face.

There it is again: that feeling that I've read something important, but didn't make the connection. The whiteness of the snow burns into my retinas and my cheeks sting from the cold. And somewhere just below the surface an insight is brooding. I know it; I just can't get hold of it. It flits away, hiding in the darkest corners of my consciousness like a shy animal.

As I go back to the police building, it finally comes to me. And suddenly I'm so afraid I'll forget it that I have the impulse to go over to the security guard and ask to borrow a pen and paper. But I decide to trust myself to remember, and hurry towards the lifts. I half-run through the corridor to my colleagues.

'Kapellgränd,' I say to Manfred, who's standing in the middle of the floor with a coffee cup. 'Emma Bohman grew up on Kapellgränd. And when she was questioned by the police about the stolen ring she said Orre lived on Kapellgränd.'

'Yeah?'

Manfred looks confused. Sanchez and Peter join us. They watch me in silence.

'She's mixing fantasy and reality, and for some reason the apartment on Kapellgränd, where she grew up, is meaningful. We're looking for a place where she feels at home. Safe. Kapellgränd could be that place.'

Sanchez raises a hand to us. She looks tired and has dark circles under her eyes from old, smudged make-up.

'You do realise we have another problem on our hands?' she says quietly. 'Angelica Wennerlind's five-year-old daughter Wilma is also missing.'

Emma

One week earlier

The street is quiet and still. Large heavy snowflakes fall from the darkening sky. The red Volvo is parked in front of the house. I walk down the pavement towards the car with a firm grip on Jesper's upper arm. At the rhododendron bush I stop and clean myself off with snow. I bury my face in the cold whiteness and rub away the blood. Jesper is standing next to me. Panting like a dog.

I pull out the keys I took from the woman. I unlock the car, give him yet another shock and press him down in the passenger seat. He says nothing. His face is completely drained of emotion and his eyes resemble wet black stones.

The black leather interior is worn and smells like a stable. For the first time in hours I allow myself to relax. Just a little, so that the cramping pain in my chest releases a little.

'Where's Mummy?'

The voice comes from the back seat. For a second I go numb with surprise and fear. Then I turn around and look at the girl's face with a steady gaze. It's quiet for a moment, while we inspect each other. She looks like she's just woken up, but doesn't seem afraid, just curious. Behind her, I catch a glimpse of suitcases in the luggage compartment.

'Mummy's had to go to the doctor,' I say and start the car. 'Jesper and I are going to be your babysitters.'

'Wilma,' Jesper says in a thick voice.

'Shut up!' I say to him and give him another shock.

He jerks and ends up sitting with his head bent forward and saliva running out of his mouth.

'Jesper's also a little ill,' I say, facing the back seat. 'We'll take care of him at home.'

It's strangely quiet in the car. I'd expected the girl to have an arsenal of questions and protests for me, but she sits silent and wide-eyed.

'Is your name Wilma?' I try.

She puts her thumb in her mouth without answering and looks out through the dark window.

'You shouldn't suck your thumb. There's dirt and bacteria on your fingers,' I say, trying not to sound too strict. She silently meets my eyes in the rear-view mirror.

'Well, my name is Emma.'

We drive a few hundred yards in silence. Maybe it's the stress, but I take a wrong turning. The road looks unfamiliar and the houses give way to snow-covered trees and vast fields. There's not a living soul in sight.

I have no idea where I am.

'I want my mummy!' the girl screams suddenly.

I hesitate, turn on the radio and think. I start to turn around to tell her to be quiet. But before I can, Jesper throws himself at me and pushes me away from the steering wheel. Somehow he must have got out of his restraints, because his hands are free. He fumbles for the wheel and the handbrake.

The car slips as I accidentally press the accelerator, then flies over a bump and runs into a birch tree. The bang is deafening, and the smell of burnt plastic spreads through the passenger compartment.

Jesper lies in my lap with his head against the window. Large cracks run across the glass. It looks like a spider's web.

I turn around reflexively.

The girl seems shocked but unharmed.

I put my hand gently against Jesper's neck, searching for a pulse but don't feel anything. There's blood flowing from his head down onto the dashboard. Everything is quiet, except for the sound of Wilma breathing in the back seat.

I gently shake Jesper but he doesn't react. Isn't breathing.

I look out into the darkness. All I can see are snow-covered bushes and fields. Slowly it dawns on me that I can't go on with Jesper in the car. I have to leave him behind.

But can I just leave him lying here, in the middle of the road?

I stare out into the darkness. In the distance, I can just make out a square box with white text.

'GRIT.'

She's lying in my bed, sleeping peacefully as if she's already forgotten yesterday's events and images: the crash; Jesper's limp, bloody body; me dragging it out of the car and after many attempts managing to push it down into the grit container; then driving on as if nothing had happened and parking among the hundreds of cars in the car park at Danderyd Hospital, where the falling snow quickly spread out like a protective blanket over the cracked window and collapsed front. The only thing she asked on the short metro ride was where I'd taken Jesper. I calmly replied that he'd had to go to the doctor, just like Mummy.

I don't know if she believed me, but she didn't say anything. Just nodded seriously. Wilma's small pale face is eerily perfect: round cheeks, long dark lashes, a half-open kiss of a mouth. I gently touch her cheek. Her skin is soft and warm.

So beautiful, I think. So perfect and unspoiled. She really is a little miracle. There's just one problem: she's not mine. My child is dead and lost for ever, disappeared before we even met.

I sleep next to her that night. Several times I wake up when she turns and kicks me with her small, strong legs. Still, it's taken root in me: the feeling that I'm part of something amazing and unique.

That this child, all children, are the meaning of life. That the core of existence fits inside that small chubby body next to mine, and that some kind of truth lives inside those pale blue, remarkably round eyes.

Maybe I can keep her, I think. Maybe we can run away together. Start all over again somewhere where no one knows us.

Maybe she can be mine for real.

Wilma wakes up before me. When I open my eyes, she's fiddling with one of my earrings on the bedside table. Her arms are pale, almost like marble.

'Are you hungry?'

She doesn't answer.

'Wait here. I'll go and get us something to eat.'

I go into the kitchen. The fridge is empty, except for a dried-up onion and a pack of rancid butter. I search the larder. No crackers. No cereal. Nothing a child might like. The freezer is almost empty, too. But on the lowest shelf, I see something. I bend forward and take out a tub, open a kitchen drawer and reach for a spoon.

Wilma sits obediently on the floor eating the ice cream. She spills it on her clothes and on the carpet, but that doesn't bother me. She's so perfect, and again the thought returns.

What if she were mine?

I go into the bathroom and look in the mirror. My short hair is standing straight up. Black make-up is smeared on the pale skin under my bloodshot eyes. Bloodstains cover my neck and arms. I rub myself down with soap, get into the shower, let the hot water run over my shoulders. Wash away the mess.

From the kitchen I hear the cutlery drawer rattling. I guess that Wilma is exploring. I've just decided I should go out and see what she's doing when I hear an excited shriek from the kitchen. Then Wilma shouts:

'I've found a treasure. Look!'

I dry myself off and wrap a towel around my body. Go out into the kitchen. Wilma looks excited. She's jumping up and down.

'You've found a treasure?' I ask.

'Look!'

At first I don't understand what she's pointing at, but then I see the bundles of cash lying here and there on the floor. I sink down on my knees. Small red rubber bands hold the banknotes in place. And suddenly I understand. This is the money I inherited. The money that disappeared without a trace. I recognise those rubber bands.

'Where did you find these?' My voice sounds hollow, as though it belongs to someone else.

'There.'

Wilma bounces up and down as she points to a narrow cabinet to the left of the oven, where I keep baking sheets. It must have been months since I've opened that cupboard. In fact, I know exactly the last time I did. It was the night Jesper and I were supposed to have our engagement dinner. And I was going to make canapés in the oven. I bend forward and stare into the dark space. It takes a few seconds for my eyes to adjust. There are more bundles lying inside. I take them out, count them and consider a moment. It actually seems as though all the money is still there.

'How . . .? Was the door open?'

Wilma shakes her head with an air of importance. She has big ice cream stains on her chin and T-shirt.

'When I opened it, I found the treasure.'

I nod, collapse onto the cold floor. Trying to work out what happened. Jesper must have put the money back. But why would he put it in the cupboard in the kitchen? The only explanation I can see is that he actually didn't want me to find the money. He hid it on purpose.

As if he wanted to drive me crazy.

Just as I'm about to close the long narrow door, I catch sight of something else hidden in the dark. It looks like a tray standing on end, leaning against the wall. I grope inside and grab hold of it. The edge is made of wood. I gently pull it into the light, put it on the floor in front of me. Trying to understand.

It's the Ragnar Sandberg painting.

I'm standing in front of the mirror in the bathroom again. Searching my memory. Could I have put the money and the painting in the kitchen and not remembered it? Something flutters by. A vague recollection of a dark kitchen. The weight of the painting in my hands as I crouch in front of the cabinet.

Am I going crazy?

I sit down on the toilet and pee. I decide I must have dreamed it all. I think of Mum instead.

Think of the fact that she never answered my question.

The woman in green scrubs put her hand comfortingly on my arm. She was young. Very young. It said 'Soraya' on her name tag.

'Emma. It's good you could come right away. I'll show you where she is.'

We walked in silence through the corridor. Outside the windows, I saw the treetops. The delicate green foliage danced in the wind. Broken clouds chased one another across the blue sky. We passed by some kind of kitchen. On the round laminate table stood a black plastic pot of withered daffodils. The smell of coffee and microwave dinners leaked out into the corridor.

The nurse's steps were quiet but determined. She stopped outside a door and turned to me.

'Before we go in . . . I need to warn you, your mother is hooked up to a respirator which is helping her breathe. It may look a little scary with all the tubes and machines, but they aren't making her suffer. She's been given a lot of morphine, so she's not in pain, but it may be difficult to communicate with her. She's not quite conscious all the time.'

'Will she recognise me?'

The nurse smiled. I couldn't decide if it was because my question was stupid or if she was just trying to be friendly.

'If she wakes up, she'll definitely recognise you. There's nothing wrong with her mind, as you know. It's just her body that . . .'

She left the sentence unfinished.

'Can I touch her?'

'Absolutely. You can talk to her, hold her hand. Kiss her. It's not dangerous and you won't hurt her. But as I said, I don't know how aware she'll be. She has developed both liver and kidney failure in the last few days, so she's very . . . fragile.'

In the distance I could see an old man tottering out into the corridor, aided by an assistant. He was pulling an IV pole behind him. Life's end station: this is the way it looked. A white hospital corridor with shiny linoleum floors and stainless-steel adjustable beds. A silence punctuated only by the sucking and hissing of machines.

The nurse opened Mum's door. I put my hand on her arm, felt I had to ask. 'Will she wake up again?'

'It's impossible to say.'

Her dark-brown eyes met mine. Then she gave me a brief smile and disappeared down the corridor in her silent white clogs.

Halfway down, she turned back to me. 'I'll be at the nurses' station if you need anything.' I nodded and walked into the room.

I almost didn't recognise her. It was as if her whole body had swollen up. Mum was big as it was, but this was something else. Her body seemed engorged with liquid. Her skin was shiny and glazed, almost transparent. Suddenly I was afraid I'd make a hole in her if I touched her. That all the liquid would ooze out, like water from a balloon.

Tubes were connected to her, and the only sound in the room was the hiss of the respirator painstakingly pumping air in and out of her chest.

I wasn't prepared for the shock.

I think I'd somehow assumed I wouldn't be affected, since our relationship was what it was. But I was wrong. My whole body started to shake, and when I grabbed a chair and sat down next to her, I broke out in a cold sweat. Strange memories, impossible to resist, caught me off guard: Mum, Dad and I decorating a Christmas tree we'd stolen from the park. Mum lying in my bed, holding me tight in one of those rare moments of love and closeness that I guarded like jewels. Her breath smelling sweetly of beer and cigarettes, and me not daring to move my face an inch away from her, despite the smell, filled as I was with unspoken gratitude for her affection. The blue butterfly, dead and broken on the floor, surrounded by shards of glass and dry, jagged branches.

I laid my hand gently on Mum's forearm, careful to avoid the large purple marks. She didn't react. Her face was also swollen, especially around the eyes. It was hard to make out if they were open or closed.

My tears surprised me. They ran down my cheeks and I let them, didn't even try to wipe them away. Inflammation of the kidney and liver failure, they said. And when I had asked if it could be because of the drinking, the doctor just nodded, explained that couldn't be ruled out. Told me many alcohol-related diseases end up in this department.

I leaned over her. Put my face against her chest. Felt how it rose and fell with the ventilator. And suddenly I had to know. I wouldn't get another chance to ask the question that had plagued me for so long.

I wiped my face against her yellow blanket and cleared my throat. Grabbed her arm tighter and studied her face closely.

'Mum, it's Emma.'

The puffy face showed no reaction. I gripped her arm even tighter, so that her skin whitened under my fingers and my nails left small crescent-shaped marks on her unnaturally shiny skin. I patted her face with my other hand. Maybe a touch too hard.

'Mum, it's Emma.'

One of her eyelids twitched. I didn't know if it was a reflex or if it meant she might have finally heard me. I leaned forward. Put my mouth to her ear.

'Mum. I need to know . . .'

The respirator hissed and Mum jerked as if I'd pinched her cheek.

'Mum. You have to tell me . . . And be honest. Is there something wrong with me?'

Peter

Sometimes I wish I could ask my mother for advice on these investigations. I imagine her standing in front of the evidence wall, her hands on her hips and a stern look on her face. Completely unmoved by the police crowding around her. She was unusually perceptive, in a slightly cynical way. She could see through a lie as soon as it was said, and she wasn't afraid to speak up when she disagreed with something. She could make things a little awkward, in other words. And could be a thorn in the side of the establishment – at least that's how she wanted to see herself.

Hanne reminds me a lot of her. Minus the cynicism. Strange. Why haven't I thought of this before?

I look over at Hanne, who's sitting at a desk and sorting through a pile of documents. There's even a physical resemblance, something about the hair and the finely drawn dark eyebrows. And in the way she moves, the way she tosses her head back when she laughs. As if she wants the whole sky to hear her.

Is it really that simple? Did I fall in love with my mother?

Love is a reflex, I think. Something we just do, like sleeping or eating. And maybe we fall in love with what feels familiar, like home. What reminds us of how life was before all the disappointment.

Manfred comes over to me. Punches me gently in the side. 'You look like shit. Anything the matter?'

I smile at his awkward attempt at thoughtfulness. 'Thank you. When do we head out?'

'The special investigations team and the negotiator will be here in thirty minutes. Apparently the property on Kapellgränd is vacant.

It's set to be demolished, so we don't have to worry about any neighbours. You coming with us?'

'If you keep your mouth shut.'

He snorts loudly and pounds me on the back. 'There you go, Lindgren. You do have some balls, after all.'

The apartment building on Kapellgränd is dark and apparently abandoned. On the bottom floor, plywood is nailed across the windows, with sharp pieces of glass still visible beneath. We're sitting in Manfred's car: Sanchez, Manfred, Hanne and me. Somewhere out there in the darkness the special investigations team are hiding. They've already searched the apartment and found it cleaned out, except for a number of empty bottles, a pile of old porn magazines and a few dirty blankets on the floor. They found no trace of a child, but we've decided to wait a while in case Emma turns up here.

Hanne has been right before.

Morrissey is on the radio, as usual, but at such low volume that I almost can't make out the lyrics: *You have never been in love, until you've seen the sunlight thrown, over smashed human bone.*

Is it true? I think. Did she do it out of love?

A few lone pedestrians pass by in the wind. A couple of women in veils are walking up from Götgatan, arm in arm. Maybe they're on their way to the mosque.

Manfred drums his fingers impatiently on the steering wheel and peers out into the darkness. Wipes away condensation from the inside of the windscreen with the sleeve of his camel-hair overcoat and sighs.

'Maybe she's not coming. Could we be looking in the wrong place?'

No answer.

A lone cyclist wobbles by just as my mobile rings. It's Janet.

Normally I'd send her straight to voicemail, but since I've four missed calls from her already, and I'm not doing anything at the moment, I decide to answer.

'You need to come right now!' she says breathlessly.

Something clicks inside me, but I keep my voice even. 'Has something happened?'

Manfred turns towards me with a questioning look. I understand immediately that he doesn't think this is the right time to discuss family problems. But Janet has never cared about such considerations.

'It's Albin,' Janet sobs. 'They've taken him.'

I breathe. 'Taken him?'

'Yes, the police have taken him.'

I try to think a step ahead, but I come up blank. 'The police? Why?'

'He . . . They . . . found . . .'

'Settle down. What happened?'

My concern is mixed with embarrassment. This is what Janet has done countless times – called in the middle of something important, expecting me to drop everything. She's never shown any understanding of the job I have to do. Even though I've sent her money every month for fifteen years.

My colleagues' eyes burn into me, but the image of Albin's face steadies me. His lean teenage body and his ears protruding through his thin hair. Janet's ears. And I remember his words that night when he came home to see me in Farsta with a skateboard in one hand and a carrier bag in the other:

Had a fight with Mum. Can I crash at your place?

Then I think of his eyes, the look he gave me as Janet led him out to the car, and how I jumped behind the curtain so he wouldn't see me.

When have I ever been there for him?

'They found marijuana in his backpack, Peter. And now he's sitting in jail with that awful gang from Skogås. You have to do something. You are his father, after all. You have to . . .'

Her voice rises into a falsetto, and I instinctively take the phone from my ear to avoid that sharp sound.

'Well . . . what? What do you want me to do?' I shout.

I hear her roar though the phone in my lap. Everybody in the car hears. It's the same shriek as when she found the wedding invitations in my desk drawer. A roar from the abyss, filled with the same bottomless anger and disgust. And suddenly it's as if I see myself through her eyes. I see the monster she thinks I am. The spineless creature who left her to bring up Albin alone.

A moment later I hear my mother's voice. Weak and a little thick, as if eternity has deprived her of her sharpness. *Responsibility, Peter. Isn't it time you took a little responsibility?*

'Janet, I'll call you right back.'

She begins to protest.

'No,' I say, and – though it must sound absurd to her to hear it from me – 'Trust me. I'll call you right back.'

Hanne's gaze rests heavily on me as I climb out of the car. She opens the door and walks over to me. Puts her hand on my arm.

'I want you to stay,' she says quickly.

'I can't,' I say and meet her eyes.

I should explain what happened. Tell her about Albin and Janet and the debt that has to be paid back one day. Explain that the day has come, as I probably always knew it would.

'I'm begging you,' Hanne says. 'I'm sure she's on her way here.'

'I have to go,' I say, and I leave.

On Götgatan I pass by a pub. The red neon sign flashes in the darkness, screaming out its promise of warmth and oblivion, and suddenly I yearn for a beer. Just one glass inside that warmth, instead of heading directly to the police station in Farsta or back to Hanne. A refuge from all the choices that make life so incredibly hard to navigate.

But refuge isn't what I need now – and it certainly isn't what I deserve. What I need is a quiet place where I can make an important call.

I step inside, quickly take the place in: the people slung over their drinks, the sport playing on muted TVs, the vinyl-covered sofas and the beer glasses glistening in the dim yellowish light.

I put the phone to my ear.

Emma

I don't understand Wilma. I've spent the whole week trying every-thing to get her settled into my home. I've read books to her, made pancakes and done craft projects. We've fed the pigeons at Karlaplan and watched the dogs playing in the snow at Gärdet Park. And when someone rang the doorbell, we hid under the bed playing the quiet game. But instead of getting closer to me, she's become increasingly difficult to make contact with. Slipped into herself in a strange way. She's sat for hours just staring at her hands or methodically cutting paper into tiny pieces, then tossing them down like flower petals onto the floor around her.

Many times we've passed by newspapers with Jesper's image on them, but she hasn't seen them, or if she has, she didn't understand. I myself looked away when I saw the photos above the headline 'Famous CEO Wanted for Murder'. Couldn't meet his eyes, didn't want to think about everything he did to me.

The last few nights, Wilma has been waking up screaming in terror, and when I shake her lightly awake from her nightmare she asks for her mother and pushes me away. I wish I could make her feel safe with me, but I just don't know how. Several times I've found myself getting angry with her for being so ungrateful and had to remind myself she's just a child. She can't help that she's ended up in this situation. It's my responsibility – my duty – as an adult not to lose my patience.

We are on our way to McDonald's, which is the only thing that seems to put Wilma in a good mood. She has her sticky little hand in mine and is babbling on about how she found the treas-ure last week. I think there's one positive thing about the money and painting surfacing: my financial problems are solved. At least for the short term. And yes, I'm happy I've found the painting. It means a lot to me, not just because of its value, but because in some strange way it connects me to my past, is a bridge to my childhood. To a world that no longer exists. To Mum and my aunts and their merry tea parties. To sugary, slightly burnt cinnamon buns; the smell of cigarette smoke; feeling safe on Aunt Agneta's knee, wedged between her enormous breasts.

The snow falls over Karlaplan. Big woolly flakes cover the drained fountain. The large trees stand in a silent, serious circle, as if guarding the square and all of the city's inhabitants. Fake Christmas trees and sacks of firewood are lined up outside the hardware store. People stream in and out of the Fältöversten Mall carrying bags of Christmas gifts. It strikes me that I'll neither give nor receive any presents this year, now that Mum is dead. Christmas will come, but a different kind of Christmas. At the corner shop I see the headline: 'Five-Year-Old Kidnapped'. The picture doesn't look much like Wilma, but still I hold her more tightly. Pull her away.

'Can I get a Happy Meal? Please, I want a Happy Meal. Please.'

'OK,' I say without really thinking.

Maybe it's a bad idea to let Wilma decide for herself what to eat. Maybe she'll end up with bad eating habits.

'And a milkshake? Please.'

I hesitate a moment. I decide to worry about her diet later. It's more important to take advantage of those moments when Wilma is communicative and friendly to me.

'Sure.'

We eat in silence in the noisy restaurant.

The ice cream stains on Wilma's clothes are complemented by ketchup and grease stains from the fries. It's crowded and humid. The floor in the restaurant is covered in a thick layer of brown slush that patrons have tramped in. Suddenly a woman slips. One of the drinks on her tray slides off and falls down towards Wilma. I catch it a second before it hits her. The woman, who's wearing a puffy coat and ski cap, has two small children in tow. She puts her hand to her mouth in horror.

'Oh no. I'm sorry. Is your daughter OK?'

At first I don't understand what she means. Then I smile widely. 'Don't worry. Everything's fine.'

Something warm spreads through my frozen body. I look at Wilma, who seems completely oblivious to the little drama that's just taken place. She licks the salt and grease from her tiny fingers with her head tilted to the side. Her fair hair falls in matted curls down onto her shoulders.

Is your daughter OK?

On the way home I can't stop thinking about it. What if she could be mine for real? Now that I have money again, maybe it's possible. We could run somewhere far away. Norrland, maybe. Hide out. Get a new cat or a small dog.

It would surely take a while for her nightmares to disappear and for her to start trusting me fully, but I'm sure she would eventually. I just have to give her some time.

I grab Wilma's hand again. It's as sticky as before.

'When are we gonna see Mummy?' she asks.

Irritation flares up inside me.

'I don't know,' I say truthfully. 'When your mummy is well again.'

'But when will Mummy be well again?'

'I don't know that either. Only the doctor knows.'

'Can we ask the doctor?'

Suddenly I just can't take her whining any more. I've answered these questions a thousand times – how long is she going to keep asking about her mother anyway?

'No, we can't, because—'

I stop abruptly, and stare at the entrance to my apartment building. Feel my legs almost give way beneath me.

There are several police cruisers parked on the street outside my house. Dark-clad figures conversing outside the door. Two German shepherds are sniffing the pavement.

We hurry back towards Karlaplan. Wilma is grumpy now. She wants to go home and look at the treasure, doesn't want to go anywhere else.

'Ouch, the scissors hurt,' she whines as I pull on her, trying to get her to hurry up.

'What scissors?'

Wilma fishes my big kitchen scissors, which she was playing with, out of her pocket. 'The ones I was cutting with.'

'Are you crazy? You put scissors in your pocket? What if you fell? They could have stabbed you.'

I pull the scissors out of her hand and put them in my pocket. Filled with an unfamiliar feeling: the fear that Wilma will hurt herself. So this is what it's like to be a parent, I think, and for some reason I feel a kind of satisfaction.

Before we go down into the metro I cast a look behind me, but nobody seems to be following us. The people outside my building don't look nearly as threatening from a distance. I slow down the pace. Exhale. Release my grip on Wilma's arm. She doesn't say anything, just pinches her little mouth.

'Can I have an ice cream?' she says as we pass by the newspaper stand. Her light-blue eyes catch mine.

'It's really cold,' I try.

'I'm not cold. I'm hot. Can I get an ice cream? Please.' She pulls on my arm.

I sigh. Go into the shop and buy her an ice cream.

I have only three hundred kronor in my wallet. I didn't take any more when we left the apartment, and now it's too late to go back. This isn't even enough to hire a car for a day, which is a shame, because if we had a car we could at least get out of town. Drive somewhere else.

We go down into the metro. Wilma eats her ice cream from the bottom up, and it drips down onto her coat. Big vanilla puddles run down her chest. I decide to ignore it. I have more pressing concerns.

The train rolls into the station and we board it. We sit opposite each other. Wilma has finished her ice cream by now, but still has the lolly stick in her mouth. She sucks and bites on it until it breaks in two pieces.

At the Östermalmstorg stop a woman in a puffy winter coat gets on. She passes through the carriage handing out some sort of sheet of laminated paper, which reads, 'Please help my daughter. She's disabled due to cerebral palsy and we have no money for a wheel-chair or physical therapy in Odessa.' I look at the picture. A smiling ten-year-old is sitting in an armchair. Her teeth and glasses look far too big for her little face. Her arms and hands are curved, as if cramping. Her legs look strangely thin, as though they belong to another, smaller body. A dog stands beside her.

'This is my daughter.'

The woman is suddenly beside me. Her accent and blue eyes remind me of someone, and the pieces fall into place and I know exactly where to go.

I give the woman back her photo and shake my head. Feel my heart pounding in my chest.

'I'm sorry. I don't have any money.'

Olga is folding jeans when we come in. I don't see Mahnoor or Björne. Maybe they're in the stockroom. Maybe on a break.

Olga hugs me tightly. The scent of her perfume hangs heavy around her and almost makes me sneeze.

'What have you done to yourself?'

She widens her pale blue eyes, and I'm struck by how similar she is to the woman on the metro. Not just the accent, but also her appearance. They could be sisters.

'What do you mean?'

She runs her hand through my short hair.

'You look like a man, Emma. Do you want to look like a man?'

Before I can answer, Mahnoor pops up behind me. Puts her hand softly on my shoulder. I turn around and she hugs me.

'You look great,' she whispers in my ear. 'Don't listen to her. I'm so sorry. We heard you were laid off. They're such arseholes.'

Then they notice Wilma. A wrinkle appears on Olga's forehead.

'This is Wilma,' I say. 'I'm taking care of her.'

'So you found a job?' Olga says. I nod.

Mahnoor and Olga look at Wilma again, but she seems to have lost interest in my colleagues. Instead, she's exploring the shop. Crawling under racks of clothes. Fiddling with the security tags. Sorting through the hairclips and earrings.

'It's just temporary. Her mother is ill. I'm taking care of her until she gets well.'

Mahnoor and Olga nod. I turn towards Olga.

'I promised her we could go to that the water park in Södertälje. You know, that thing with slides and waves. Could I borrow your car again, Olga? I'll bring it back tomorrow.'

'Sure. It's a pain in the backside finding parking anyway.' Olga rolls her eyes.

'Thank you so much.'

I follow her into the staffroom. She grabs her bag, which is encrusted in gold embroidery and rhinestones. Roots around in it. Pulls out a packet of cigarettes, a box of tampons and a hairbrush until she finds what she's looking for.

'Here. Just bring it back tomorrow afternoon. I don't need it today.'

I take the keys and give her a quick hug.

'Thank you. You're so sweet.'

She looks down at the floor, suddenly embarrassed. 'Stop. It's nothing.'

We go back out into the shop. Wilma is sitting on the jeans table helping Mahnoor fold. Mahnoor smiles and Wilma laughs. It looks idyllic. They might as well be sitting in a park or a playground.

I go over to them. Stroke Wilma's cheek. 'We have to go now, honey.'

'No. I'm working,' she protests, and manages to sound very determined. Olga and Mahnoor laugh.

'She's a real sweetie. I could take her home.'

Something glitters in Mahnoor's dark eyes. I reassure myself that she has no idea that's exactly what's happened, that I did take Wilma home with me.

Just as I'm leaving, a guy wearing a green parka enters the shop. He walks towards us and as soon as his eyes meet mine, I recognise him.

It feels as though someone has just kicked me hard in the stomach. It's Anders Jönsson, the journalist I met up with. The one who specialised in sabotaging Jesper Orre's life and career. A sort of colleague of mine, you might say.

He looks at Wilma and then me, and I know that he knows.

I turn around and the car keys drop from my hand onto the floor, but I ignore them. Instead I take Wilma by the hand and run out of the shop towards the metro.

Hanne

Peter left. He got out of the car after that phone call and left, even though I asked him to stay. The weight of it settles on me.

The atmosphere in the car is heavy. Sanchez and Manfred exchange meaningful glances, but say nothing. I wonder what they're thinking, if they too are surprised by Peter's sudden outburst, and how quickly he disappeared into the darkness towards the metro.

'He does that sometimes,' Manfred says tactfully, as if reading my thoughts.

I don't respond.

'I guess something must have happened,' Sanchez says, and her eyes linger on me.

Do they know? I wonder. Have they sensed that my relationship with Peter is something more than professional?

'We'll do fine without him,' Manfred continues.

'Why are you defending him?' I ask. 'He disappears, and you seem to think it's perfectly normal. But is it? Do you really think that's OK?'

No answer.

We sit there for a moment. In silence. Then Manfred's mobile rings. He lifts up his big body to grab the phone from his back pocket and answers. Listens for a long time. After he's hung up, he turns to me.

'A witness saw Emma Bohman and Wilma half an hour ago at her former workplace. A journalist who writes articles about Orre, and who's met her before.'

'What do we do?' Sanchez says.

'We head out,' Manfred says, starting the car.

'Wait,' I say. 'Can't we stay a little longer? I still think she's going to come here.'

Manfred throws me a tired look. 'We're searching in the wrong place. We should go back now.'

'No. I'm staying.'

'You're coming with us,' Manfred says, an edge in his voice. I open the car and step out. It's dark and a hard crust has formed on top of the slush.

'I'm staying,' I say, facing Manfred. He and Sanchez exchange a glance.

'Do what you want,' Manfred says. 'But I think you should take the opportunity to go home and grab a few hours' sleep. There's nothing you can do here alone anyway.'

Then the car takes off in a cloud of exhaust.

I'm freezing. The cold penetrates my damp winter coat, and I realise I've forgotten both my gloves and my hat in the car. Luckily I have my notepad with me; it's lying safe and sound in the inside pocket of my coat. The idea of Manfred and Sanchez reading my notes – the names and physical descriptions of the members of the investigative team – and finally realising the extent of my problems feels far more frightening than the cold. The shame of the unmentionable is beyond everything else.

Dementia.

A case for the memory clinic.

On her way to becoming a vegetable.

I clench my hands in my pockets. I try not to think about the disease or the cold biting my cheeks. Instead I focus on the Inuit. How they survived winter after winter, in bitter cold. Fishing and hunting even though they lived in total darkness for months. How they made sacrifices to the sea goddess Sedna, so she'd let them catch sea creatures without pulling them down into the depths.

Half an hour goes by without anything happening. I pull up my hood and push my hands down into my pockets. Stamping on the spot, unsure what I should do. The house on Kapellgränd stands empty and dark in front of me, the shards of glass behind the plywood glistening in the moonlight like sharp teeth.

Maybe Manfred was right. Maybe I should go home to Gunilla's. Take Frida for a walk, crawl into bed. Sleep without setting an alarm clock. Forget this day – Peter leaving the car, my mittens and hat still in the back seat.

The thought of calling Owe pops into my head for a second. But even here, alone in this intense cold, it doesn't feel like a serious option. I'd rather stand alone outside an abandoned house on Kapellgränd all night than go back to that prison on Skeppargatan.

I start to walk down towards the glittering lights of Götgatan. I stop outside a pub, unsure of what to do – go home or stay.

Then I see her.

She's walking up Högbergsgatan holding a little girl by the hand. Her steps are slow, almost lumbering. Her eyes are on the ground. And I know I have to make a choice. Should I make myself known and try to talk to her, or just let her pass?

The girl's steps are heavy, too. She drags her boots in the slush, pulling on Emma's arm as if she wants to get free. Her jacket is open and she has no hat on.

If I do nothing, I know that anything might happen to the girl. She might freeze to death tonight or be hidden away somewhere. And then we might never find her again. But if I make contact with Emma, I'm risking my life.

But what kind of life do I have anyway? What's left for me to do when this investigation is over?

The memory clinic?

I approach Emma and the girl.

'I know what Jesper Orre did to you,' I say.

Emma Bohman freezes mid-step and shoots me a wary look. The girl stops, too. Stares at me with her mouth open, but says nothing. Her fair hair hangs in tangles over her shoulders, as if it hasn't been brushed for weeks. The jacket is covered with spots in a rainbow of colours. Her free hand is in a fist, and I can tell she's freezing.

'What?' Emma says.

'I know he betrayed and deceived you. He's done the same to others.'

She blinks and looks up at the moon hanging large and heavy in the night sky. 'Who are you?' she asks.

'Just somebody who knows a lot about Jesper and what he's done.'

'OK. And what are you doing here?'

Her voice is harsh; I sense tears in it.

'Hmmm. What am I doing here?' I say. 'I'm waiting for a man. A man who's never going to come . . .'

She meets my eyes. Nods slowly.

'I understand completely,' she says slowly, emphasising every word. I gently put my hand on her arm.

'Come on, we'll sort this out.' She looks around nervously. 'We have to go.'

'Let's just go inside and warm up for a little bit?' I propose. 'You can't run forever, Emma.'

Her gaze hardens when I say her name, and I realise I've made a mistake.

'Who are you really? Are you with the police?'

'No. I'm—'

'Get your fucking hands off us,' she says, and pulls away from my grasp with unexpected force.

I take a step towards her. But she's faster, gives me a hard shove and I fall helplessly sideways onto the icy kerb. A crunching sound emanates from my jaw and my mouth fills immediately with blood. Searing pain radiates from my shoulder.

I grab hold of her legs, clinging to her.

'Leave me alone, you bitch,' she screams and starts kicking.

Then she's on top of me. Sits astride my chest staring into my eyes. Something is shining in her hand. I don't understand what it is, don't see what's about to happen. Then I see: she has a large pair of kitchen scissors in her hand. As they hurtle towards me, life seems to stop and I see everything with surprising clarity. The rage in Emma's face. Wilma watching us silently with her mouth open. The snow crystals beside my head sparkling under the streetlamps.

And something else.

Through the window of the pub, I see Peter standing, phone in hand. He seems to be roaring into it.

But as the scissors pierce my coat, he looks out and sees me. His gaze reveals a mixture of horror and surprise, and he drops his phone and begins to move.

That's all.

Then only pain and the hard chill of the pavement exist. I close my eyes, immediately overcome by a numbing fatigue. The pain fades away, replaced by a sensation as soft as down, as if I'm lying in freshly fallen snow or hovering a few inches above the hard stone ground, weightless and completely indifferent to what's happening around me.

Everything becomes delightfully quiet.

And in the midst of all this, I feel it anyway: Peter's presence, like a warm hand around my soul.

Emma

Four months later

I'm sitting in a small room staring out the window. I catch glimpses of small green buds on the trees on the other side of the thick glass. On the street below a pregnant woman waddles past. A man supports her forearm. My guess: she's about to give birth, but has been sent outside to walk-start the labour. The maternity ward is located in the building next door. Further away, behind the large red-brick buildings, I can glimpse the water. It's blue-grey, and there's foam on the peaks of the waves.

They say it's cold outside.

They say it looks much warmer and more inviting than it really is. I can't decide if that's true. It's been exactly seven weeks since I set foot outside this brick building. For seven weeks I've stared out the same window, watched the hard little buds of the trees swell and the migratory birds return.

There's a knock on the door.

Urban pops his head in. 'Would you like a cup of coffee?'

'Tea, thank you,' I say, and marvel at how he never seems to learn I don't drink coffee. Even though we've spent every day together for weeks, he still asks me if I want coffee. But that's just so typical of Urban. Despite his sharp intellect and his obvious interest in me, he sometimes gets confused. Sometimes his thoughts just seem to wander, like he's not really present.

He disappears and the door closes with a sigh. He comes back a few minutes later. He carries two cups of tea and a notepad tucked under one arm.

'Your tea.'

'Thank you kindly.'

He sits down on the stool opposite me and puts on his thin steel-framed glasses. Then he rubs his hand over his stubble and looks at his notes.

The whole thing is quite comical. It's like he's trying to maintain some kind of facade. As if our relationship is defined solely as doctor and patient. Like he's denying the truth. I smile; I can't help it – the situation is so absurd. Just a few days ago we lay in my bed as close as two people can get. And now he's pretending to go through my medical records like he's just some random doctor.

He meets my eyes again.

'What's so funny? Have I missed something?'

I shake my head. 'No, it's just . . .'

I leave the sentence unfinished because I see how it is.

If we're going to dance this dance, then it's got to be on his terms. He probably feels guilty about what he did. Perhaps he'd even get fired if this came out. If he thinks it's better to pretend it never happened, then I just have to accept that.

He takes off his glasses and puts the notepad on the table. Meets my eyes. 'So, how are you feeling today, Emma?'

I push out my breasts and let my top slip down a little over one shoulder, as if by chance.

'Well, where should I begin?'

Hanne

This is how I imagine eternity.

Everything is white, silent and lacking in any contours. And the cold, which is ever present, doesn't even bother you. It's just there, like the sea and the birds and the goddess Sedna, brooding in the blue-black depths.

Kulusuk's cemetery spreads out in front of me, and beyond those simple white wooden crosses, the sea presides. Married to the sky on the horizon. Mountains are reflected in the calm waters of the Torsuut Tunoq sound, and large turquoise blocks of ice float on its surface.

The crosses of the Inuit are nameless.

When someone dies, their name is given to a newborn and life goes on. I like that. I too want a nameless white wooden cross one day, instead of some bulky granite stone with a gold inscription. Maybe I'll be buried here, on this hill, where the permafrost never melts and the land has to be carved open to accept you.

Peter stands next to me. Puts his arm around my waist and stares out across the sound. I feel a shiver of happiness that he followed me here, travelling halfway around the world to visit the land I've dreamed of for so long.

The deep scissor wound in my stomach has healed. But the doctors say I was lucky. Incomprehensibly lucky. If my notebook hadn't been in my pocket, partially blocking the scissors, I probably wouldn't be alive today. The stab was a powerful one, and the liver, which survived by a margin of a few millimetres, is a sensitive organ.

I was saved by my own sense of order and my fear of losing control. It's almost comical.

It bought enough time for Peter, who came rushing out of the pub, to overpower Emma and call for help.

Peter went to see Albin later that evening, after Emma had been arrested and Wilma had been taken to a safe place. But he still won't tell me why his relationship with his son is what it is. It's something I have to accept. Learn to relate to. Just as he has to learn to relate to my illness.

I meet his eyes. He might be smiling a little, I don't know. Or maybe just squinting against the intensely bright light.

I know he's hoping I'll get better. He doesn't want to lose me to the disease. But I also know that's not how things will go. One day I'll slip into oblivion and become exactly what he fears.

But not today.

And really, isn't that the only thing that matters?

Acknowledgements

I'd like to give my sincere thanks to all the people who helped me with *The Ice Beneath Her*, especially my publisher, Sara; my editor, Katarina; everyone at Wahlström & Widstrand; and my agents, Astri and Christine at Ahlander Agency.

In addition, I am forever grateful to all the people who read this book in manuscript form and contributed their knowledge in various important ways with facts and insights into everything from forensics to police procedures, especially Eva von Vogelsang, Martin Csatlos, Cina Jennehov and Kristina Ohlsson.

Finally, I would like to express my gratitude to family and friends for their understanding and encouragement while I was in the process of writing this book. Without your love and patience, no book!

Camilla Grebe

About the Author

Camilla Grebe was born near Stockholm. She co-founded audio-book publisher Storyside and has written four celebrated crime novels with her sister Åsa Träff, the first two of which were nominated for Swedish Crime Novel of the Year by the Swedish Crime Writers' Academy. Camilla has also written the popular Moscow Noir trilogy with Paul Leander-Engström. *The Ice Beneath Her* is Camilla's debut novel.